IRL

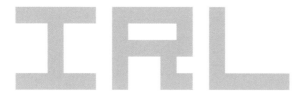

ENTER
52%
LOADING

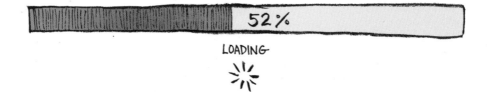

IN REAL LIFE

Cory Doctorow
Jen Wang

:01
First Second
New York

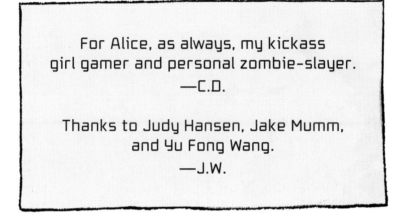

For Alice, as always, my kickass
girl gamer and personal zombie-slayer.
—C.D.

Thanks to Judy Hansen, Jake Mumm,
and Yu Fong Wang.
—J.W.

HAIRY
LONGPO TUSK
+15 GOLD

INVENTORY
HAIRY LONGPO TUSK
LOBOK
SKY ELIXIR
CATSEYE
PINECONE
BEACH STONE
ANTS NEST
OMUSUBI
THYME

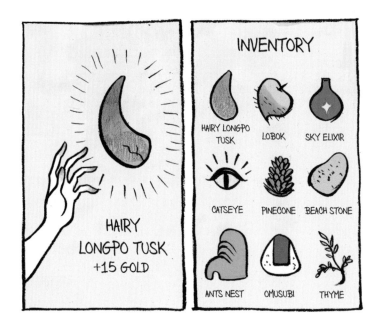

INTRODUCTION

by Cory Doctorow

In Real Life is a book about games and economics. A lot of us pay attention to games, but think of them as trivial—mere amusements that help us fill the long, dismal stretch between the cradle and the grave. As for economics, well, yeah, people think economics is important, but it's also one of those intimidating no-go areas that scares people away, despite the fact that economics—the study of why people do things, really—is the subject that has the most to say about the circumstances in which they find themselves.

When you put economics and games together, you suddenly find yourself in the middle of a bunch of sticky, tough questions about politics and labor. *In Real Life* connects the dots between the way we shop, the way we organize, and the way we play, and why some people are rich, some are poor, and how they seem to get stuck there.

I hope that readers of this book will be inspired to dig deeper into the subject of behavioral economics and to start asking hard questions about how we end up with the stuff we own, what it costs our human brothers and sisters to make those goods, and why we think we need them.

But it's a poor politics that can only be expressed by choosing to buy or not buy something. Sometimes (often!), you need to organize to make a difference.

This is the golden age of organizing. If there's one thing the Internet's changed forever, it's the relative difficulty and cost of getting a bunch of people in the same place, working toward the same goal. That's not always good (thugs, bullies, racists, and loonies never had it so good), but it is fundamentally *game-changing*.

It's hard to remember just how difficult this organizing stuff used to be: how hard it was to do something as trivial as getting ten friends to agree on dinner and a movie, let alone getting millions of people together to raise money for a political candidate, get the vote out, protest corruption, or save an endangered and beloved institution.

When I was an activist in the 1980s, ninety-eight percent of my time was spent stuffing envelopes and writing addresses on them. The remaining two percent was the time we spent figuring out what to put in the envelopes. Today, we get those envelopes and stamps and address books for free. This is so fantastically, hugely different and weird that we haven't even begun to feel the first tendrils of it. Moments like the Occupy movement and the Gezi uprising in Istanbul will be remembered as the tiniest tremors of what happens when people can organize more cheaply.

Working together is the secret origin story of our species. We diverged from our hominid ancestors when we started to divide up labor—you watch the kids, I'll watch for tigers, and that guy's going to go and forage for fruit. The most modern part of our brains, the neocortex (the "new bark," which wraps around all the more ancient parts of our

brains), developed around this time and is strongly impli-
cated in managing our social relationships. Everything from
language and literacy to corporations and countries are just
structures for organizing human labor.

The games we play with other people all tickle this organizing mechanism. When you play hide and seek, you try
and outguess where your opponents will look (or where
they'll hide when they're trying to out outguess you!). When
you do a mass raid on some huge instance in an MMO (a
massively multiplayer online game), the "game" isn't just
killing the boss, it's figuring out how to convince a couple

dozen of your friends to work with you, coordinating your schedules so that you can raid together, agreeing on tactics, even coming up with a chain of command and hammering out its legitimacy.

It's not surprising that gamespace has become a workplace for hundreds of thousands of "gold farmers" who undertake dreary, repetitive labor to produce virtual wealth that's sold to players with more money and less patience than them. The structural differences between in-game play and in-game work are mostly arbitrary, and "real" work is half a game, anyway. Most of the people you see going to work today are LARPing (live-action role playing) an incredibly boring RPG (role-playing game) called "professionalism" that requires them to alter their vocabulary, posture, eating habits, facial expressions—every detail all the way down to what they allow themselves to find funny.

The most amazing thing about the moment we're living through is the degree to which it allows us to abolish all the boring stuff that used to be required for any kind of ambitious project. We're at a point where we can build an encyclopedia with the kind of organizational structures that were once only good enough to run an ambitious fun fair or bake sale. Hierarchy and injustice are far from dead, but the justification for continuing them gets weaker with every passing moment.

The net doesn't solve the problem of injustice, but it solves the first hard problem of righting wrongs: getting everyone together and keeping them together. You still have to do the even harder work of risking life, limb, personal fortune, and reputation.

Every wonderful thing in our world has a fight in its history: our rights, our good fortune, our happiness. All that is sweet was paid for, once upon a time, by principled people who risked everything to change the world for the better.

Those risks are not diminished one iota by the net. But the rewards are every bit as sweet.

LEVEL 2

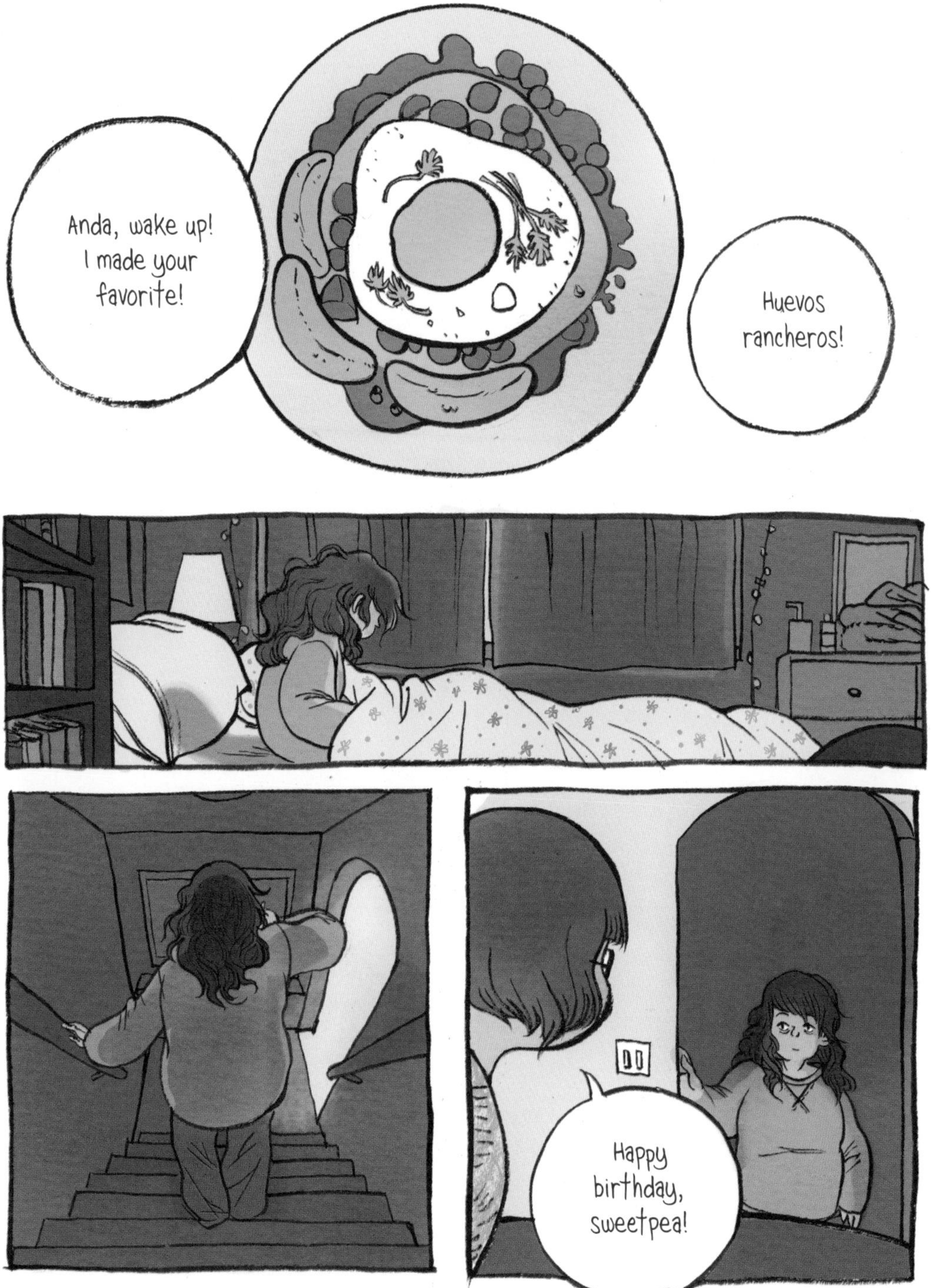
Anda, wake up! I made your favorite!
Huevos rancheros!
Happy birthday, sweetpea!

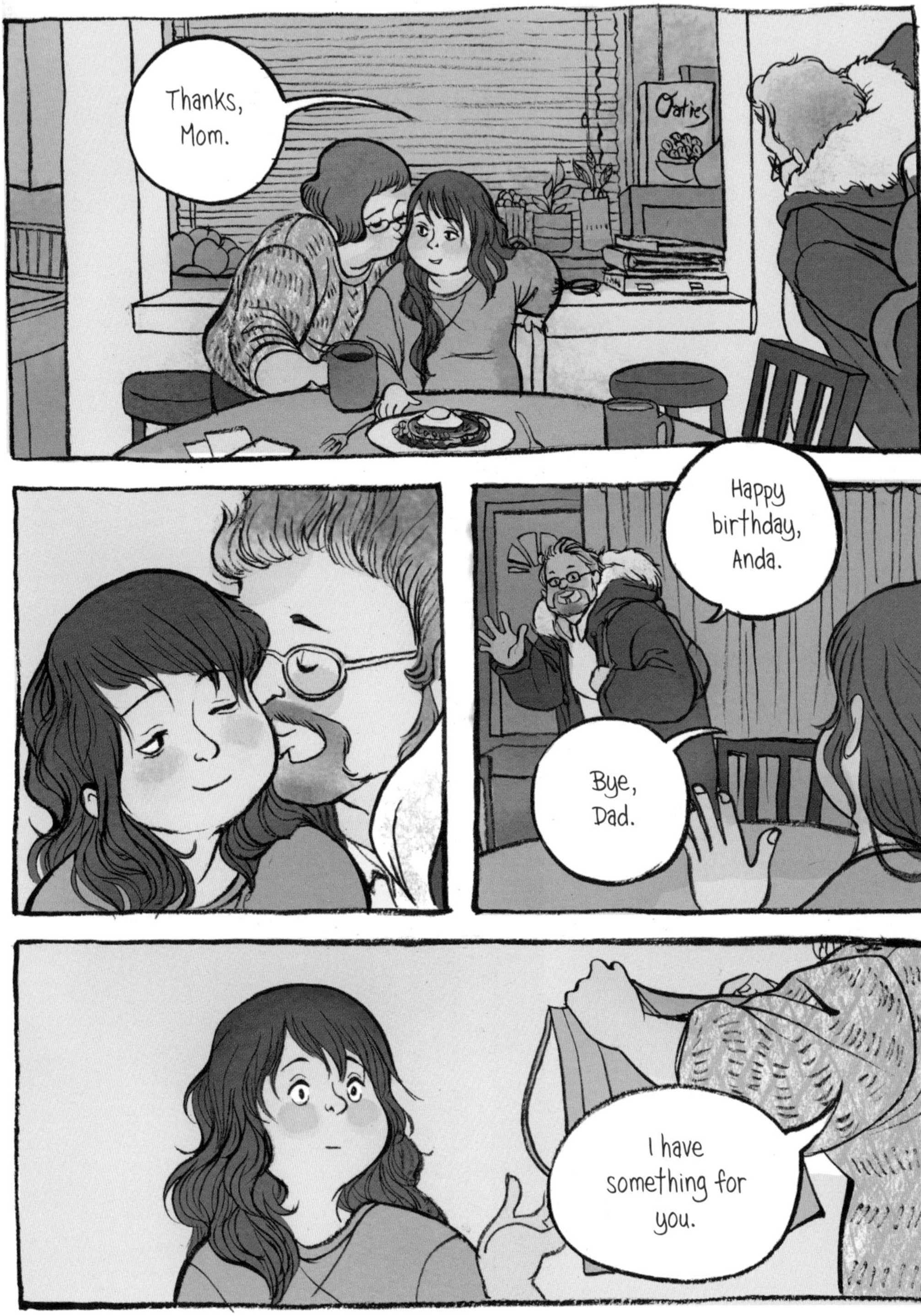
Thanks, Mom.
Oaties
Happy birthday, Anda.
Bye, Dad.
I have something for you.

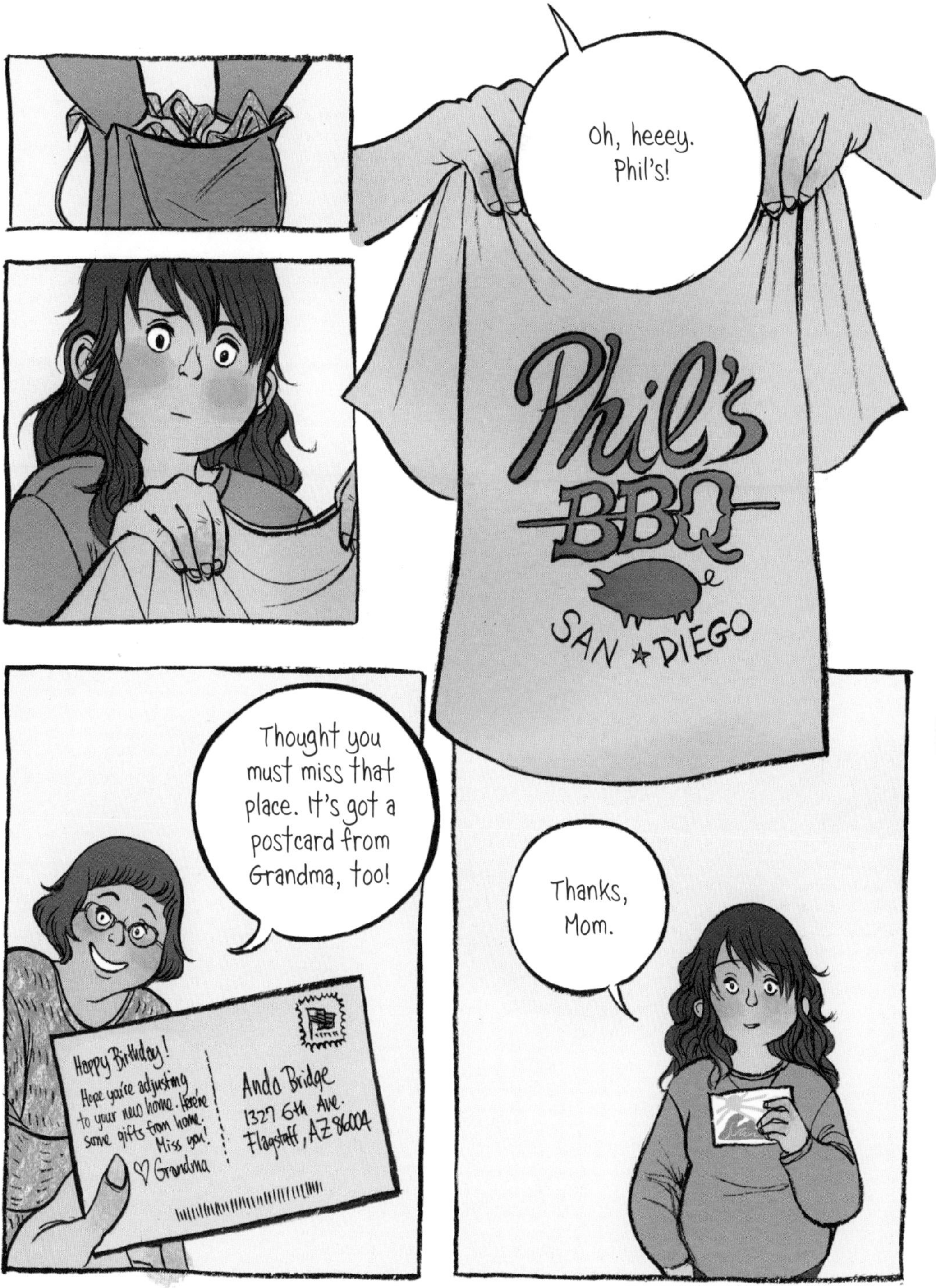
Oh, heeey. Phil's!
Phil's BBQ
SAN ★ DIEGO
Thought you must miss that place. It's got a postcard from Grandma, too!
Happy Birthday! Hope you're adjusting to your new home. Here're some gifts from home. Miss you! ♡ Grandma
Anda Bridge 1327 6th Ave. Flagstaff, AZ 86004
Thanks, Mom.

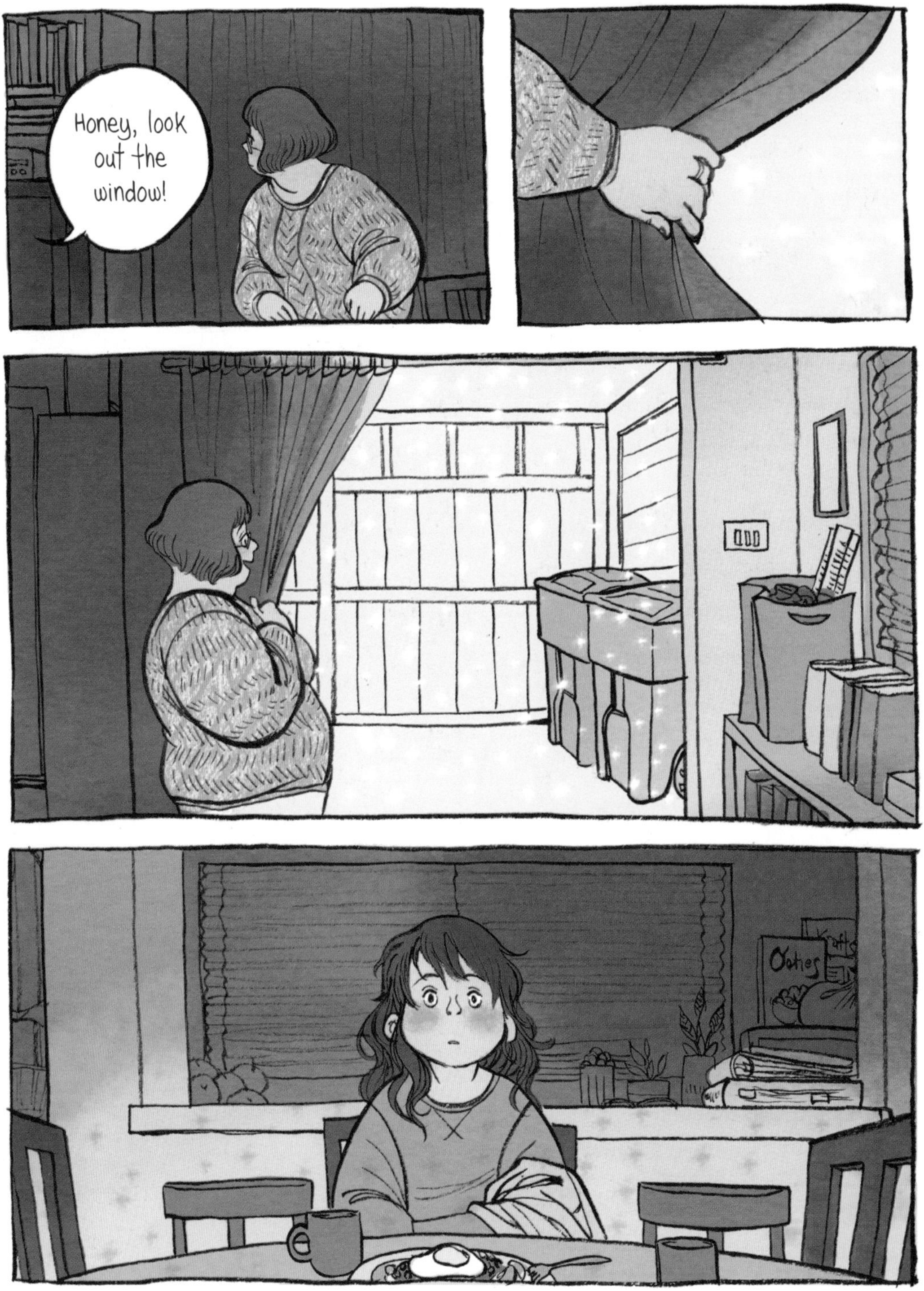
Honey, look out the window!

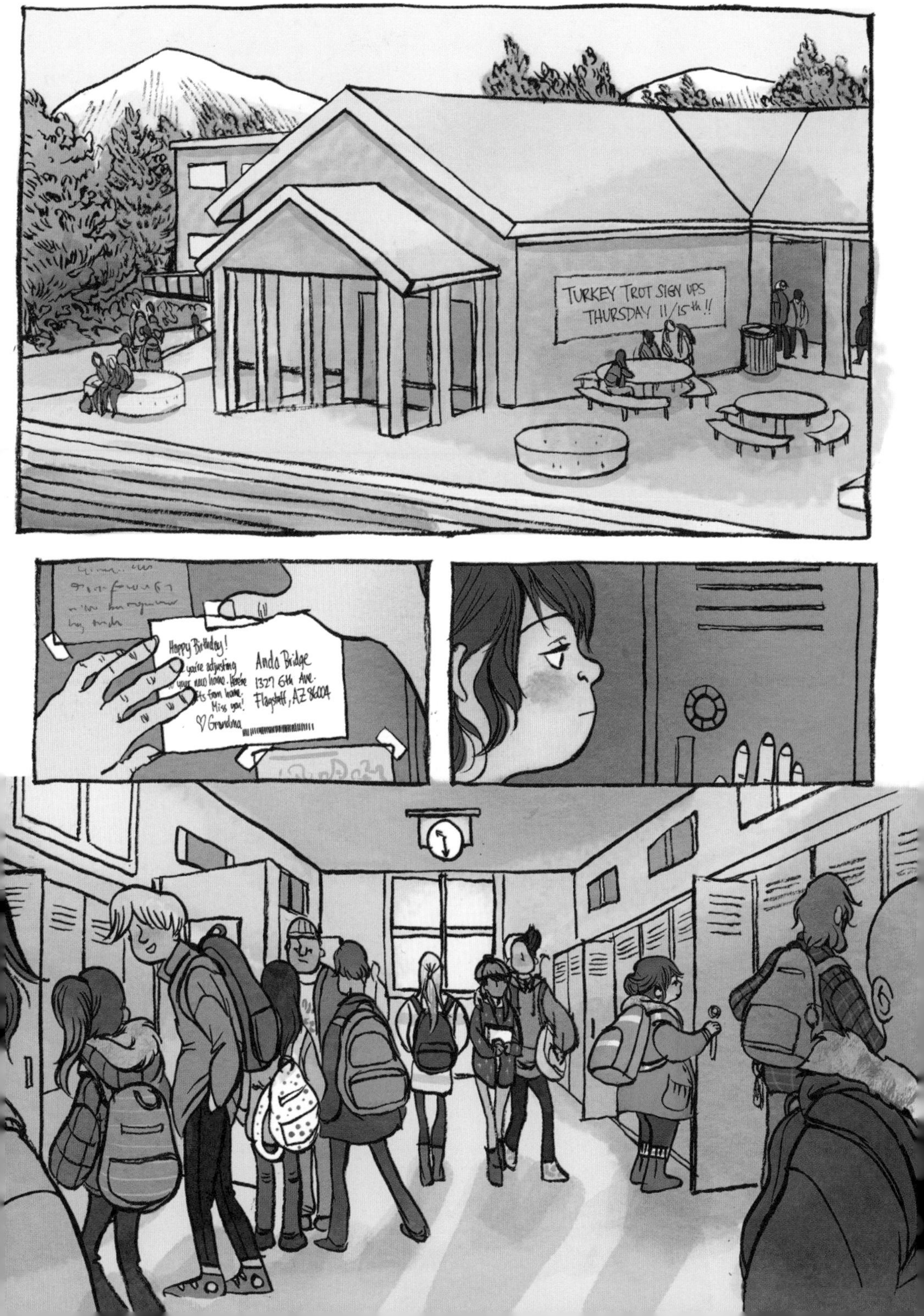
TURKEY TROT SIGN UPS THURSDAY 11/15th!!
Happy Birthday!
you're adjusting
your new home. Here're
ts from home.
Miss you!
♡ Grandma
Anda Bridge
1327 6th Ave.
Flagstaff, AZ 86004

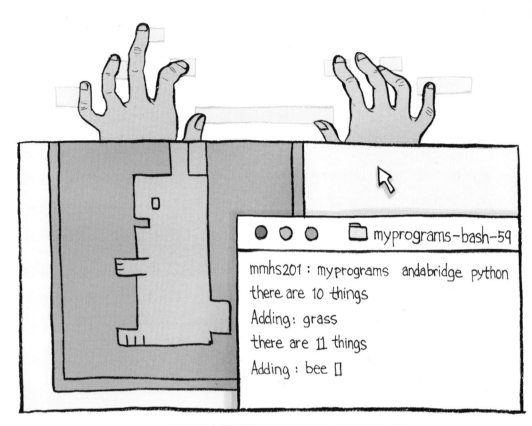

```
mmhs201: myprograms   andabridge  python
there are 10 things
Adding: grass
there are 11 things
Adding : bee []
```

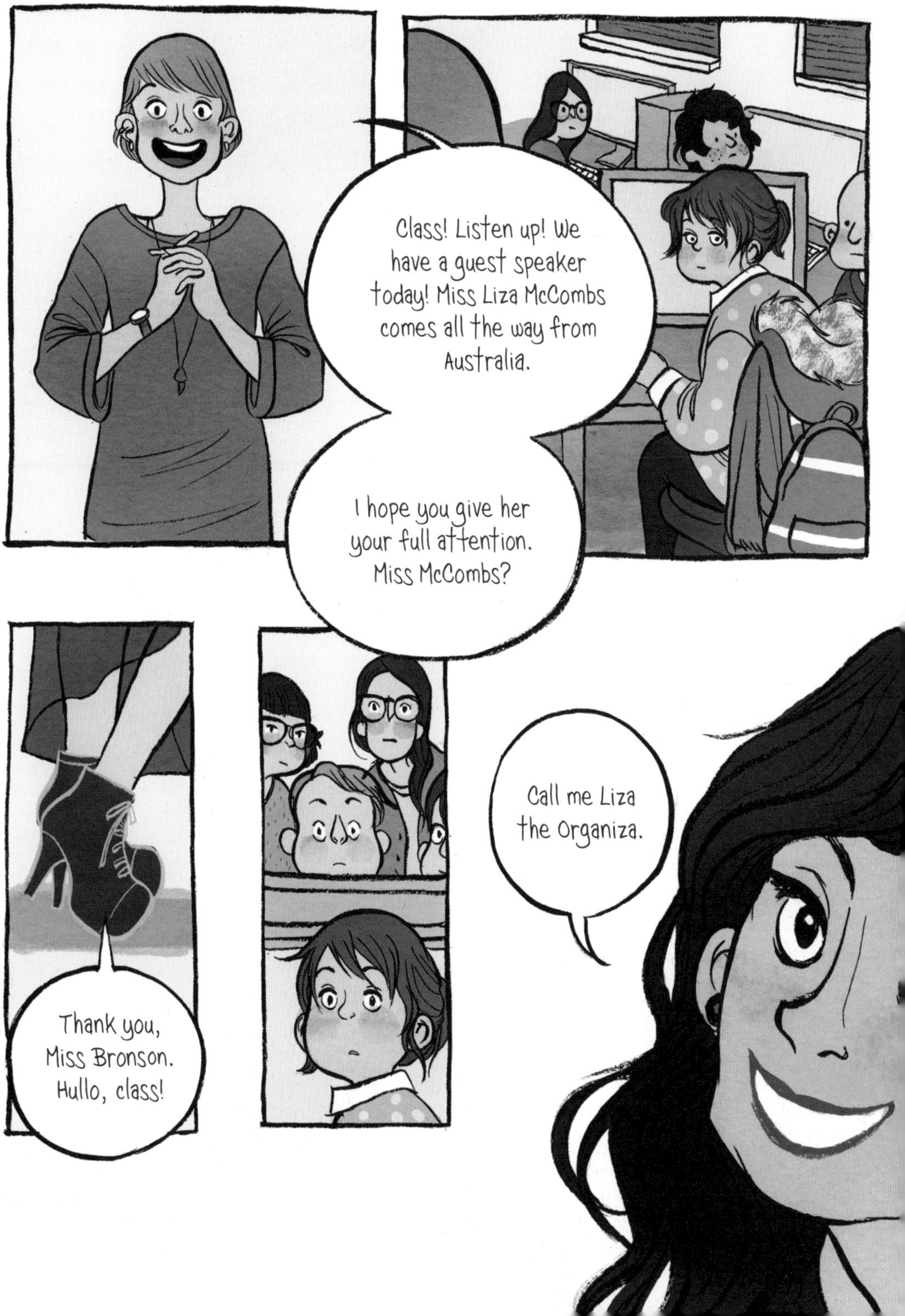
Class! Listen up! We have a guest speaker today! Miss Liza McCombs comes all the way from Australia.
I hope you give her your full attention. Miss McCombs?
Thank you, Miss Bronson. Hullo, class!
Call me Liza the Organiza.

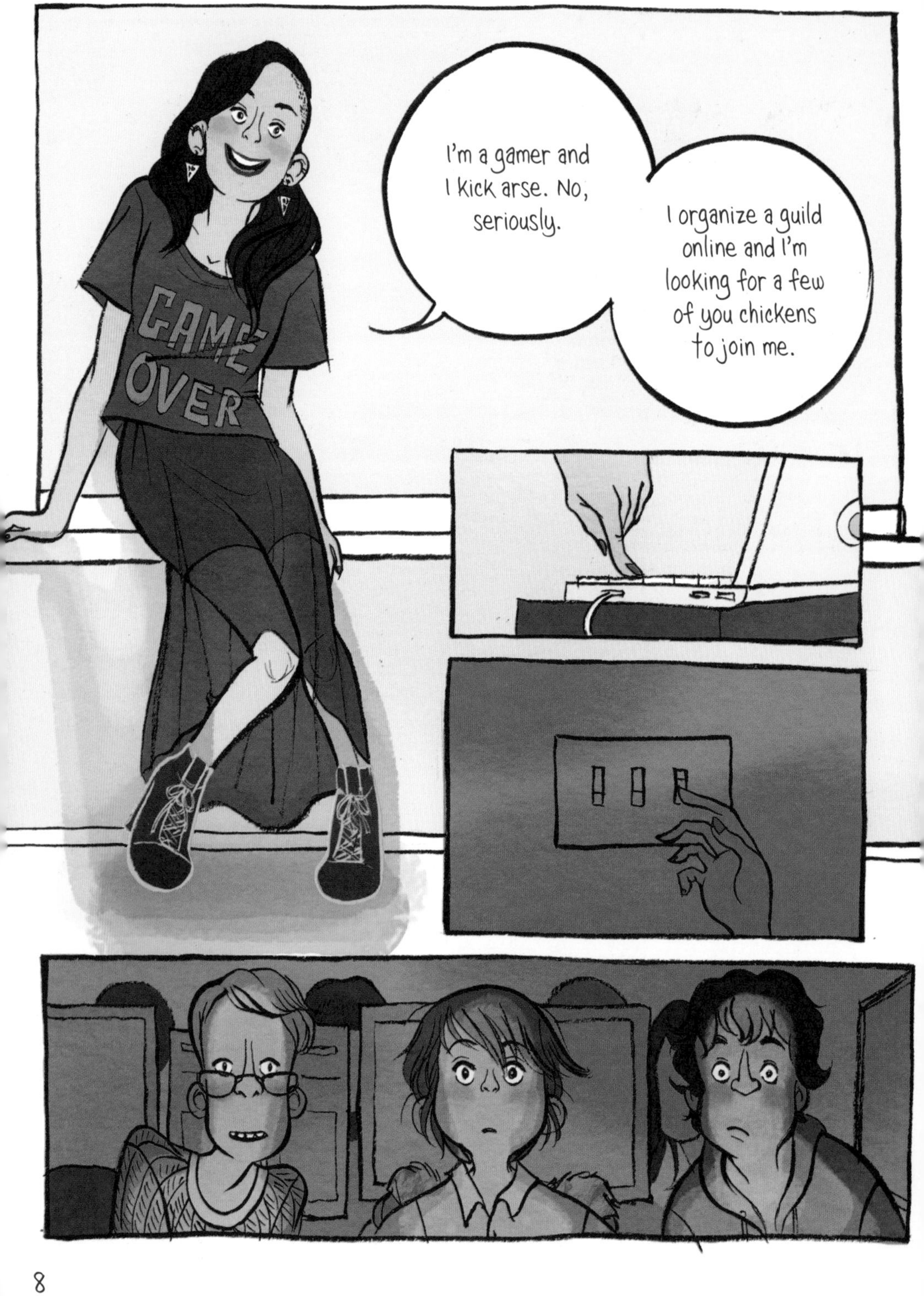
I'm a gamer and I kick arse. No, seriously.
I organize a guild online and I'm looking for a few of you chickens to join me.
GAME OVER

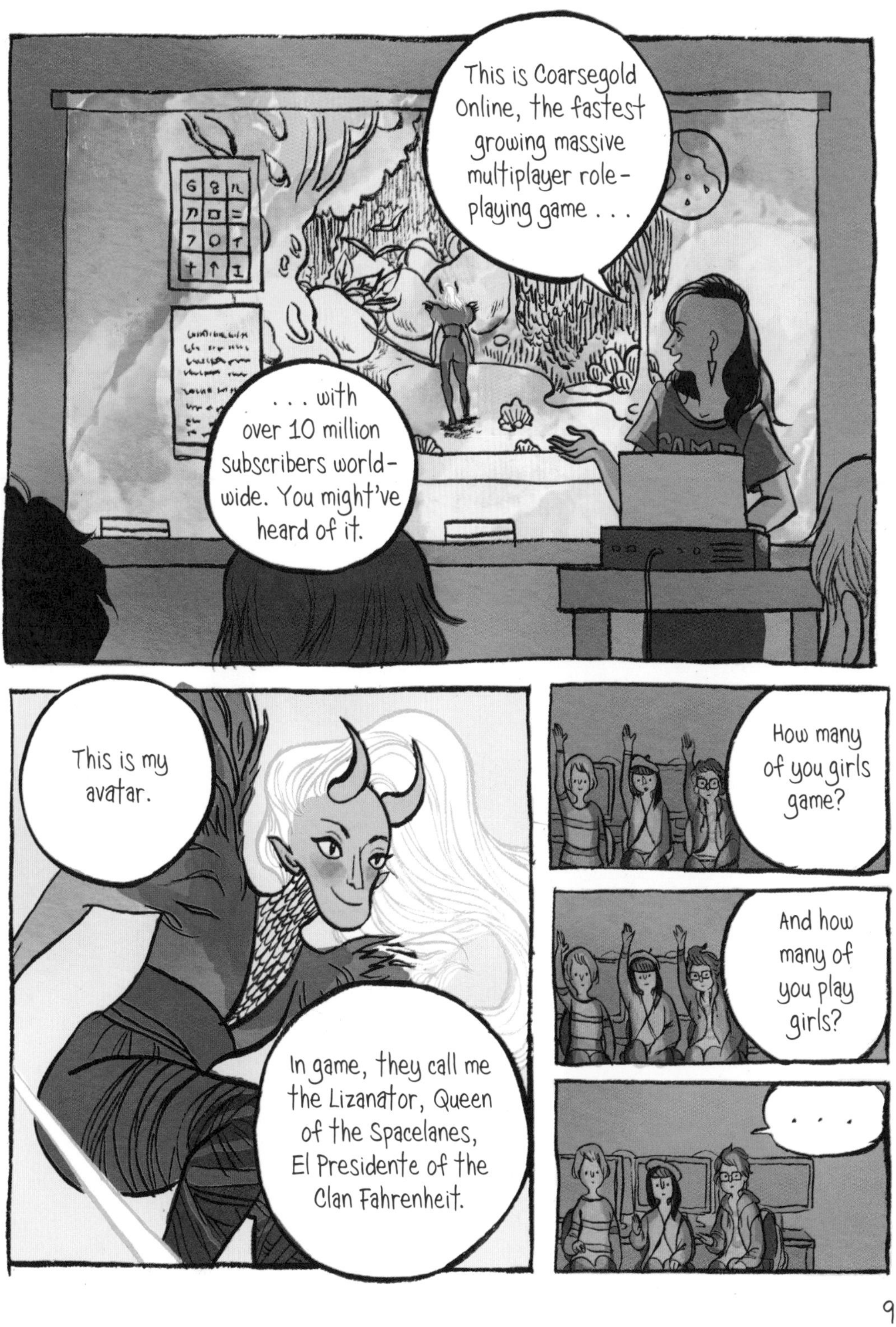

This is Coarsegold Online, the fastest growing massive multiplayer role-playing game . . .
. . . with over 10 million subscribers world-wide. You might've heard of it.
This is my avatar.
In game, they call me the Lizanator, Queen of the Spacelanes, El Presidente of the Clan Fahrenheit.
How many of you girls game?
And how many of you play girls?
. . .

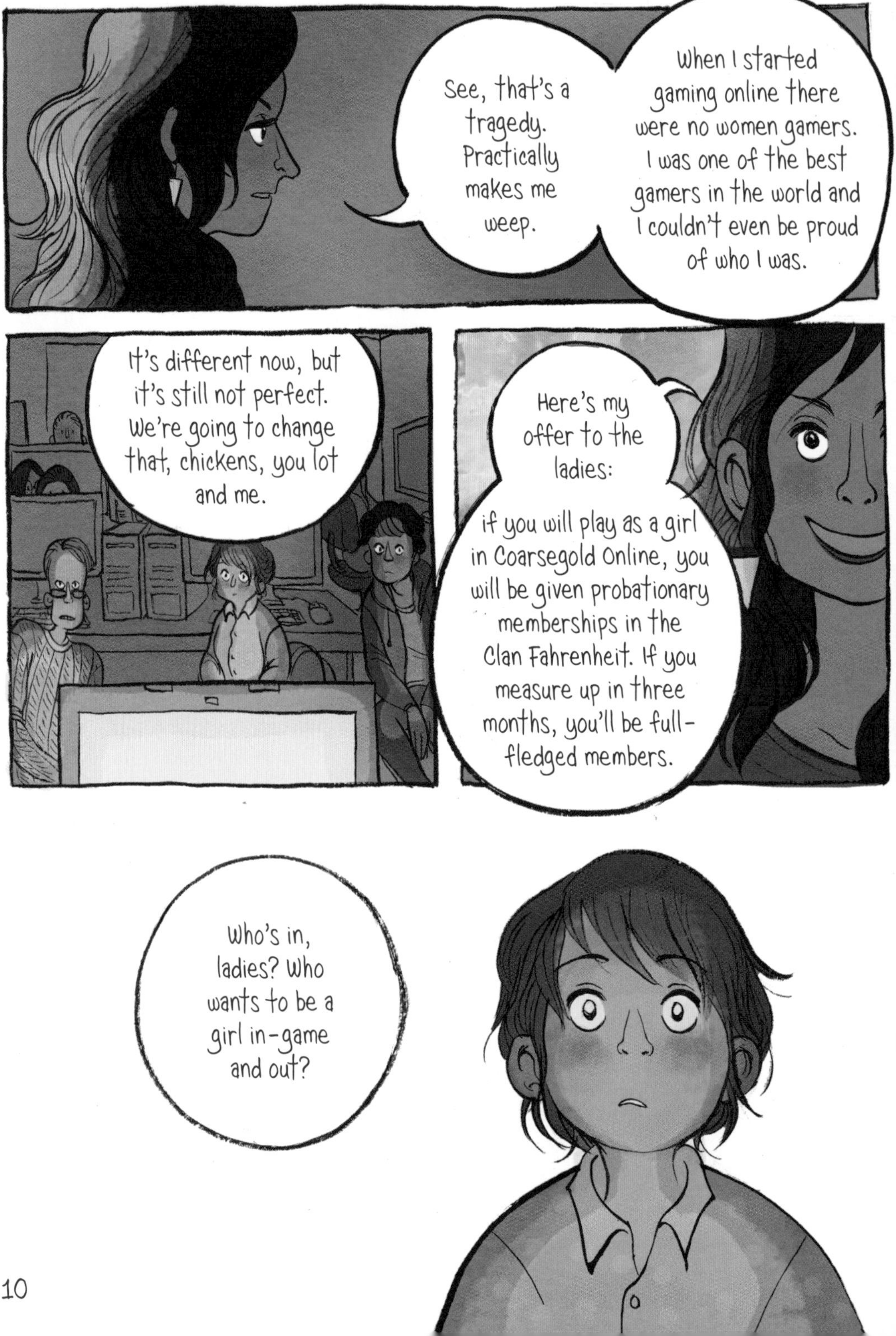
See, that's a tragedy. Practically makes me weep.
When I started gaming online there were no women gamers. I was one of the best gamers in the world and I couldn't even be proud of who I was.
It's different now, but it's still not perfect. We're going to change that, chickens, you lot and me.
Here's my offer to the ladies:
if you will play as a girl in Coarsegold Online, you will be given probationary memberships in the Clan Fahrenheit. If you measure up in three months, you'll be full-fledged members.
Who's in, ladies? Who wants to be a girl in-game and out?

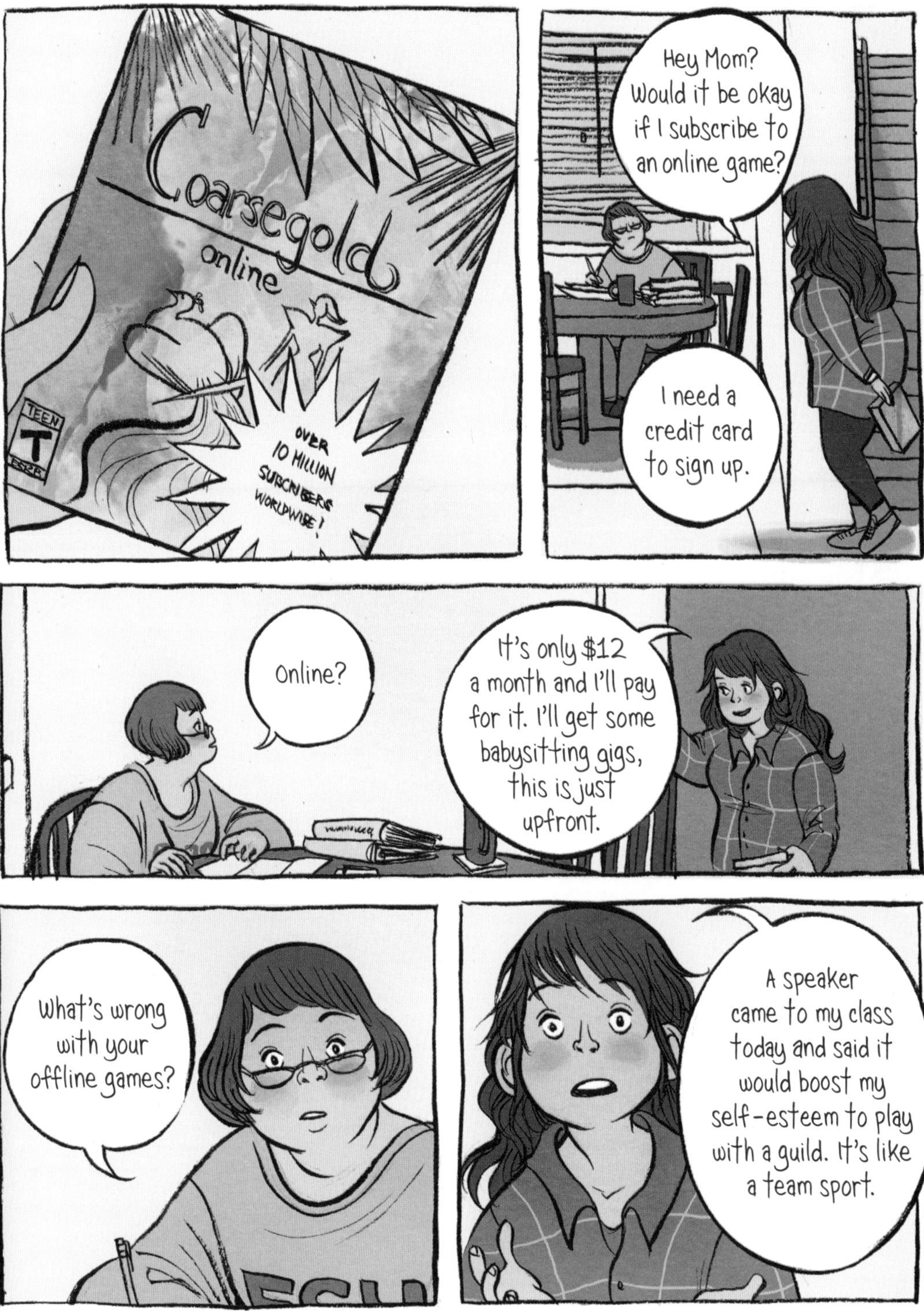
Coarsegold online
TEEN T ESRB
OVER 10 MILLION SUBSCRIBERS WORLDWIDE!
Hey Mom? Would it be okay if I subscribe to an online game?
I need a credit card to sign up.
Online?
It's only $12 a month and I'll pay for it. I'll get some babysitting gigs, this is just upfront.
What's wrong with your offline games?
A speaker came to my class today and said it would boost my self-esteem to play with a guild. It's like a team sport.

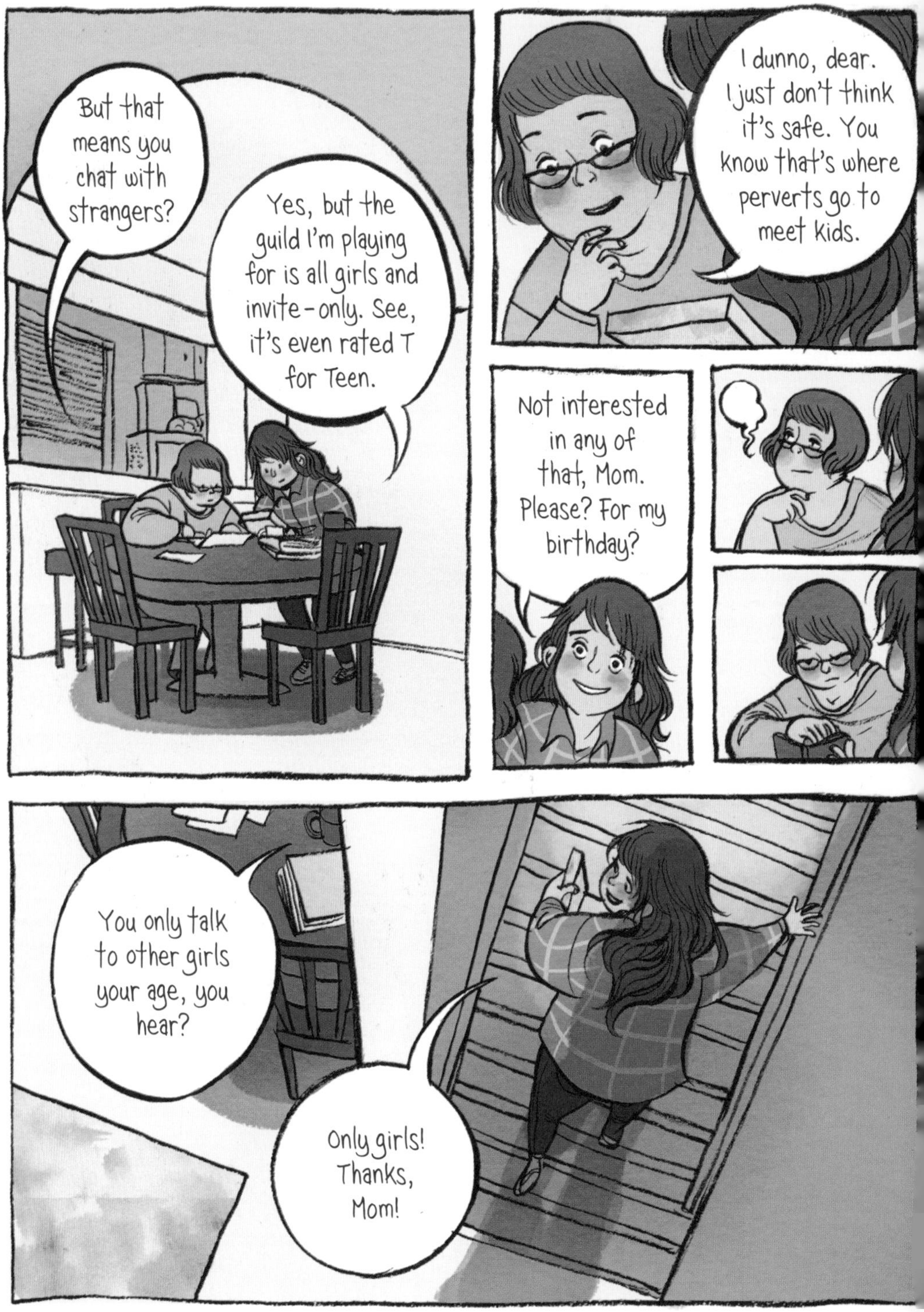
But that means you chat with strangers?
Yes, but the guild I'm playing for is all girls and invite-only. See, it's even rated T for Teen.
I dunno, dear. I just don't think it's safe. You know that's where perverts go to meet kids.
Not interested in any of that, Mom. Please? For my birthday?
You only talk to other girls your age, you hear?
Only girls! Thanks, Mom!

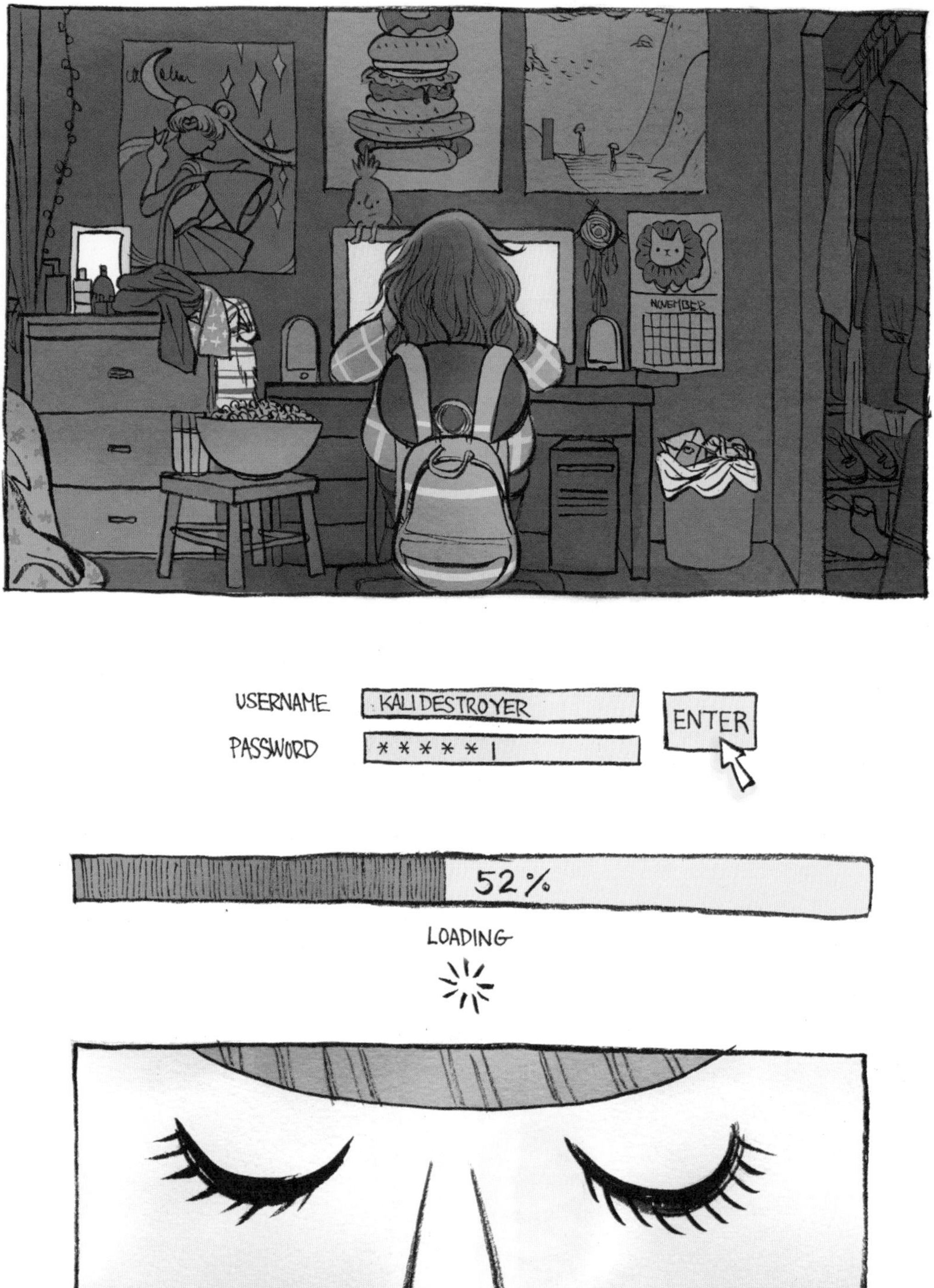
NOVEMBER
USERNAME
KALIDESTROYER
PASSWORD
*****
ENTER
52%
LOADING

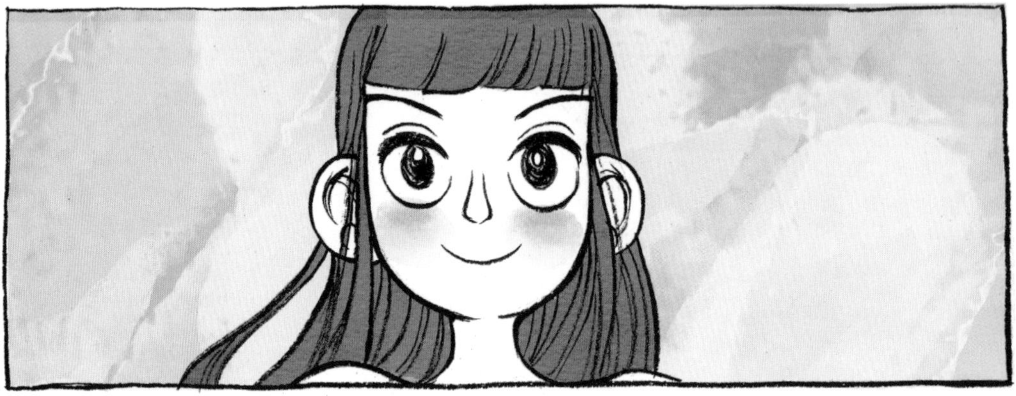

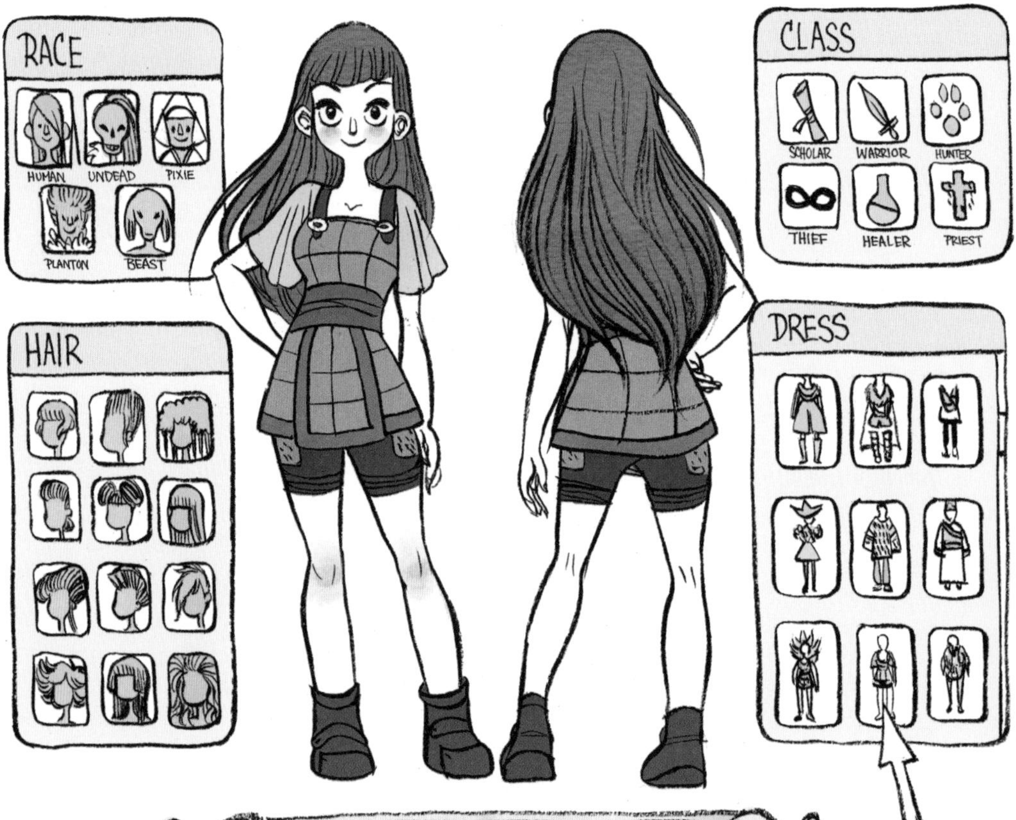
RACE
HUMAN
UNDEAD
PIXIE
PLANTON
BEAST
CLASS
SCHOLAR
WARRIOR
HUNTER
THIEF
HEALER
PRIEST
HAIR
DRESS
KALIDESTROYER

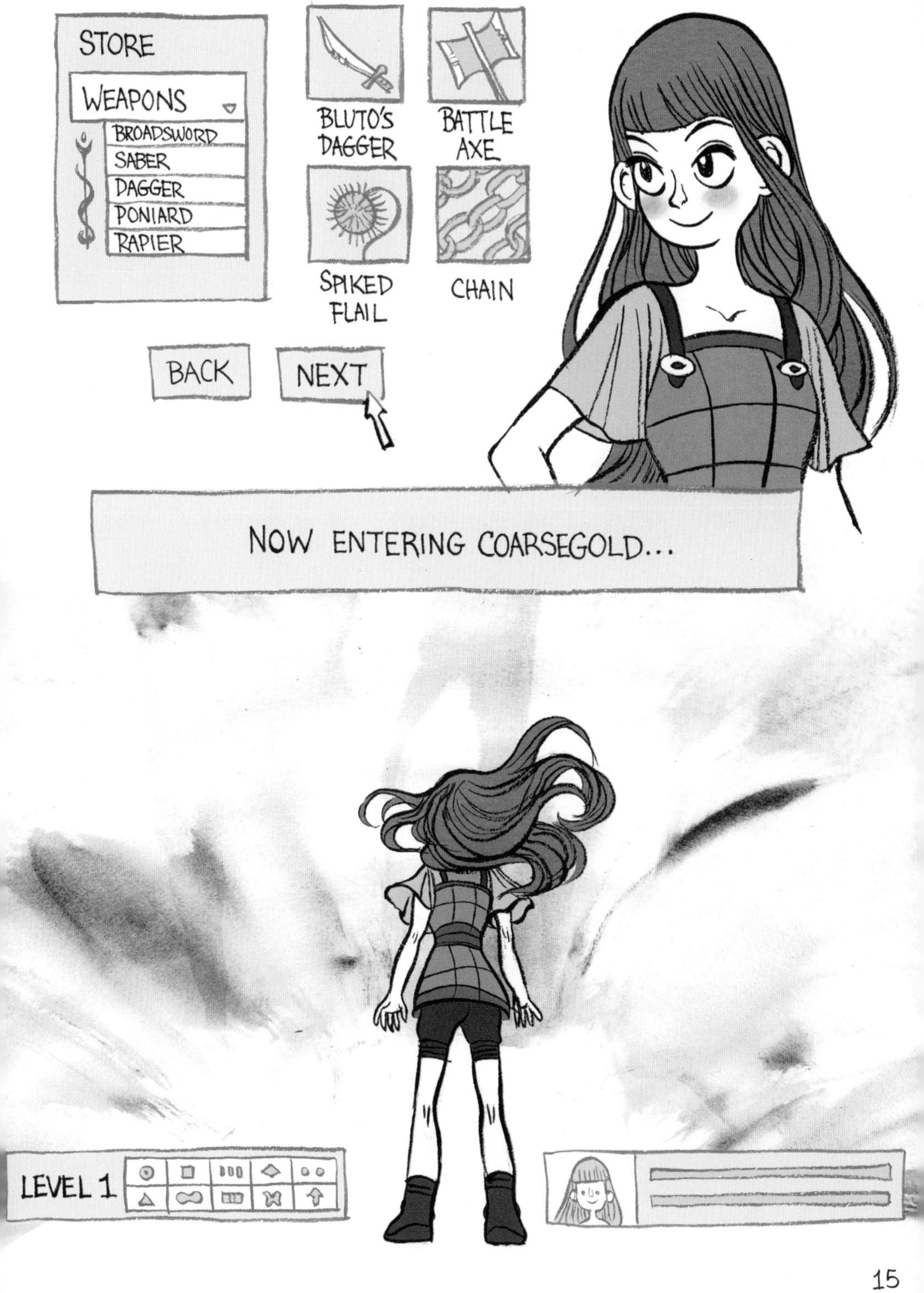
STORE
WEAPONS
BROADSWORD
SABER
DAGGER
PONIARD
RAPIER
BLUTO'S DAGGER
BATTLE AXE
SPIKED FLAIL
CHAIN
BACK
NEXT
NOW ENTERING COARSEGOLD...
LEVEL 1

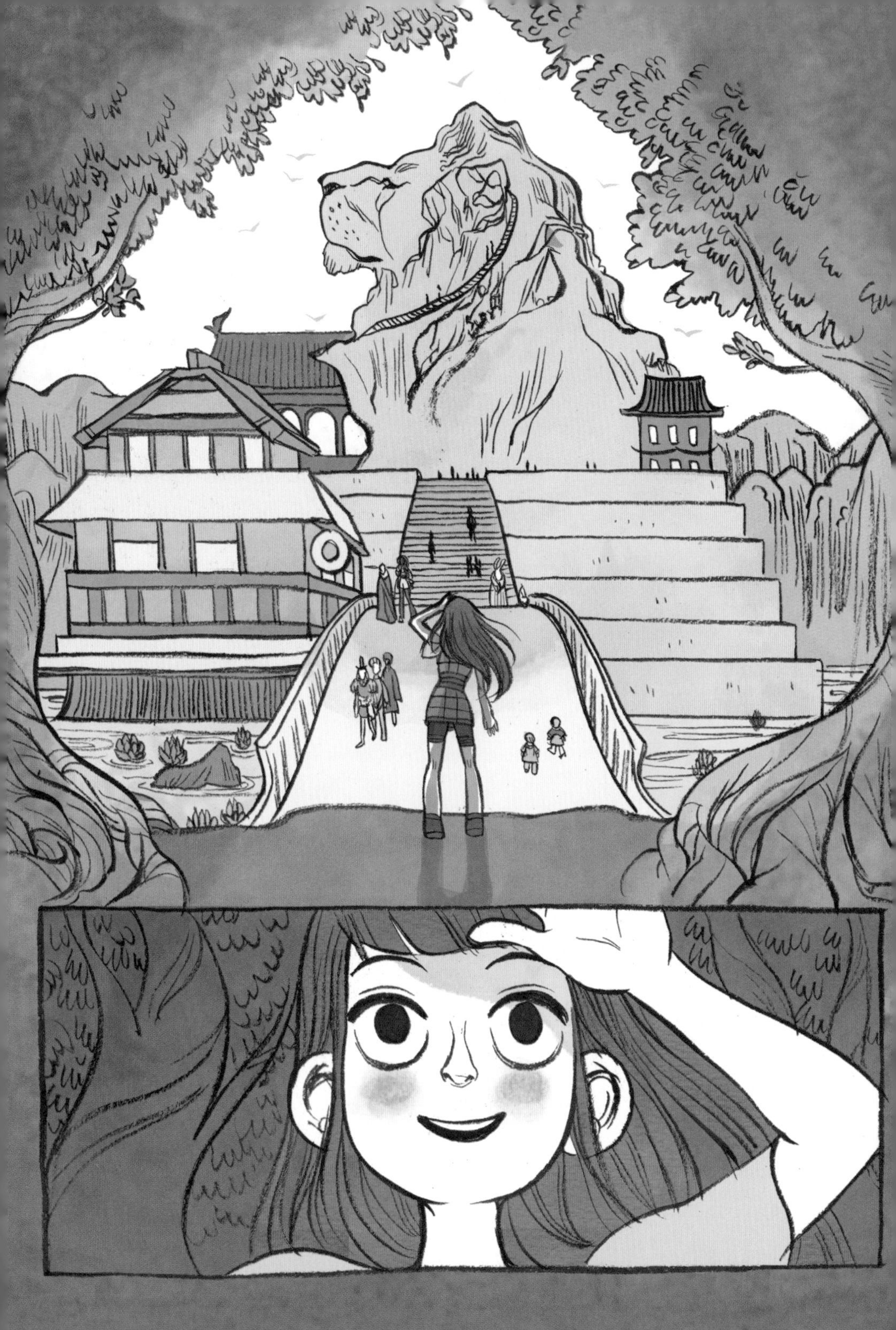

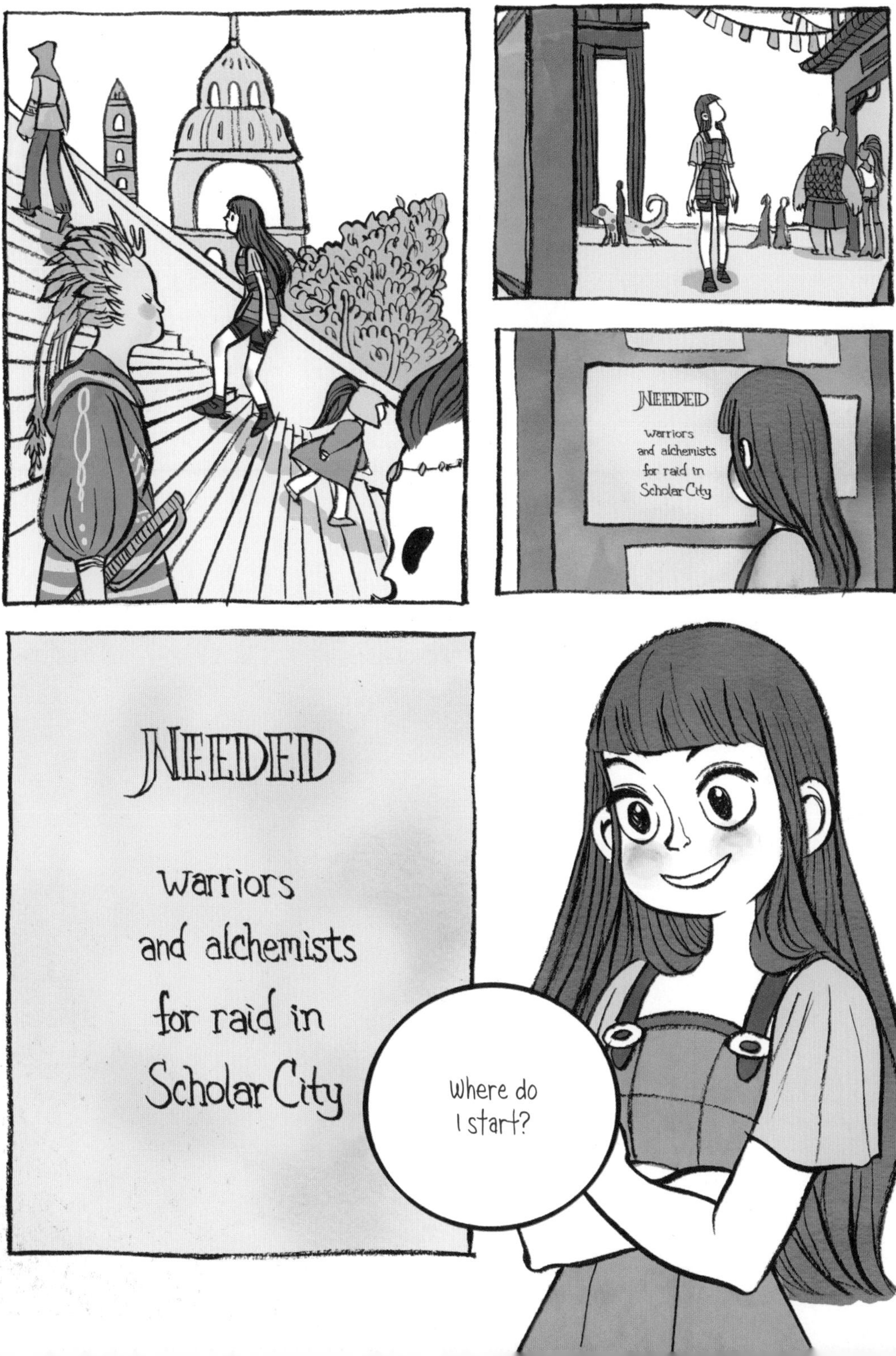
NEEDED
warriors
and alchemists
for raid in
Scholar City
NEEDED
warriors
and alchemists
for raid in
Scholar City
Where do
I start?

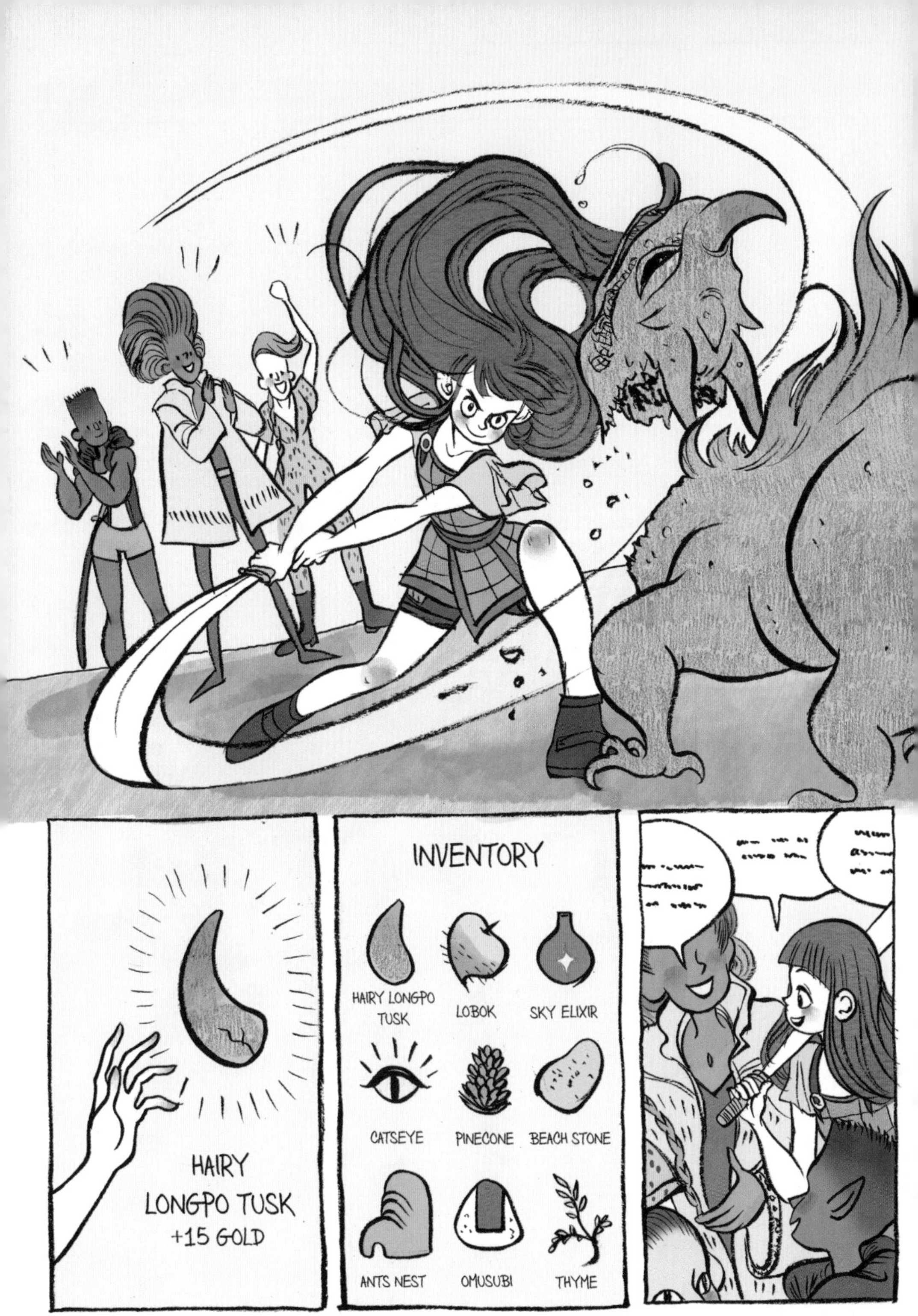
HAIRY
LONGPO TUSK
+15 GOLD
INVENTORY
HAIRY LONGPO
TUSK
LOBOK
SKY ELIXIR
CATSEYE
PINECONE
BEACH STONE
ANTS NEST
OMUSUBI
THYME

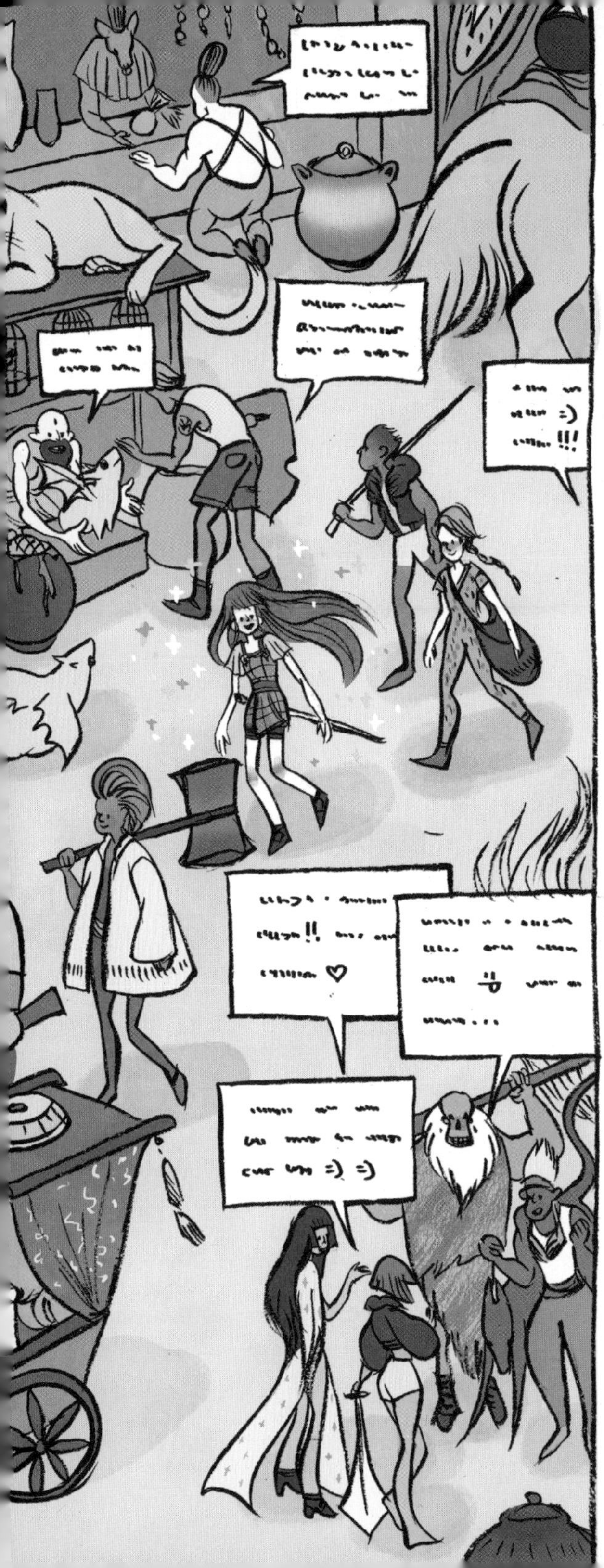

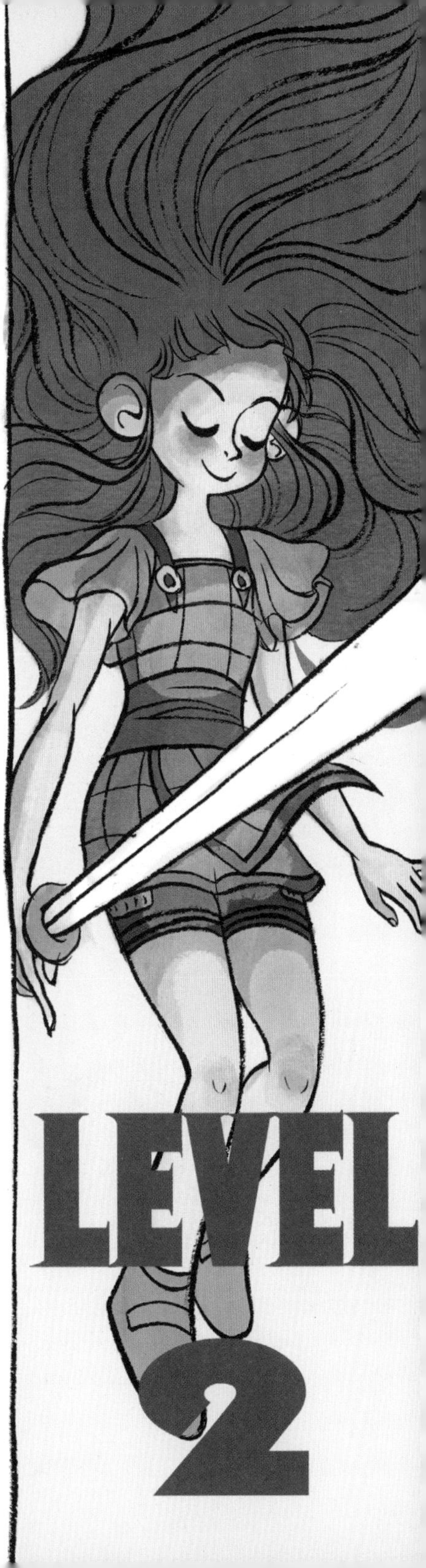

LEVEL 2

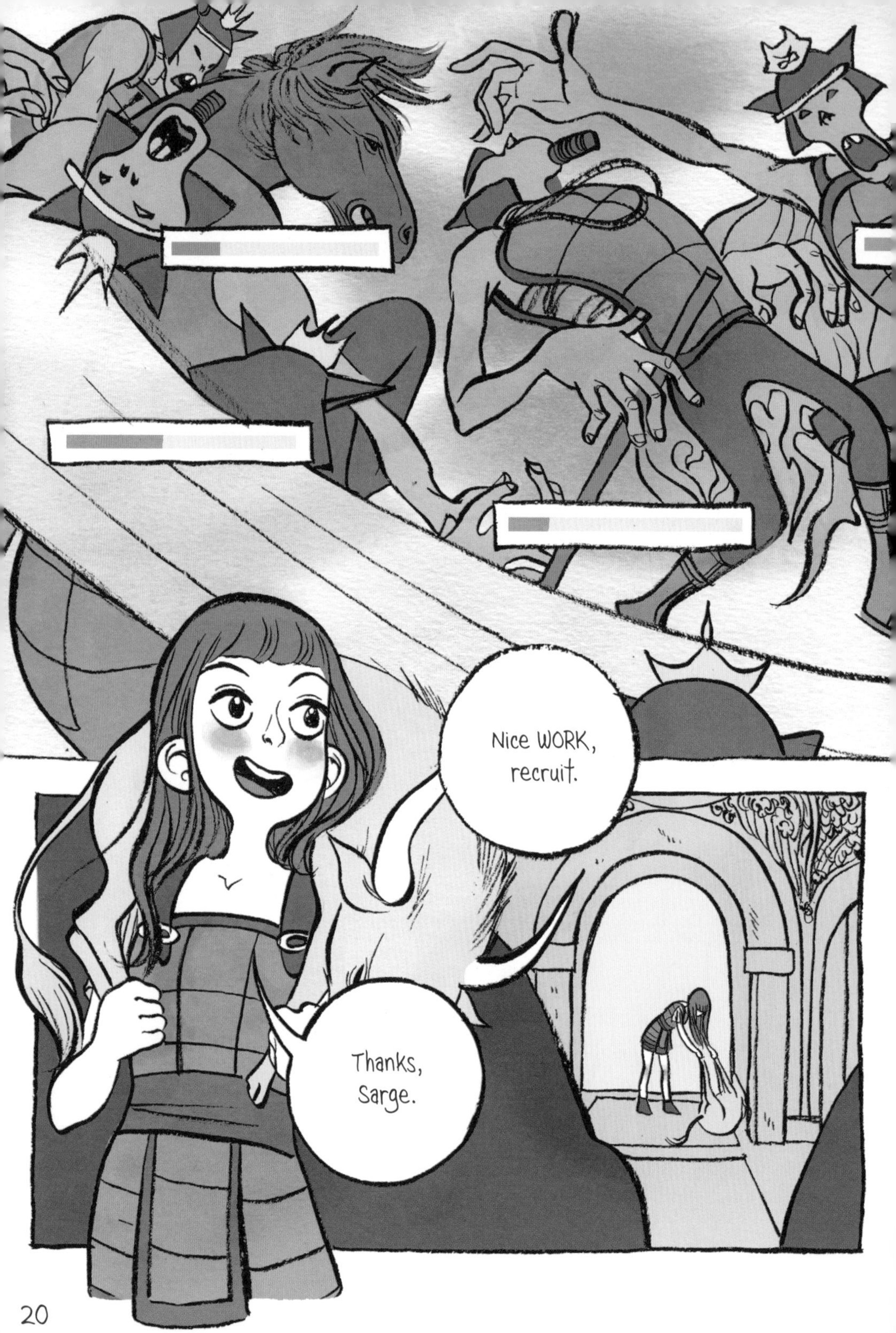
Nice WORK, recruit.
Thanks, Sarge.

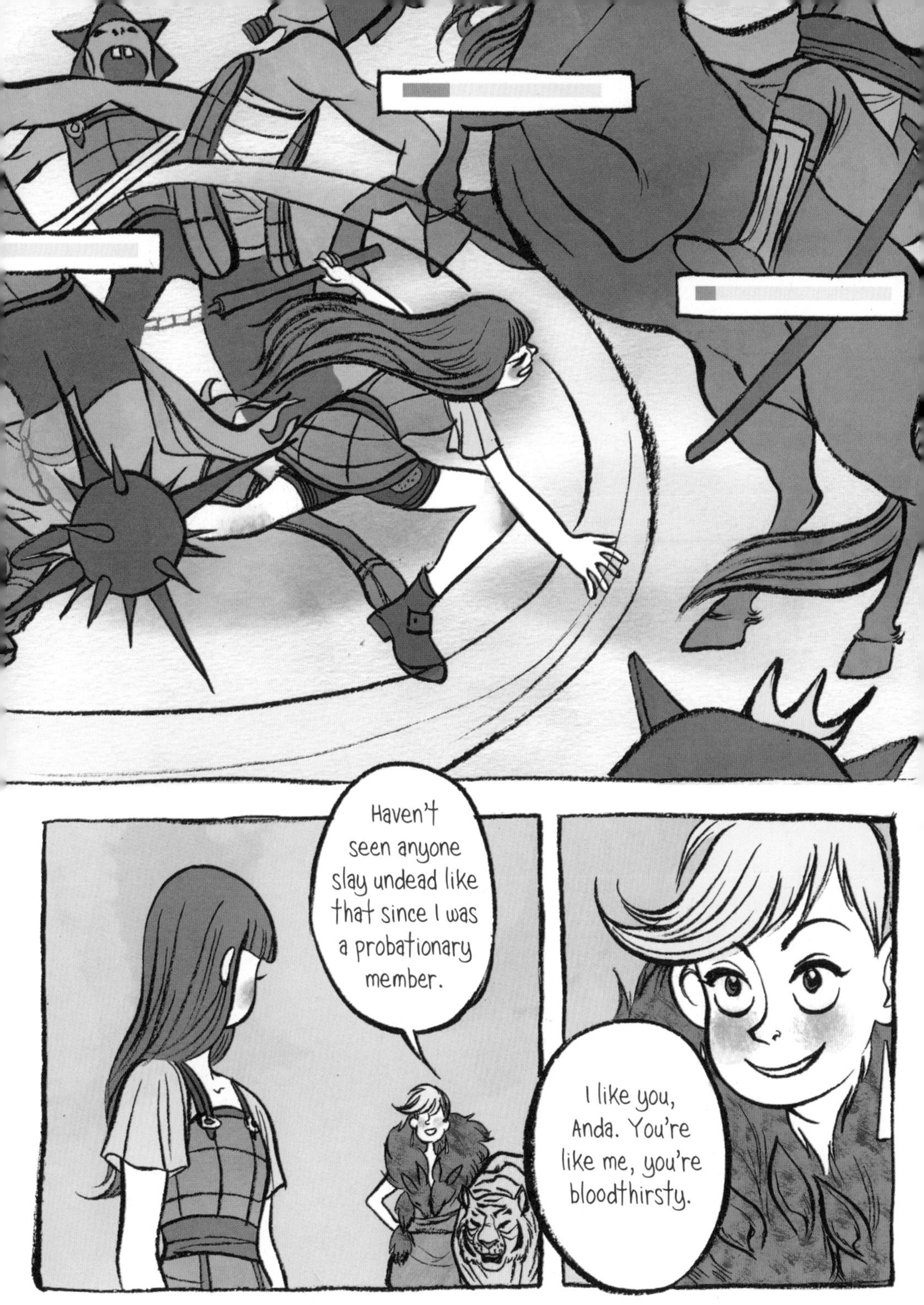
Haven't seen anyone slay undead like that since I was a probationary member.
I like you, Anda. You're like me, you're bloodthirsty.

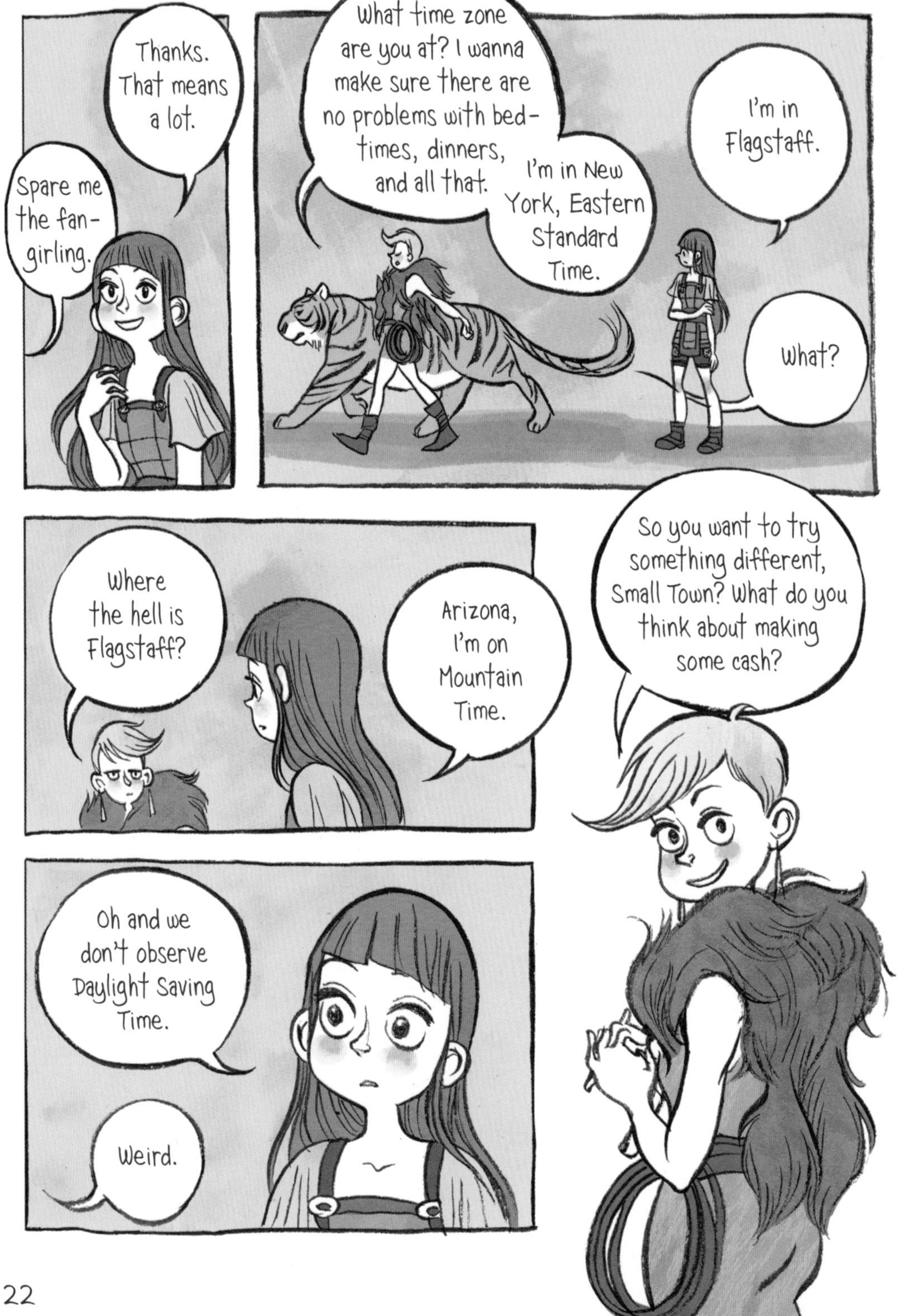
Thanks. That means a lot.
Spare me the fan-girling.
What time zone are you at? I wanna make sure there are no problems with bed-times, dinners, and all that.
I'm in New York, Eastern Standard Time.
I'm in Flagstaff.
What?
Where the hell is Flagstaff?
Arizona, I'm on Mountain Time.
Oh and we don't observe Daylight Saving Time.
Weird.
So you want to try something different, Small Town? What do you think about making some cash?

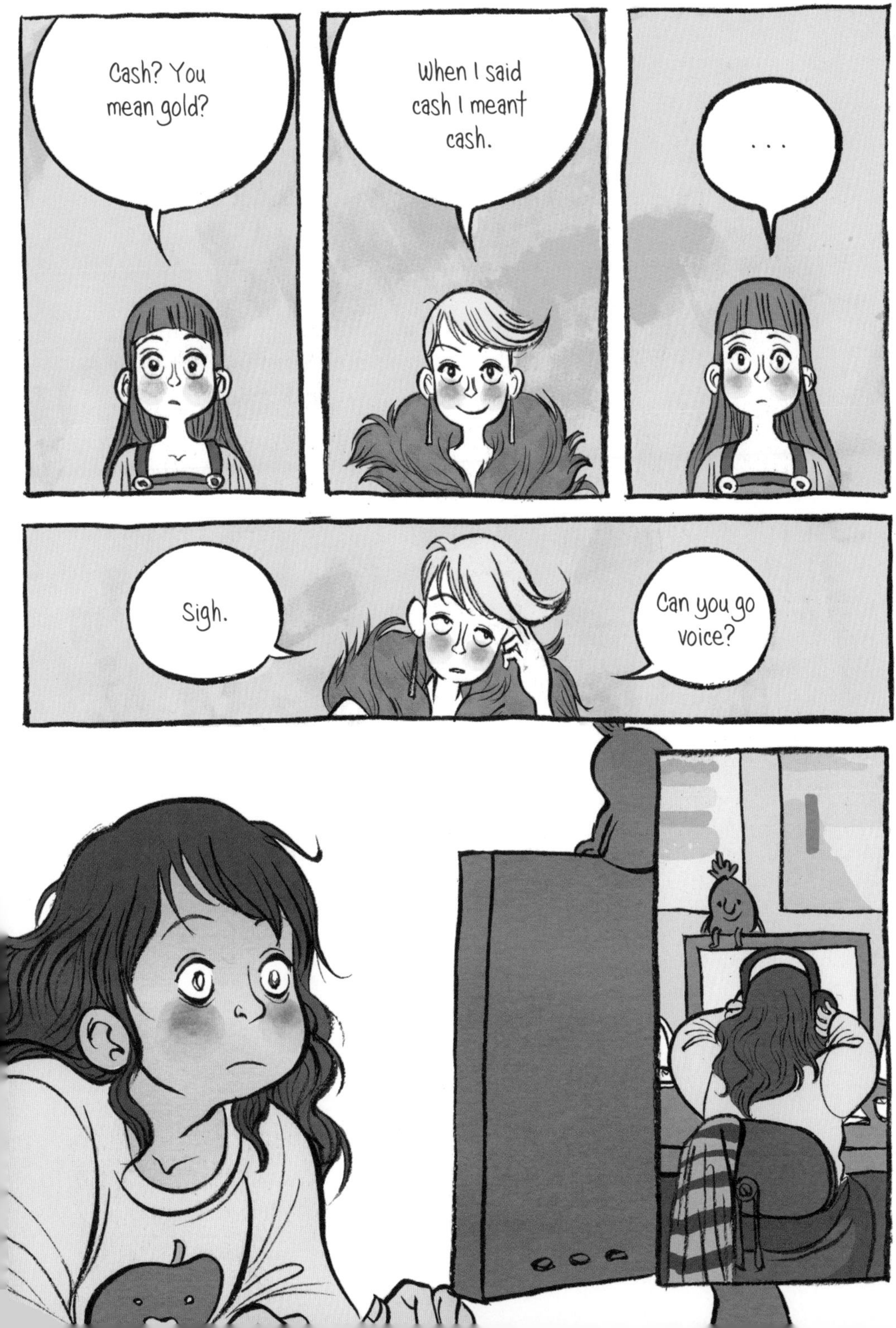
Cash? You mean gold?
When I said cash I meant cash.
. . .
Sigh.
Can you go voice?

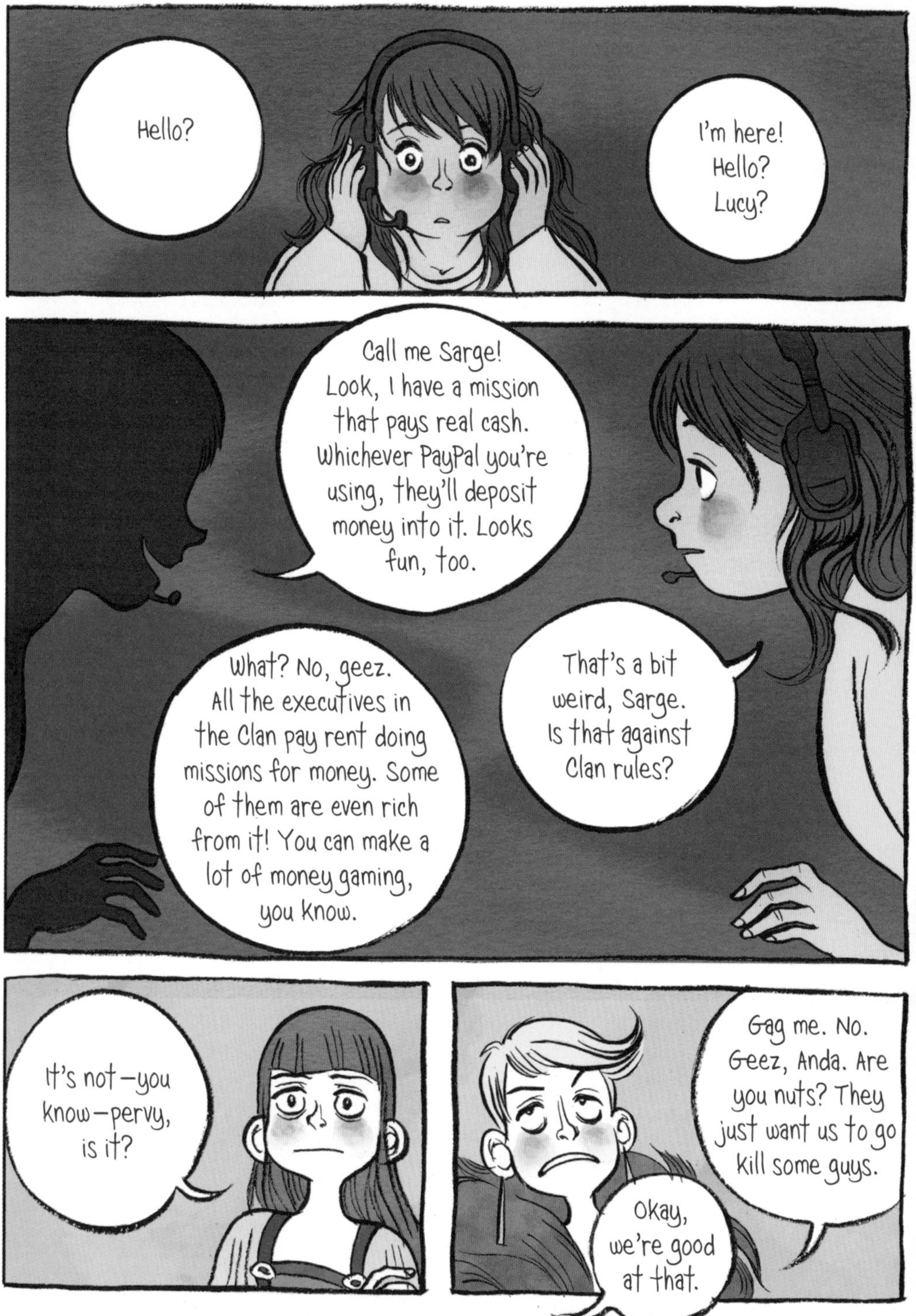
Hello?
I'm here! Hello? Lucy?
Call me Sarge! Look, I have a mission that pays real cash. Whichever PayPal you're using, they'll deposit money into it. Looks fun, too.
That's a bit weird, Sarge. Is that against Clan rules?
What? No, geez. All the executives in the Clan pay rent doing missions for money. Some of them are even rich from it! You can make a lot of money gaming, you know.
It's not—you know—pervy, is it?
Gag me. No. Geez, Anda. Are you nuts? They just want us to go kill some guys.
Okay, we're good at that.

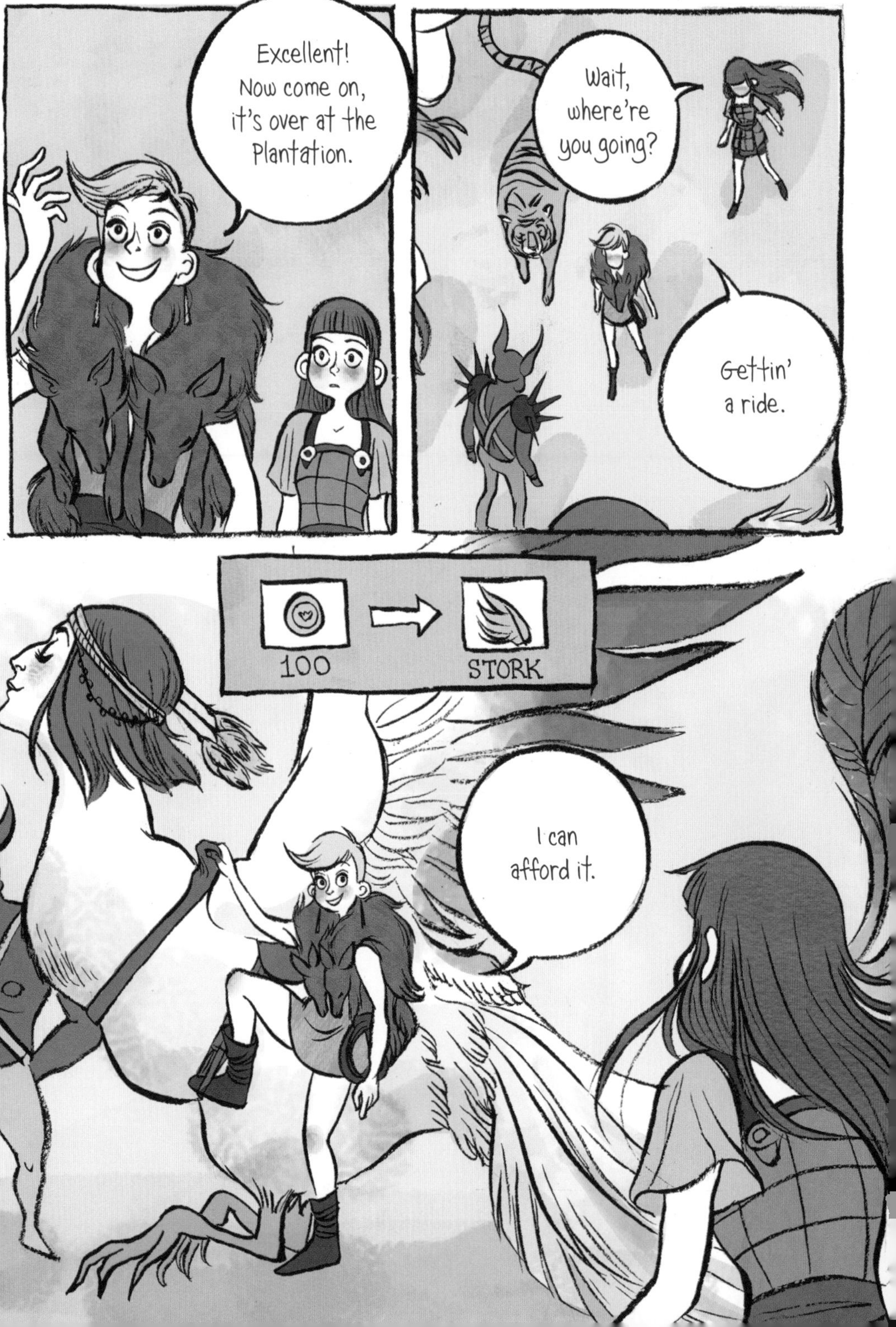
Excellent! Now come on, it's over at the Plantation.
Wait, where're you going?
Gettin' a ride.
100
STORK
I can afford it.

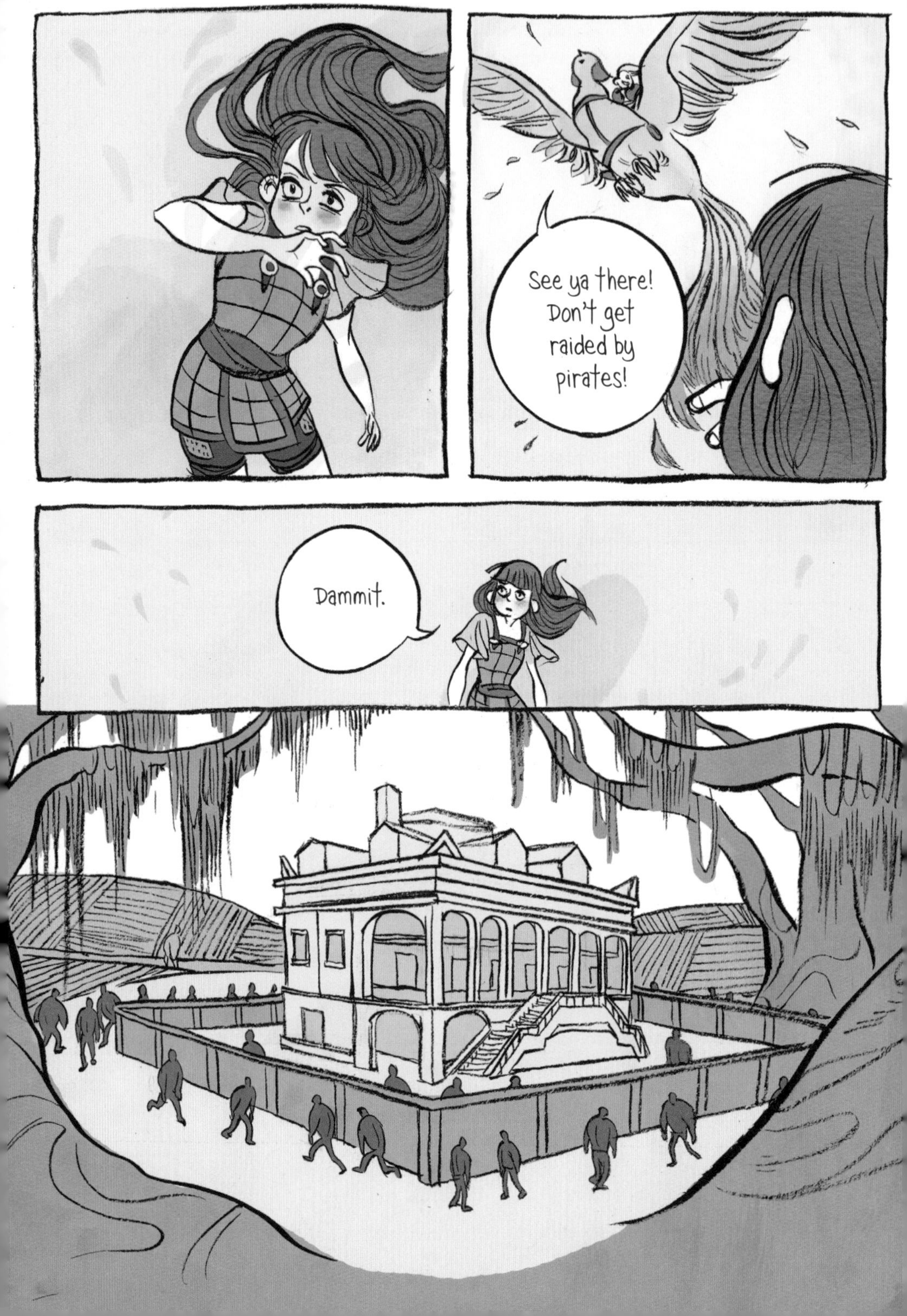
See ya there! Don't get raided by pirates!
Dammit.

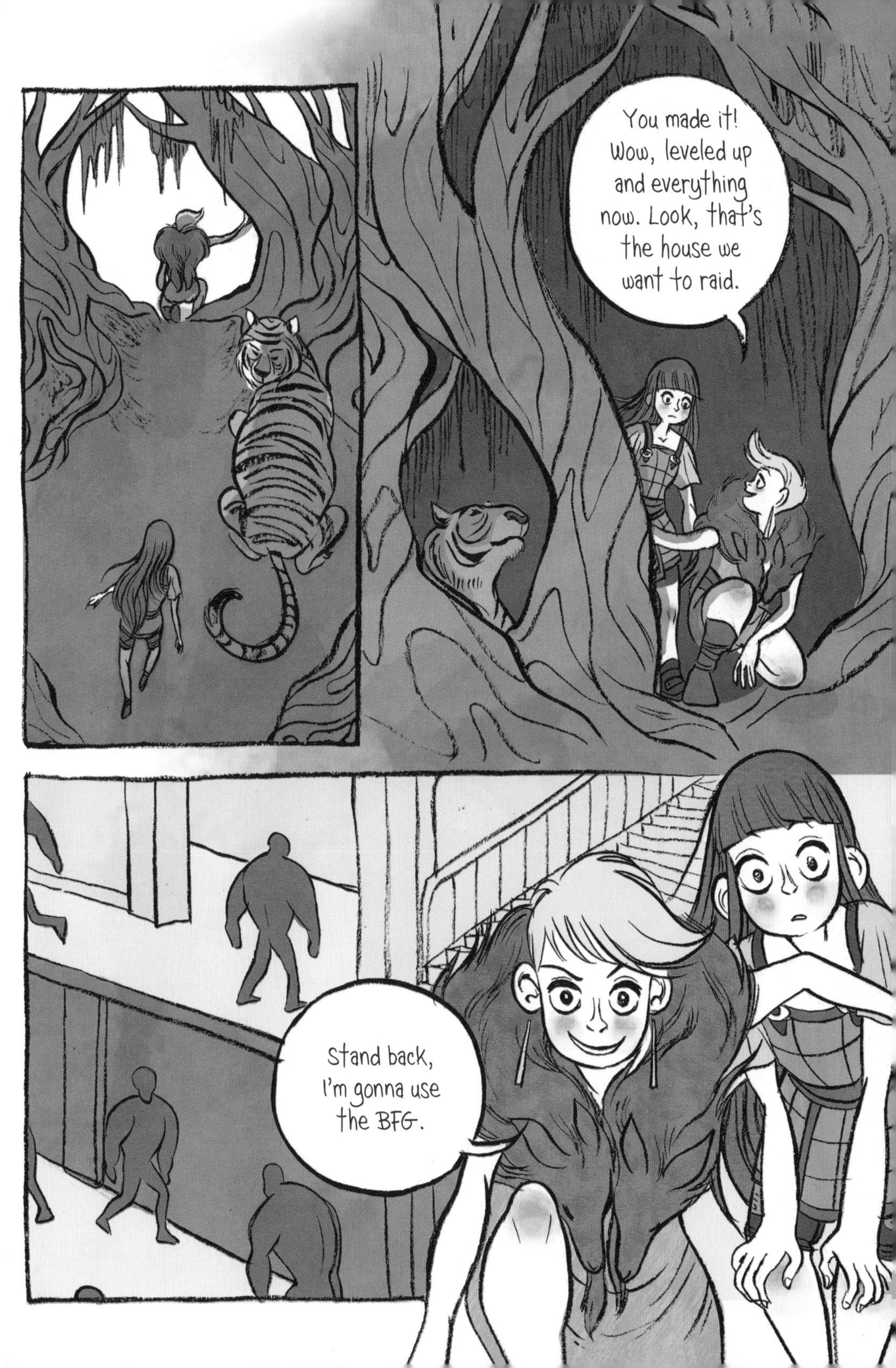
You made it! Wow, leveled up and everything now. Look, that's the house we want to raid.
Stand back, I'm gonna use the BFG.

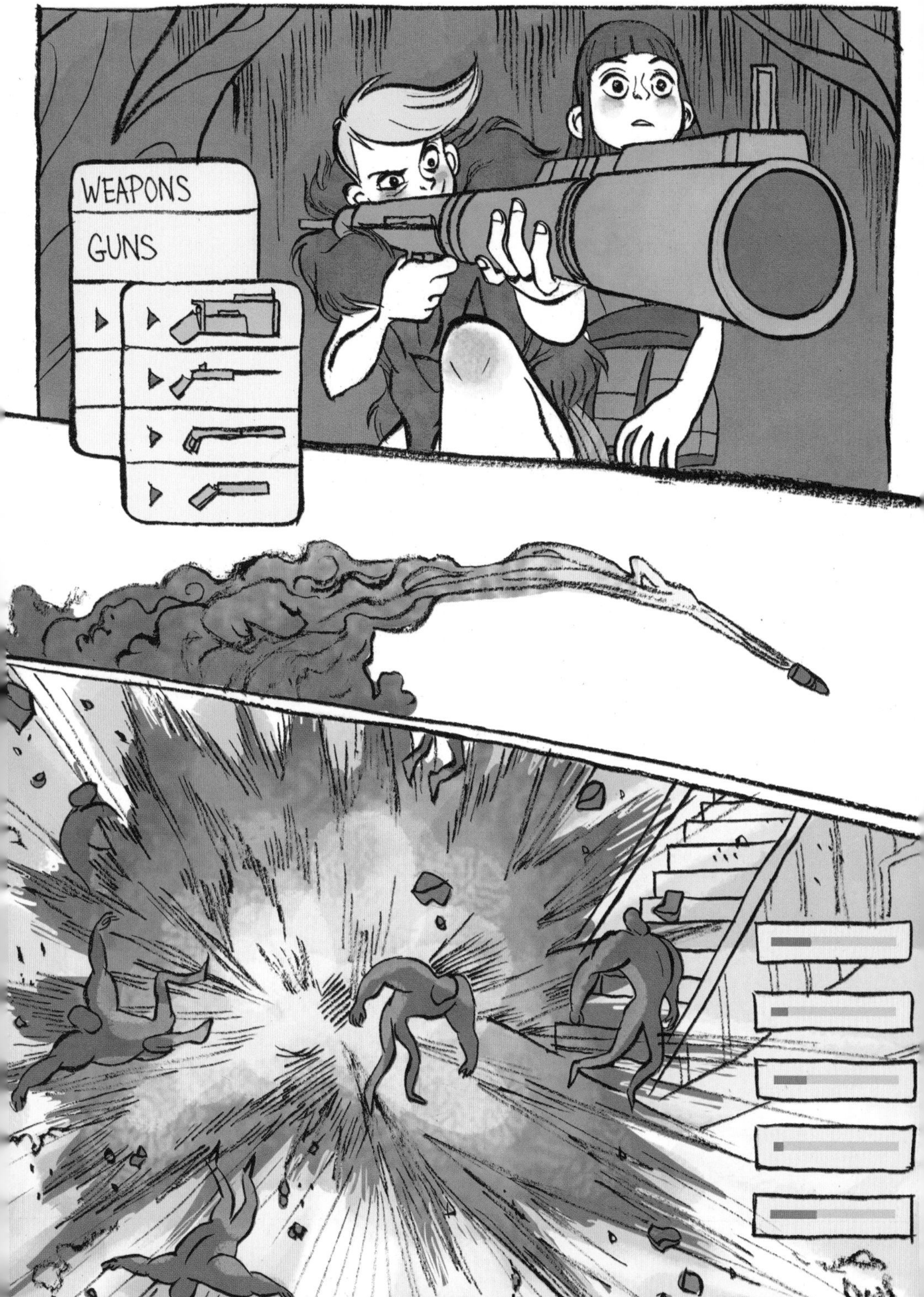
WEAPONS
GUNS

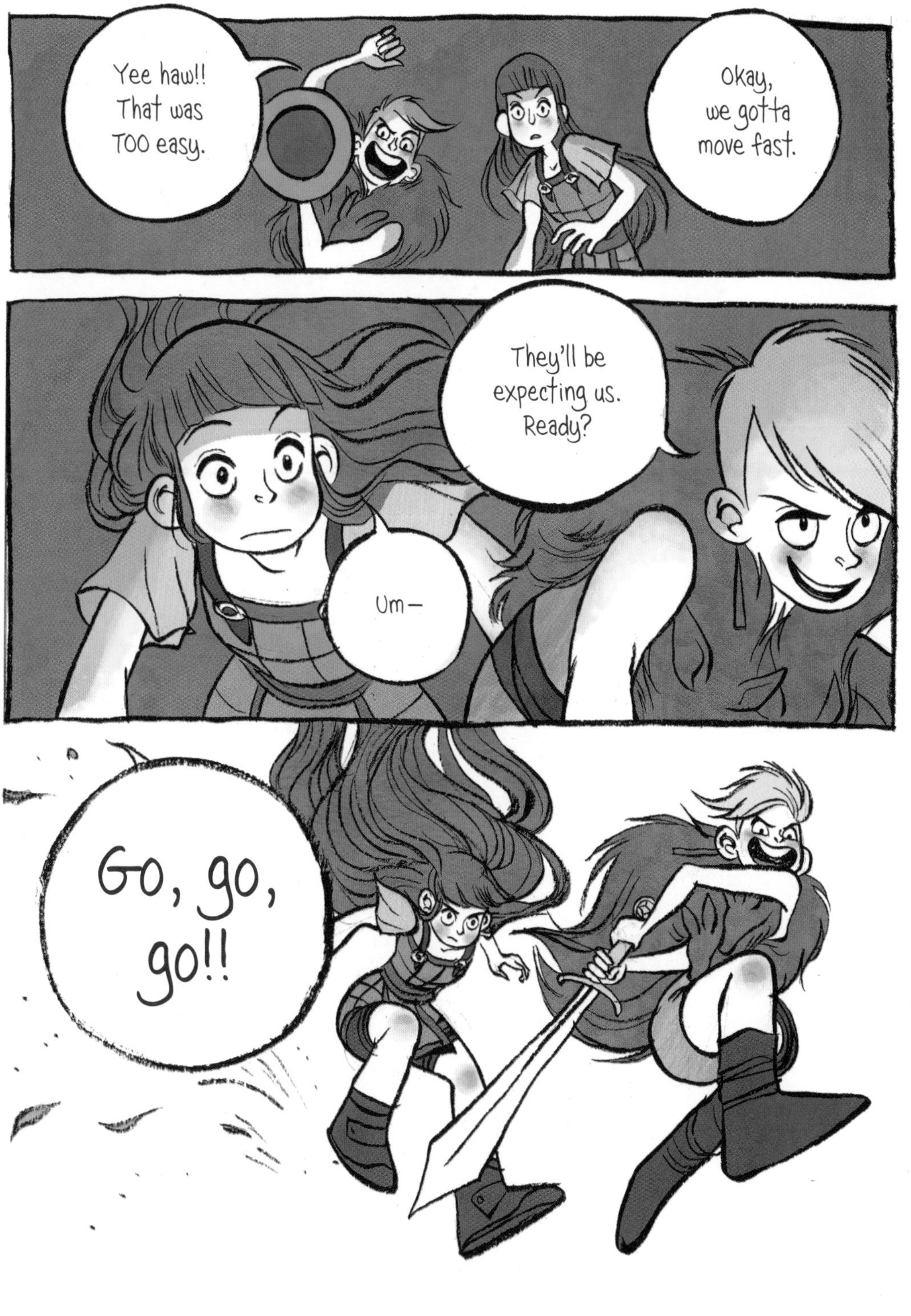
Yee haw!!
That was
TOO easy.
Okay,
we gotta
move fast.
They'll be
expecting us.
Ready?
Um—
Go, go,
go!!

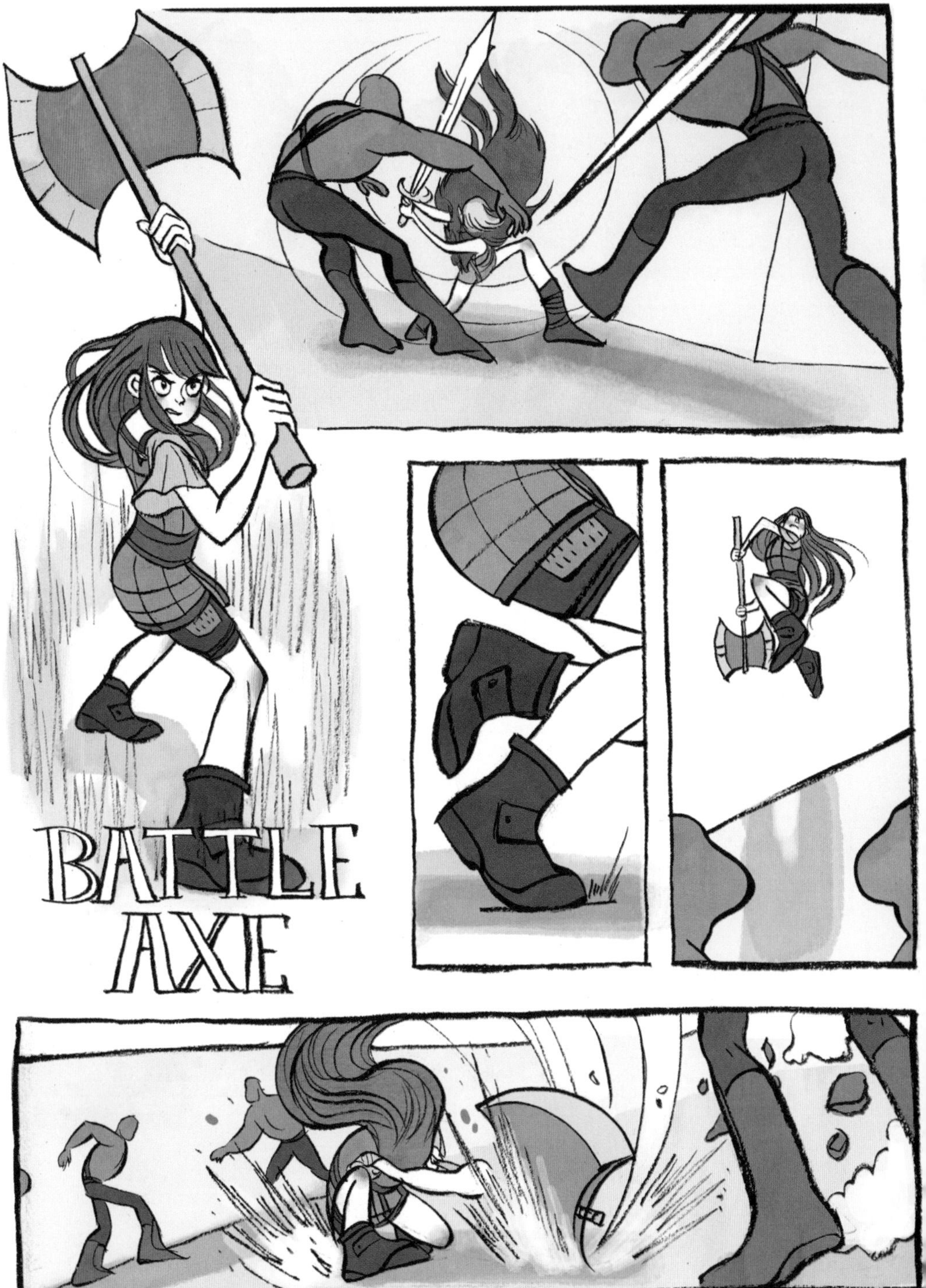
BATTLE
AXE

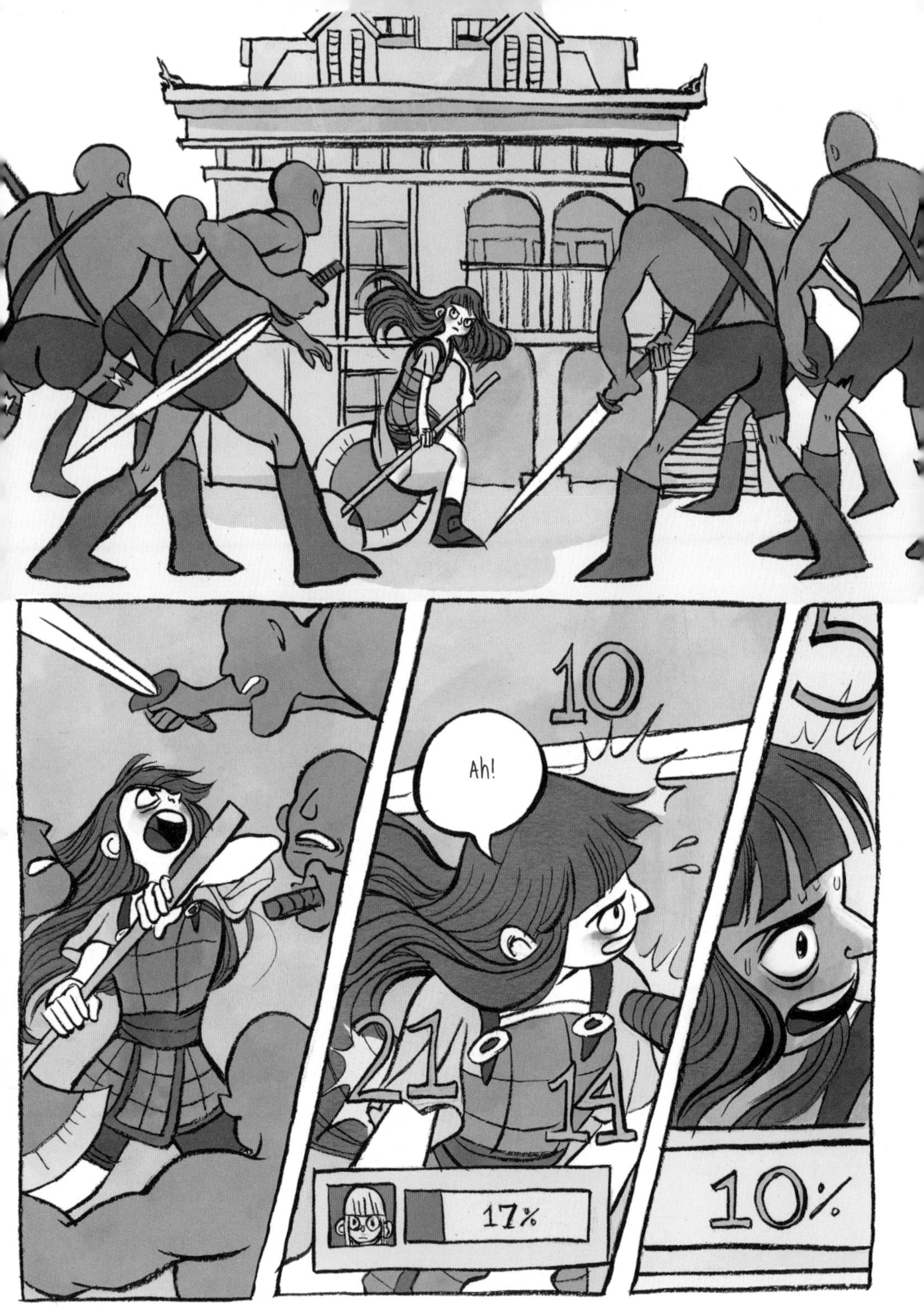
10
5
Ah!
21
14
17%
10%

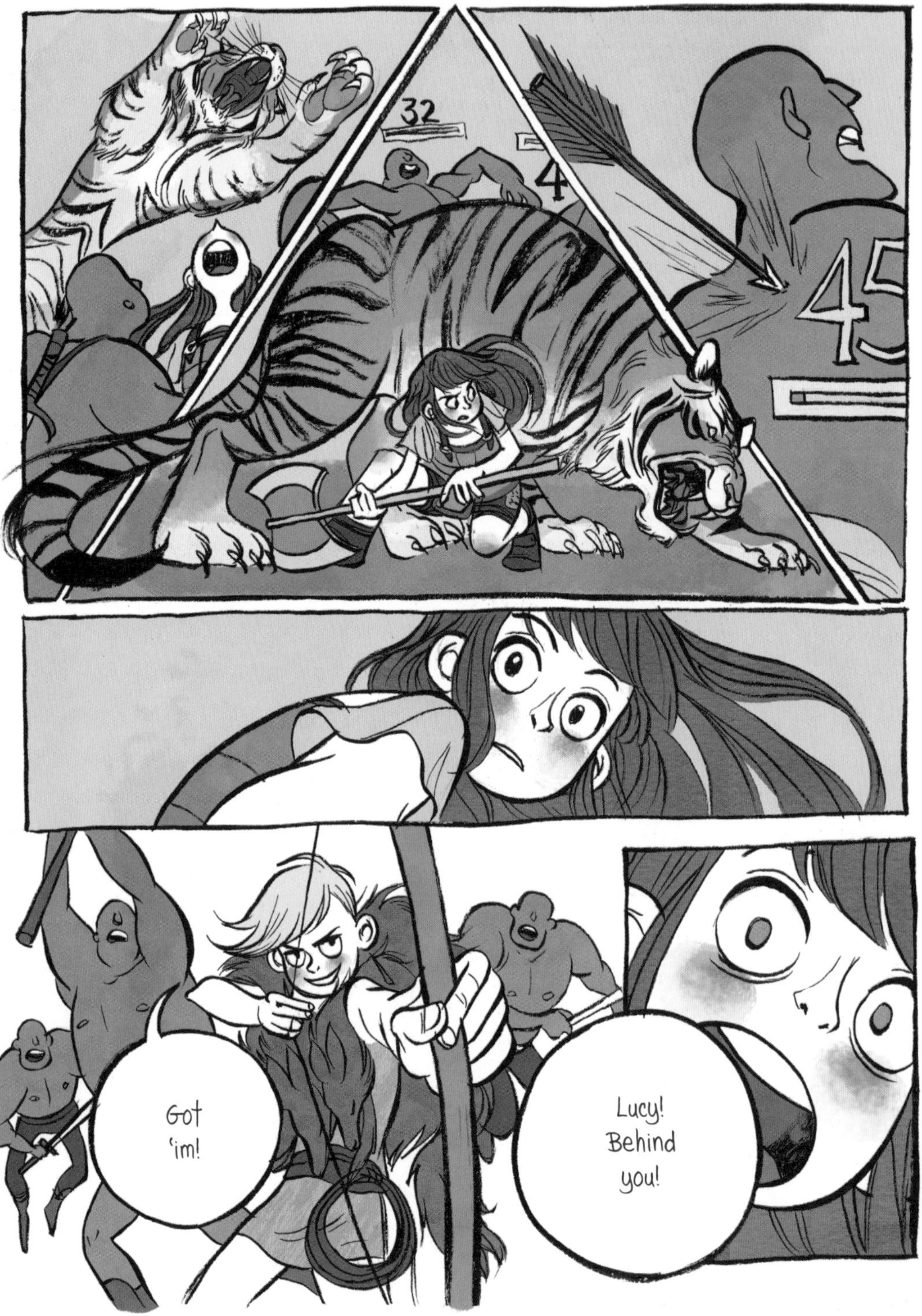
32
4
45
Got 'im!
Lucy! Behind you!

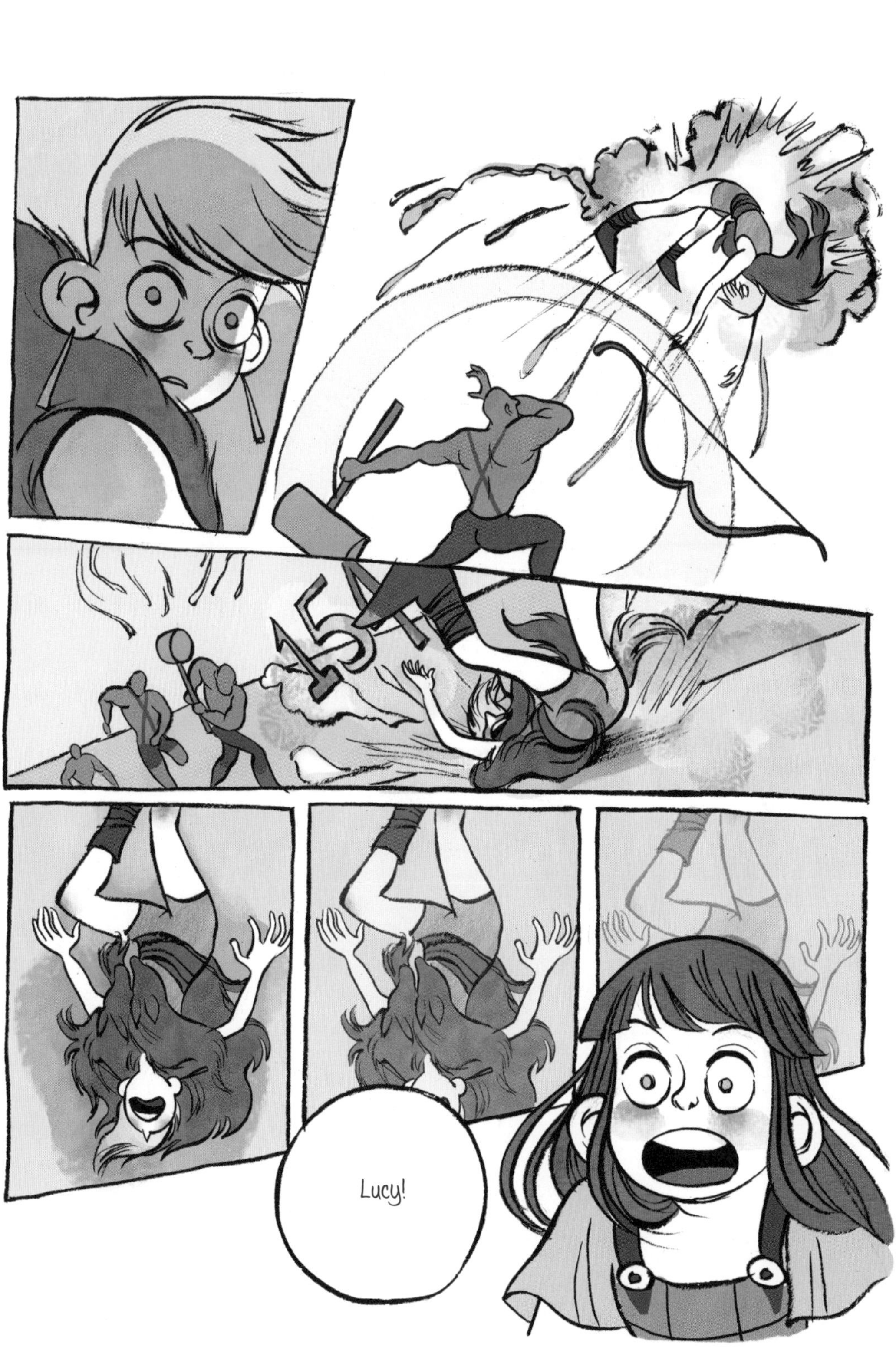
Lucy!

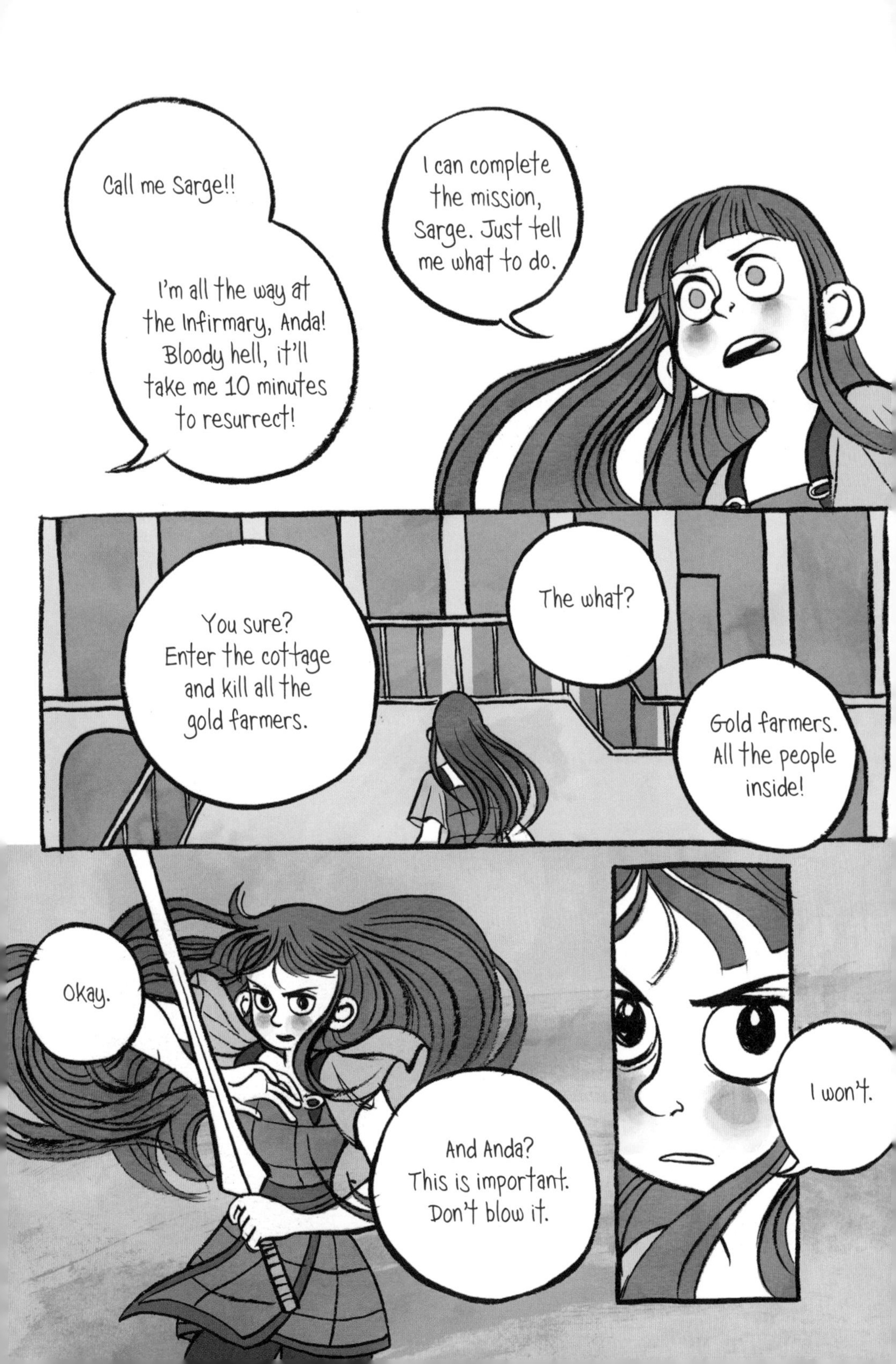
Call me Sarge!!
I'm all the way at the Infirmary, Anda! Bloody hell, it'll take me 10 minutes to resurrect!
I can complete the mission, Sarge. Just tell me what to do.
You sure? Enter the cottage and kill all the gold farmers.
The what?
Gold farmers. All the people inside!
Okay.
And Anda? This is important. Don't blow it.
I won't.

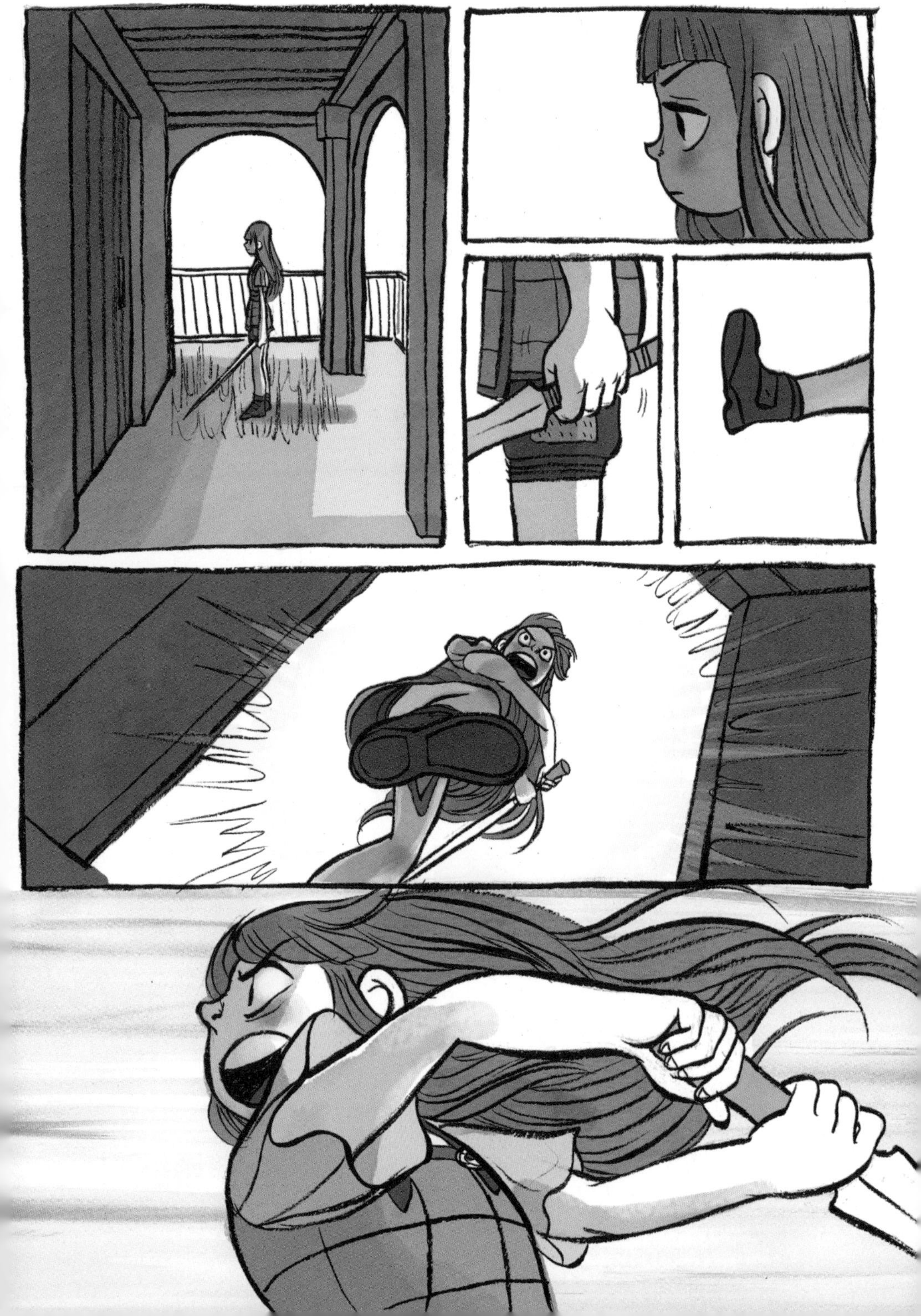

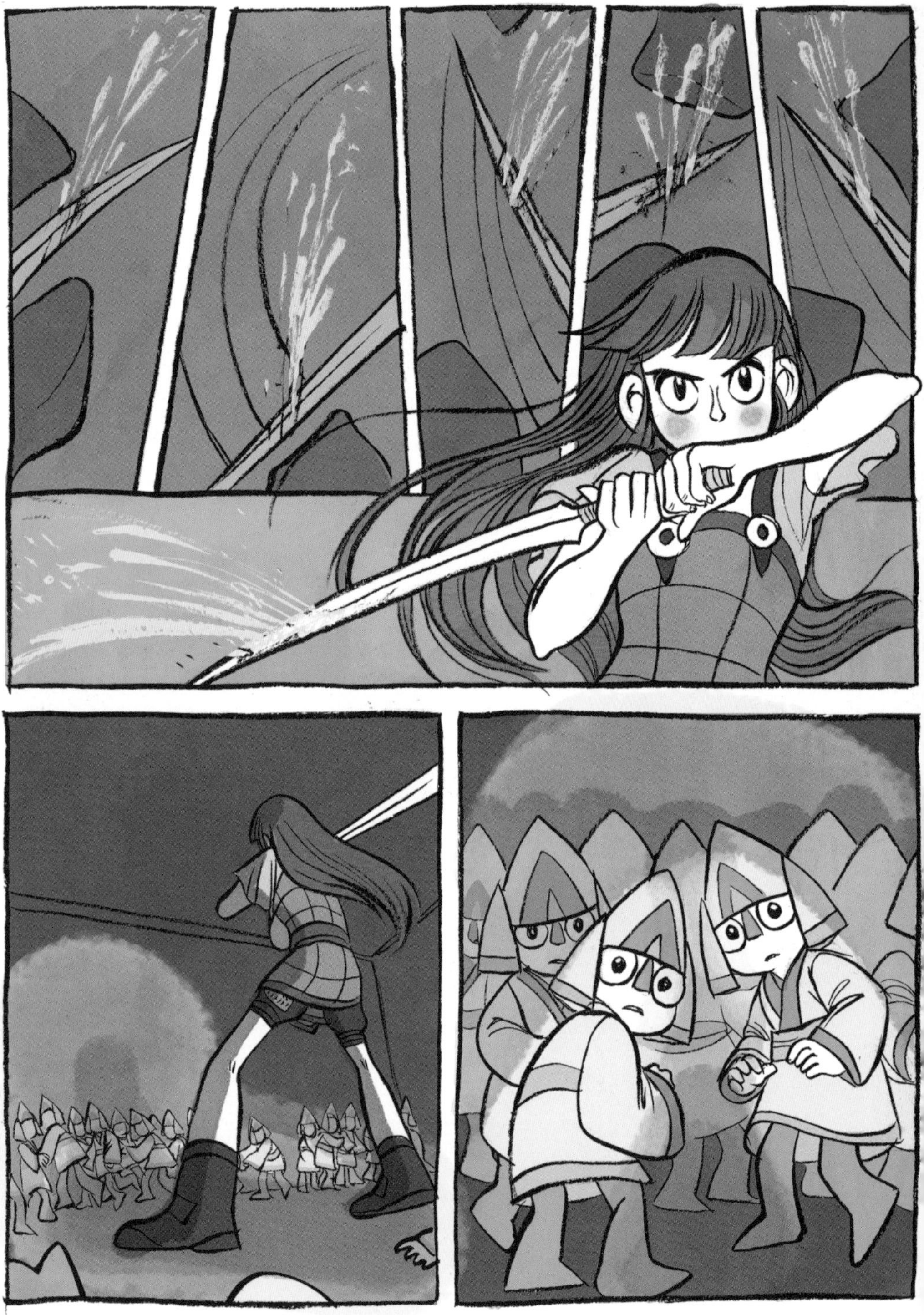

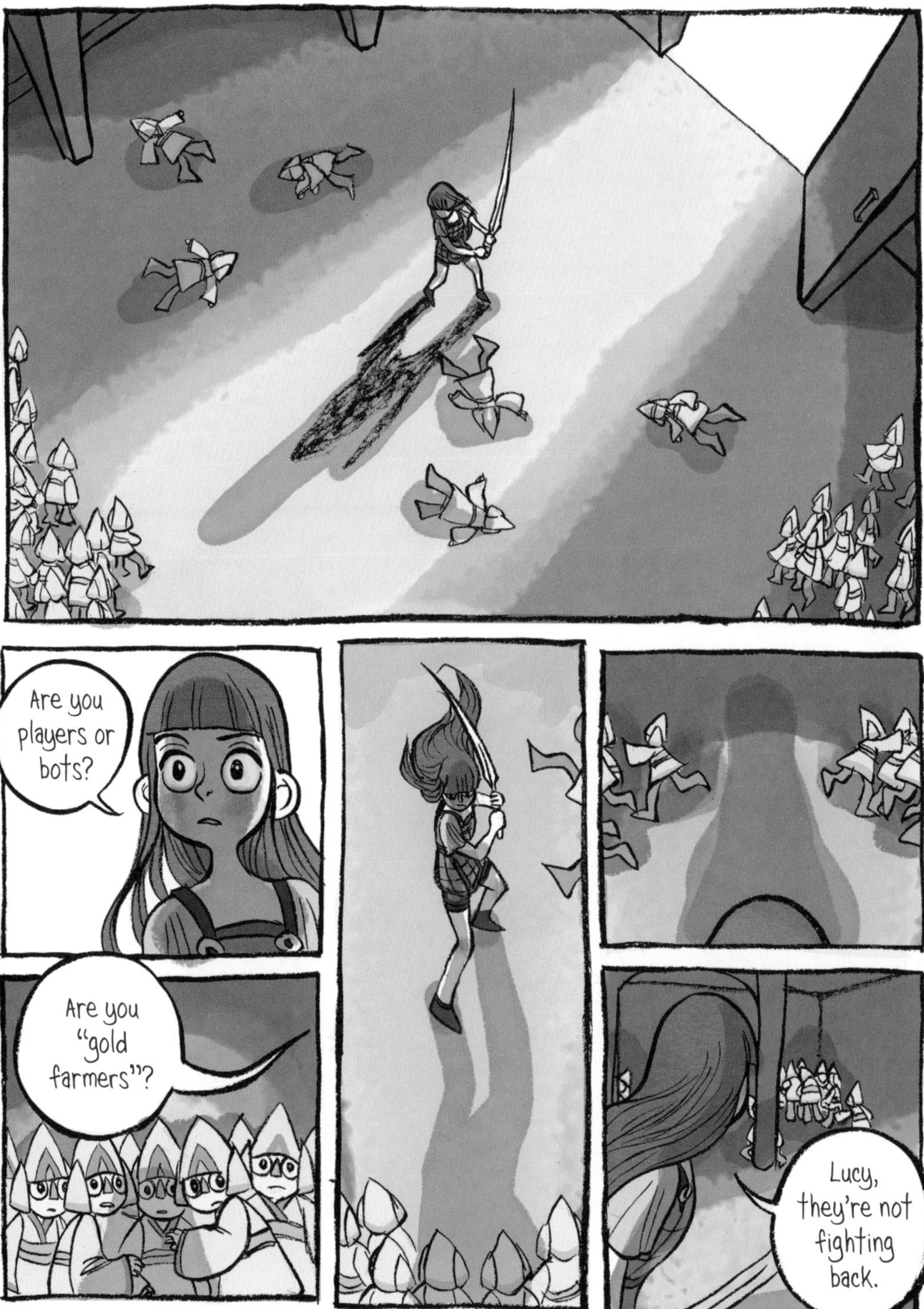
Are you players or bots?
Are you "gold farmers"?
Lucy, they're not fighting back.

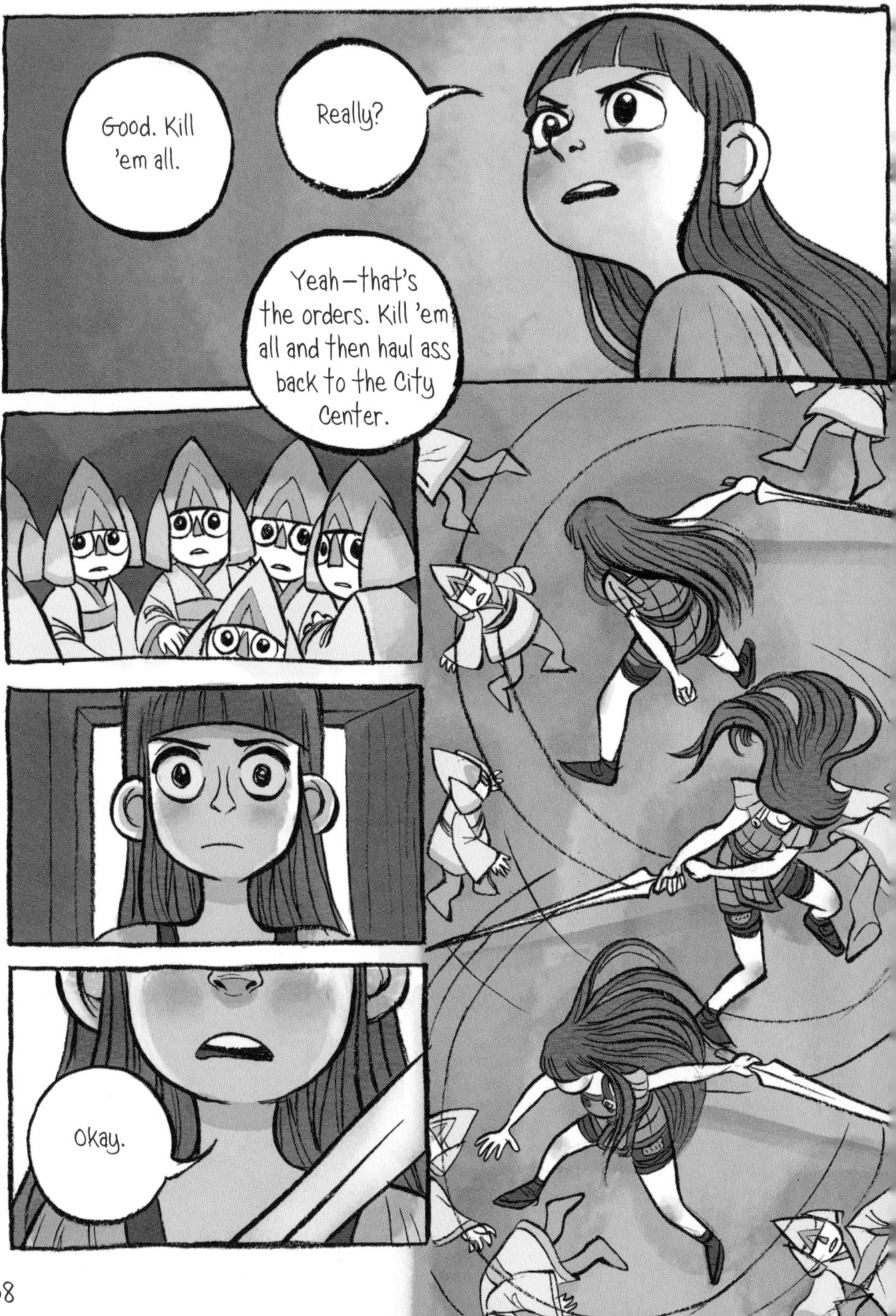
Good. Kill 'em all.
Really?
Yeah—that's the orders. Kill 'em all and then haul ass back to the City Center.
Okay.

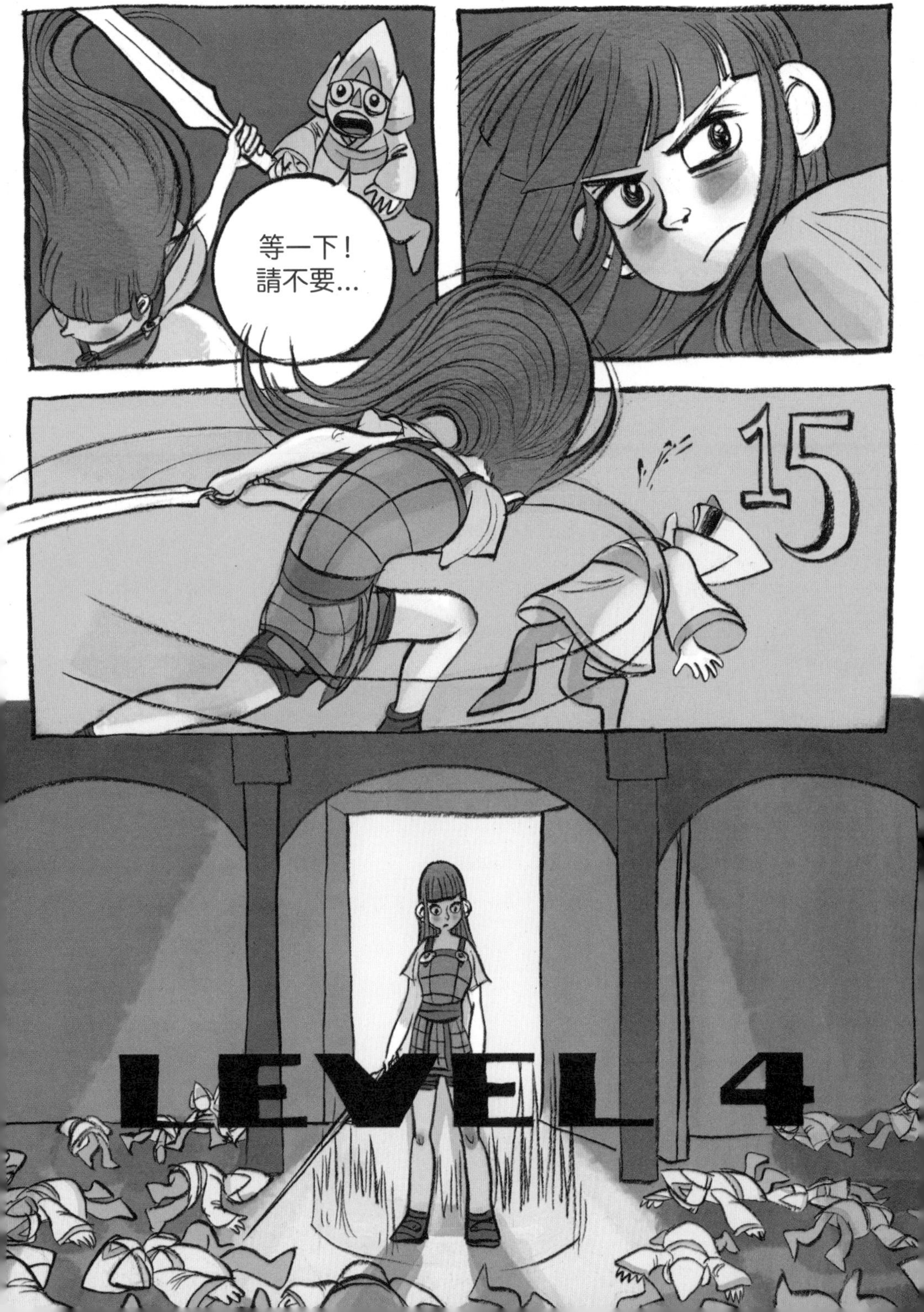
等一下！
請不要...
15
LEVEL 4

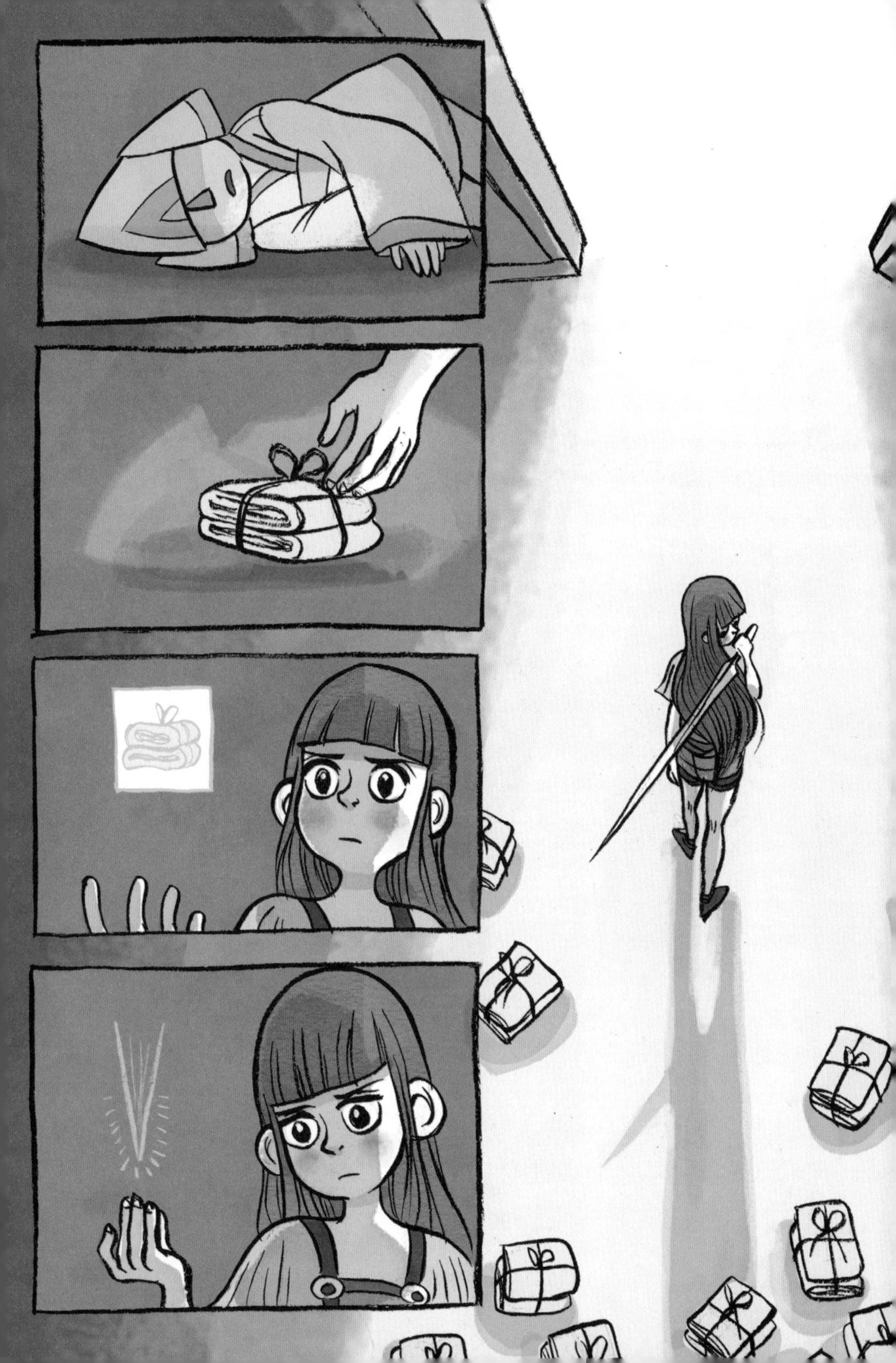

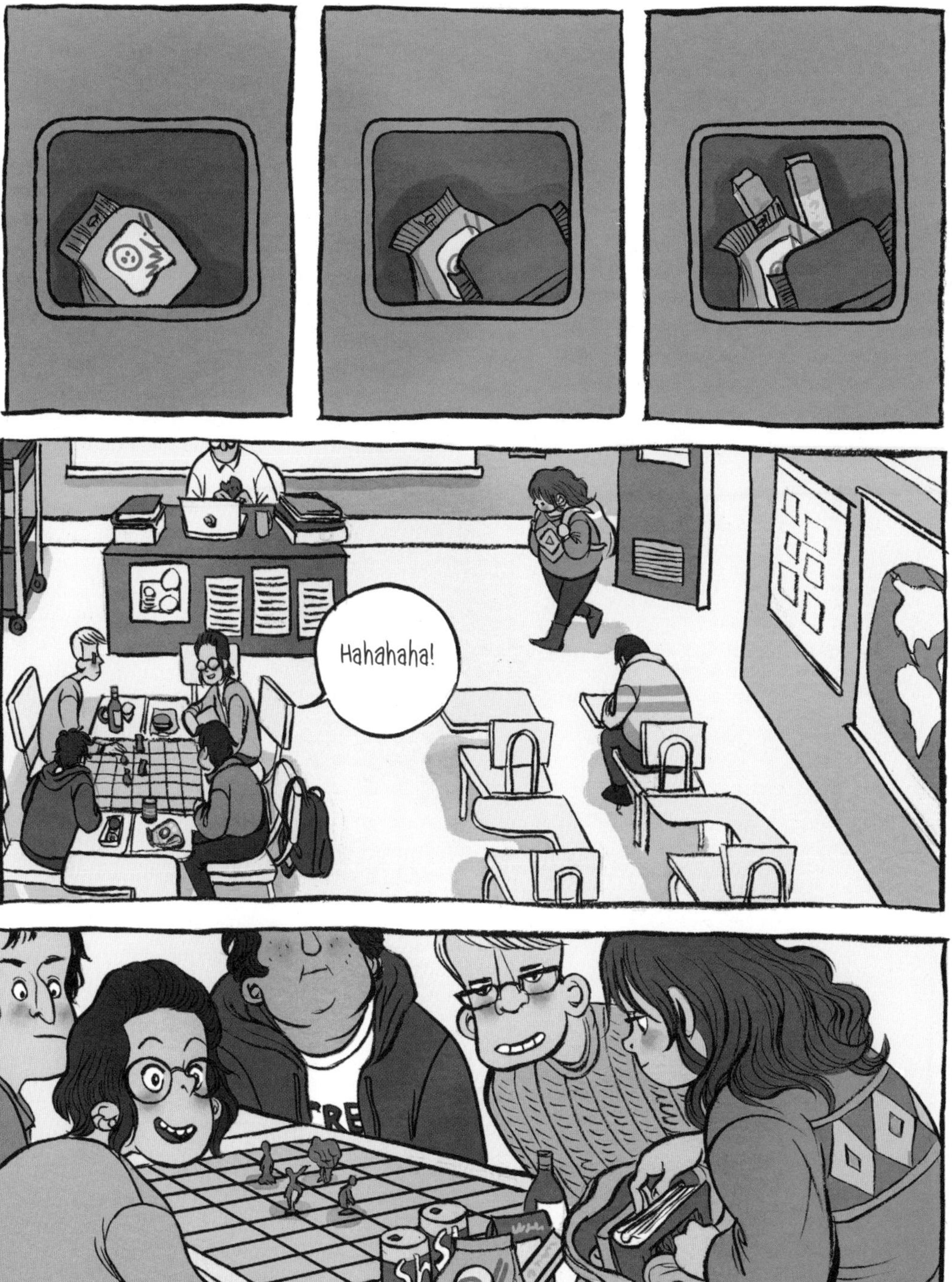
Hahahaha!

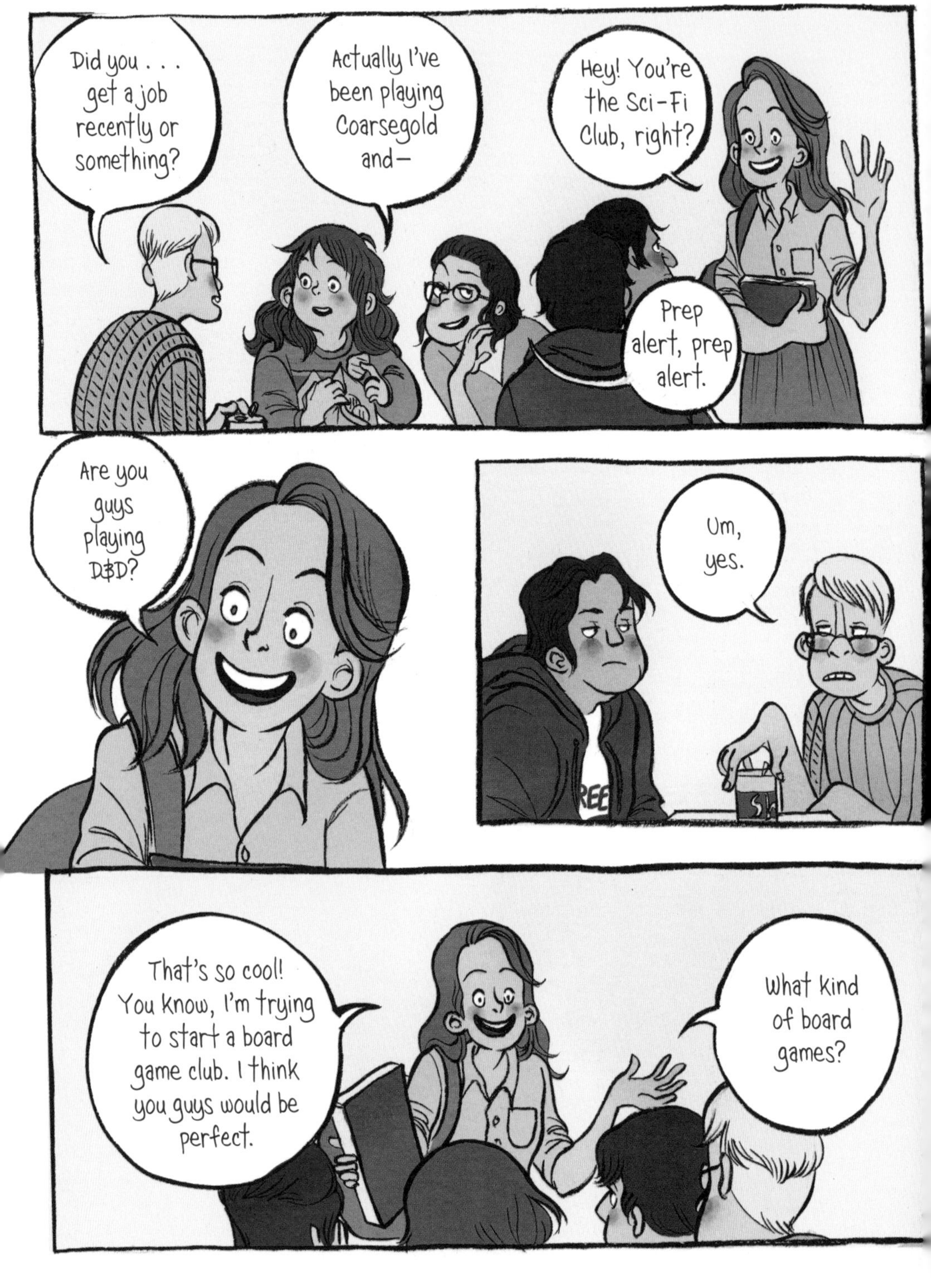
Did you . . . get a job recently or something?
Actually I've been playing Coarsegold and—
Hey! You're the Sci-Fi Club, right?
Prep alert, prep alert.
Are you guys playing D&D?
Um, yes.
That's so cool! You know, I'm trying to start a board game club. I think you guys would be perfect.
What kind of board games?

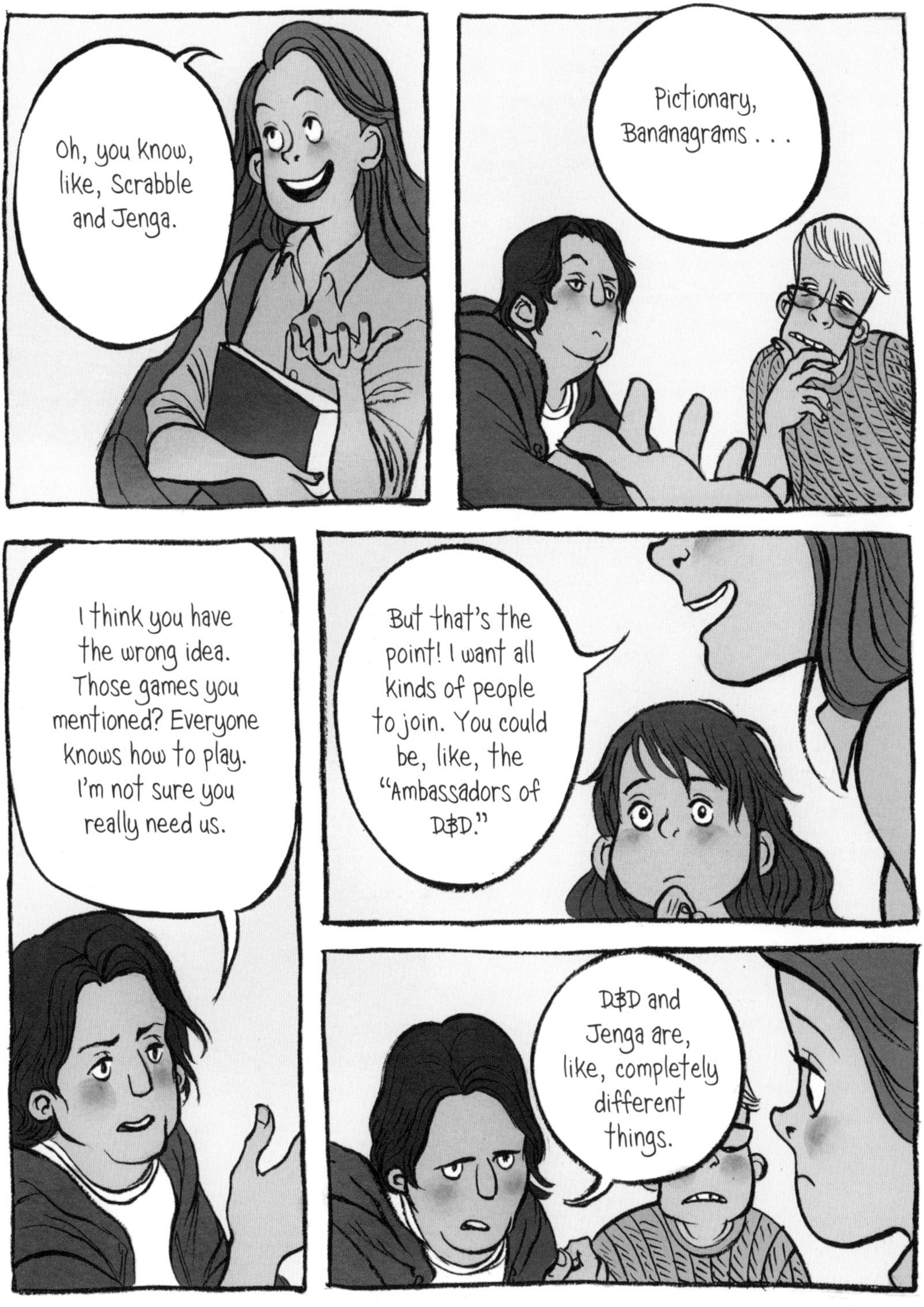
Oh, you know, like, Scrabble and Jenga.
Pictionary, Bananagrams . . .
I think you have the wrong idea. Those games you mentioned? Everyone knows how to play. I'm not sure you really need us.
But that's the point! I want all kinds of people to join. You could be, like, the "Ambassadors of D&D."
D&D and Jenga are, like, completely different things.

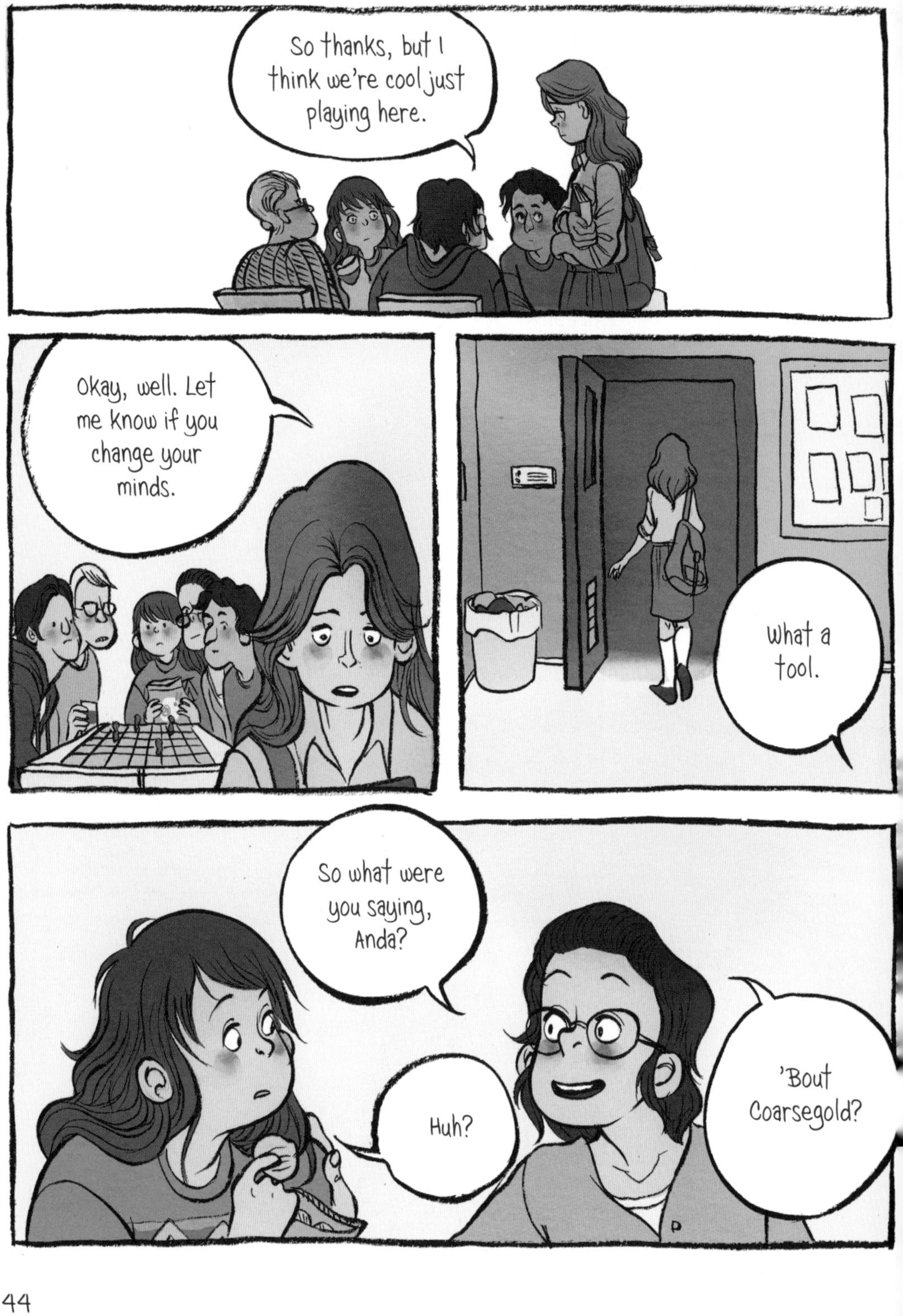
So thanks, but I think we're cool just playing here.
Okay, well. Let me know if you change your minds.
What a tool.
So what were you saying, Anda?
Huh?
'Bout Coarsegold?

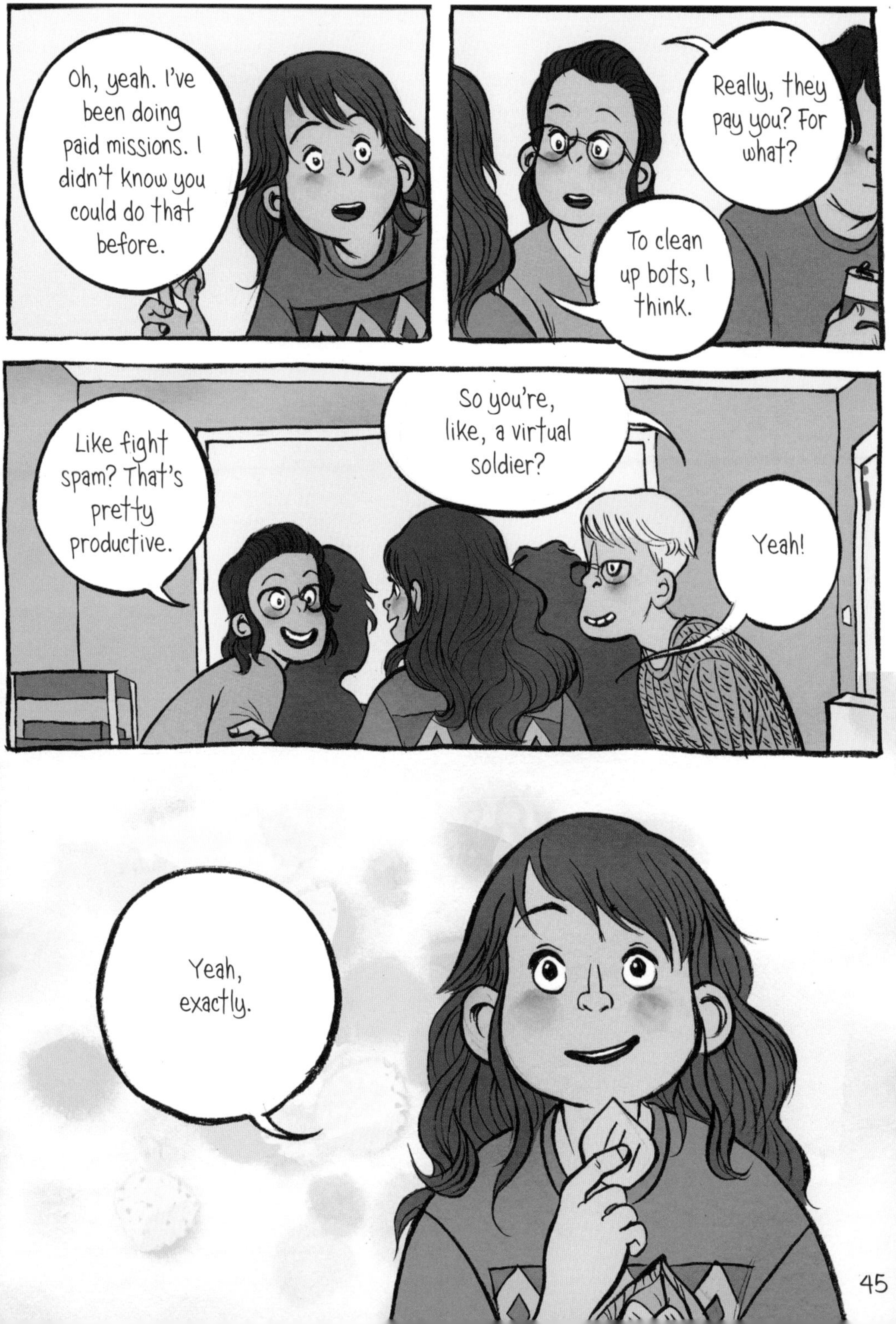
Oh, yeah. I've been doing paid missions. I didn't know you could do that before.
Really, they pay you? For what?
To clean up bots, I think.
Like fight spam? That's pretty productive.
So you're, like, a virtual soldier?
Yeah!
Yeah, exactly.

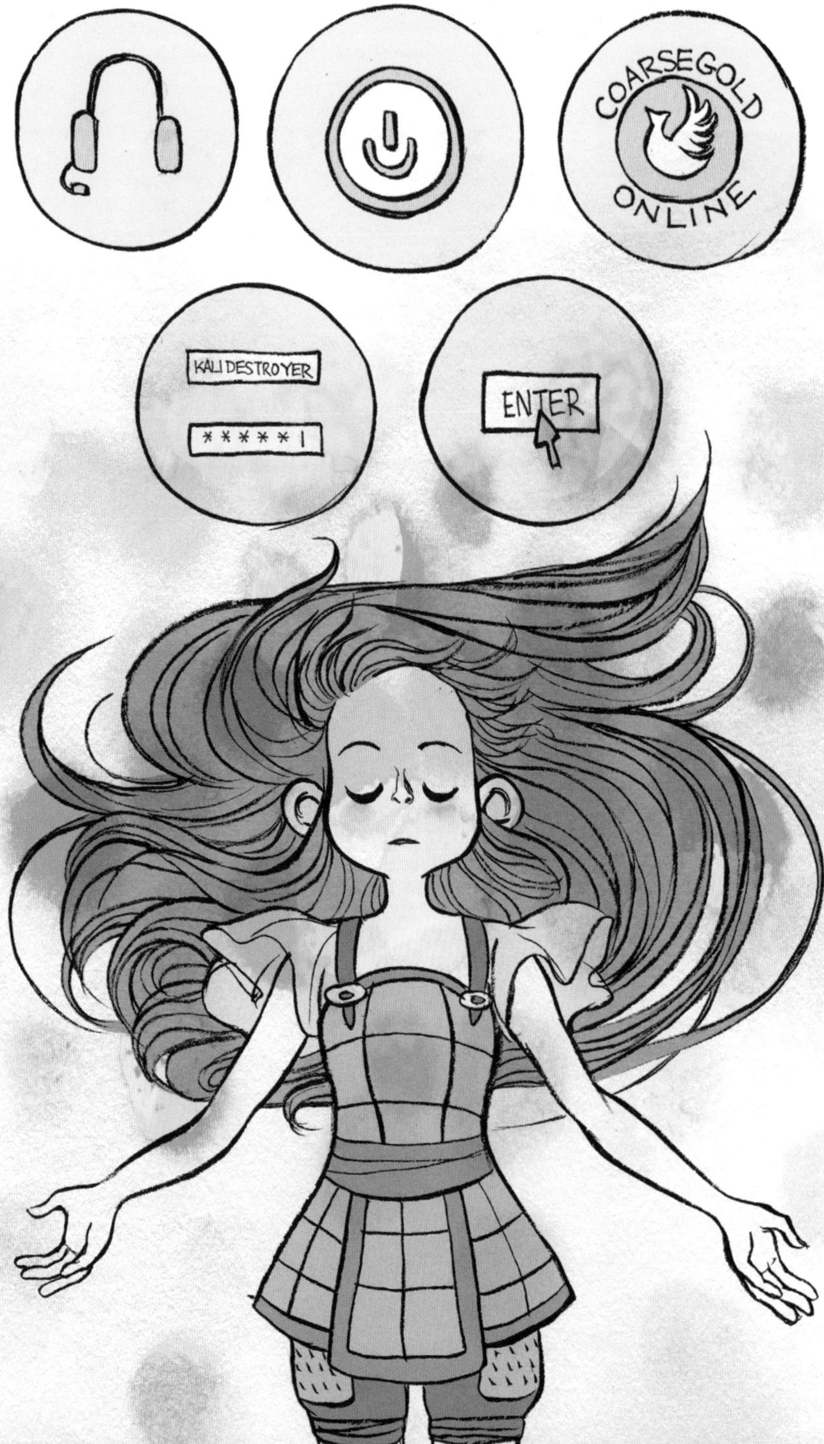
COARSEGOLD ONLINE
KALIDESTROYER
*****
ENTER

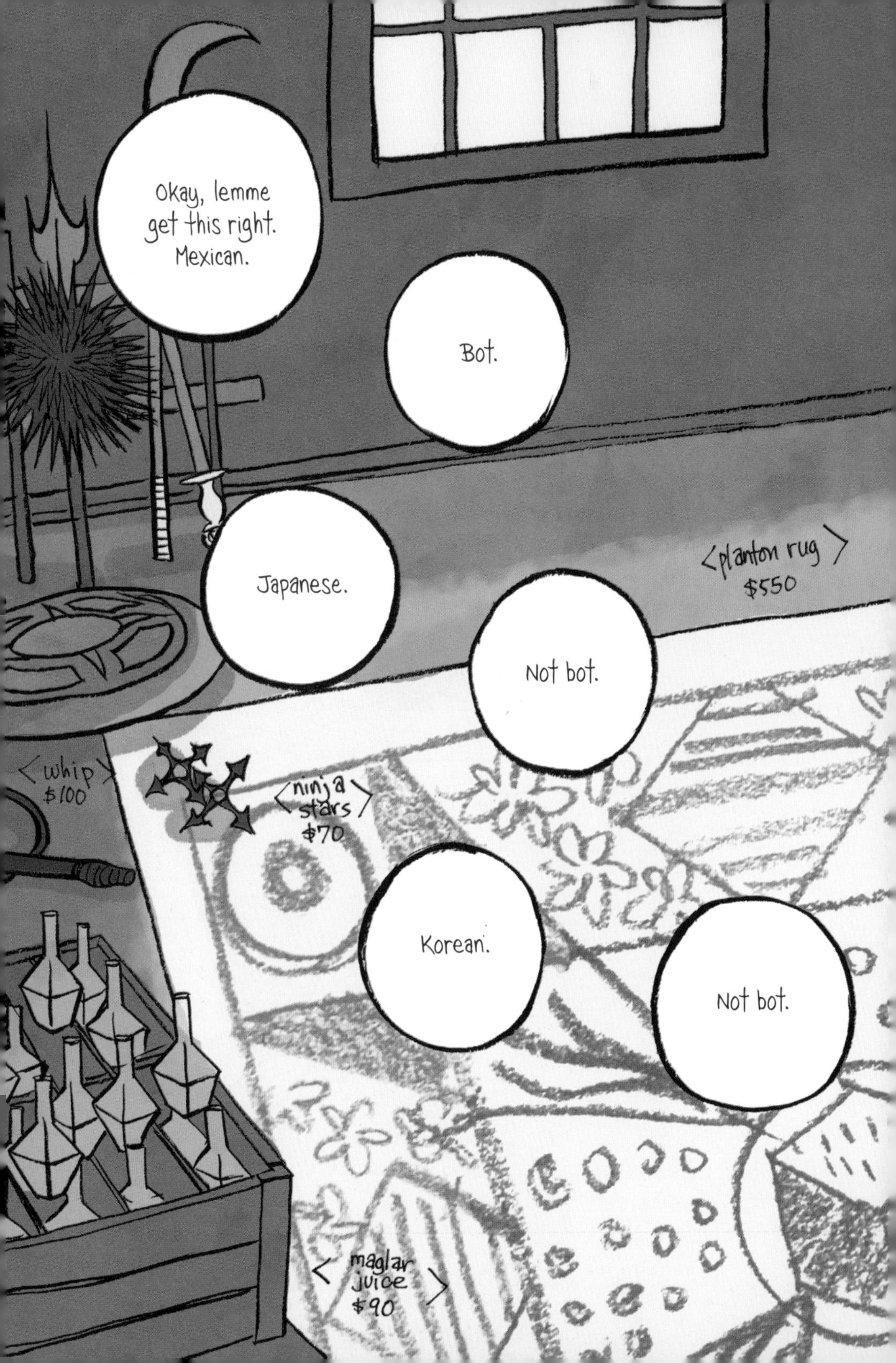
Okay, lemme get this right. Mexican.
Bot.
Japanese.
Not bot.
Korean.
Not bot.
<planton rug> $550
<whip> $100
<ninja stars> $70
<maglar juice> $90

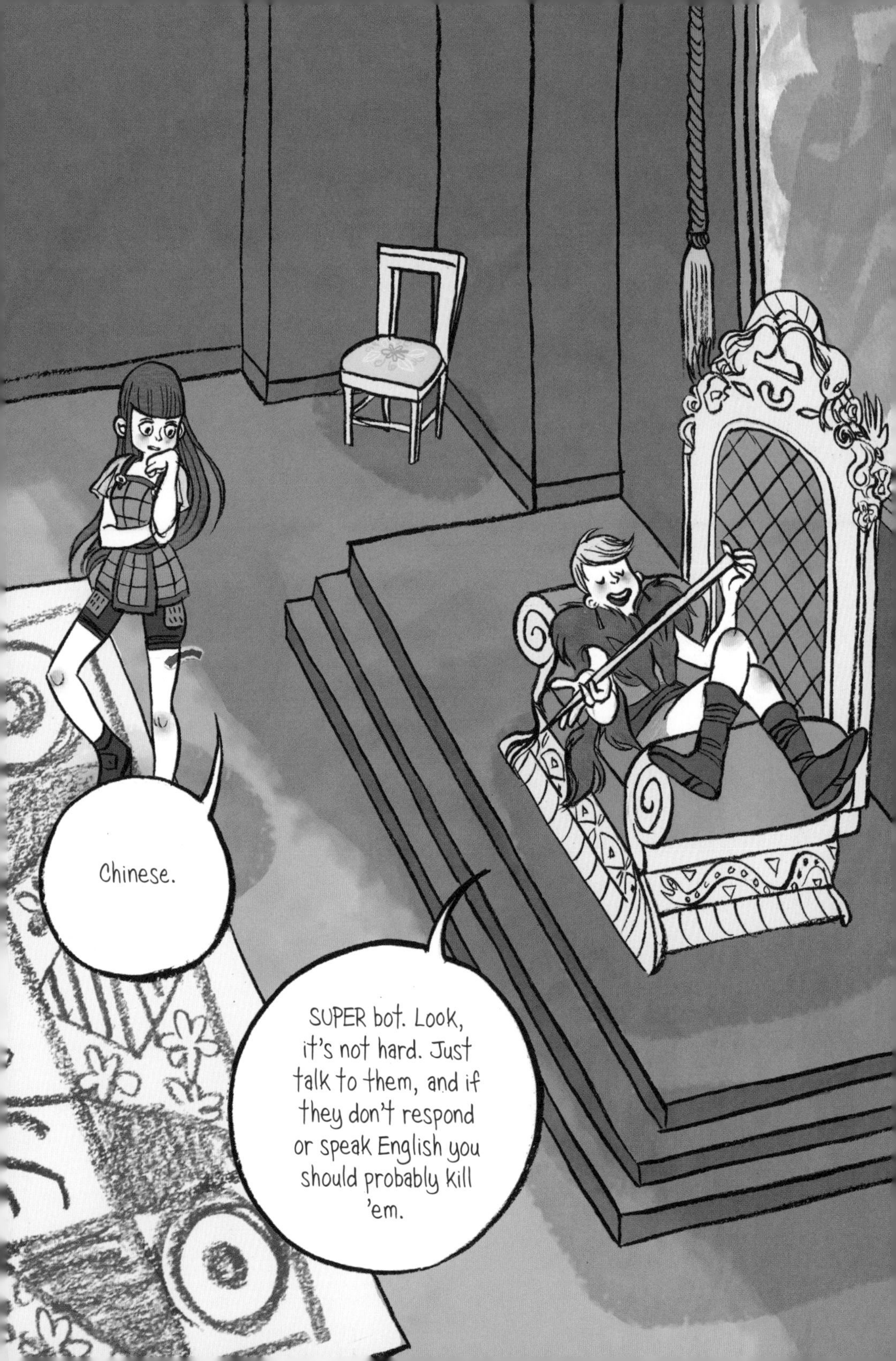
Chinese.
SUPER bot. Look, it's not hard. Just talk to them, and if they don't respond or speak English you should probably kill 'em.

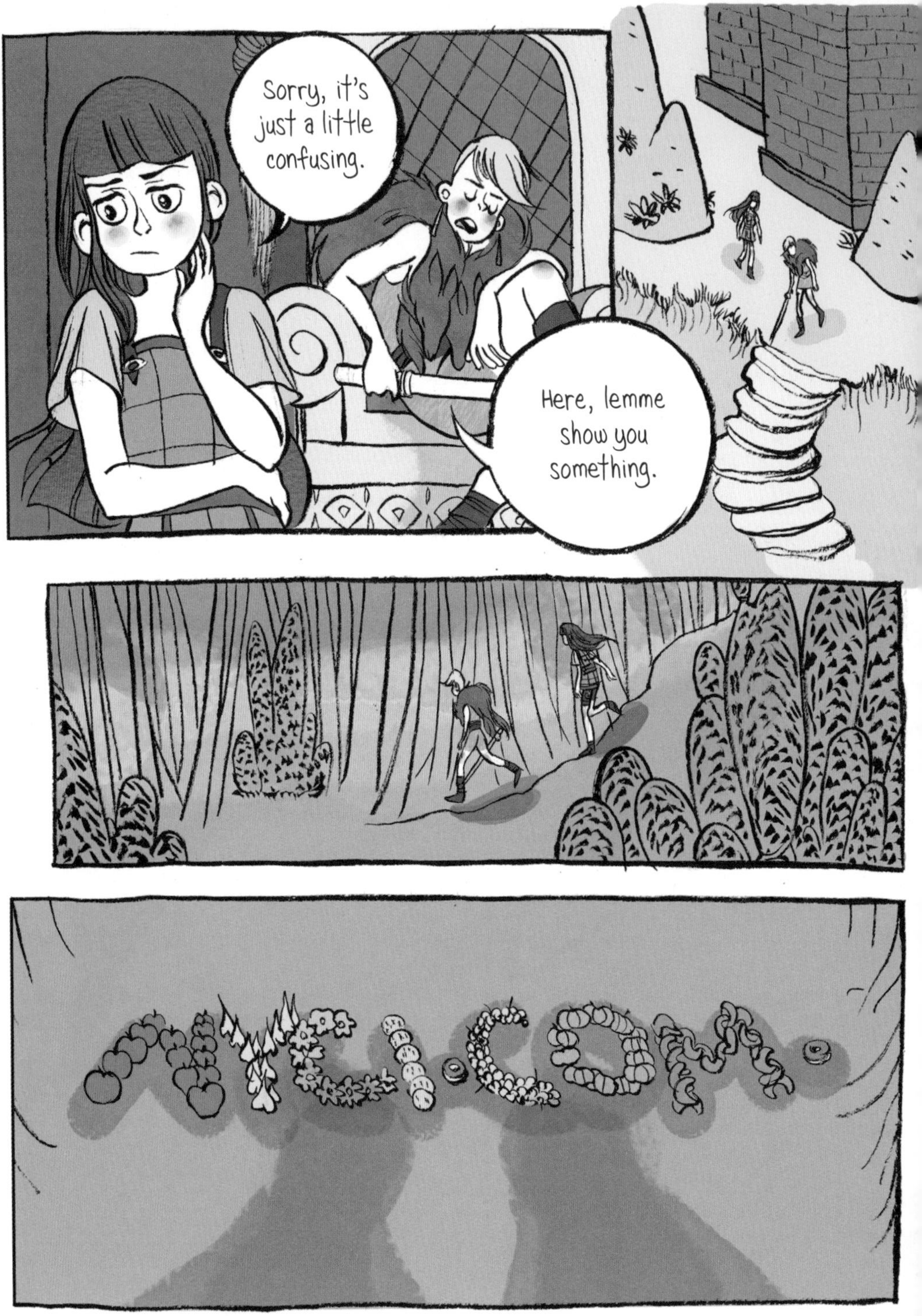
Sorry, it's just a little confusing.
Here, lemme show you something.

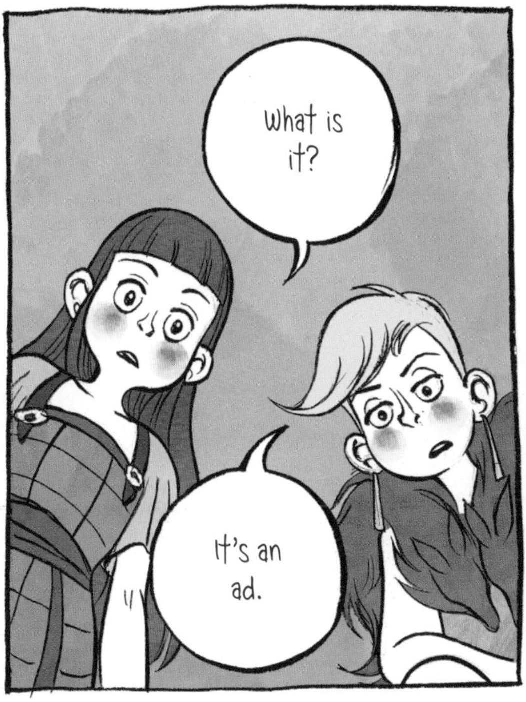
What is it?
It's an ad.

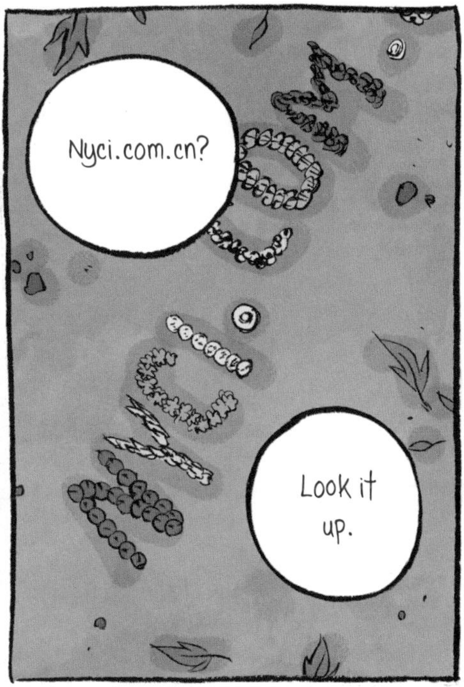
Nyci.com.cn?
Look it up.

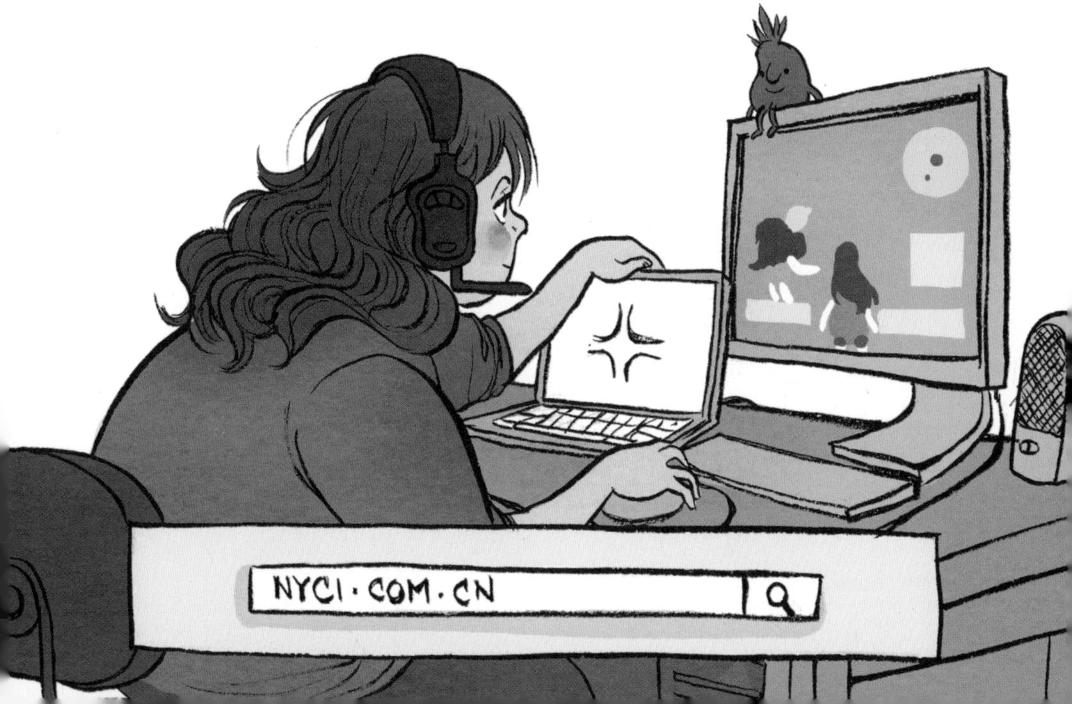
NYCI·COM·CN

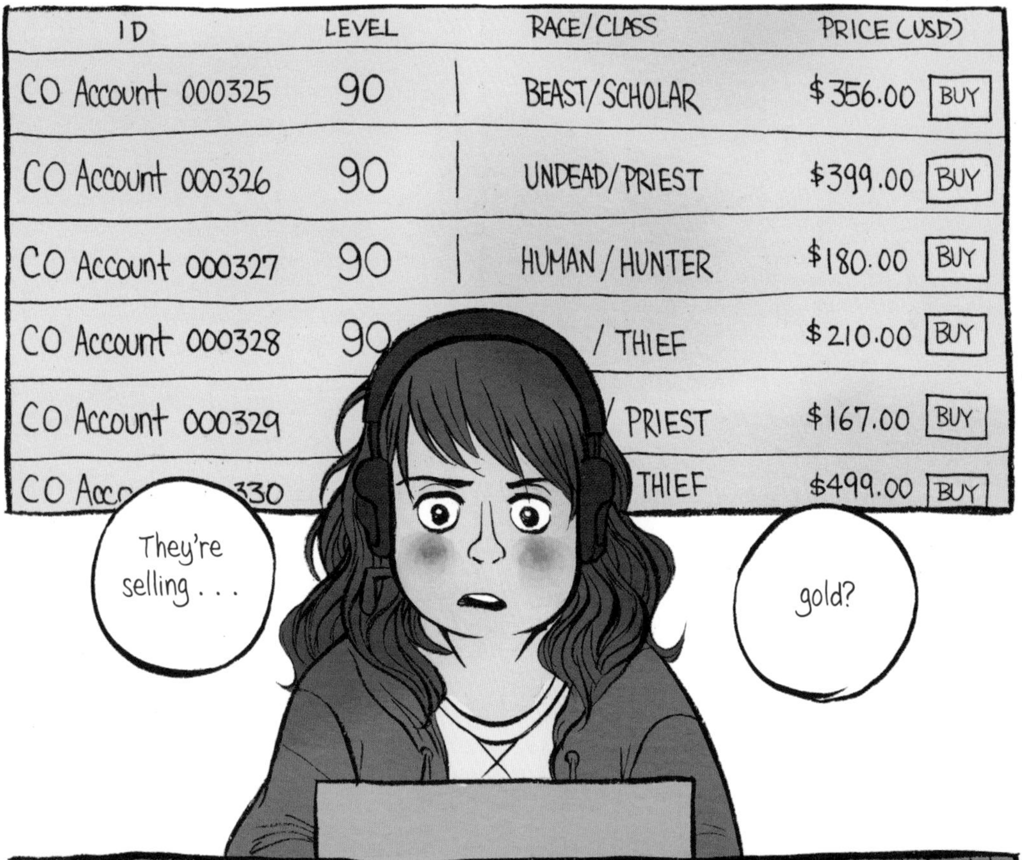
ID
LEVEL
RACE/CLASS
PRICE (USD)
CO Account 000325 90 BEAST/SCHOLAR $356.00 BUY
CO Account 000326 90 UNDEAD/PRIEST $399.00 BUY
CO Account 000327 90 HUMAN/HUNTER $180.00 BUY
CO Account 000328 90 / THIEF $210.00 BUY
CO Account 000329 / PRIEST $167.00 BUY
CO Acc 330 THIEF $499.00 BUY
They're selling . . .
gold?

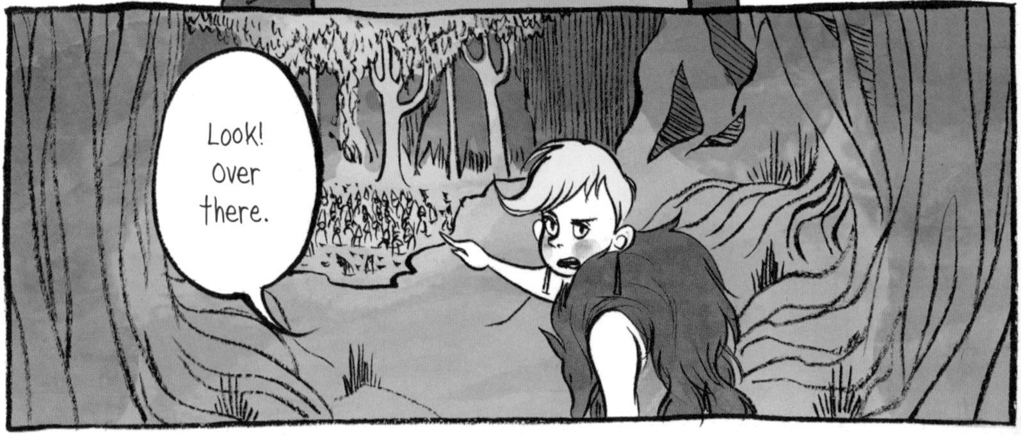
Look! Over there.

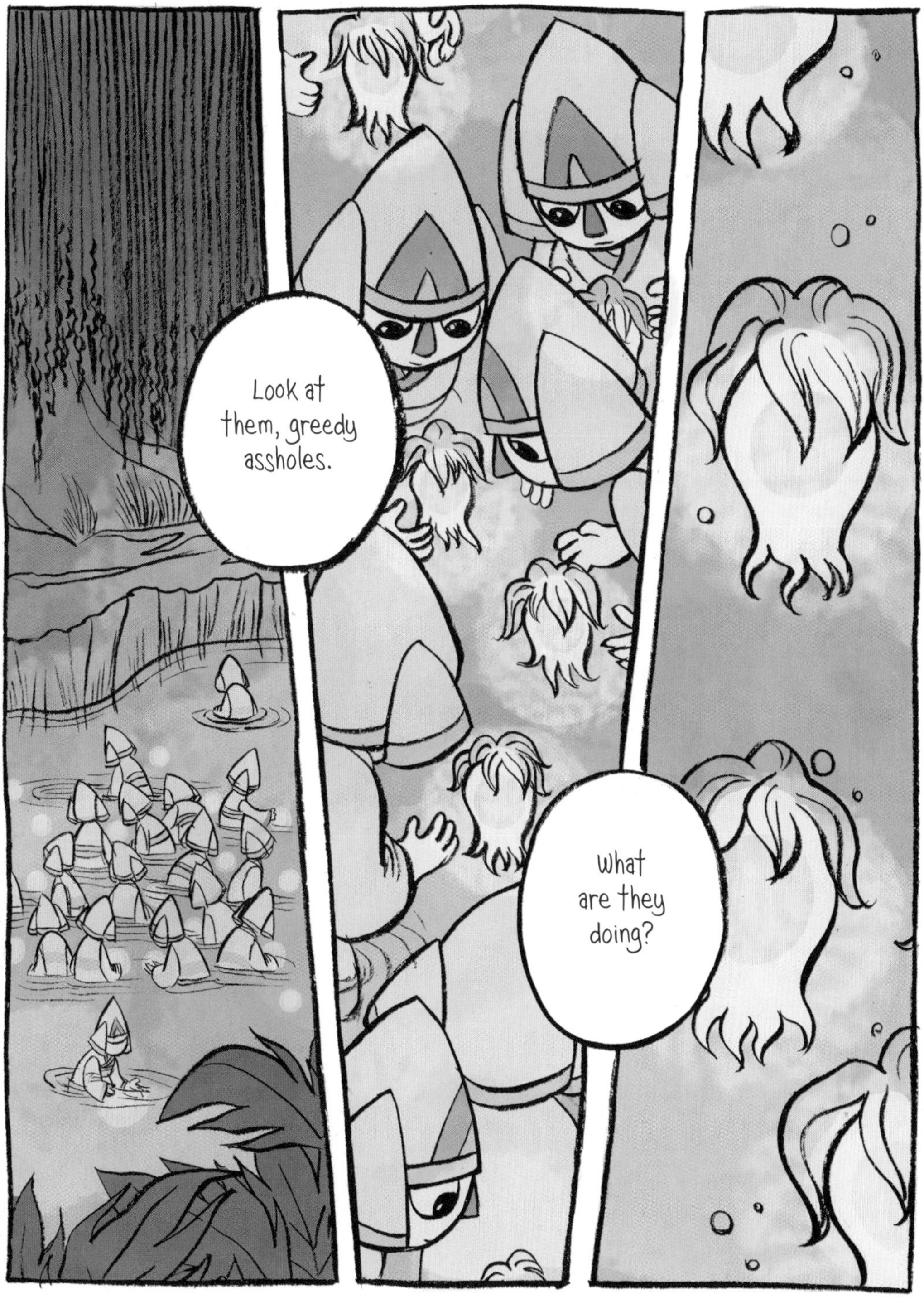
Look at them, greedy assholes.
What are they doing?

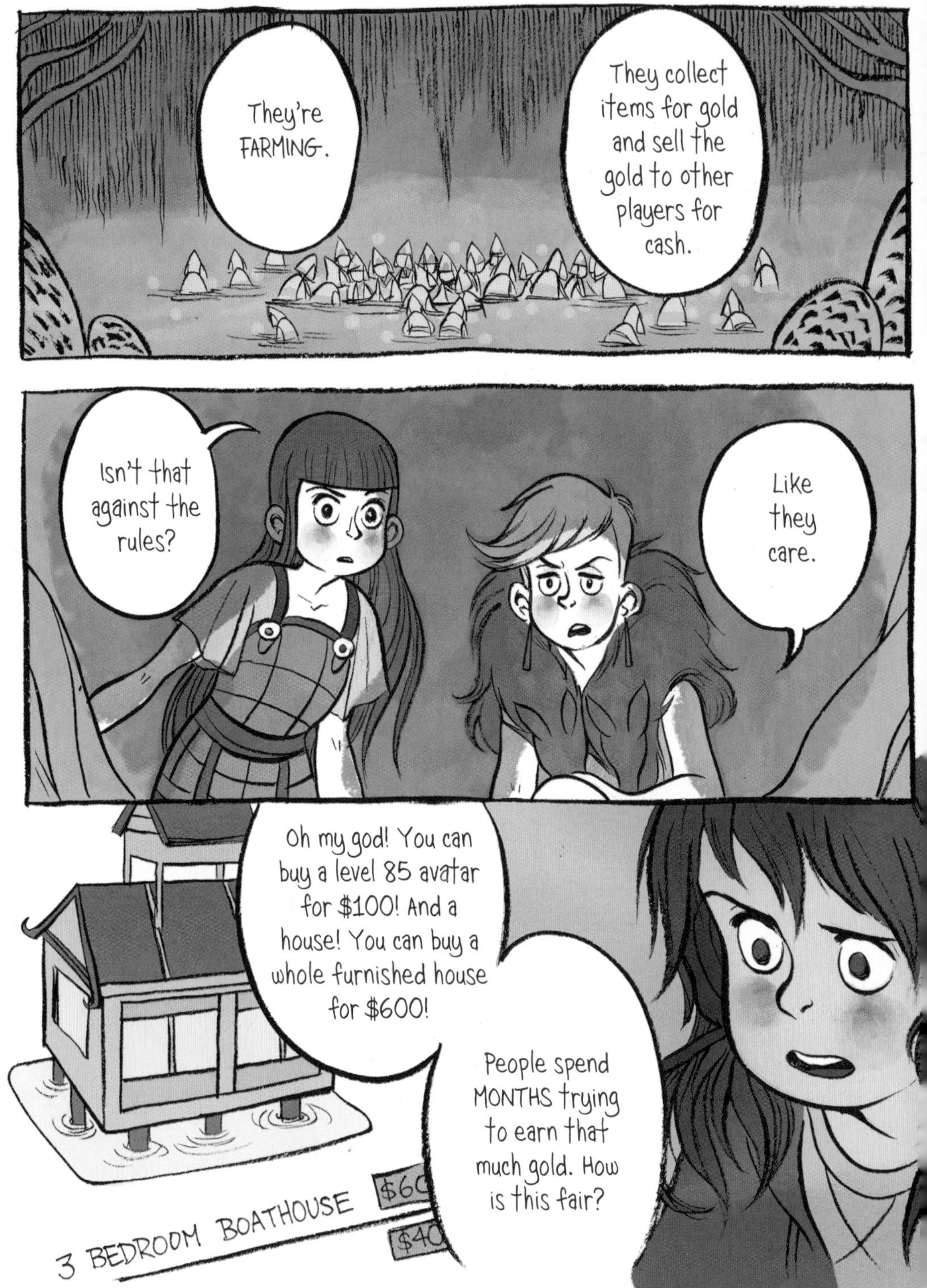
They're FARMING.
They collect items for gold and sell the gold to other players for cash.
Isn't that against the rules?
Like they care.
Oh my god! You can buy a level 85 avatar for $100! And a house! You can buy a whole furnished house for $600!
People spend MONTHS trying to earn that much gold. How is this fair?
3 BEDROOM BOATHOUSE

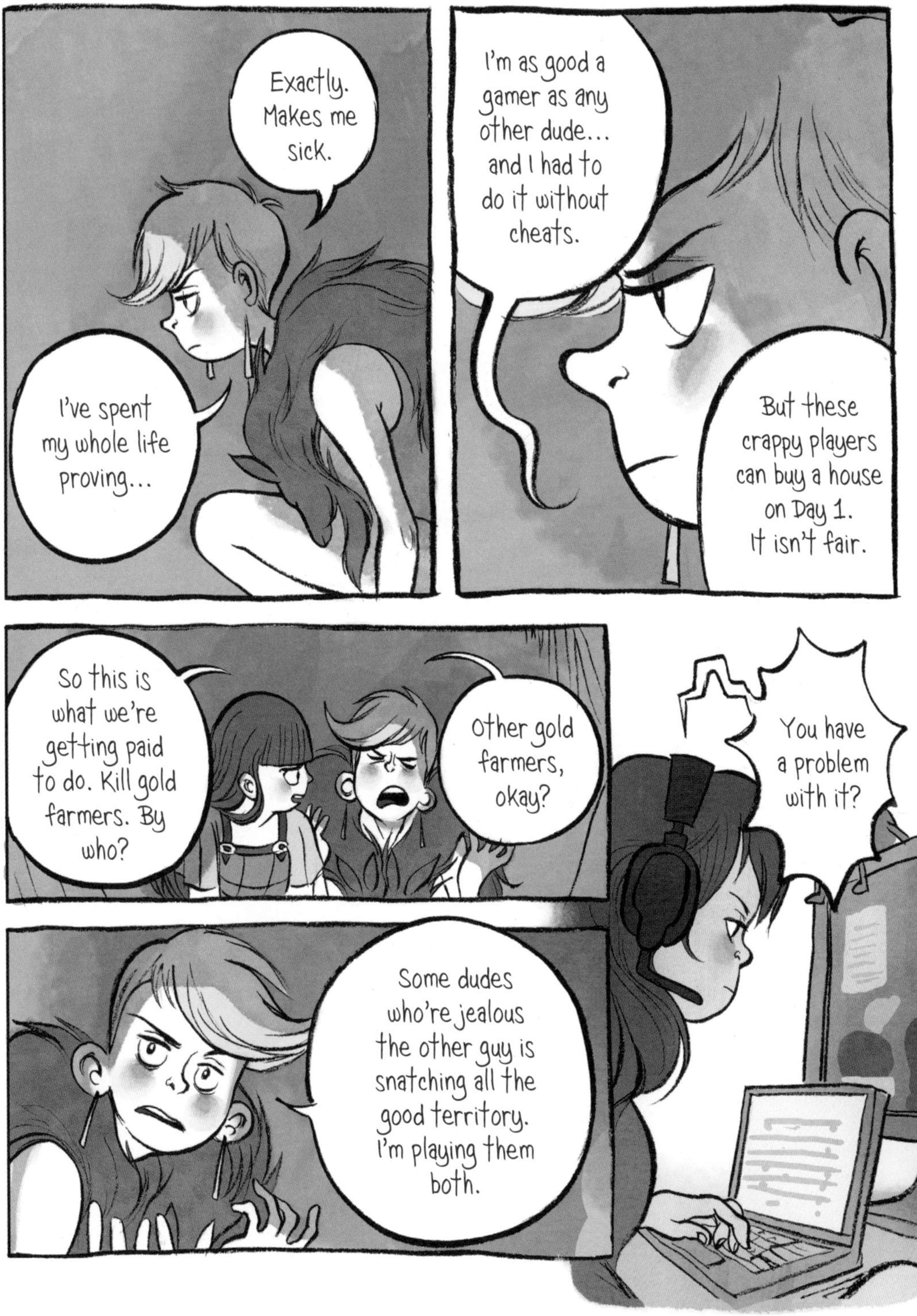
Exactly. Makes me sick.
I've spent my whole life proving...
I'm as good a gamer as any other dude... and I had to do it without cheats.
But these crappy players can buy a house on Day 1. It isn't fair.
So this is what we're getting paid to do. Kill gold farmers. By who?
Other gold farmers, okay?
You have a problem with it?
Some dudes who're jealous the other guy is snatching all the good territory. I'm playing them both.

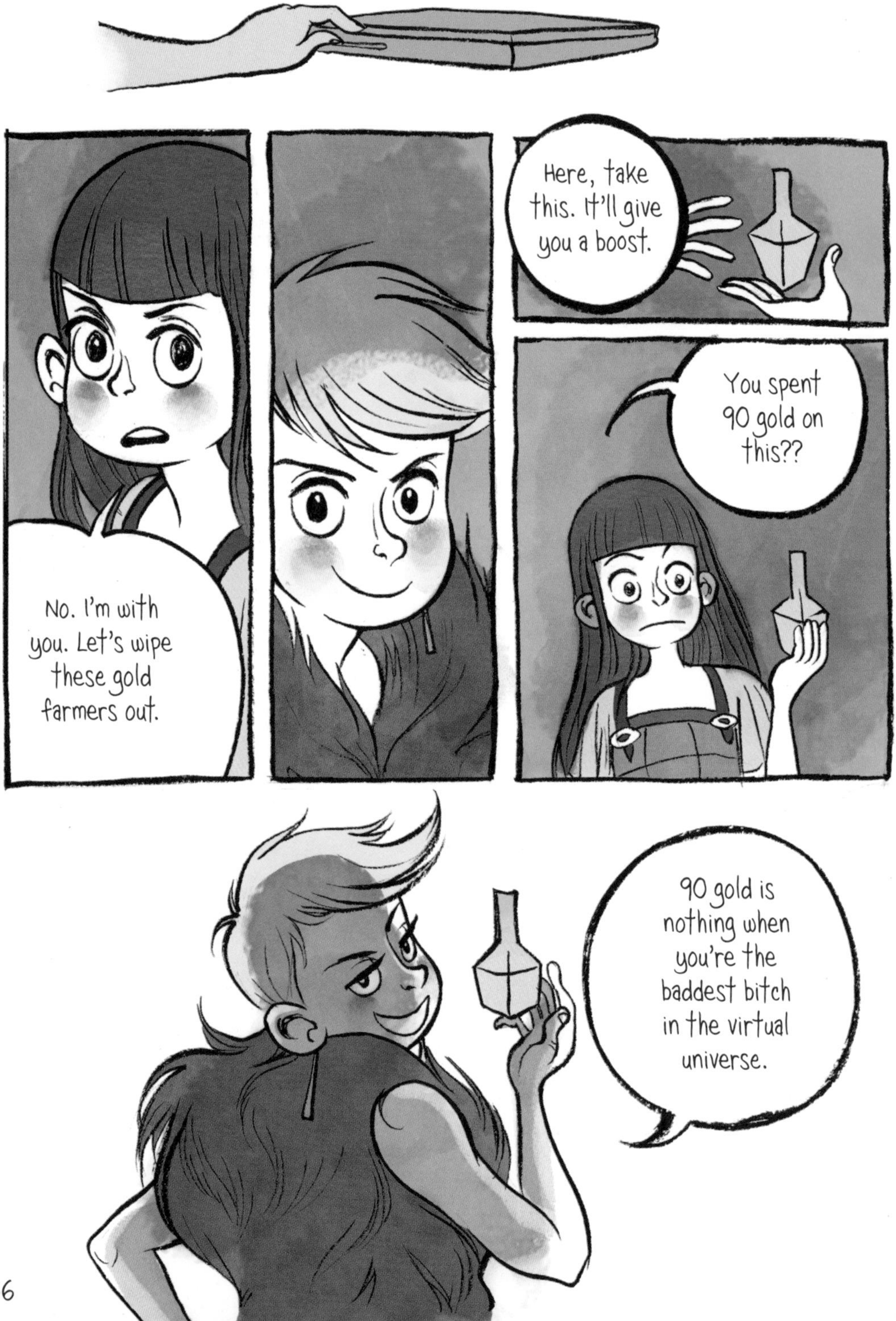
No. I'm with you. Let's wipe these gold farmers out.
Here, take this. It'll give you a boost.
You spent 90 gold on this??
90 gold is nothing when you're the baddest bitch in the virtual universe.

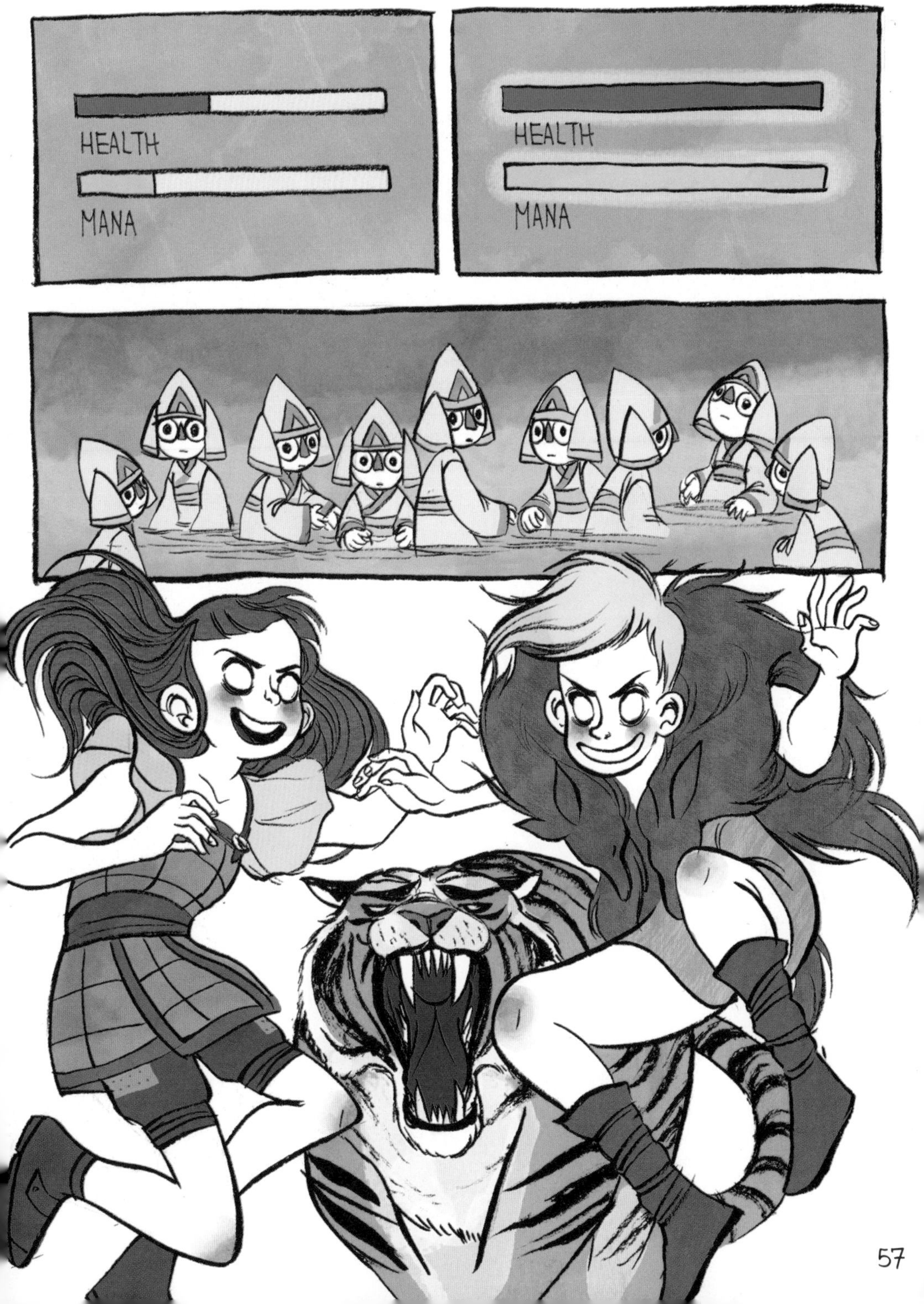
HEALTH
MANA
HEALTH
MANA

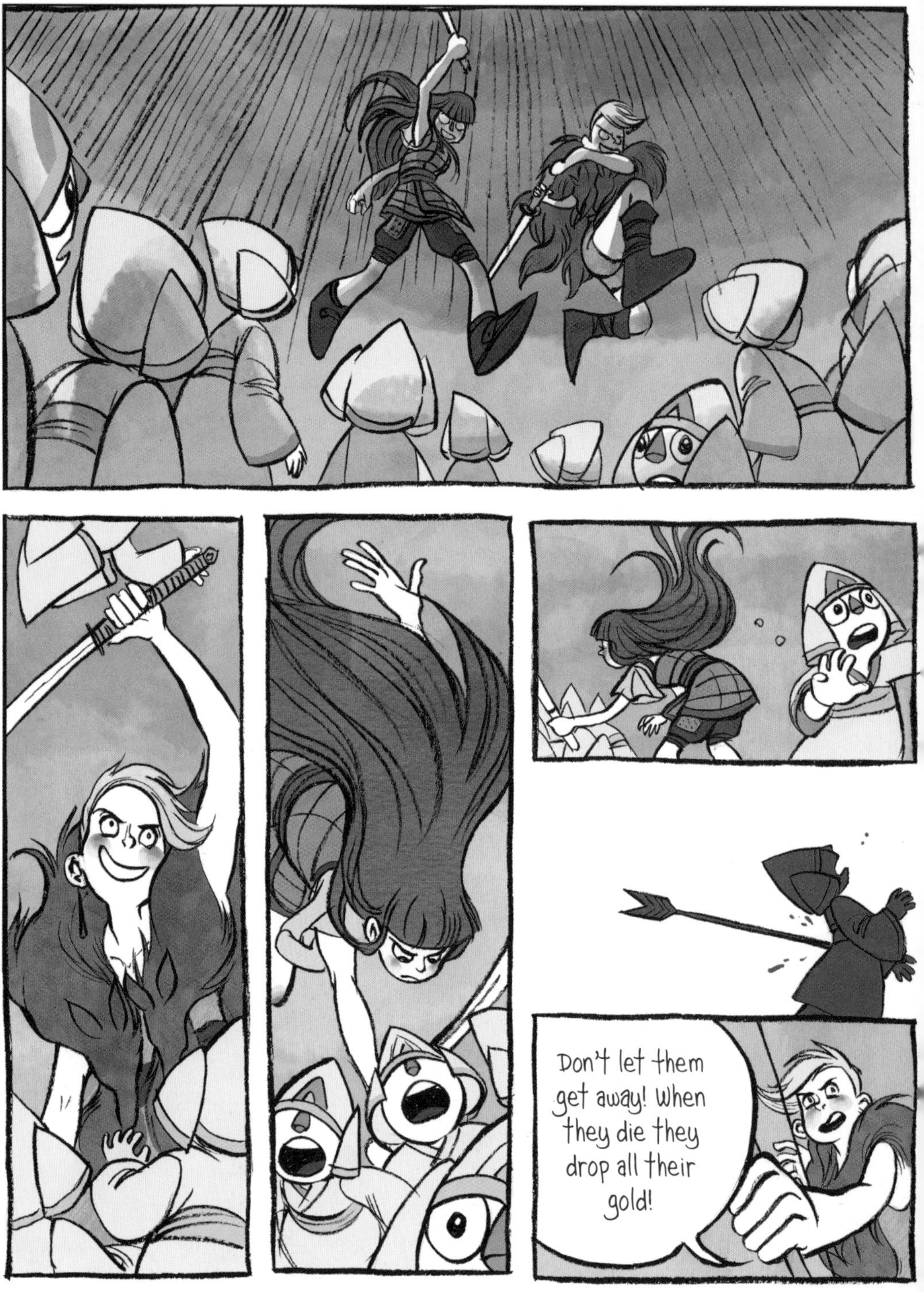
Don't let them
get away! When
they die they
drop all their
gold!

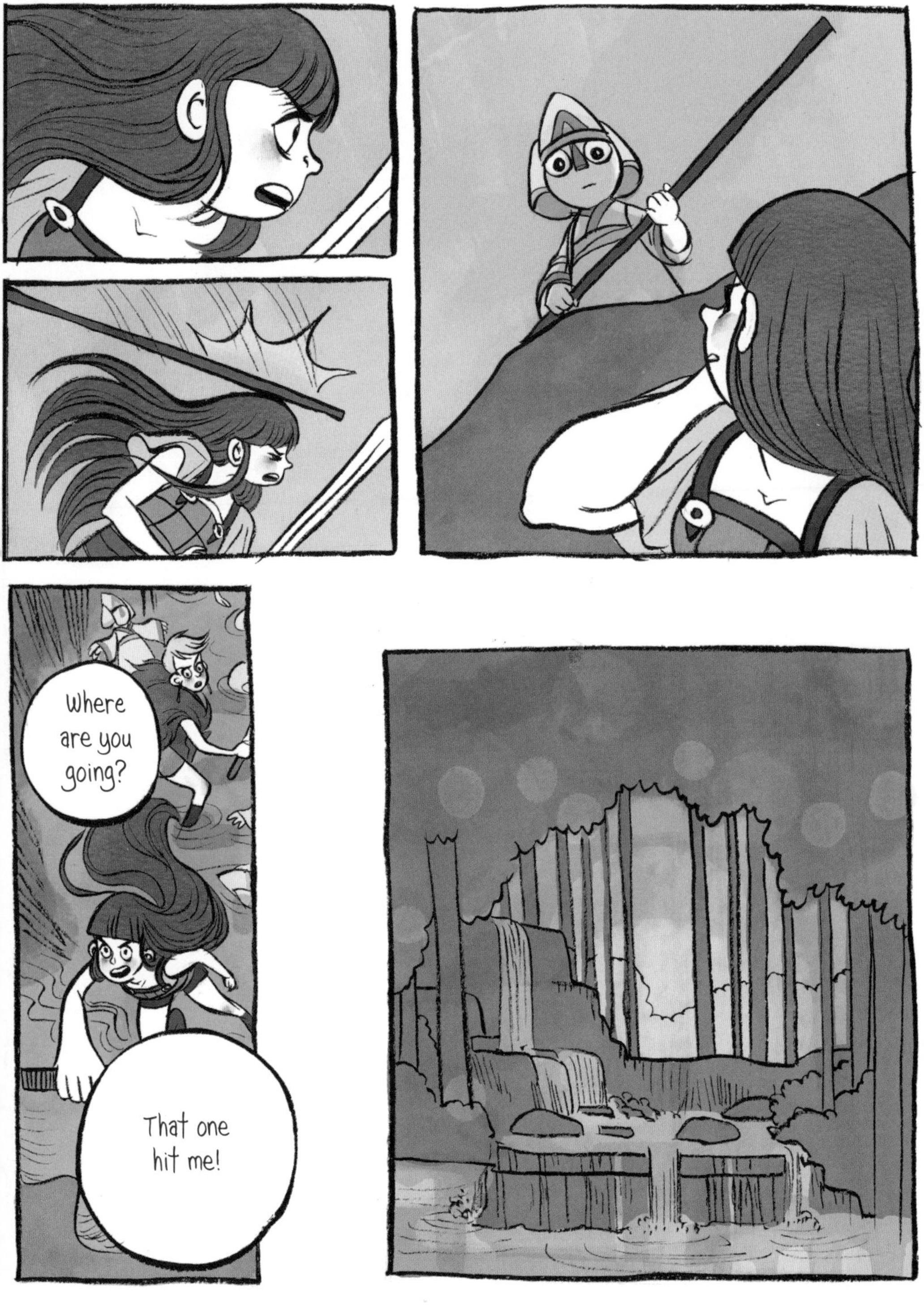
Where are you going?
That one hit me!

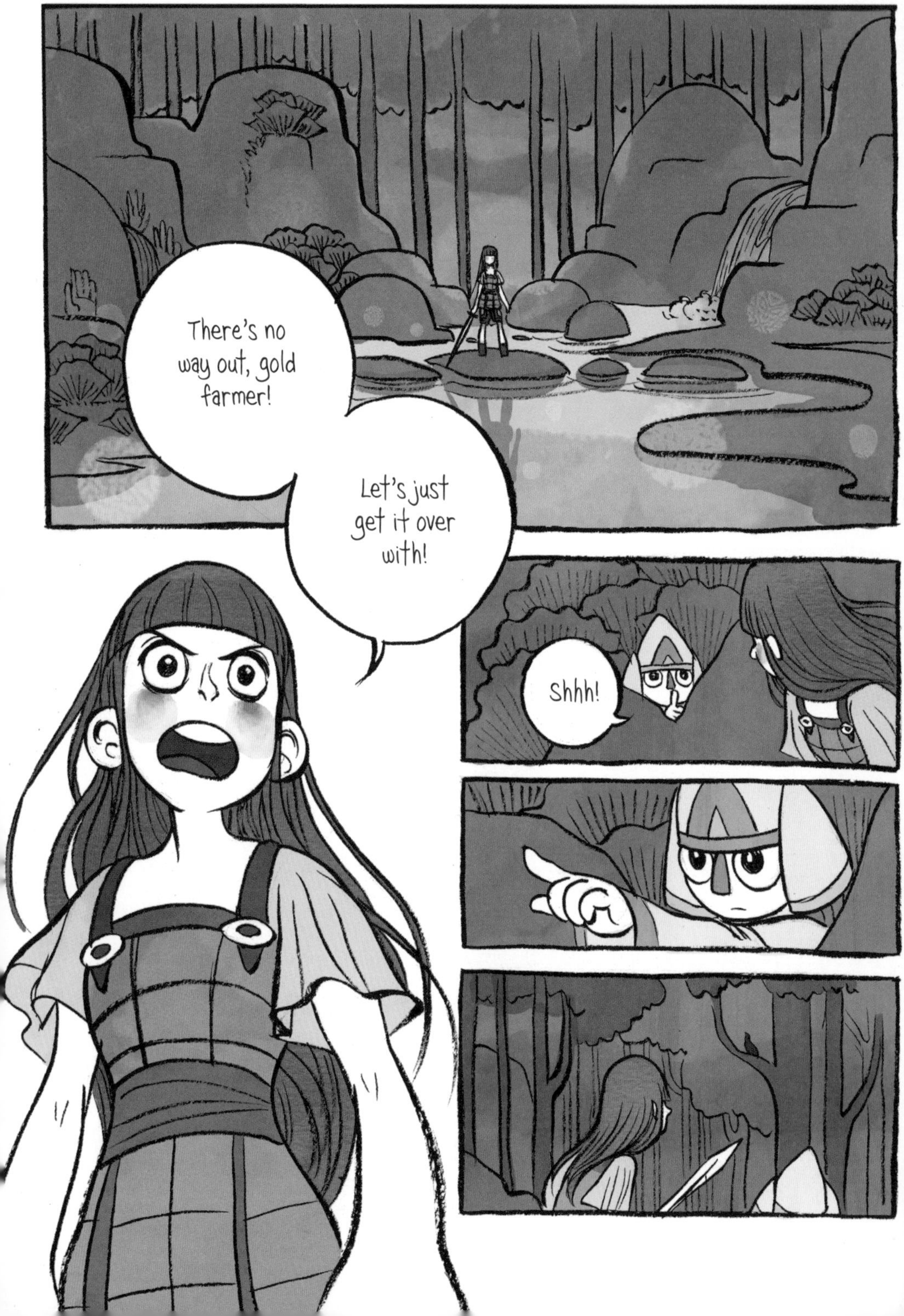
There's no way out, gold farmer!
Let's just get it over with!
Shhh!

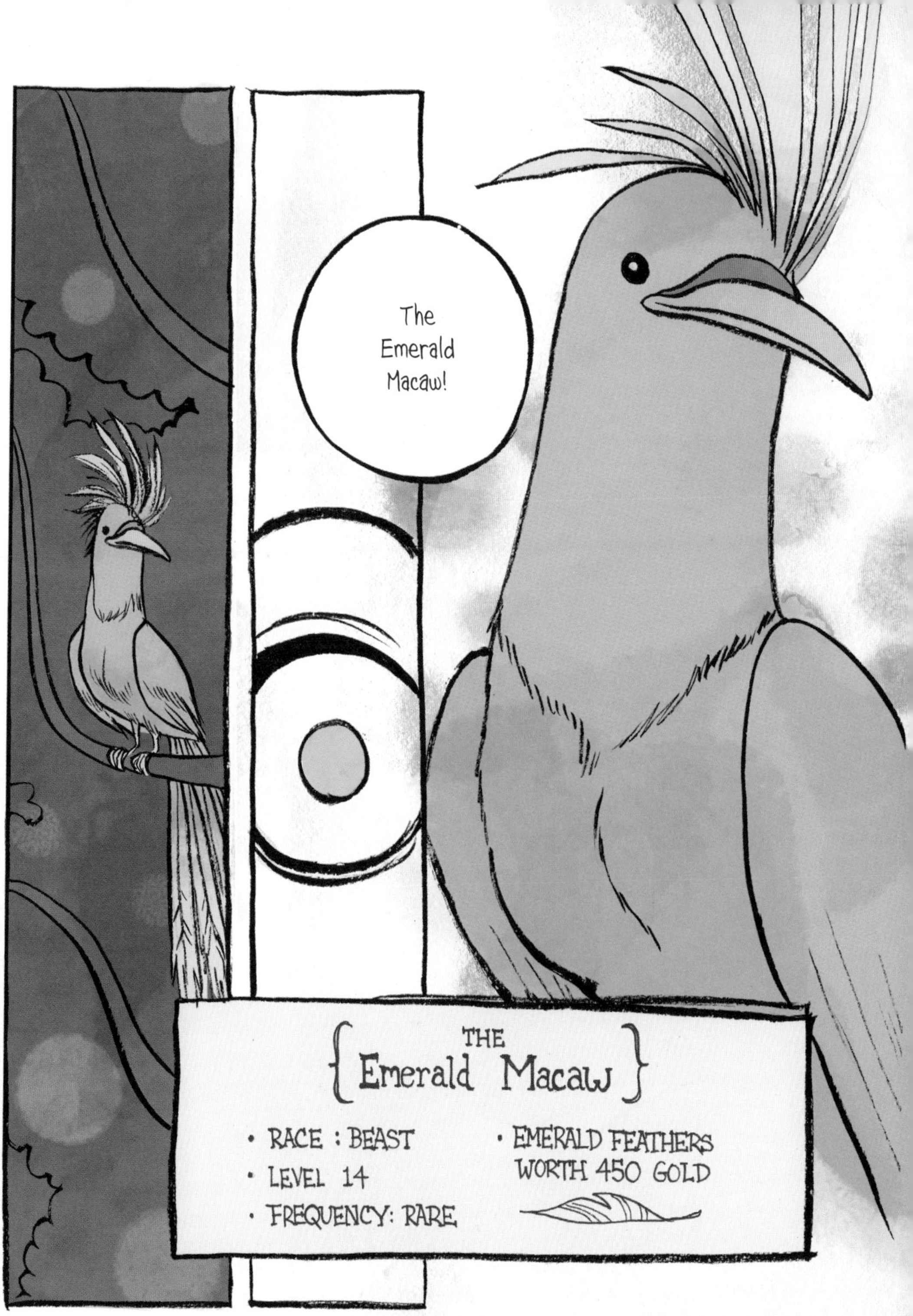
The Emerald Macaw!
THE Emerald Macaw
• RACE : BEAST
• LEVEL 14
• FREQUENCY: RARE
• EMERALD FEATHERS WORTH 450 GOLD

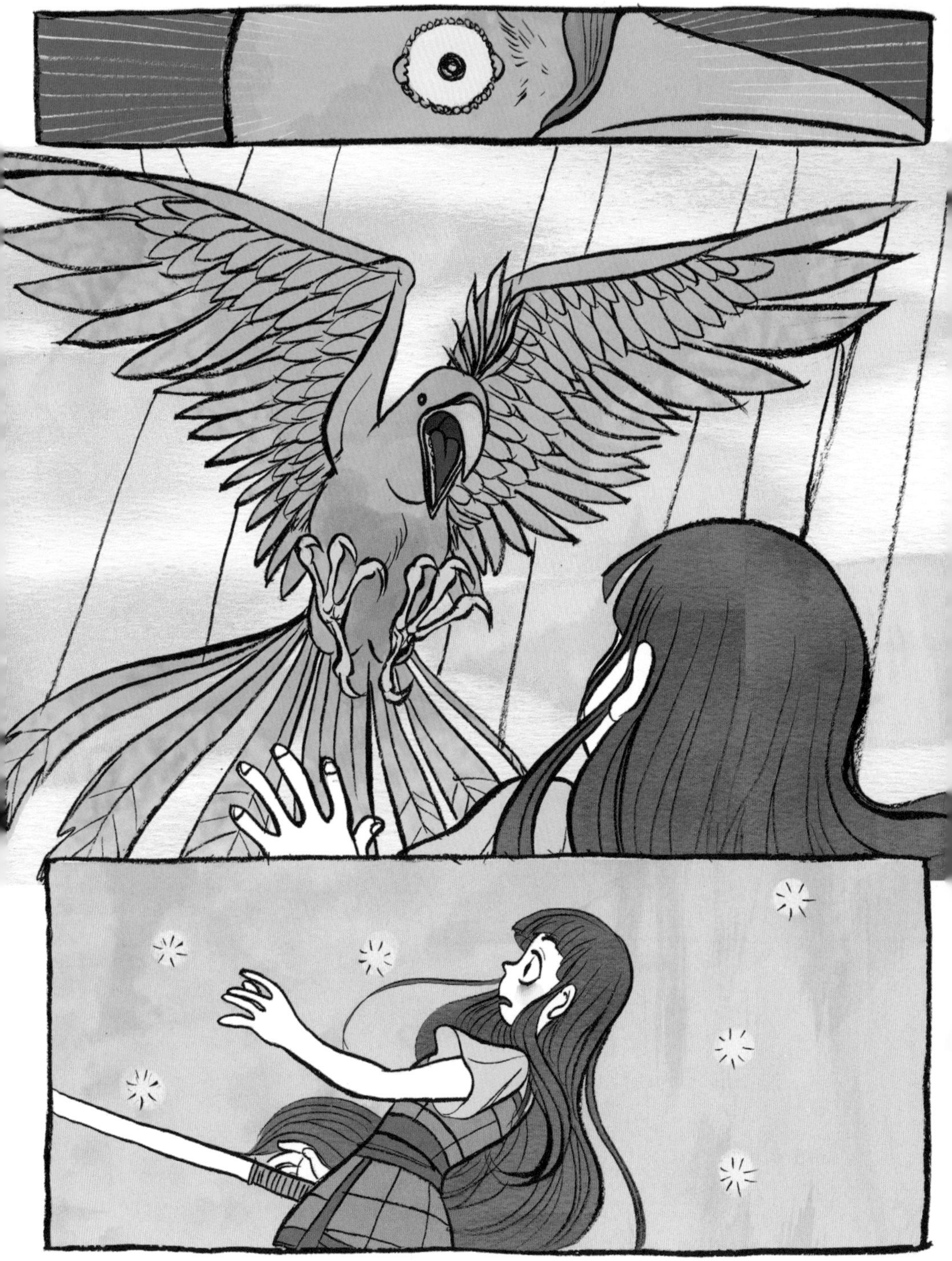

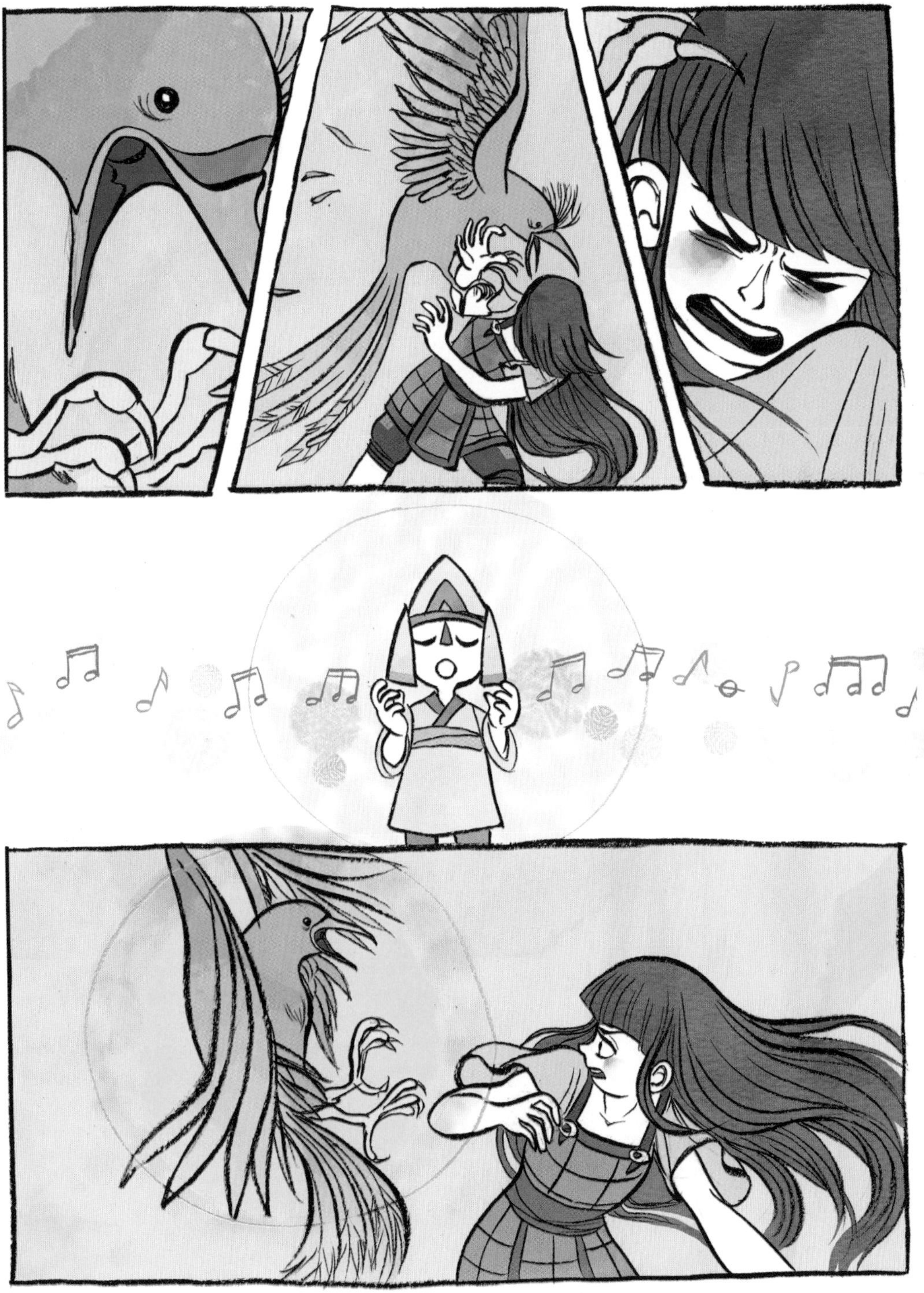

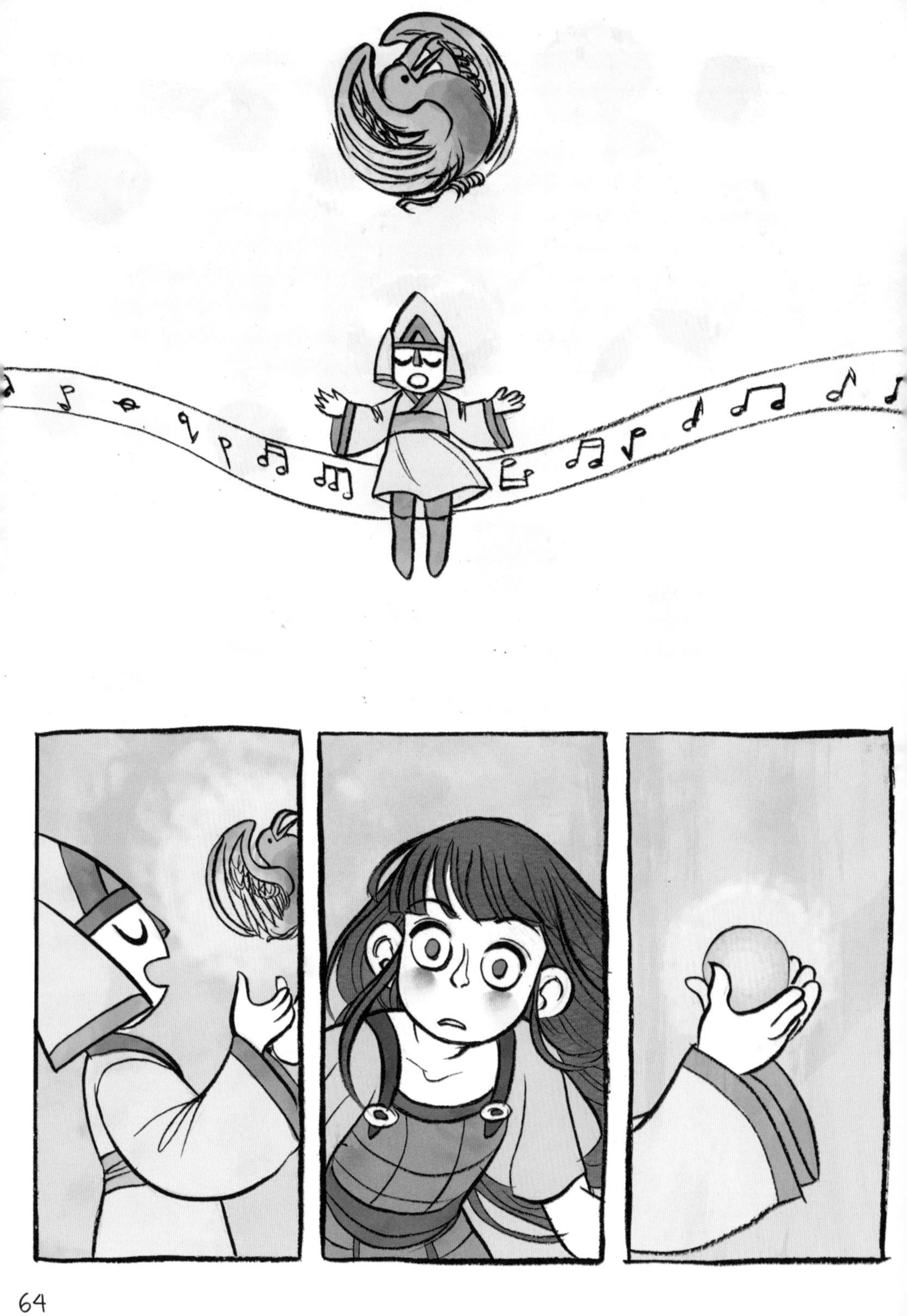

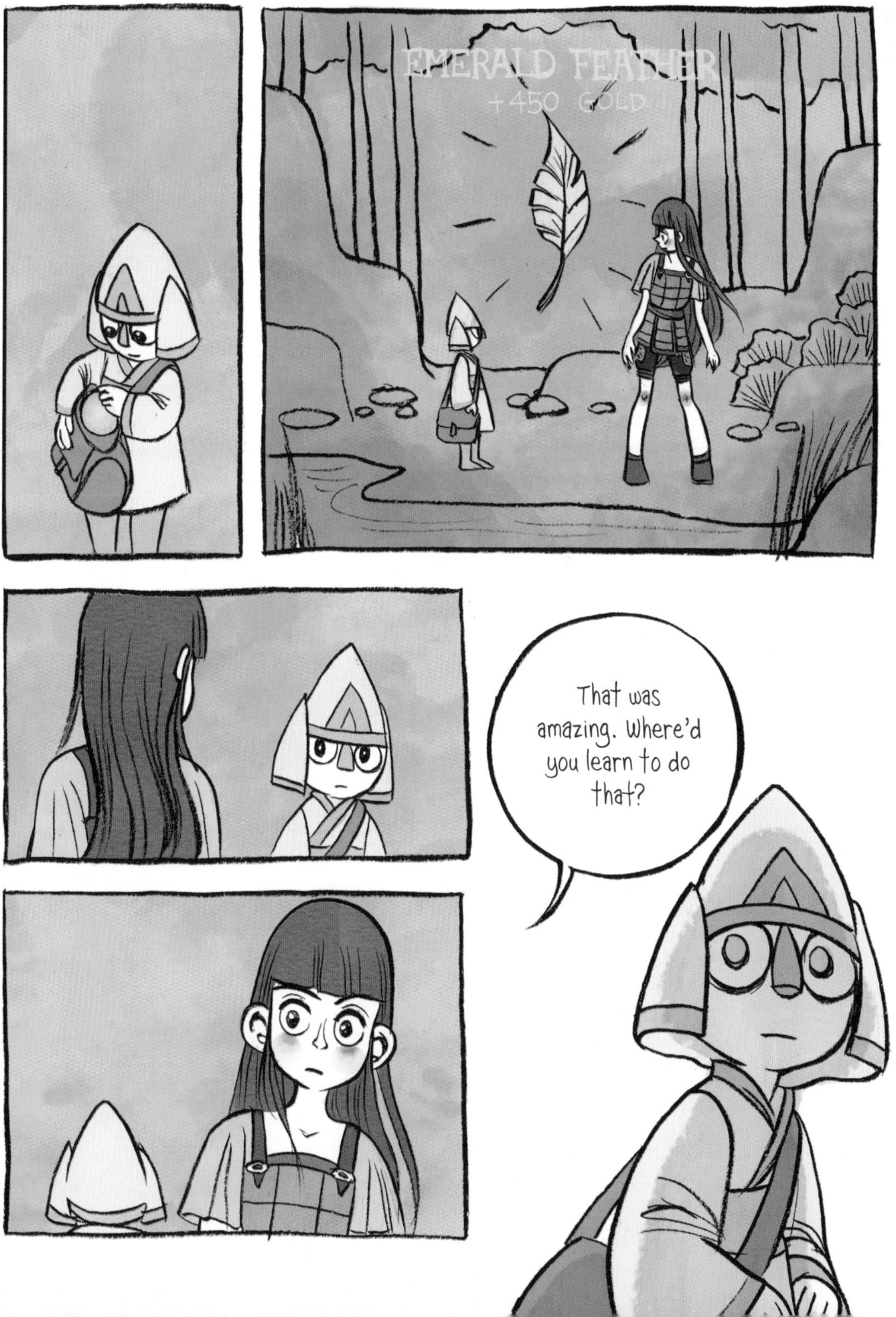
EMERALD FEATHER
+450 GOLD
That was amazing. Where'd you learn to do that?

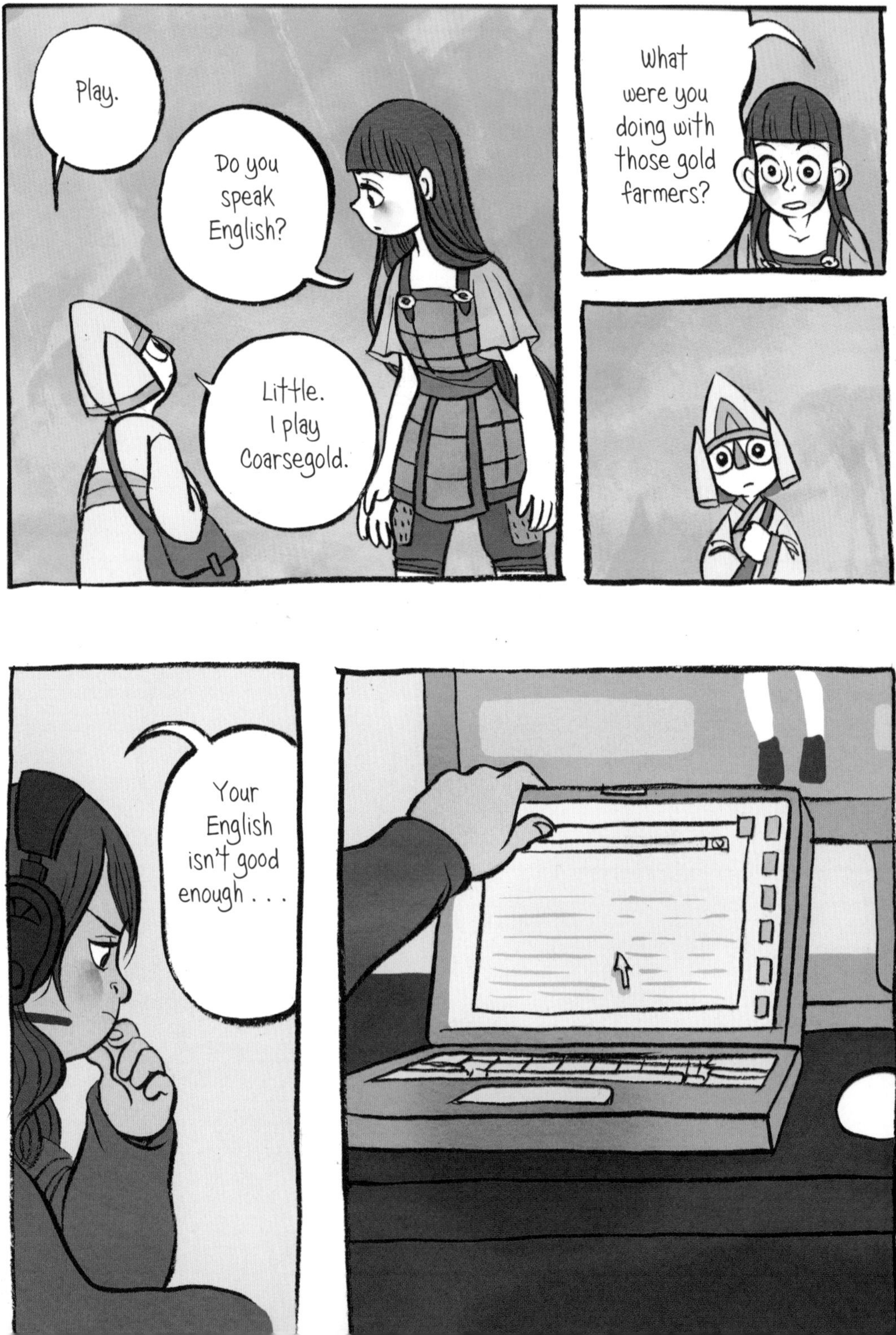
Play.
Do you speak English?
Little. I play Coarsegold.
What were you doing with those gold farmers?
Your English isn't good enough . . .

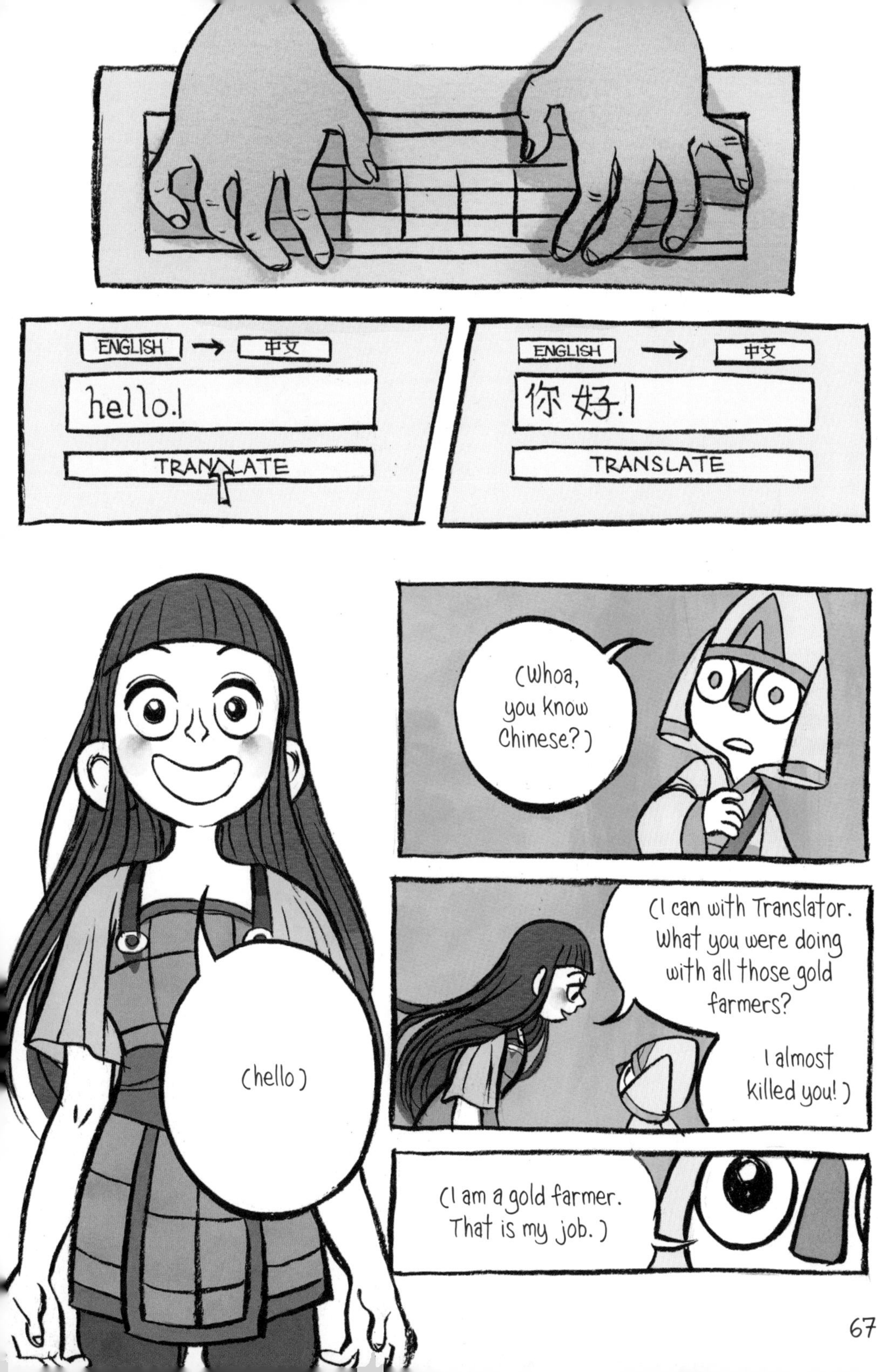
ENGLISH
中文
hello.
TRANSLATE
ENGLISH
中文
你好.
TRANSLATE
(hello)
(Whoa, you know Chinese?)
(I can with Translator. What you were doing with all those gold farmers?
I almost killed you!)
(I am a gold farmer. That is my job.)

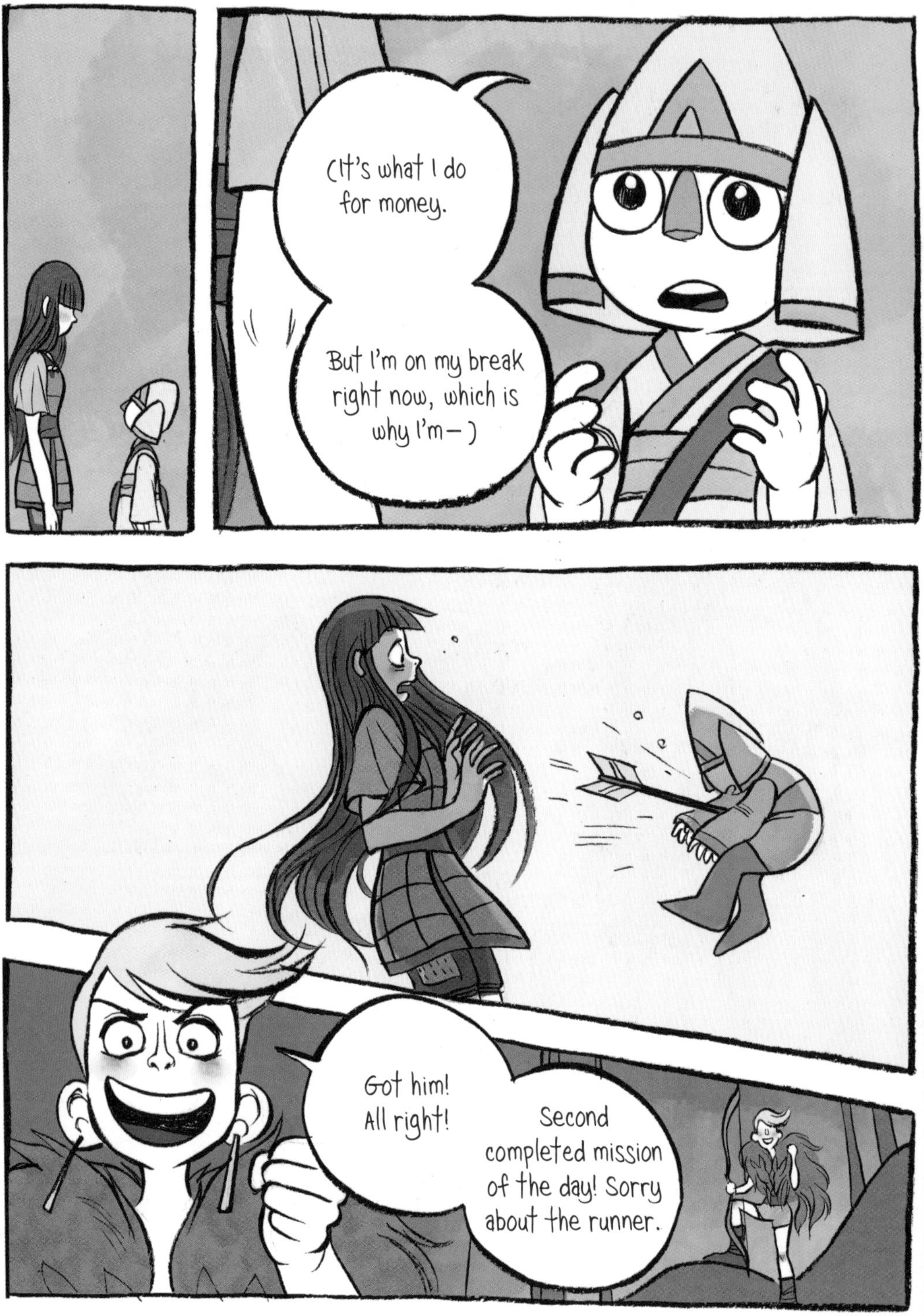
(It's what I do for money.
But I'm on my break right now, which is why I'm—)
Got him! All right!
Second completed mission of the day! Sorry about the runner.

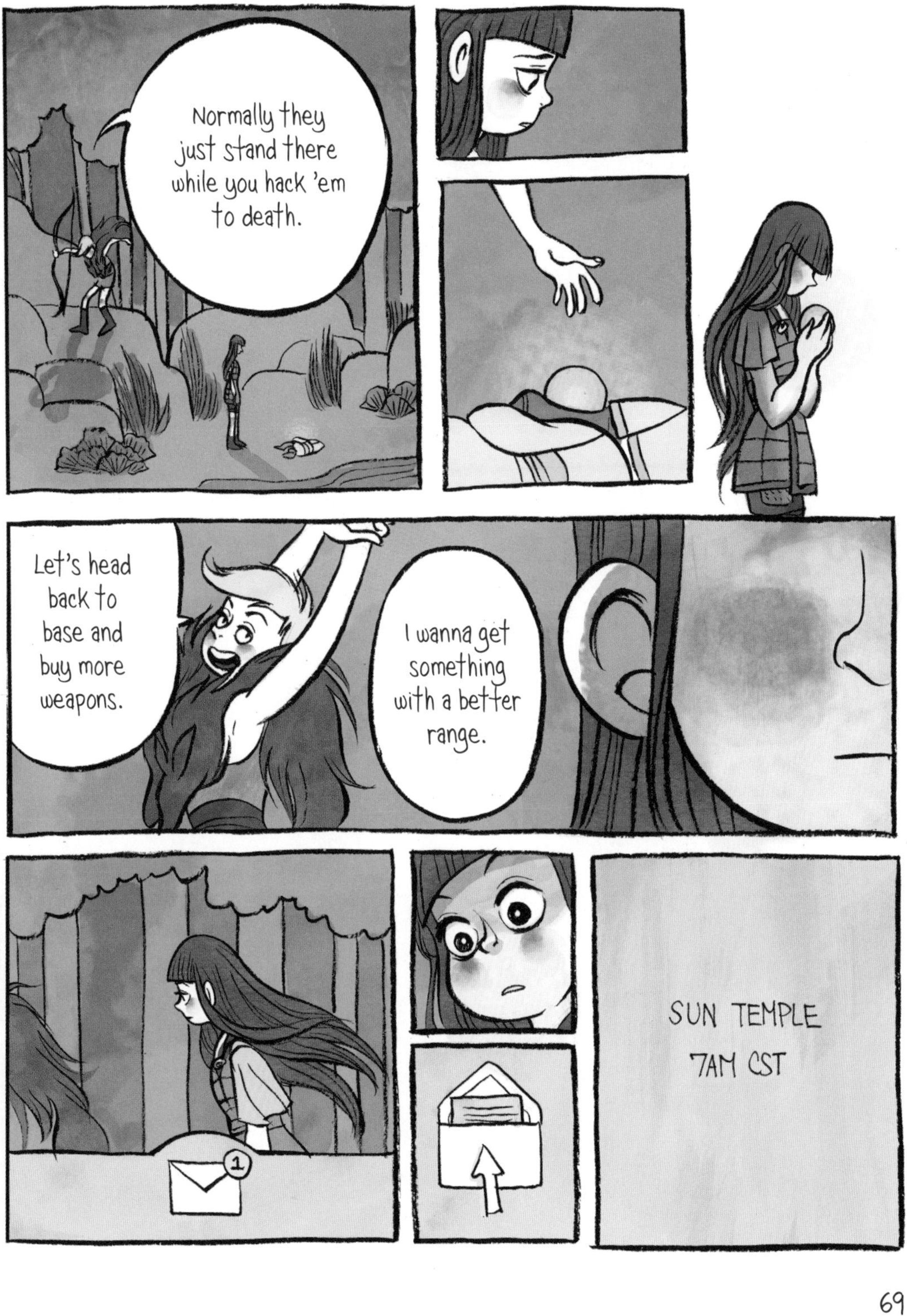
Normally they just stand there while you hack 'em to death.
Let's head back to base and buy more weapons.
I wanna get something with a better range.
1
SUN TEMPLE
7AM CST

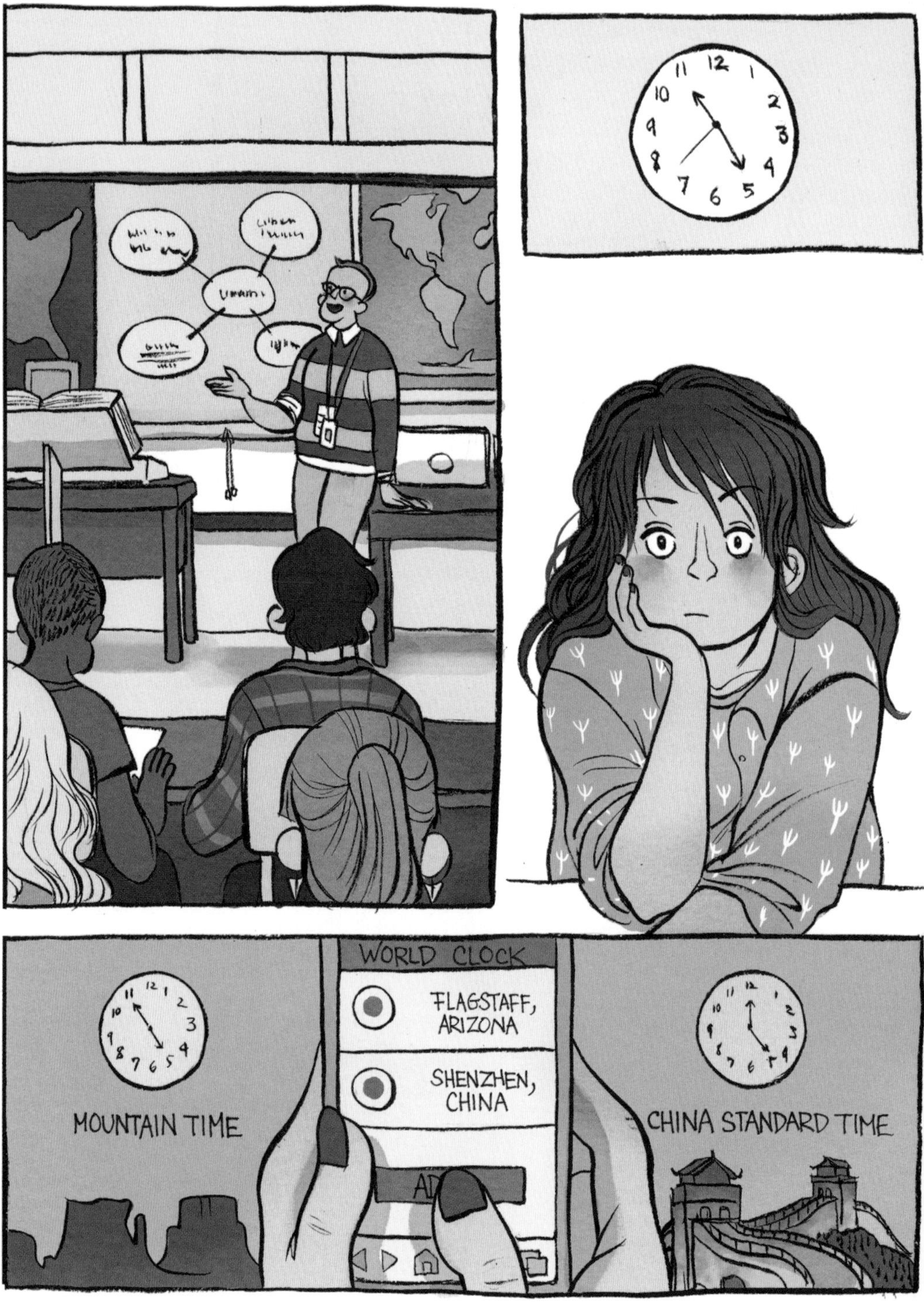
WORLD CLOCK
FLAGSTAFF, ARIZONA
SHENZHEN, CHINA
MOUNTAIN TIME
CHINA STANDARD TIME

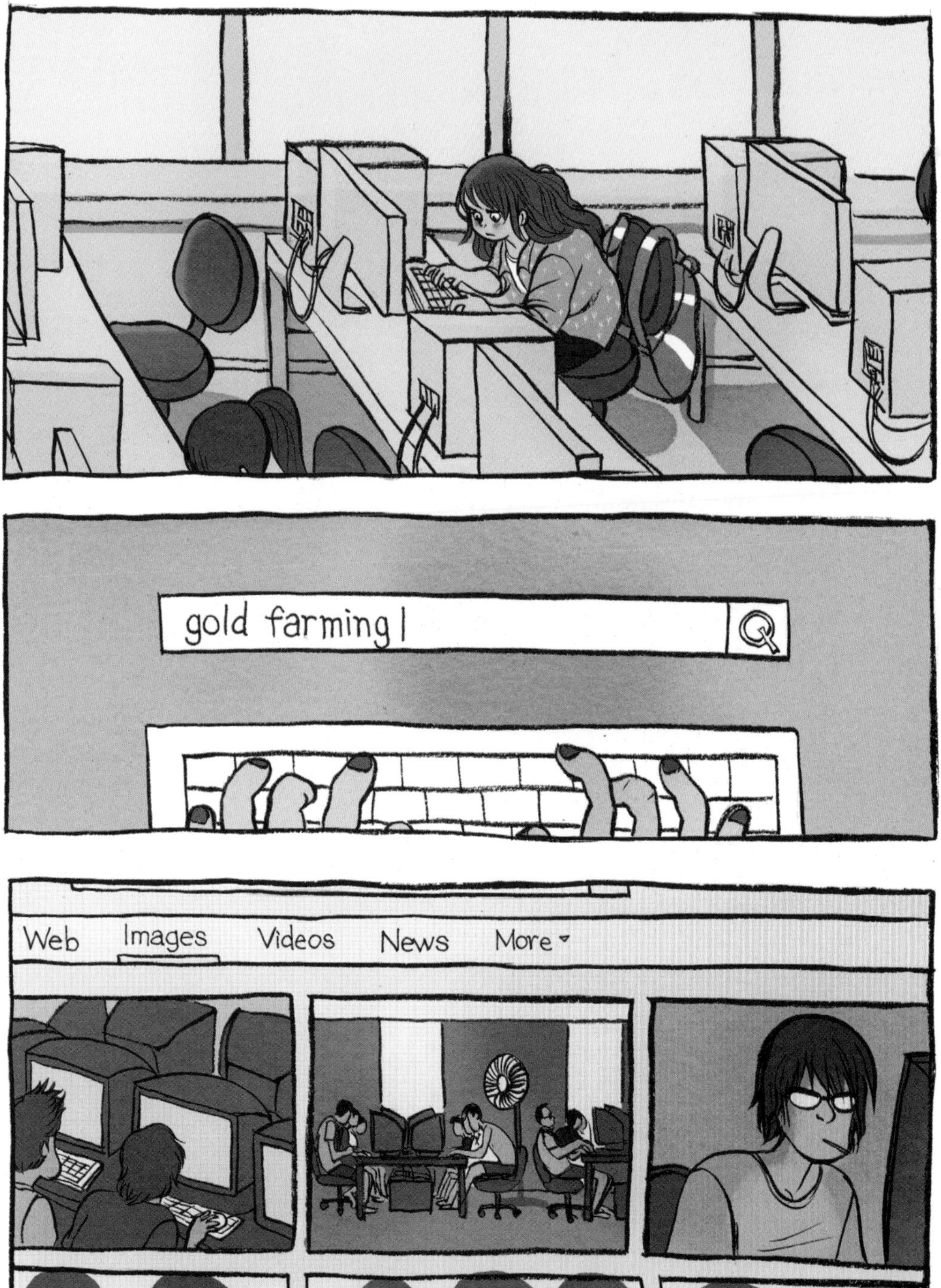
gold farming
Web
Images
Videos
News
More

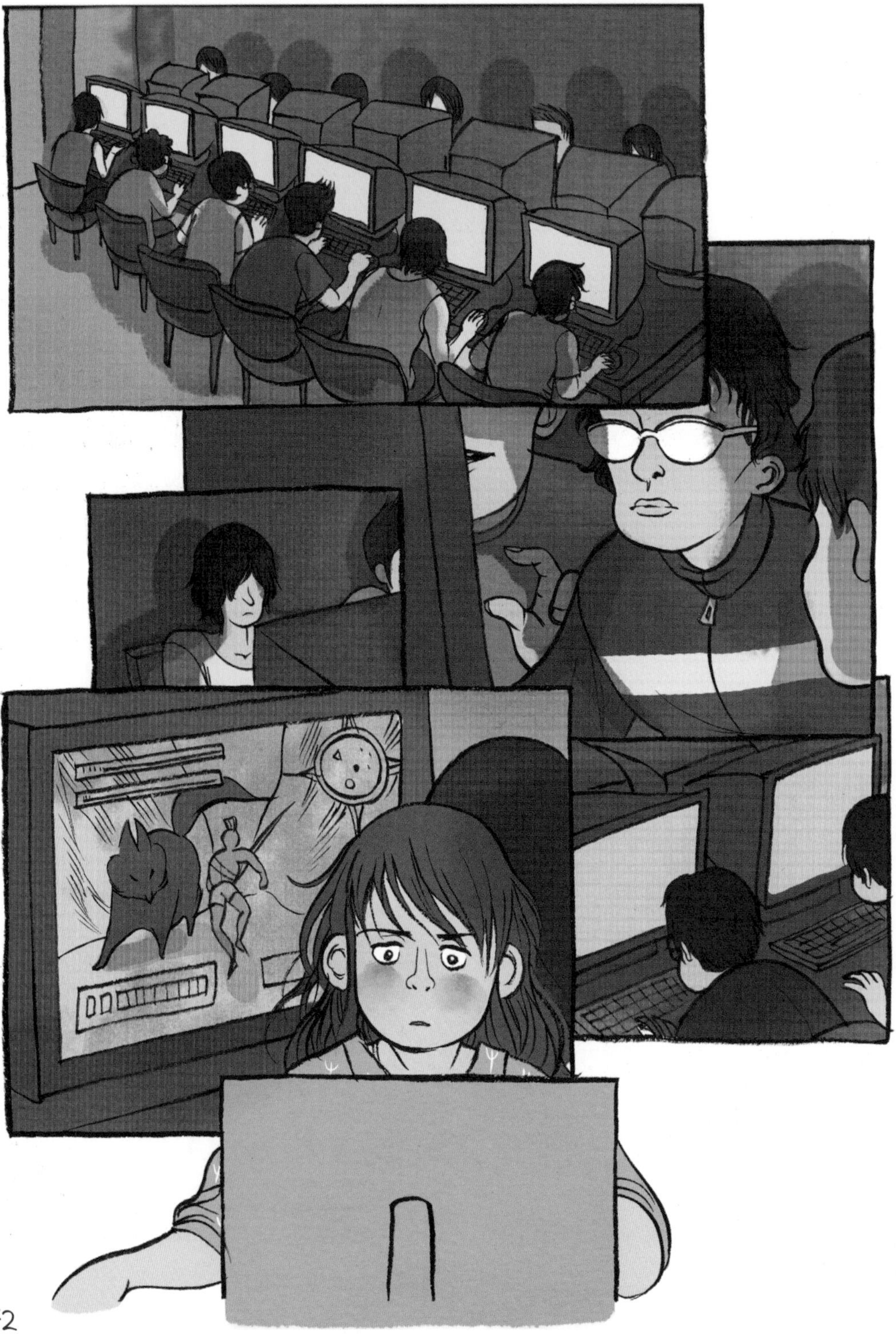

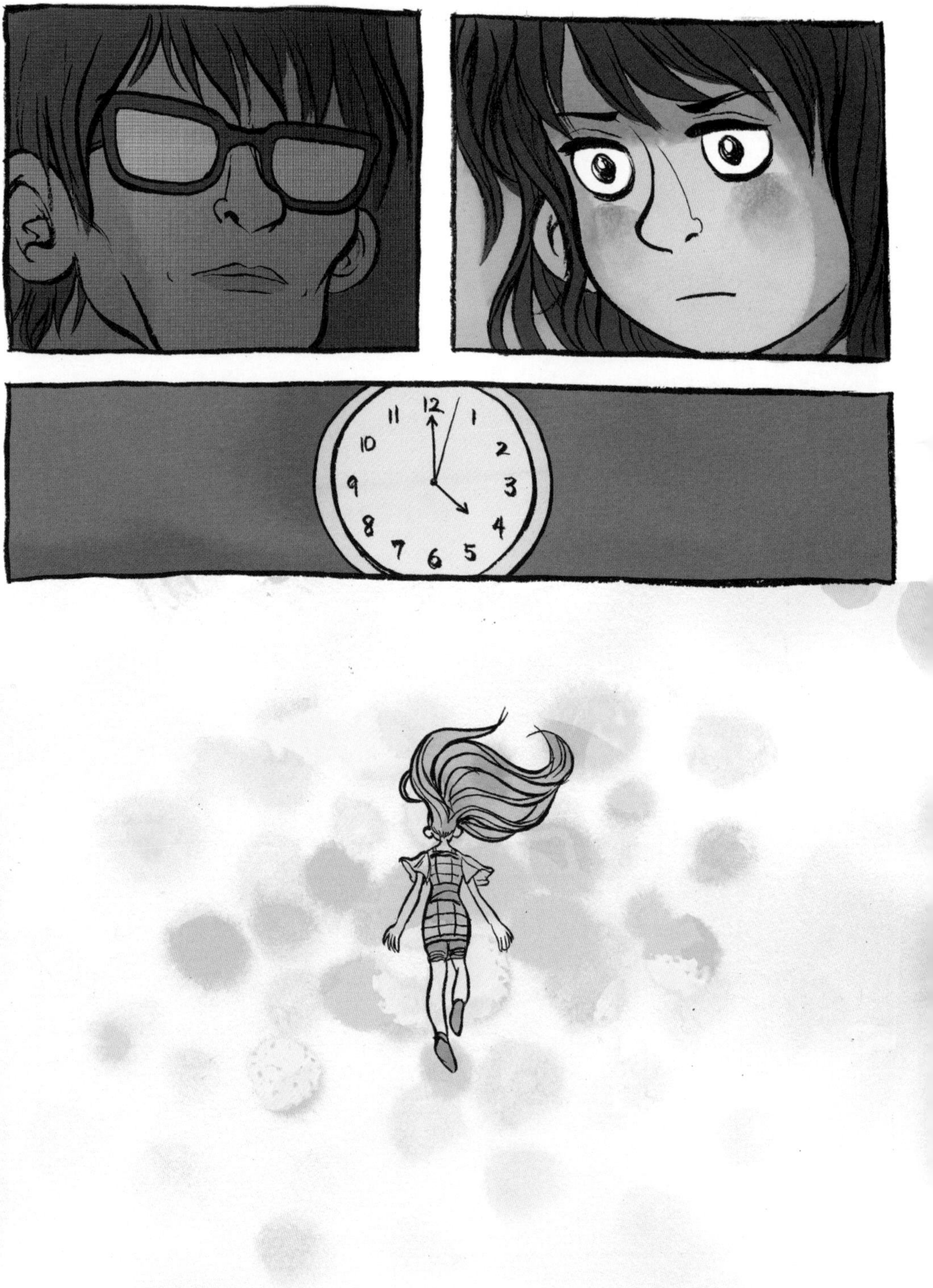

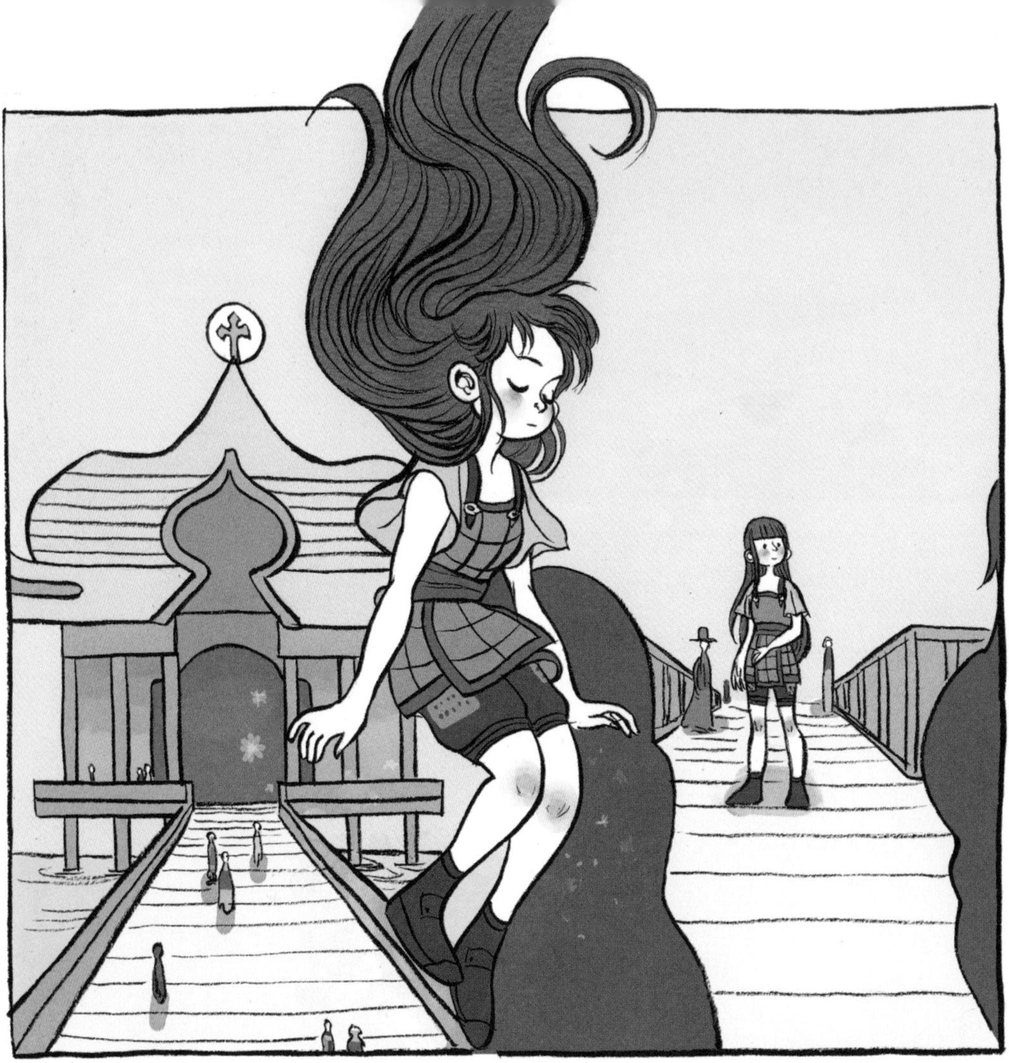

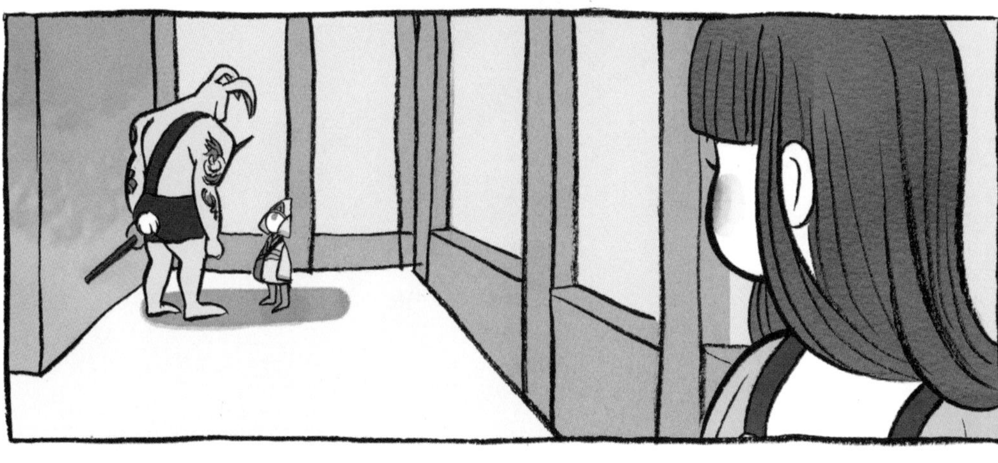

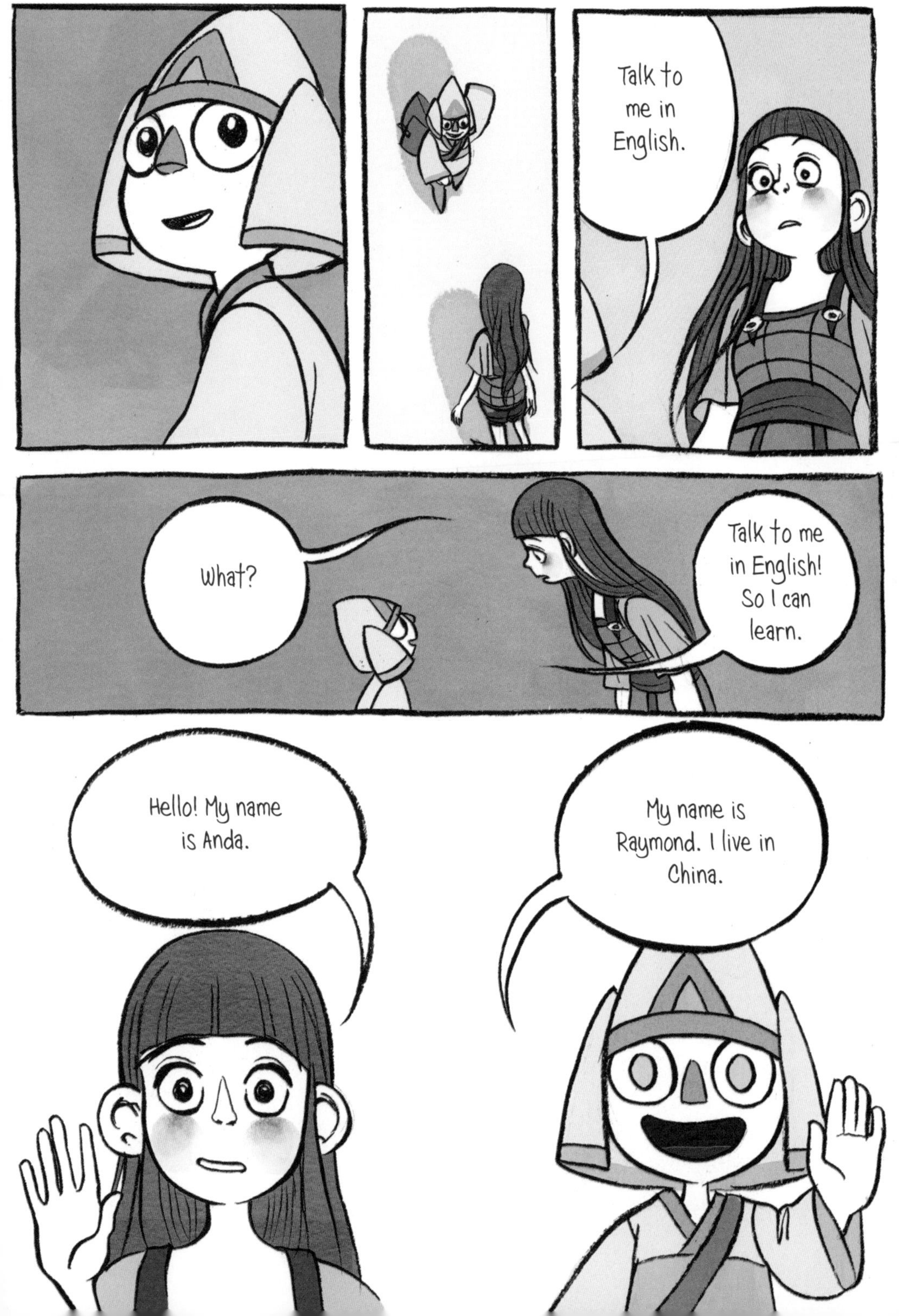
Talk to me in English.
What?
Talk to me in English! So I can learn.
Hello! My name is Anda.
My name is Raymond. I live in China.

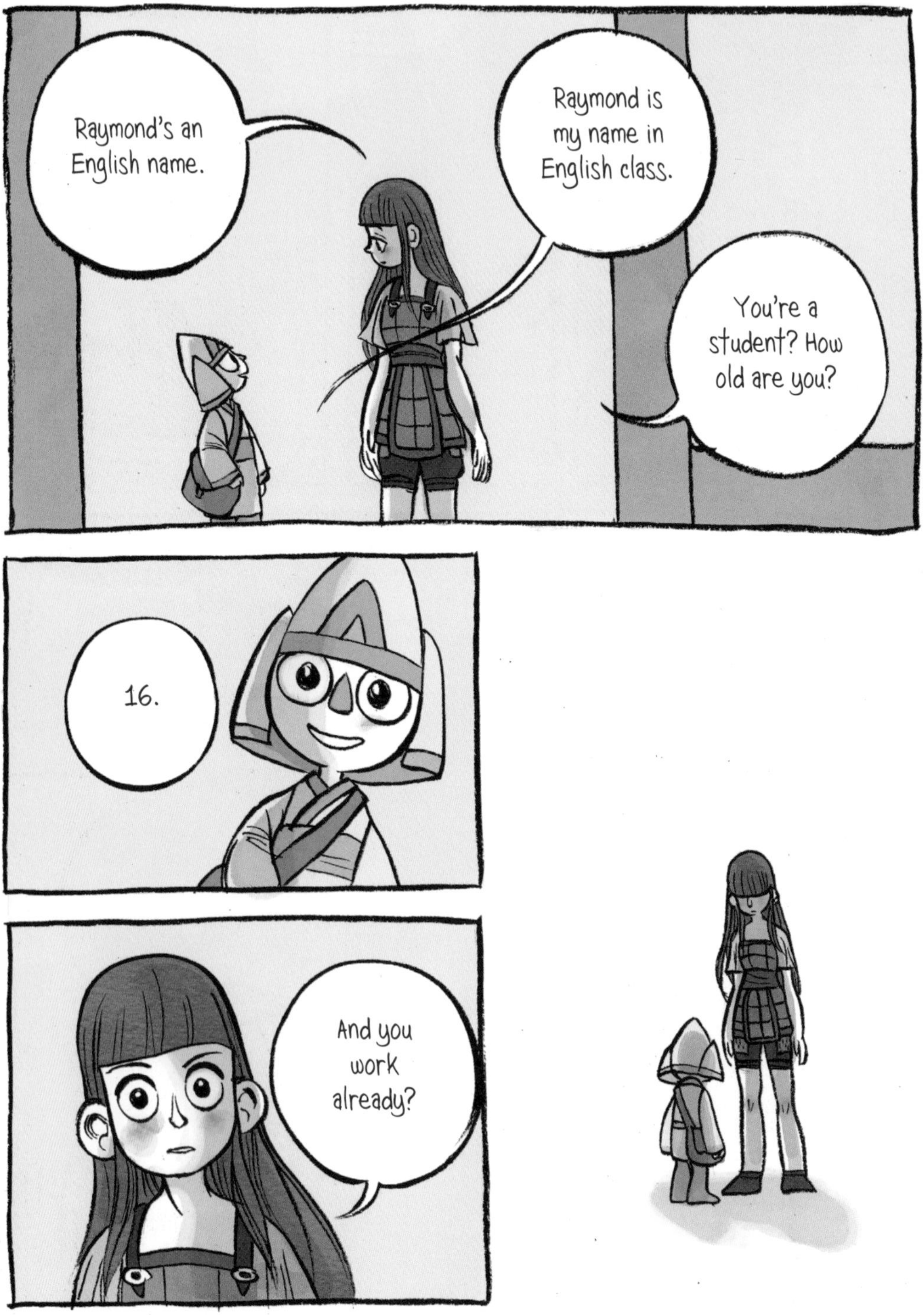

Raymond's an English name.
Raymond is my name in English class.
You're a student? How old are you?
16.
And you work already?

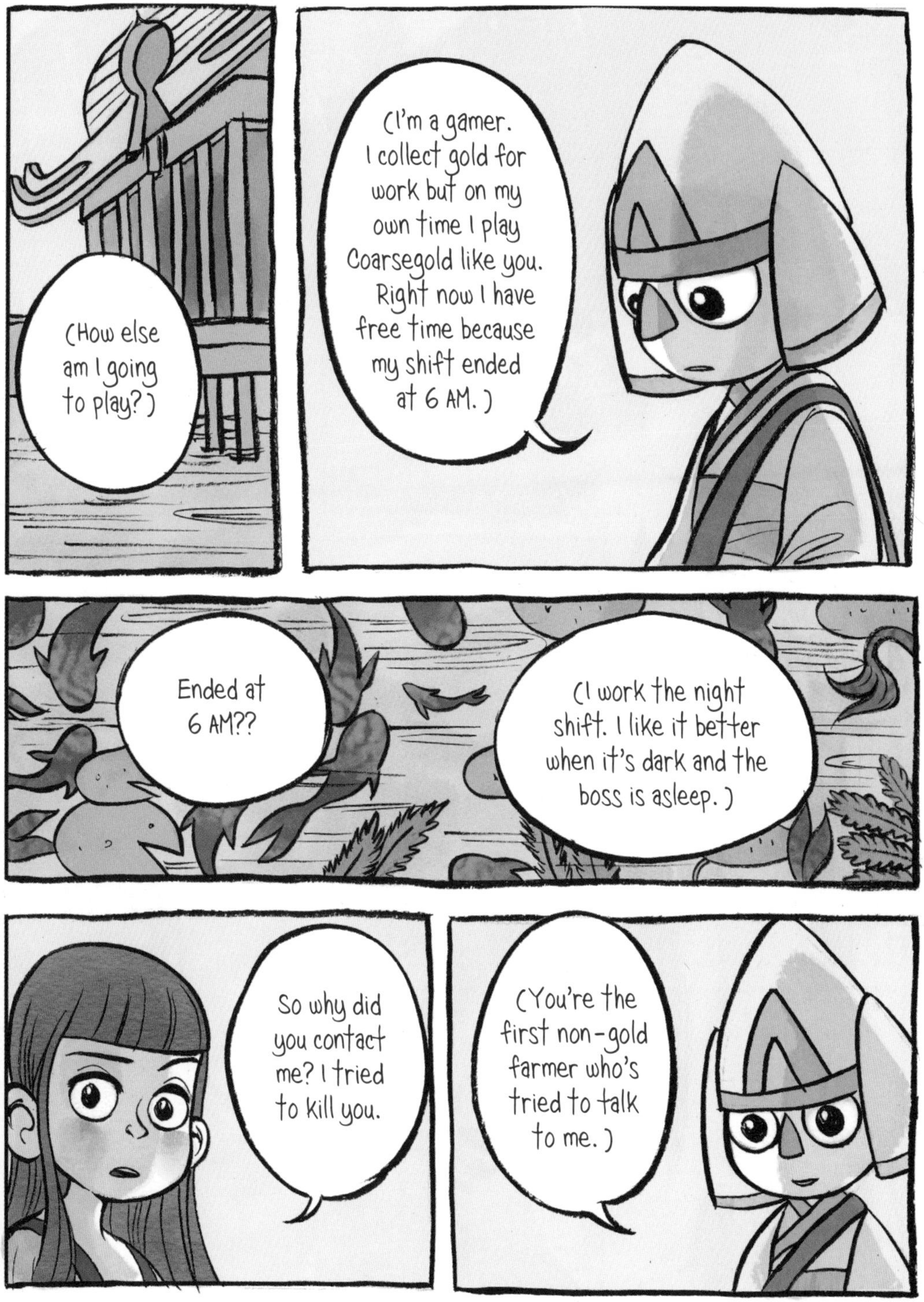
(How else am I going to play?)
(I'm a gamer. I collect gold for work but on my own time I play Coarsegold like you. Right now I have free time because my shift ended at 6 AM.)
Ended at 6 AM??
(I work the night shift. I like it better when it's dark and the boss is asleep.)
So why did you contact me? I tried to kill you.
(You're the first non-gold farmer who's tried to talk to me.)

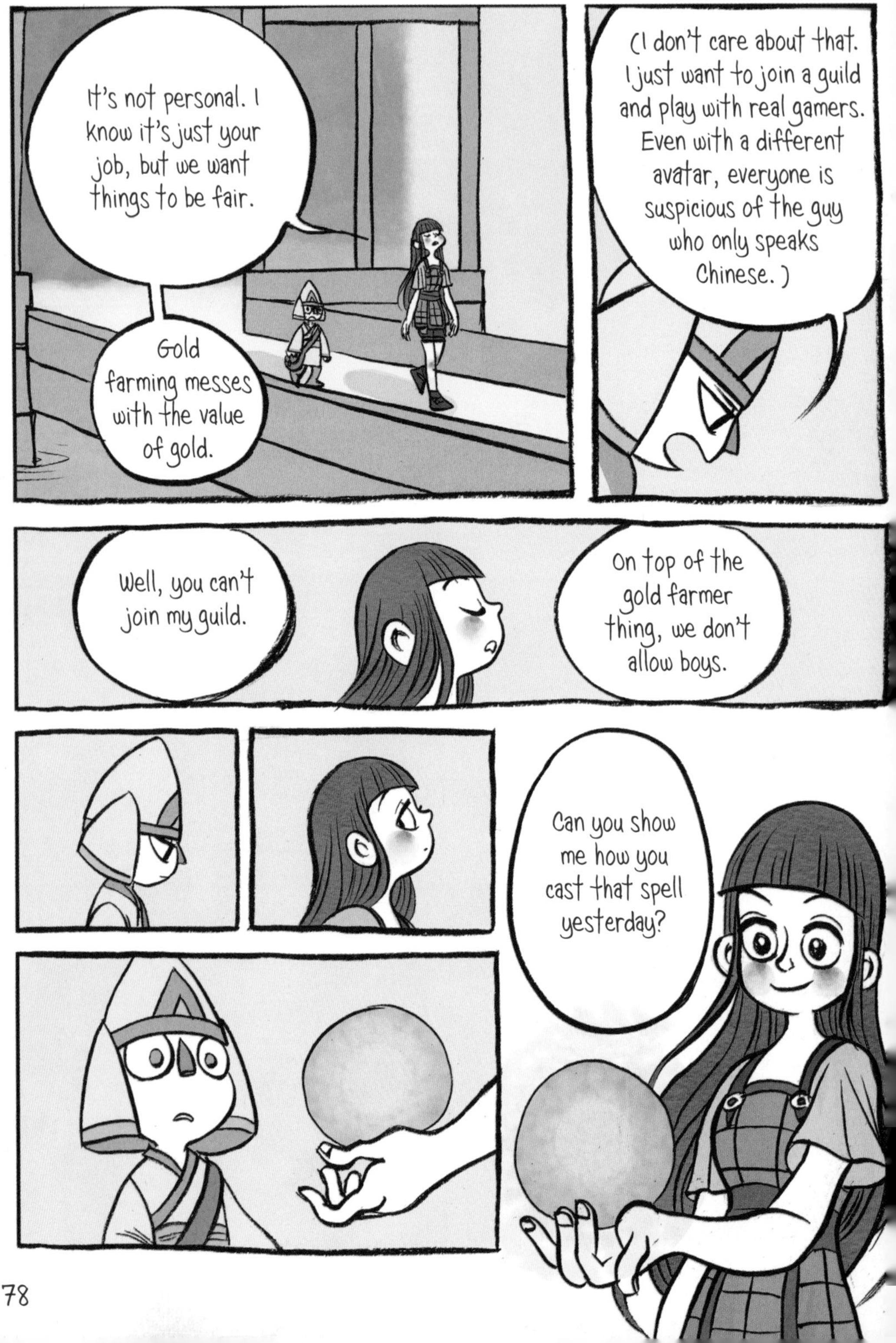
It's not personal. I know it's just your job, but we want things to be fair.
Gold farming messes with the value of gold.
(I don't care about that. I just want to join a guild and play with real gamers. Even with a different avatar, everyone is suspicious of the guy who only speaks Chinese.)
Well, you can't join my guild.
On top of the gold farmer thing, we don't allow boys.
Can you show me how you cast that spell yesterday?

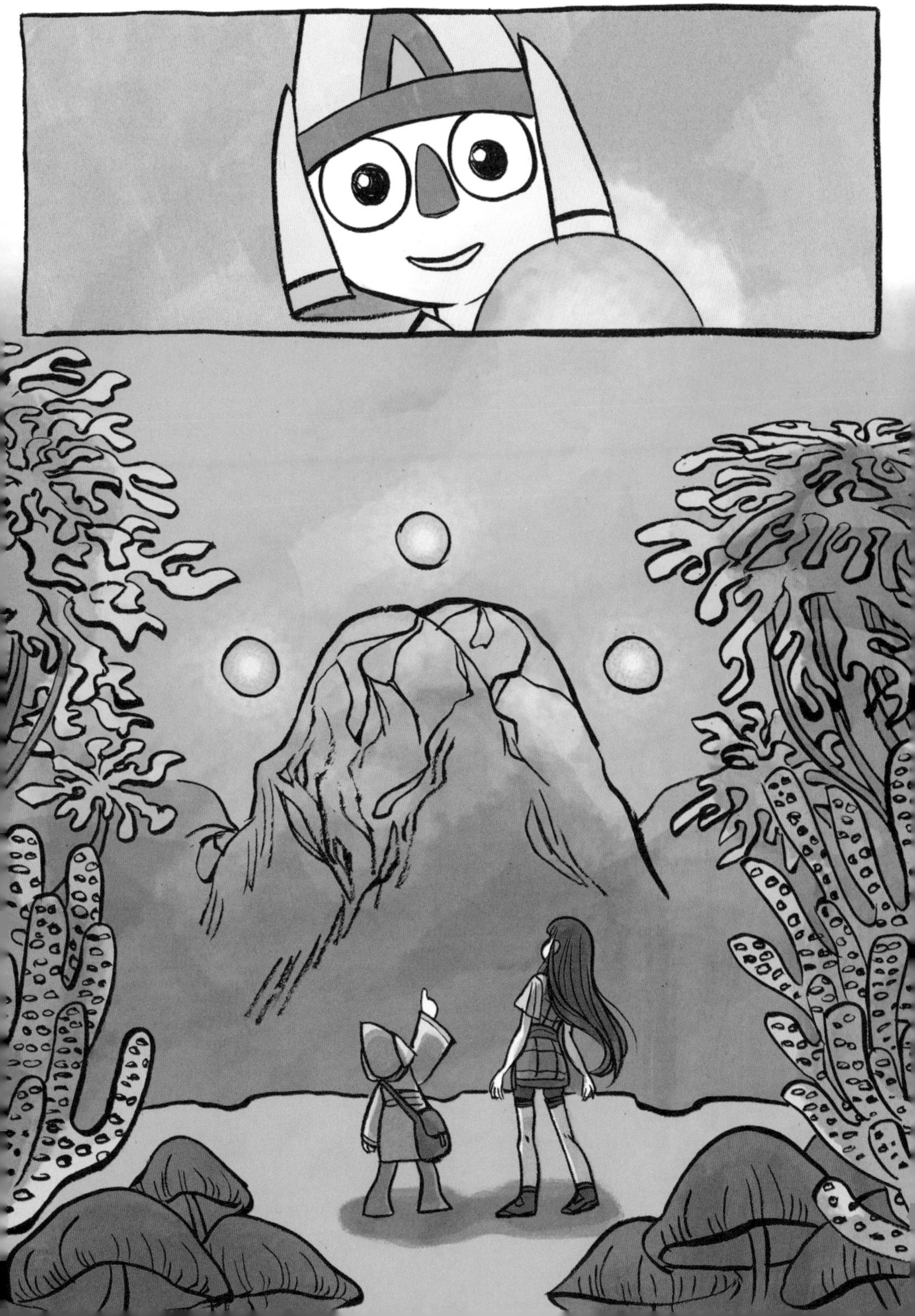

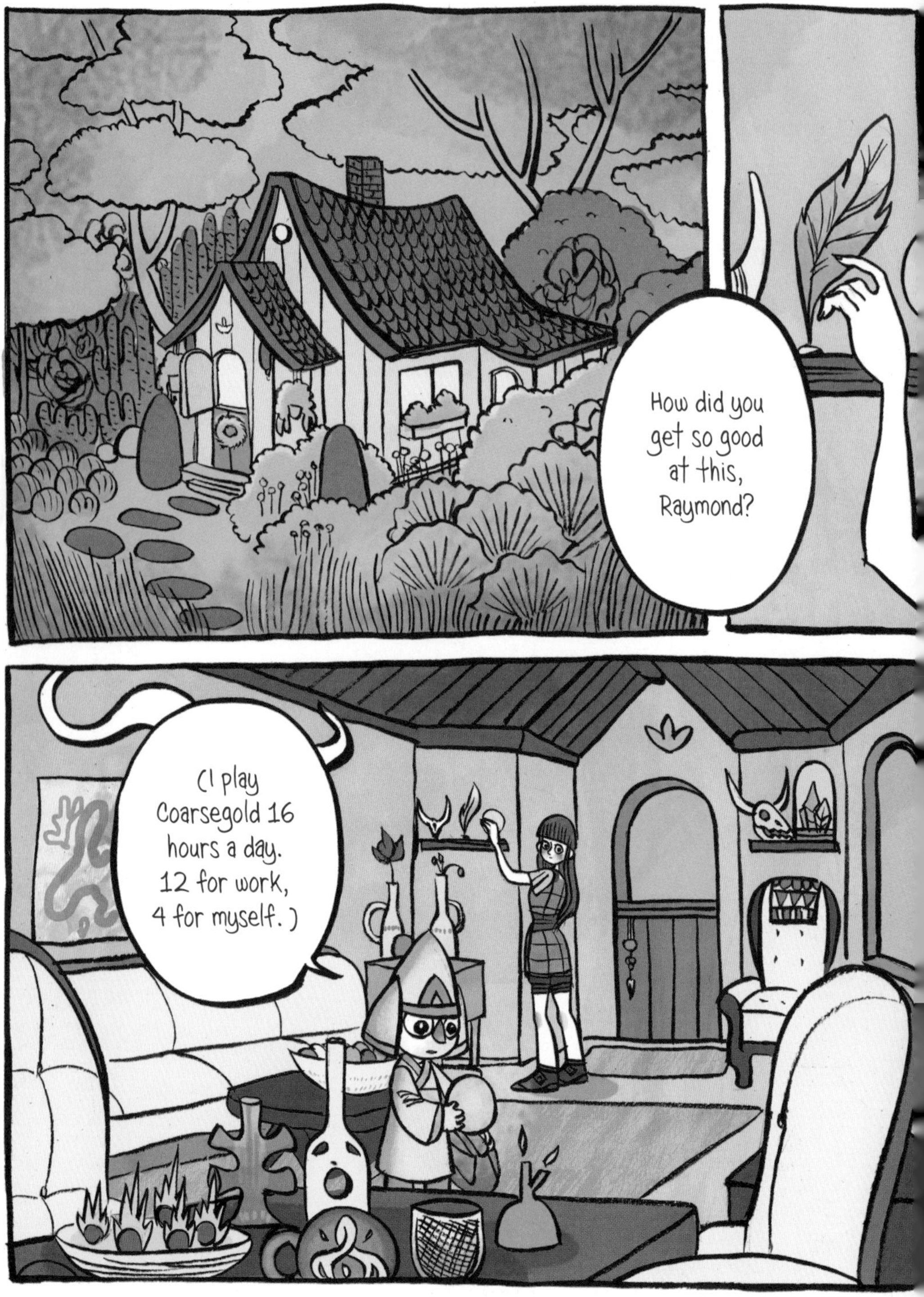
How did you get so good at this, Raymond?
(I play Coarsegold 16 hours a day. 12 for work, 4 for myself.)

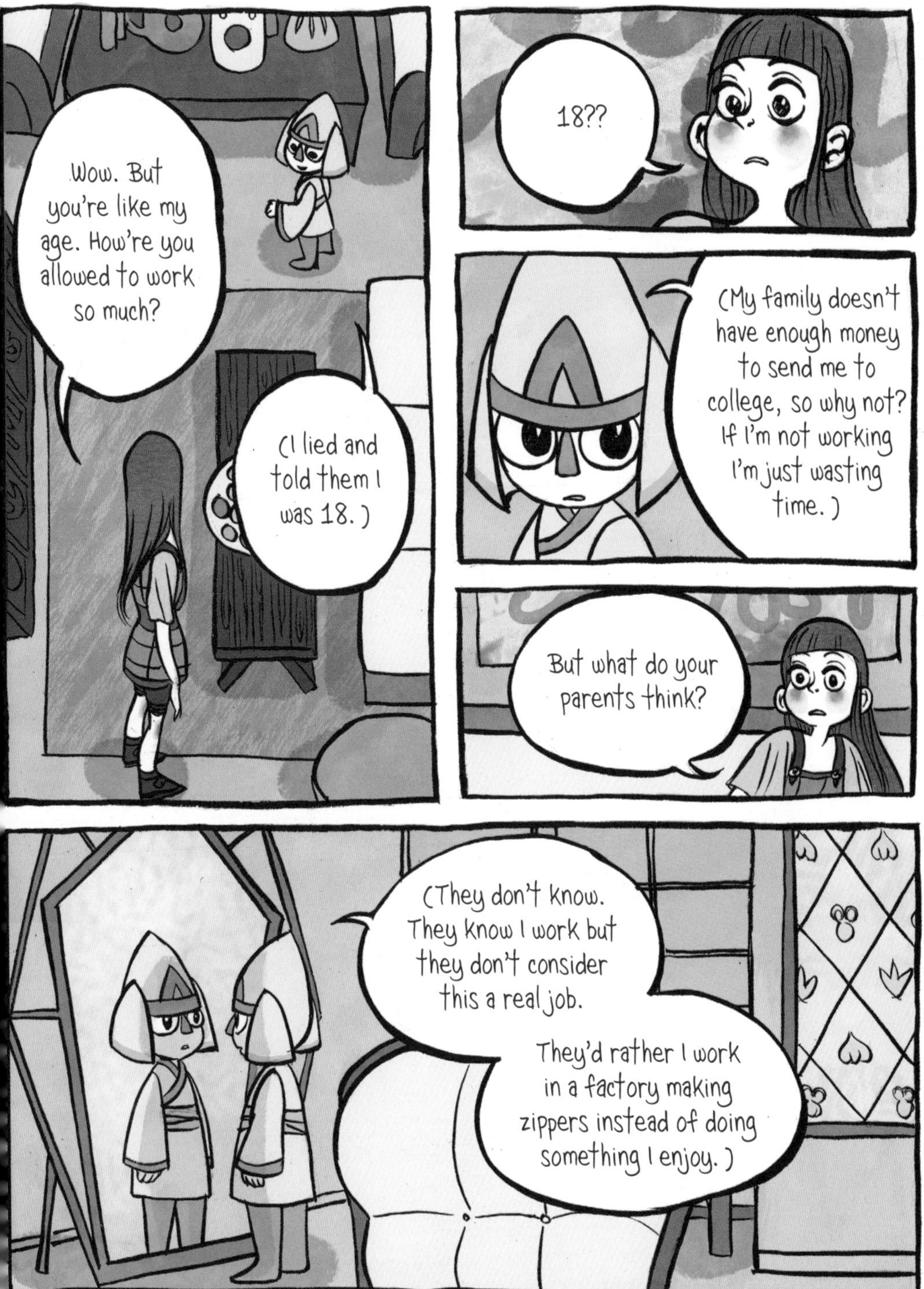
Wow. But you're like my age. How're you allowed to work so much?
(I lied and told them I was 18.)
18??
(My family doesn't have enough money to send me to college, so why not? If I'm not working I'm just wasting time.)
But what do your parents think?
(They don't know. They know I work but they don't consider this a real job.
They'd rather I work in a factory making zippers instead of doing something I enjoy.)

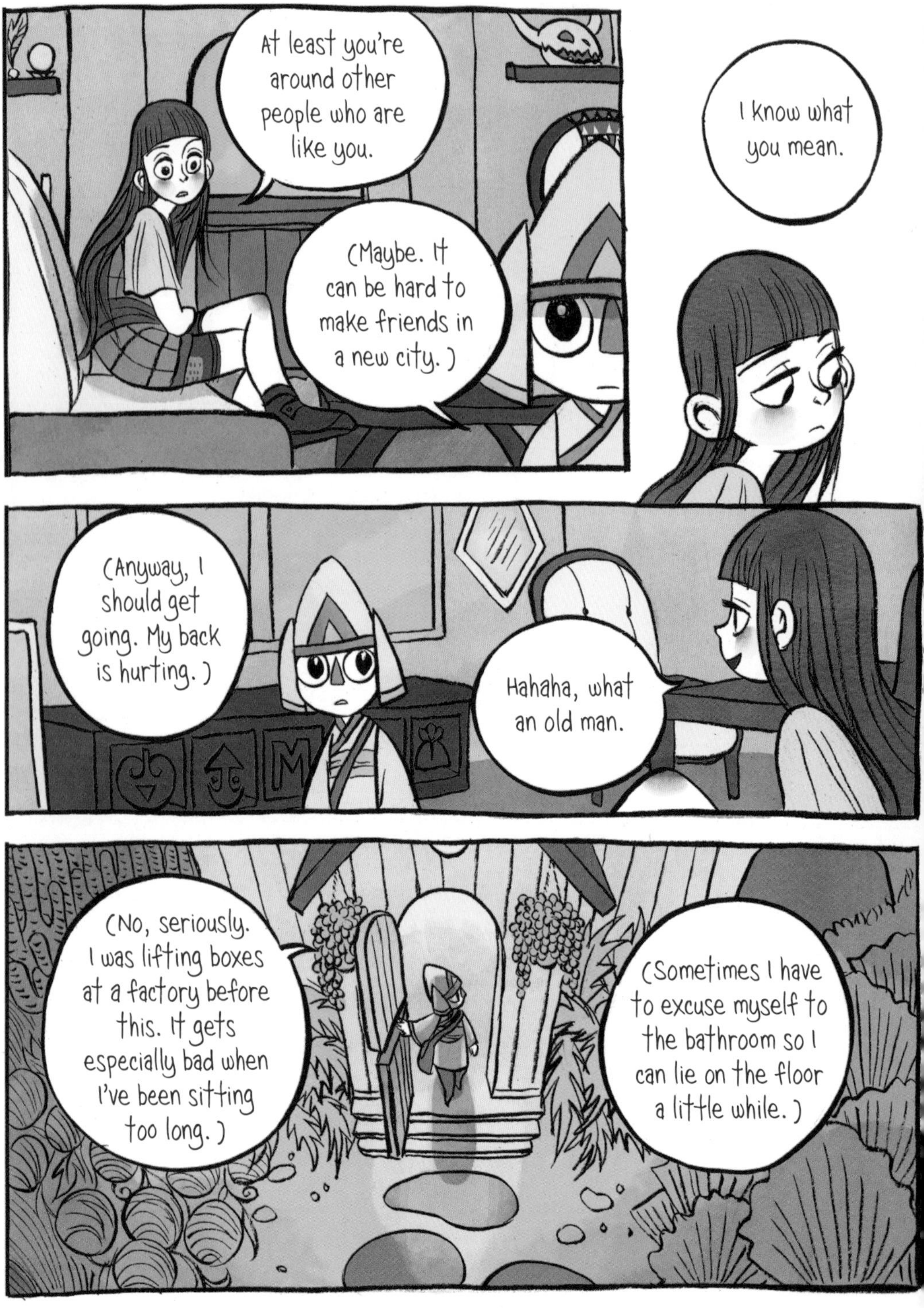
At least you're around other people who are like you.
(Maybe. It can be hard to make friends in a new city.)
I know what you mean.
(Anyway, I should get going. My back is hurting.)
Hahaha, what an old man.
(No, seriously. I was lifting boxes at a factory before this. It gets especially bad when I've been sitting too long.)
(Sometimes I have to excuse myself to the bathroom so I can lie on the floor a little while.)

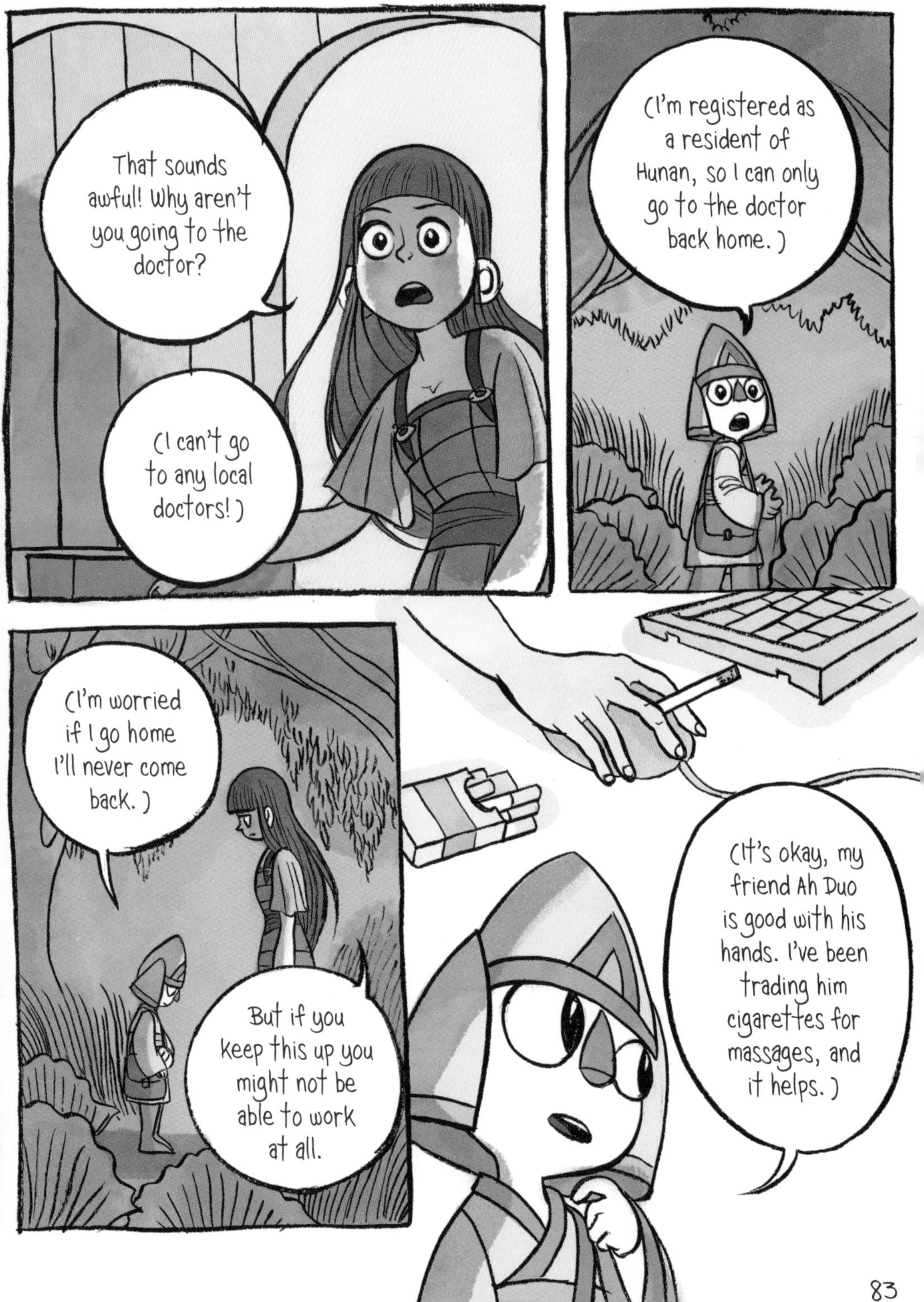
That sounds awful! Why aren't you going to the doctor?
(I can't go to any local doctors!)
(I'm registered as a resident of Hunan, so I can only go to the doctor back home.)
(I'm worried if I go home I'll never come back.)
But if you keep this up you might not be able to work at all.
(It's okay, my friend Ah Duo is good with his hands. I've been trading him cigarettes for massages, and it helps.)

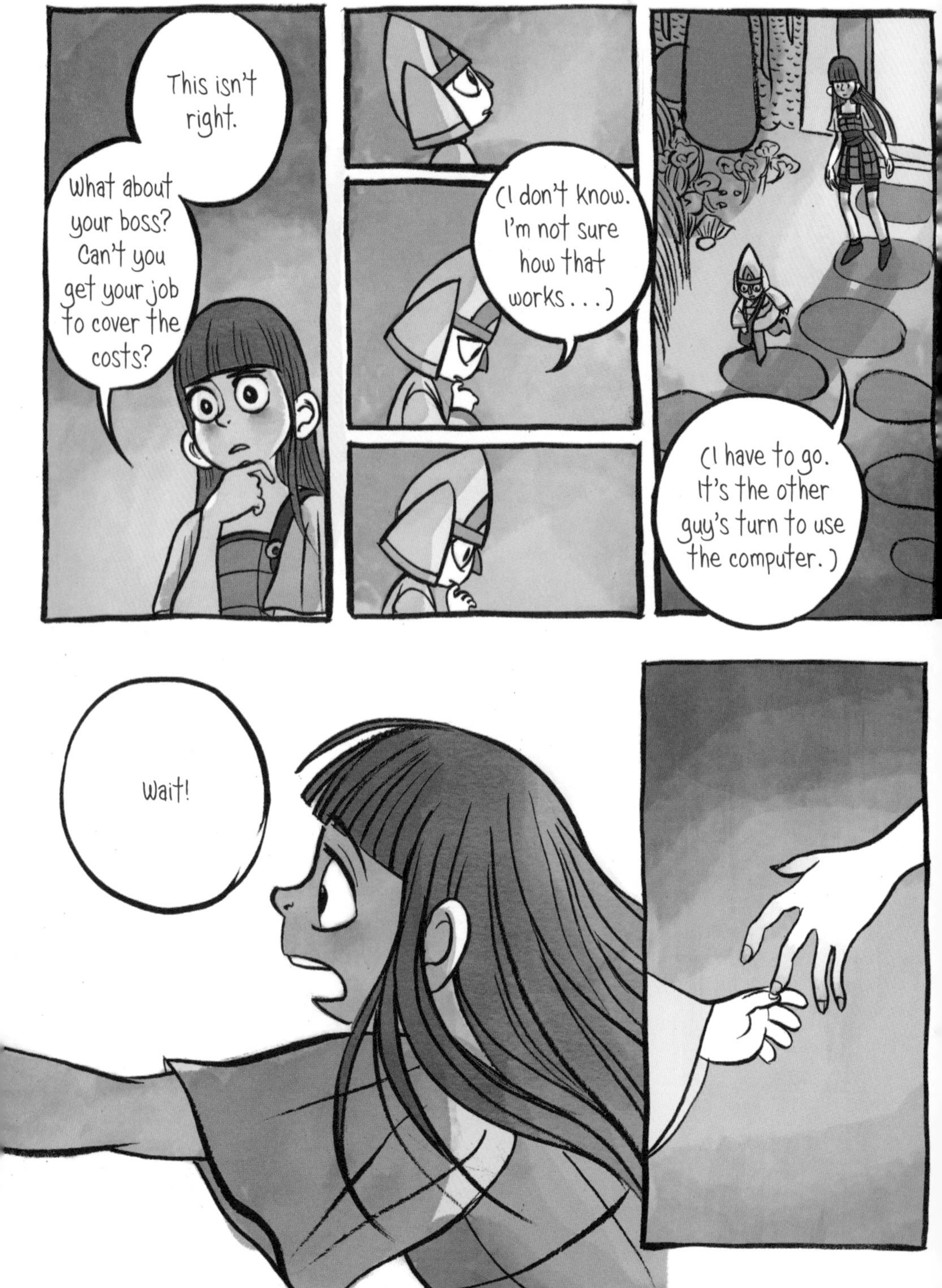
This isn't right.
What about your boss? Can't you get your job to cover the costs?
(I don't know. I'm not sure how that works . . .)
(I have to go. It's the other guy's turn to use the computer.)
Wait!

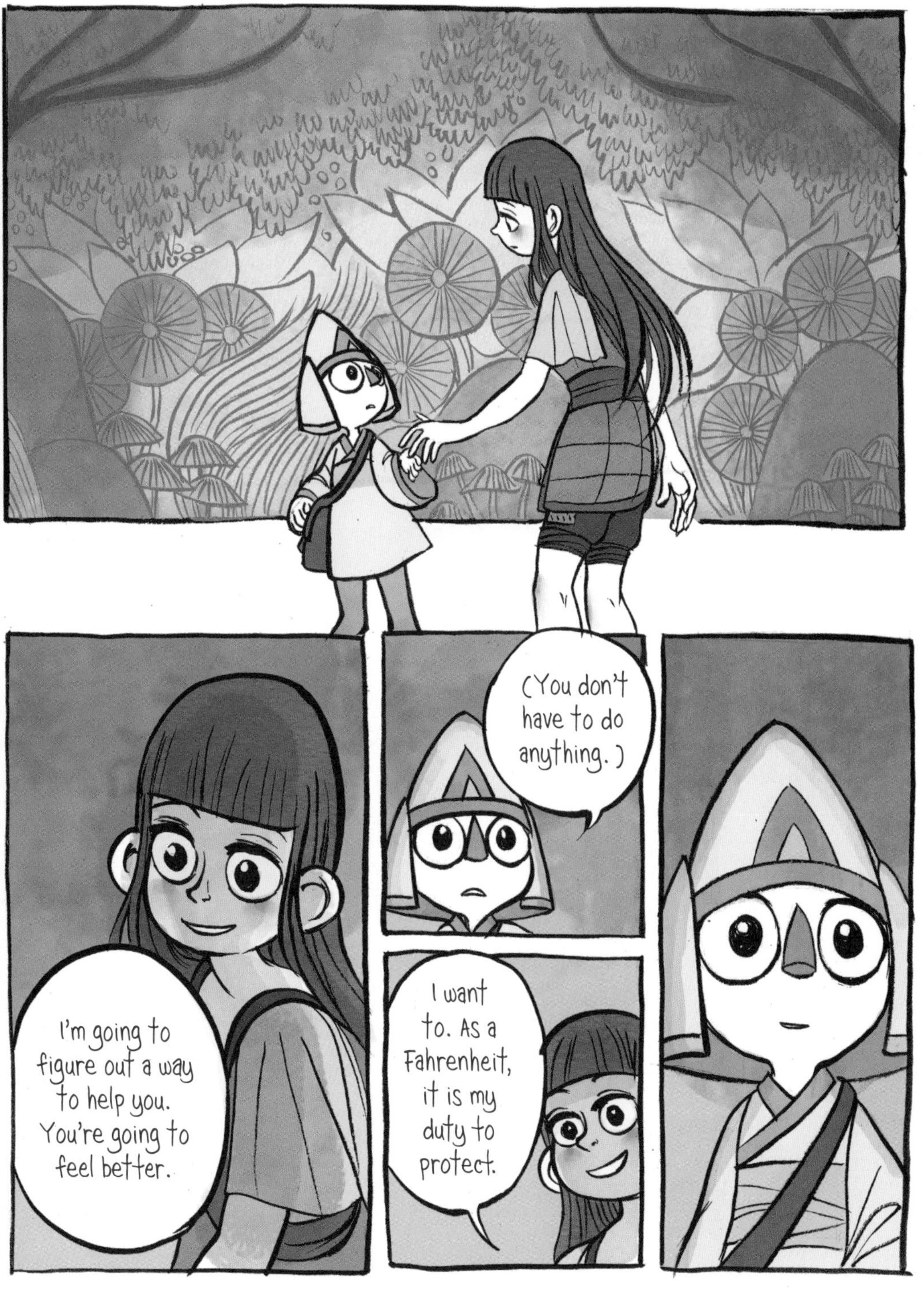
(You don't have to do anything.)
I'm going to figure out a way to help you. You're going to feel better.
I want to. As a Fahrenheit, it is my duty to protect.

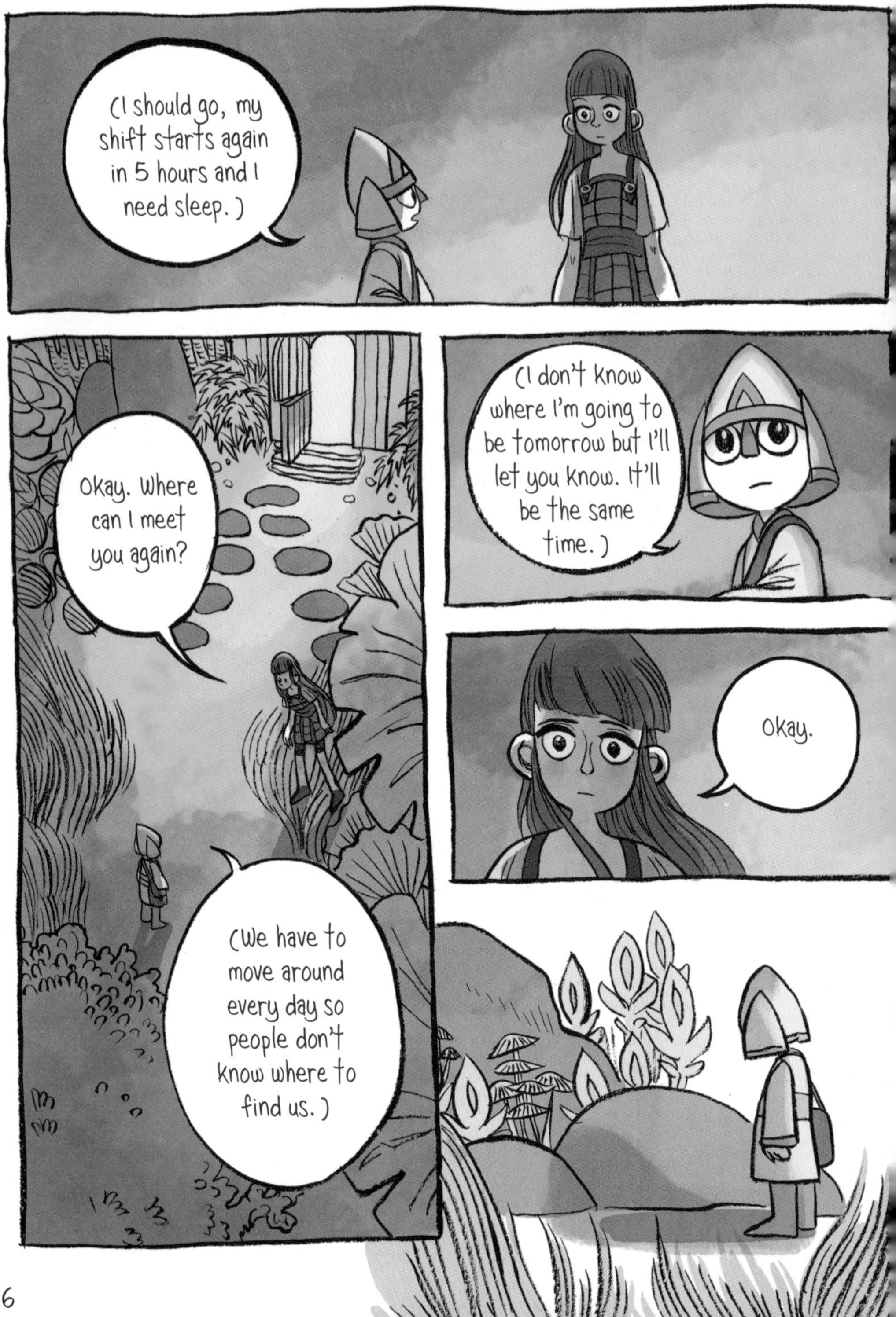
(I should go, my shift starts again in 5 hours and I need sleep.)
Okay. Where can I meet you again?
(I don't know where I'm going to be tomorrow but I'll let you know. It'll be the same time.)
Okay.
(We have to move around every day so people don't know where to find us.)

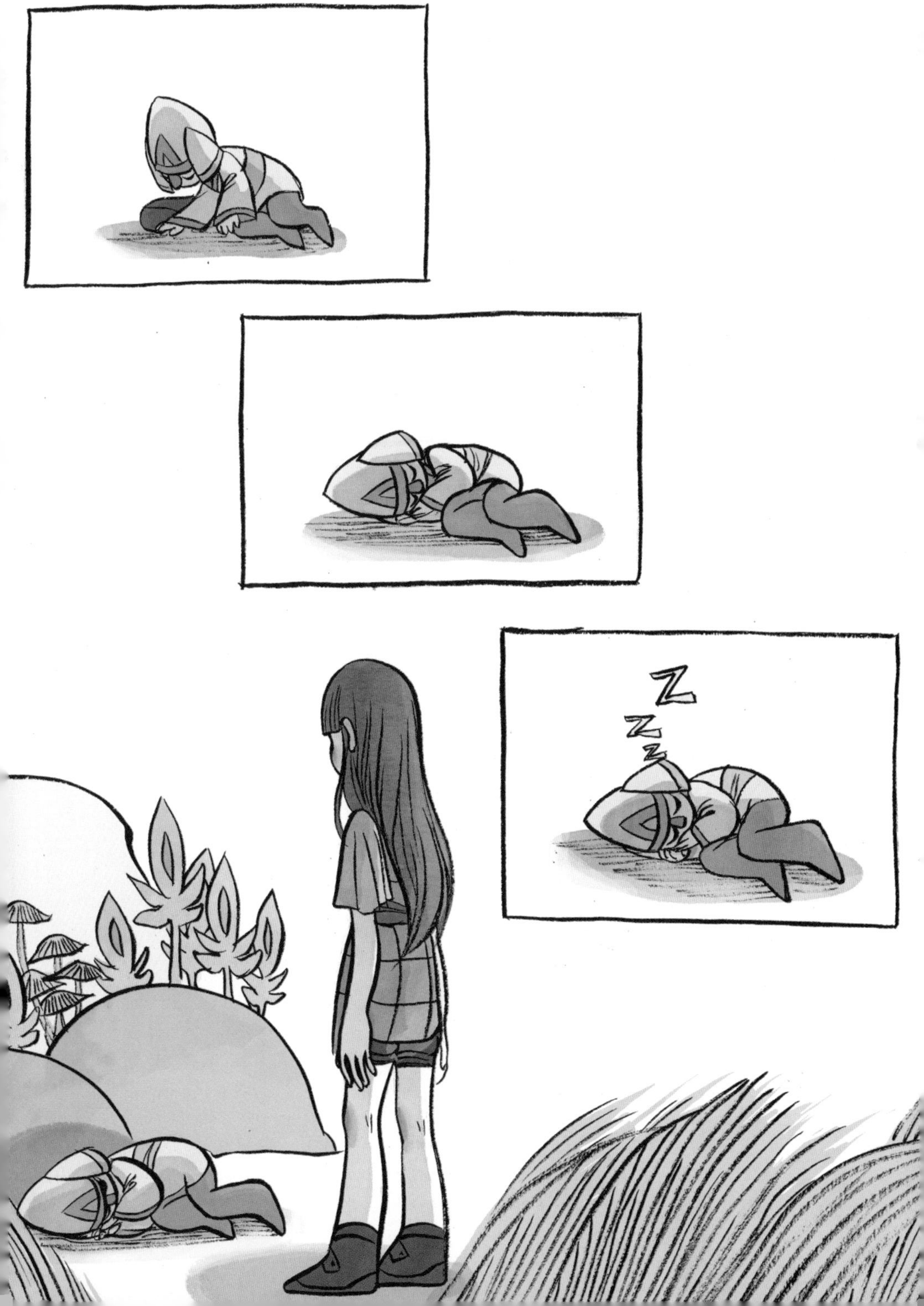
Z
Z
Z

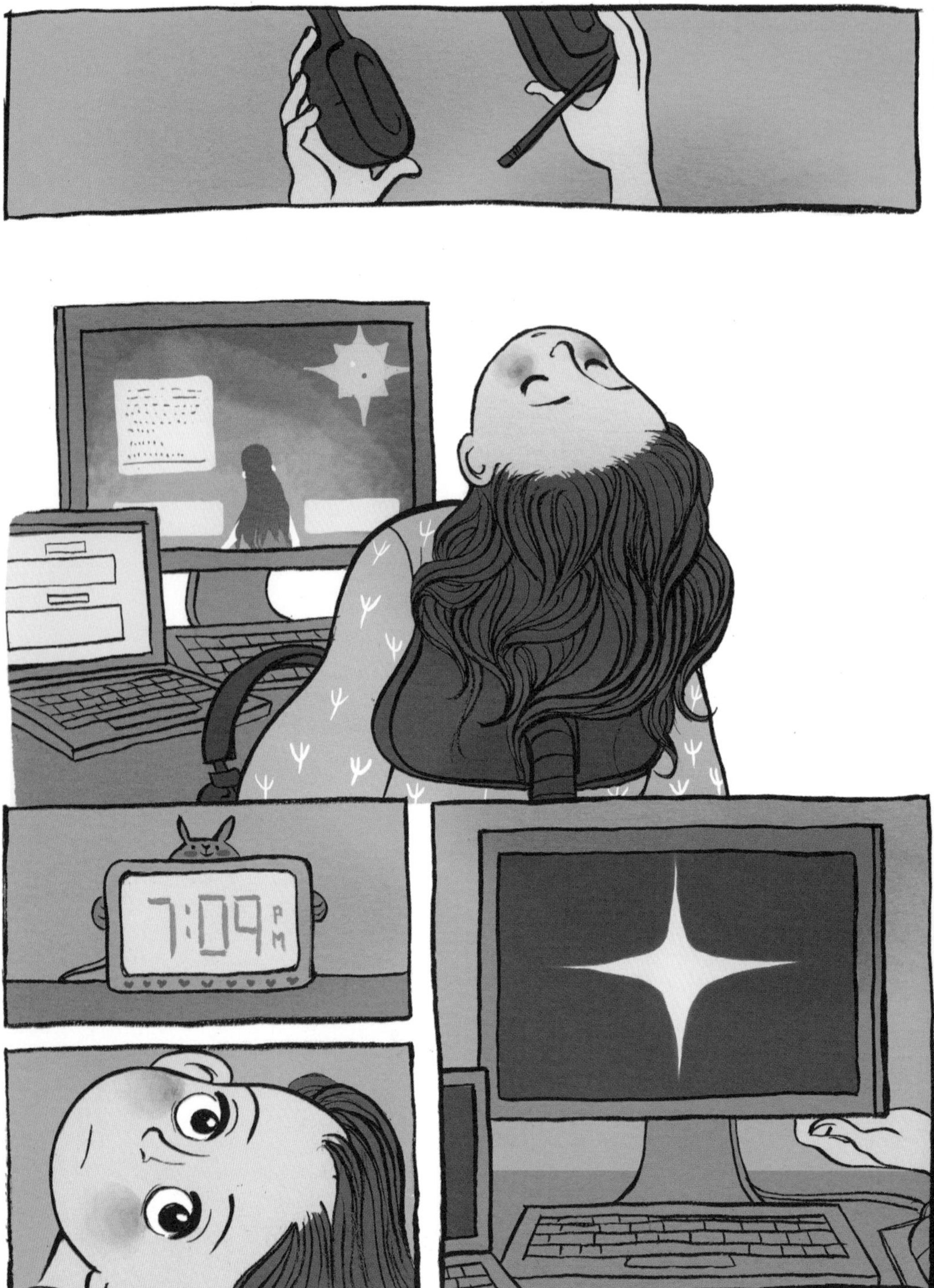
7:09 PM

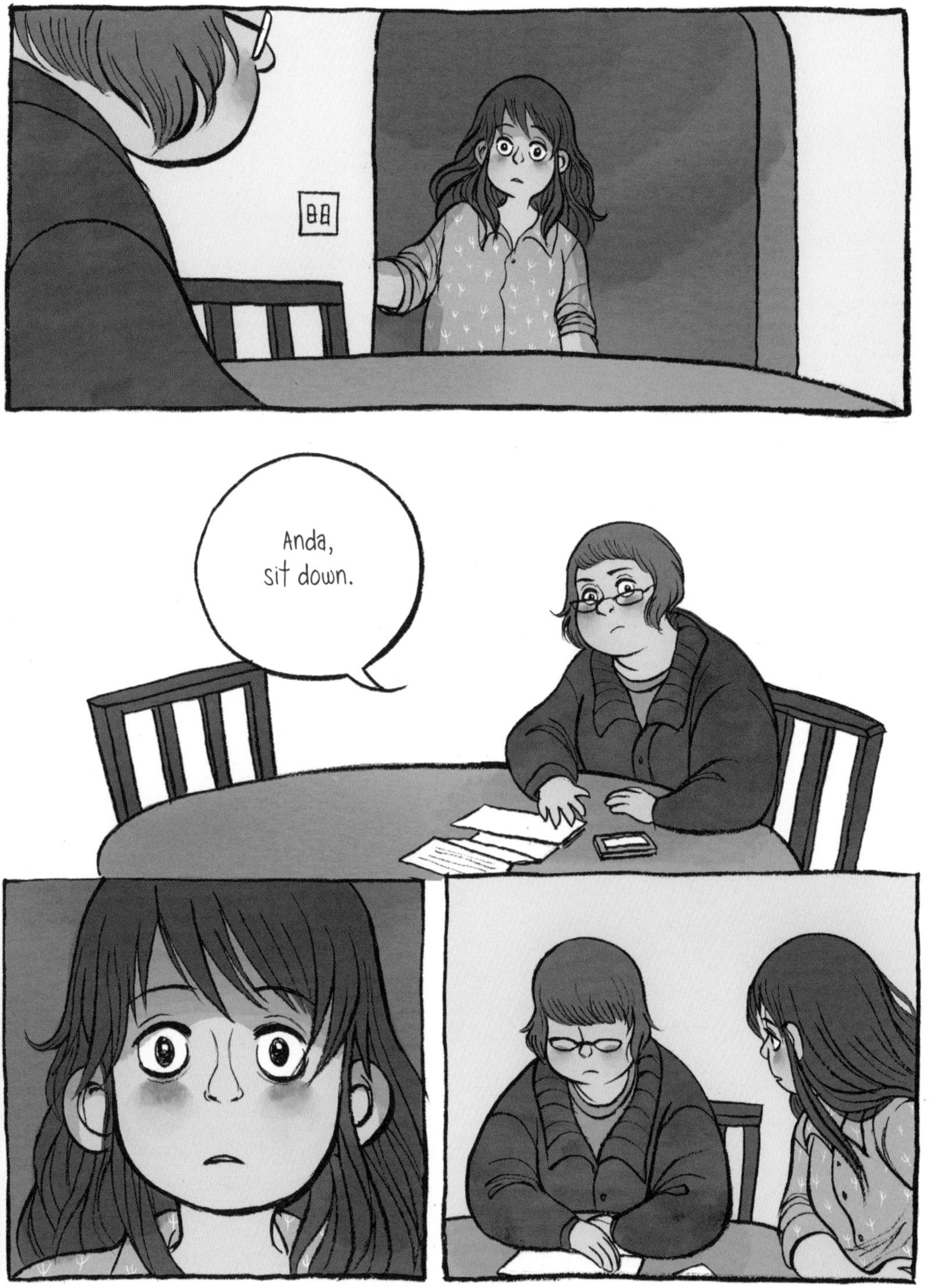
Anda,
sit down.

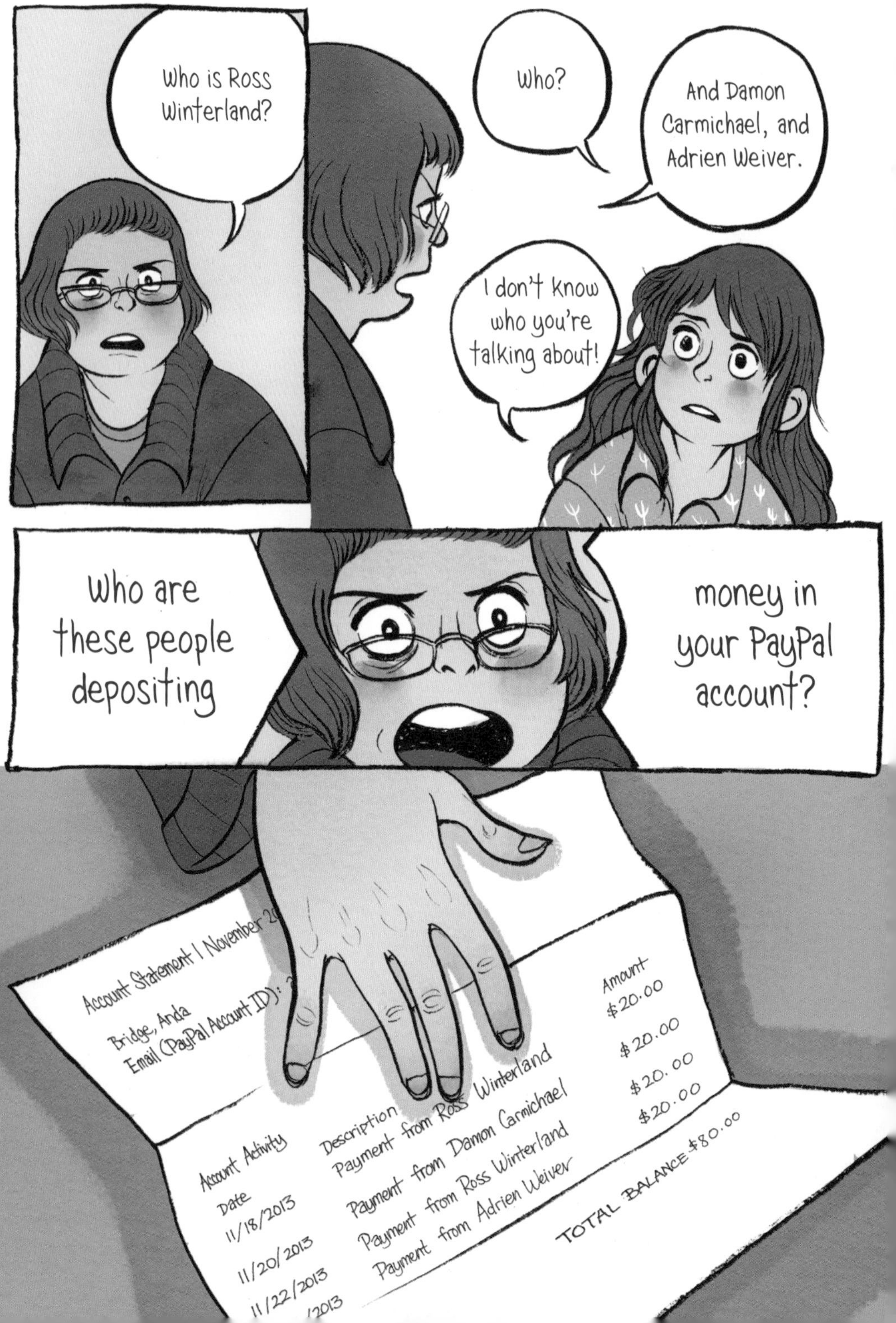

Who is Ross Winterland?
Who?
And Damon Carmichael, and Adrien Weiver.
I don't know who you're talking about!
Who are these people depositing
money in your PayPal account?
Account Statement | November 20
Bridge, Anda
Email (PayPal Account ID):
Amount
$20.00
$20.00
$20.00
$20.00
Account Activity
Date
Description
11/18/2013
Payment from Ross Winterland
11/20/2013
Payment from Damon Carmichael
11/22/2013
Payment from Ross Winterland
/2013
Payment from Adrien Weiver
TOTAL BALANCE $80.00

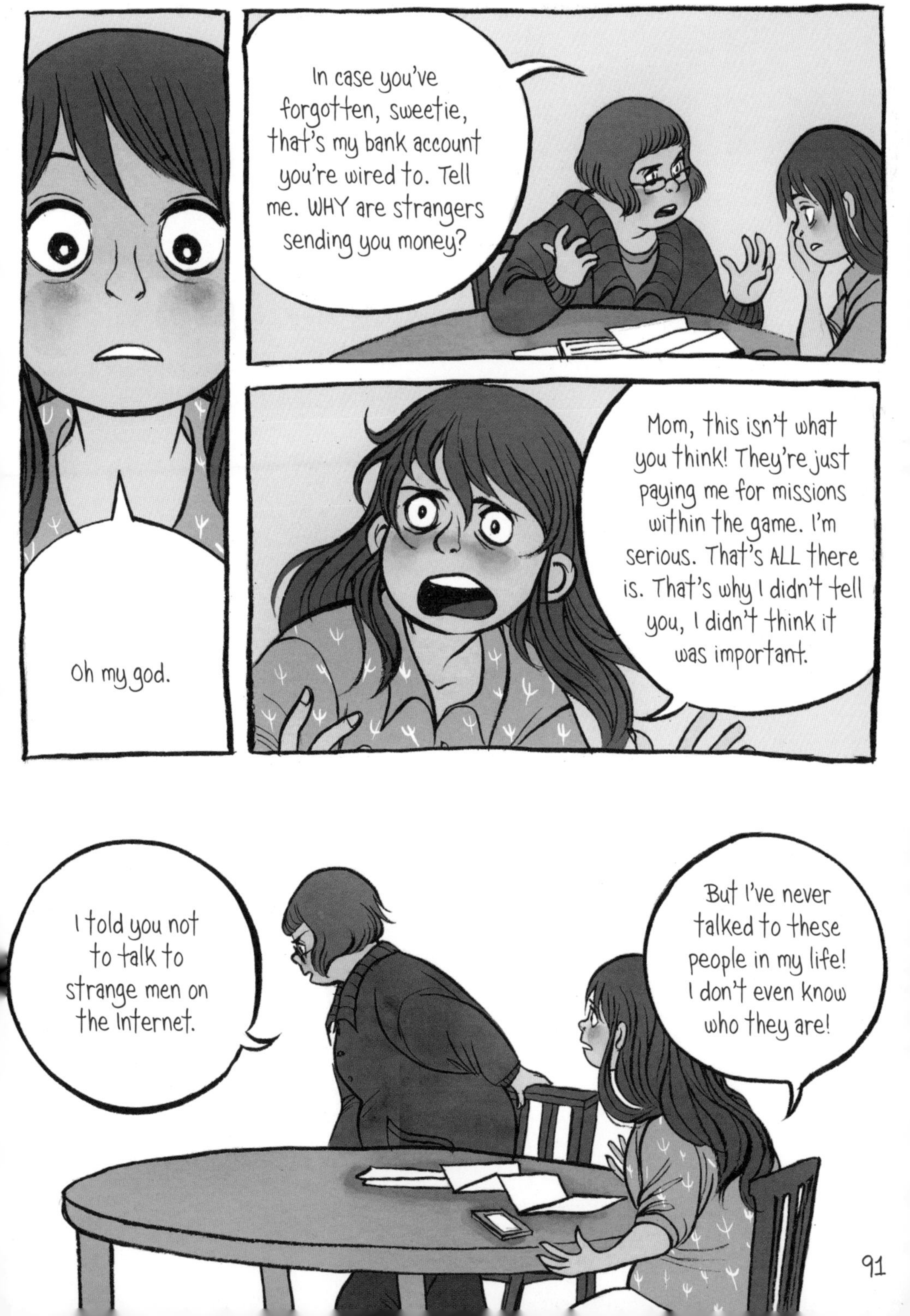
In case you've forgotten, sweetie, that's my bank account you're wired to. Tell me. WHY are strangers sending you money?
Oh my god.
Mom, this isn't what you think! They're just paying me for missions within the game. I'm serious. That's ALL there is. That's why I didn't tell you, I didn't think it was important.
I told you not to talk to strange men on the Internet.
But I've never talked to these people in my life! I don't even know who they are!

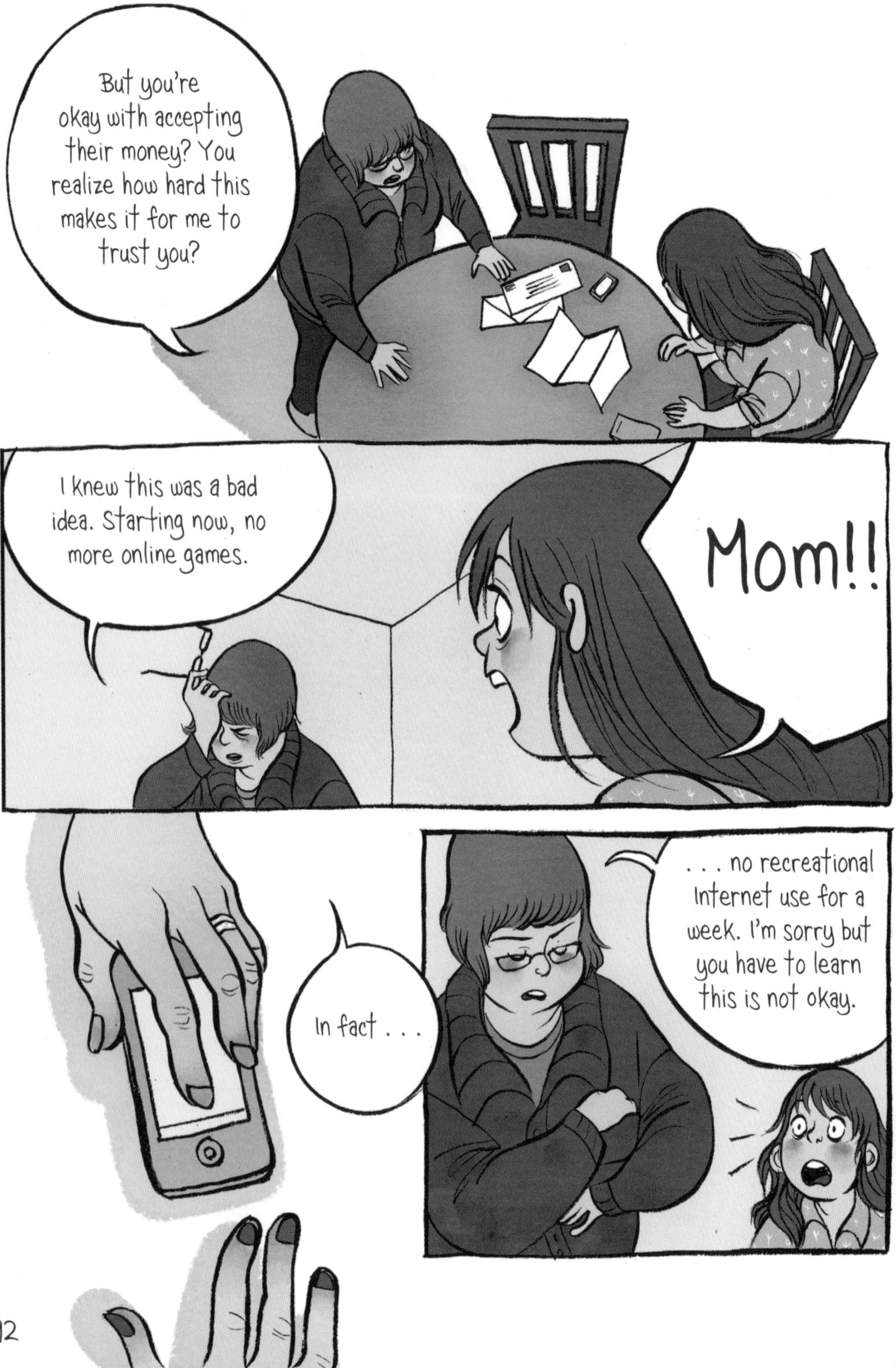
But you're okay with accepting their money? You realize how hard this makes it for me to trust you?
I knew this was a bad idea. Starting now, no more online games.
Mom!!
In fact . . .
. . . no recreational Internet use for a week. I'm sorry but you have to learn this is not okay.

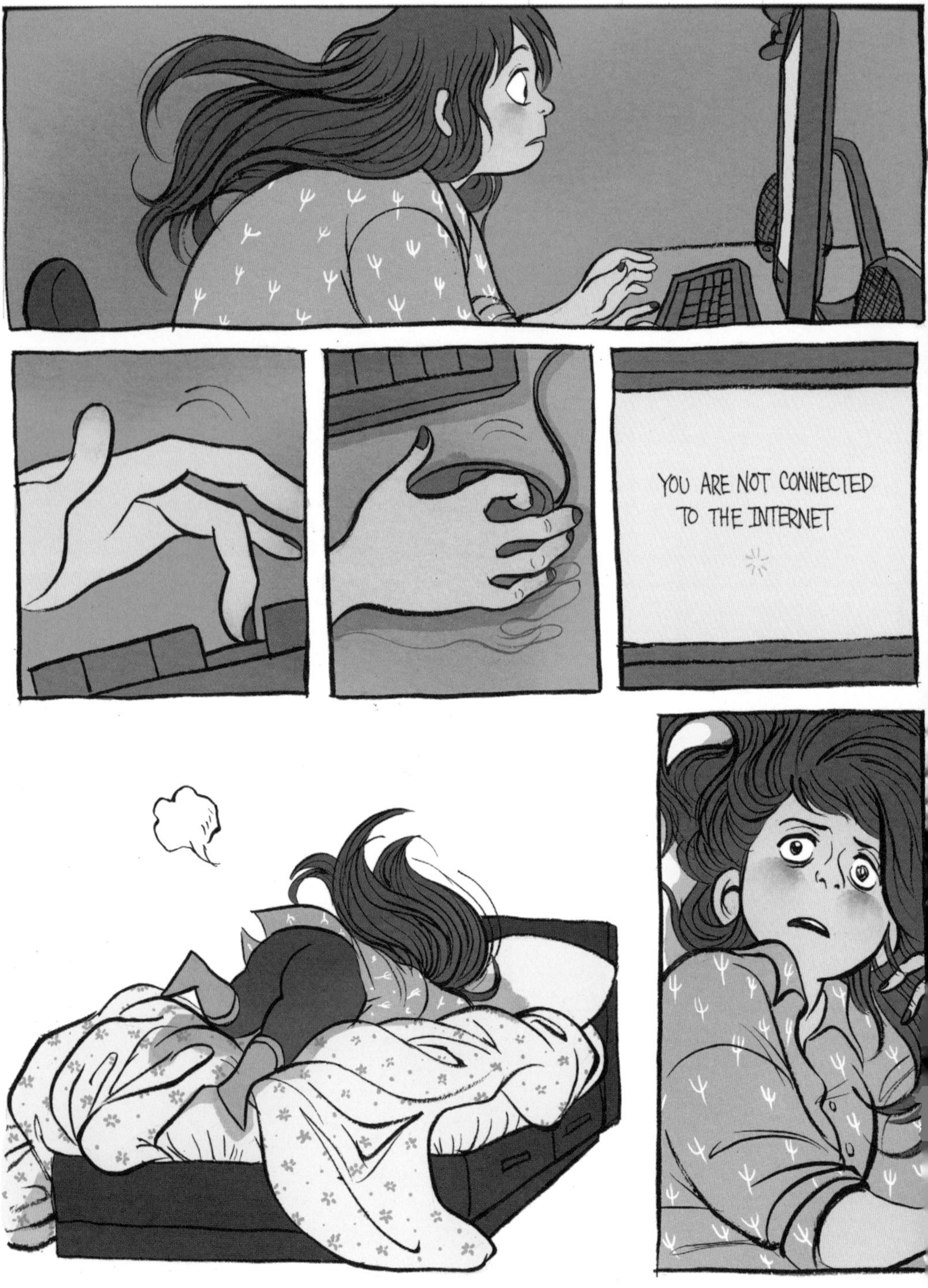
YOU ARE NOT CONNECTED TO THE INTERNET

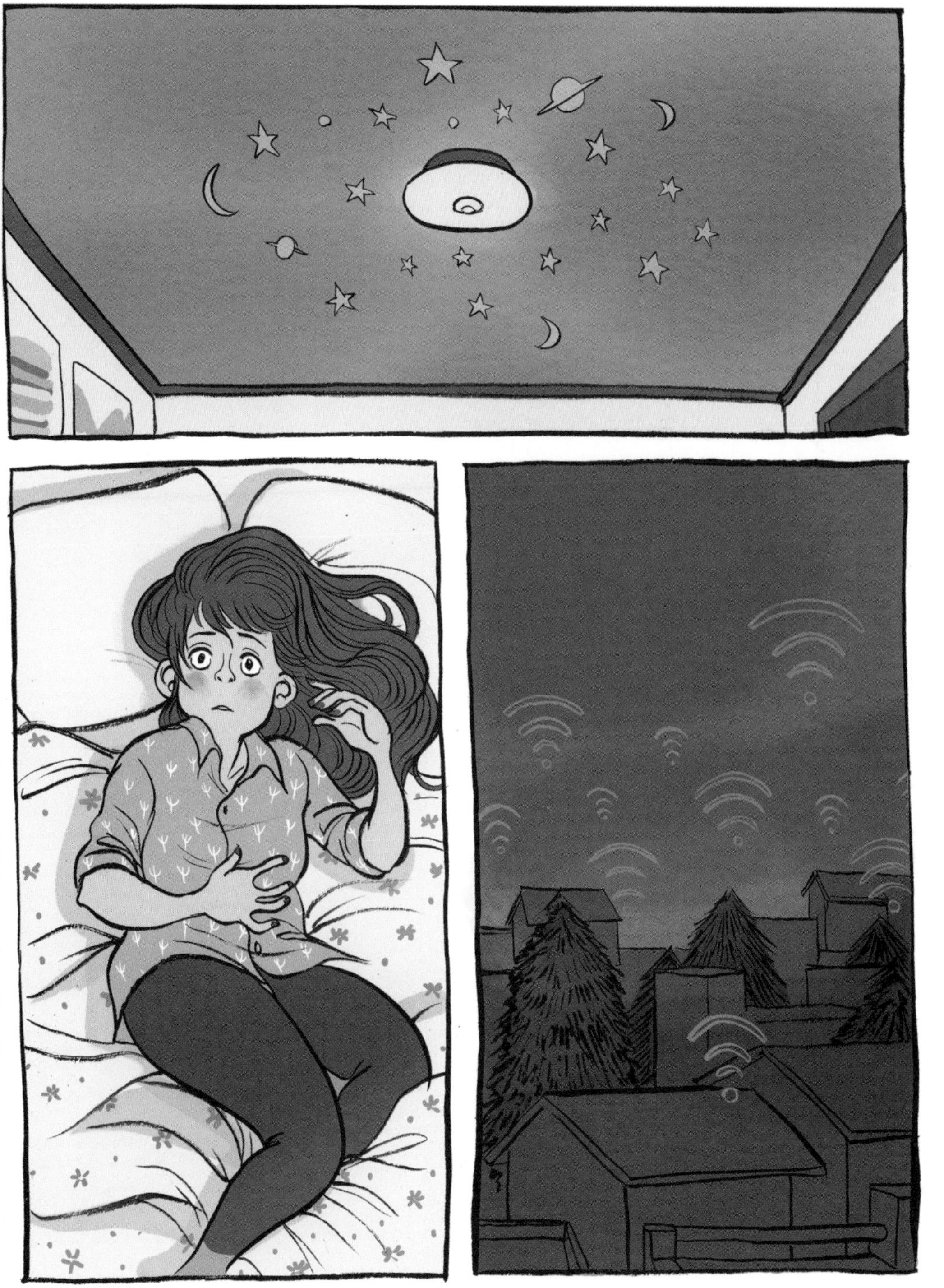

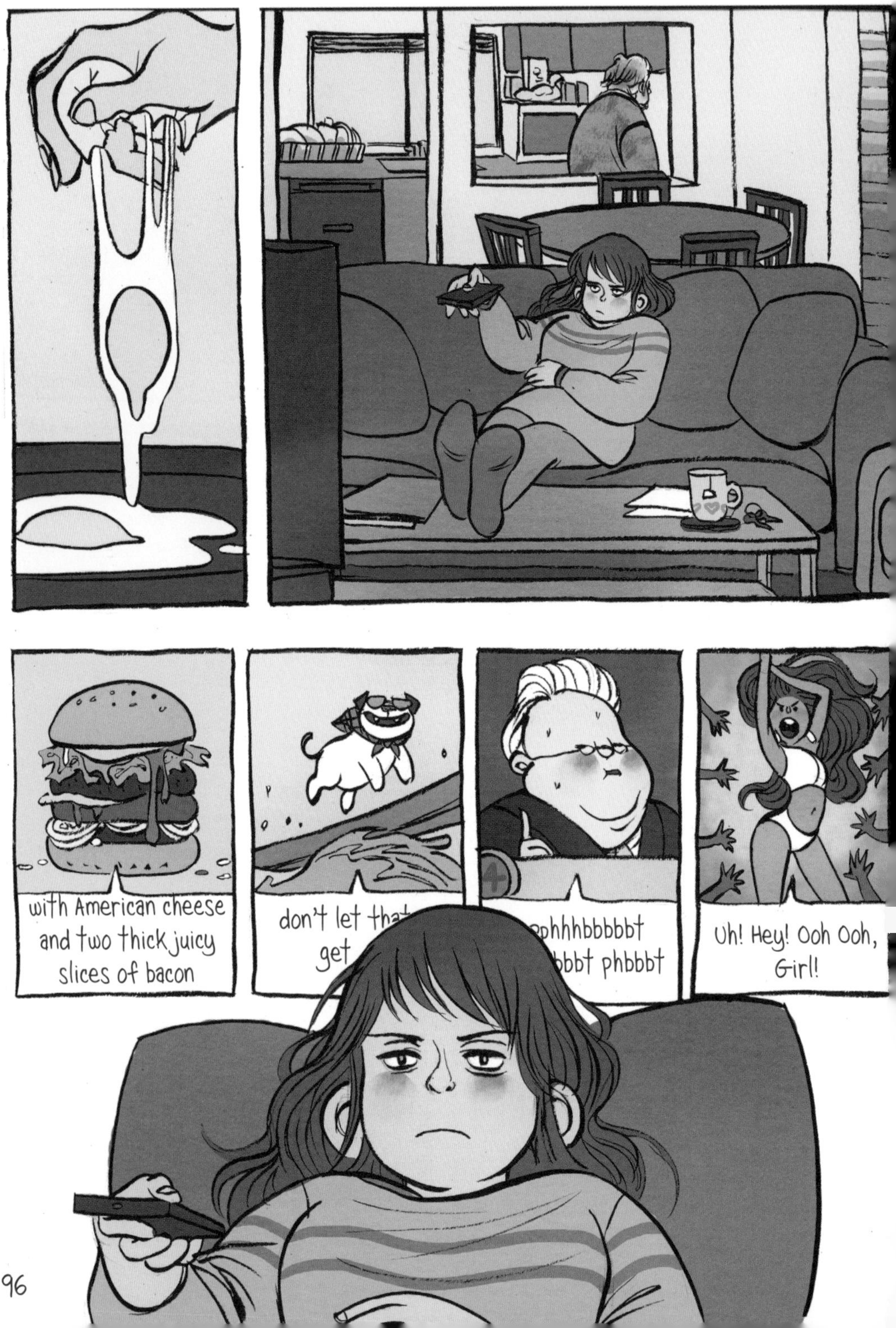
with American cheese and two thick juicy slices of bacon
don't let that
get
phhhbbbbbt
bbbt phbbbt
Uh! Hey! Ooh Ooh, Girl!

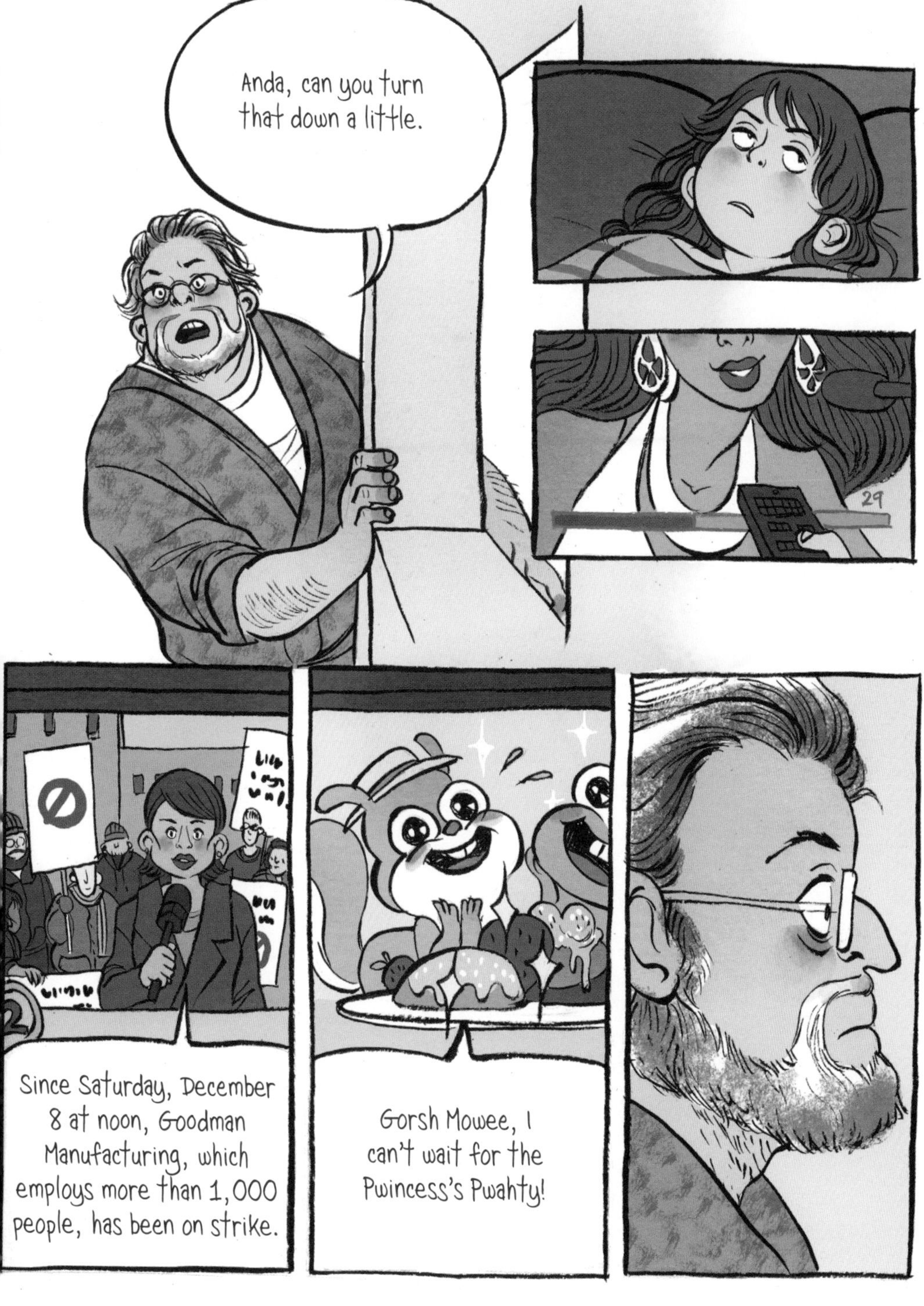
Anda, can you turn that down a little.
29
Since Saturday, December 8 at noon, Goodman Manufacturing, which employs more than 1,000 people, has been on strike.
Gorsh Mowee, I can't wait for the Pwincess's Pwahty!

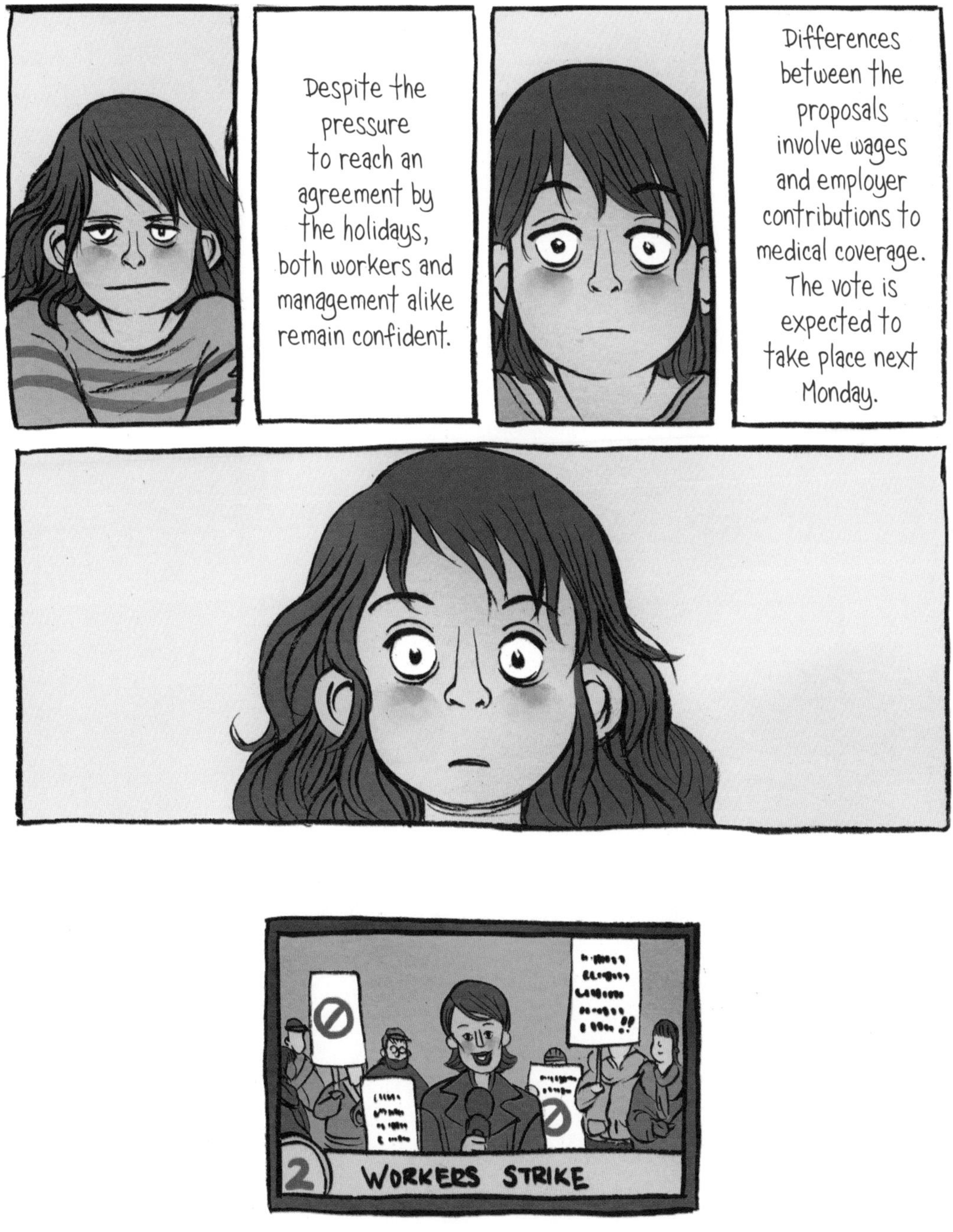
Despite the pressure to reach an agreement by the holidays, both workers and management alike remain confident.
Differences between the proposals involve wages and employer contributions to medical coverage. The vote is expected to take place next Monday.
2
WORKERS STRIKE

I'm Sarah Tanaka, Channel 2 News.

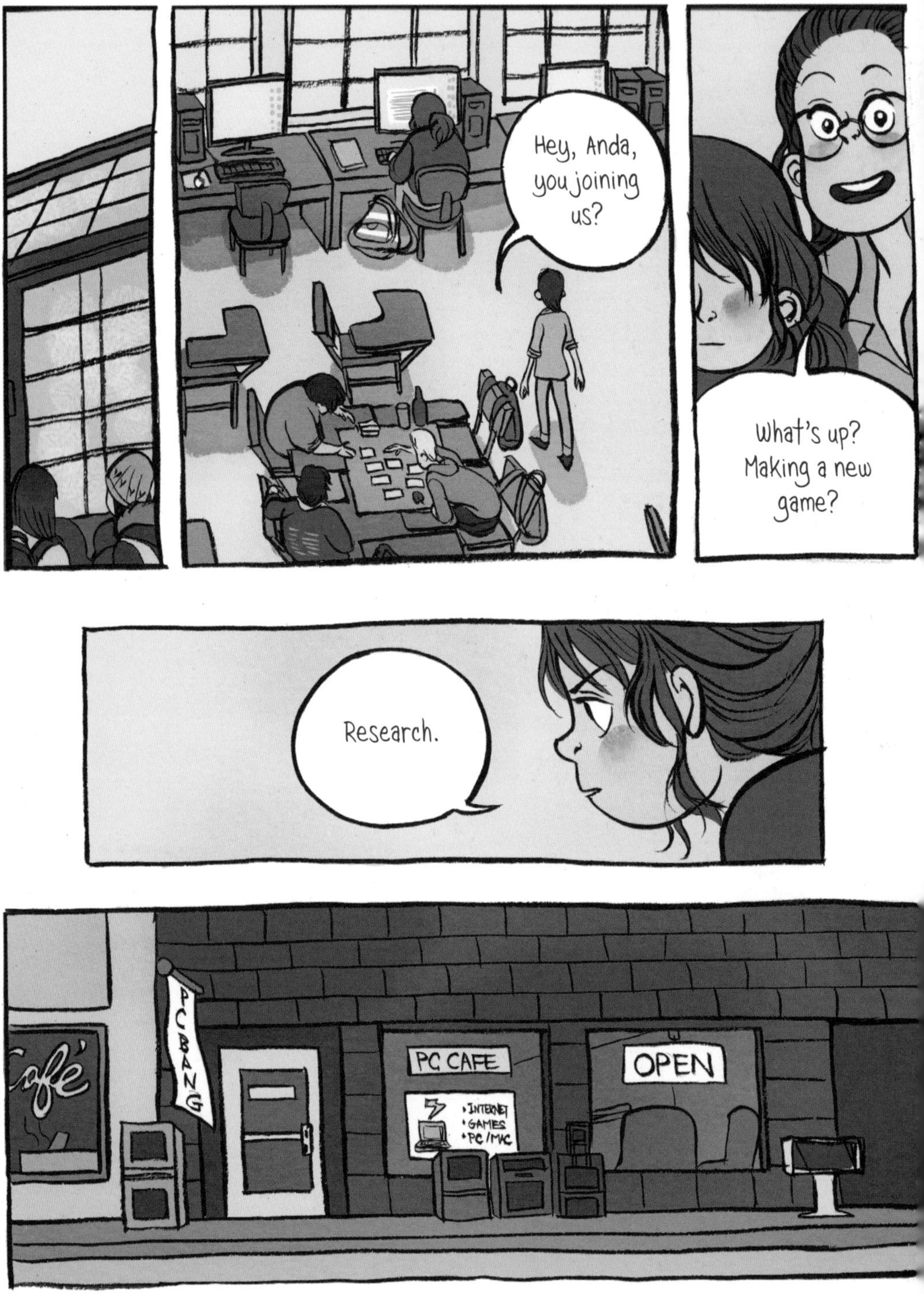
Hey, Anda, you joining us?
What's up? Making a new game?
Research.
PC BANG
Café
PC CAFE
INTERNET
GAMES
PC/MAC
OPEN

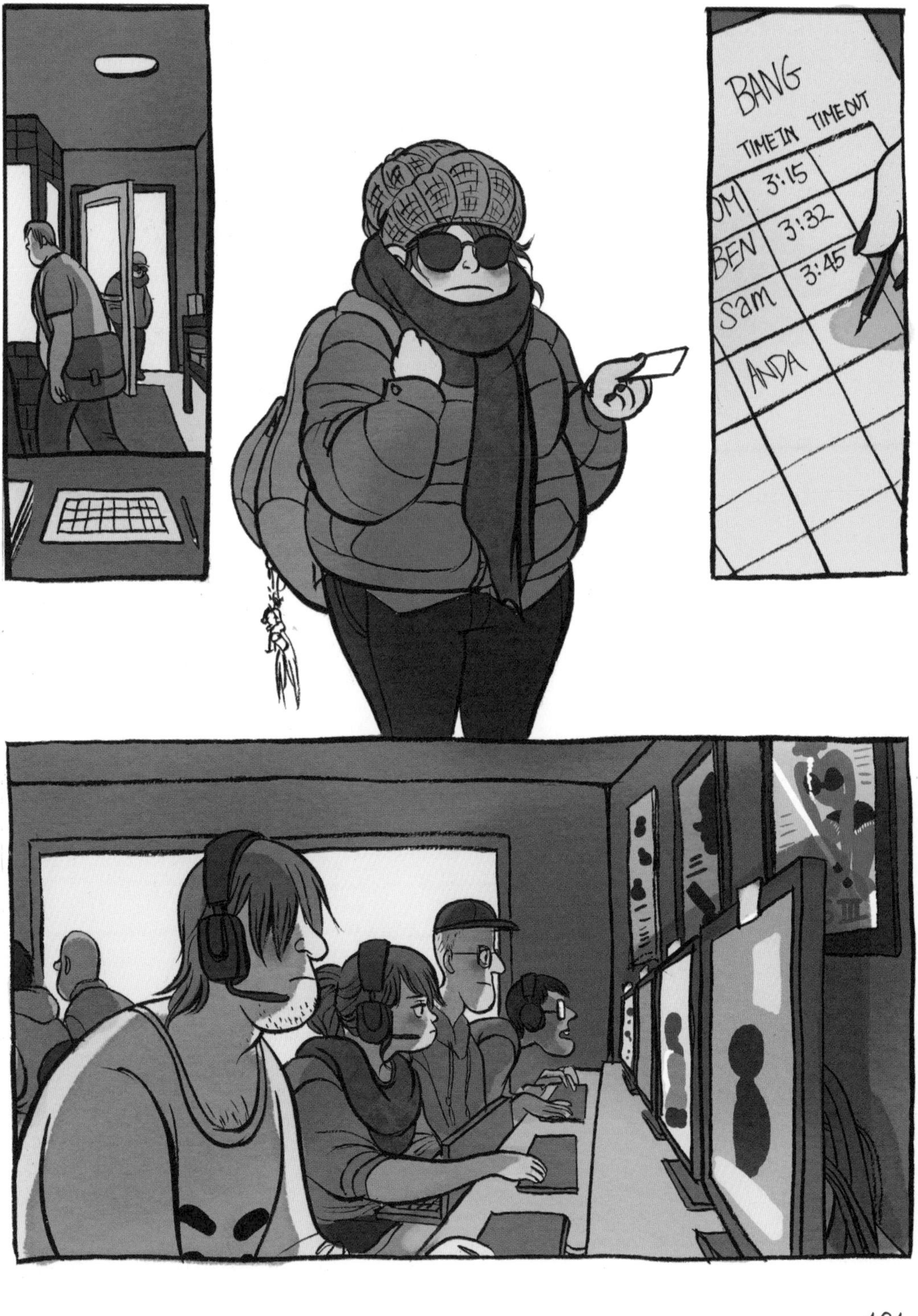
BANG
TIME IN TIME OUT
OM 3:15
BEN 3:32
Sam 3:45
ANDA

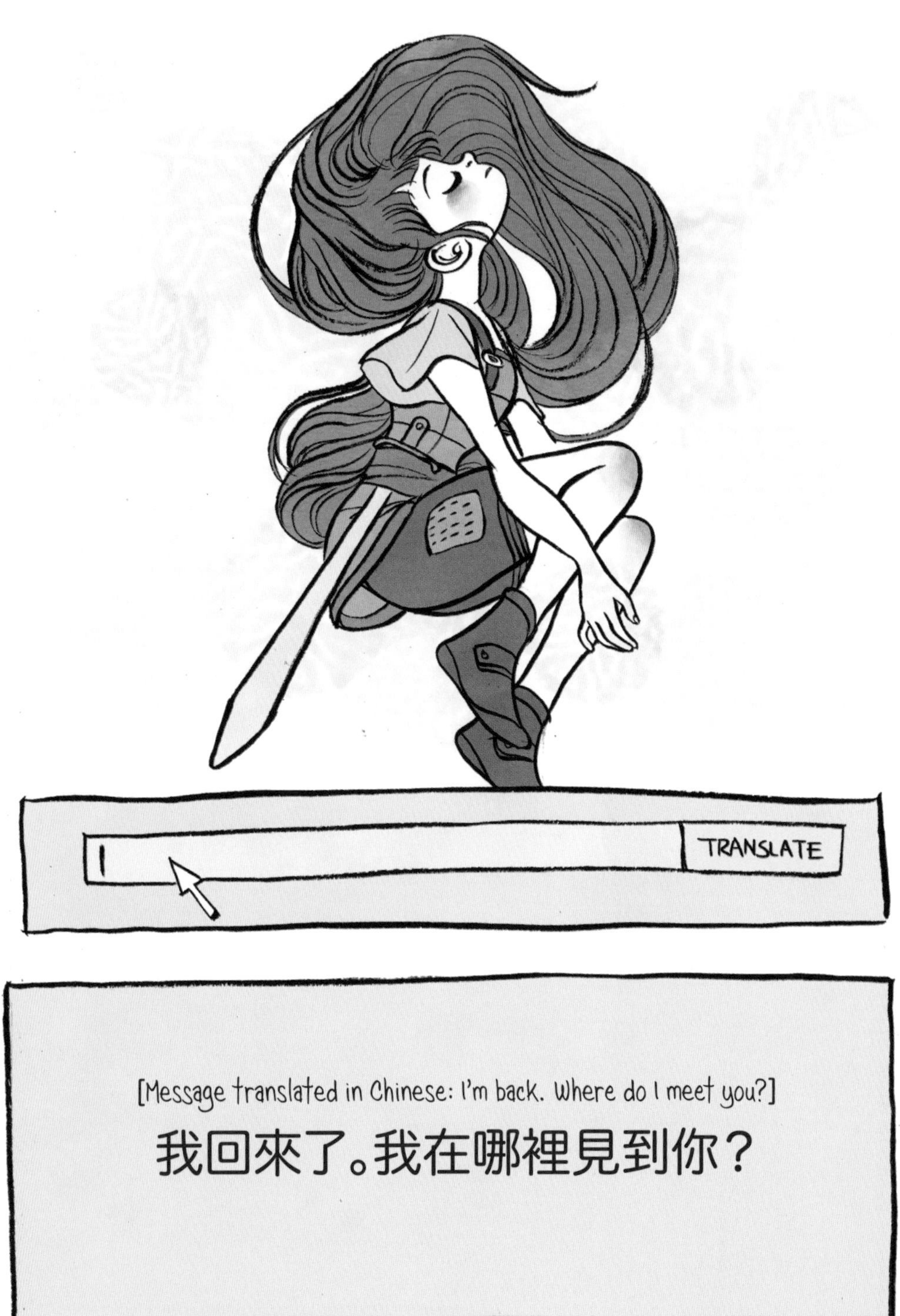
TRANSLATE
[Message translated in Chinese: I'm back. Where do I meet you?]
我回來了。我在哪裡見到你？

☑	LUCY	12/5
☑	LUCY	12/5
☑	LUCY	12/5
☑	LUCY	12/6
☑	LUCY	12/6
☑	LUCY	12/?

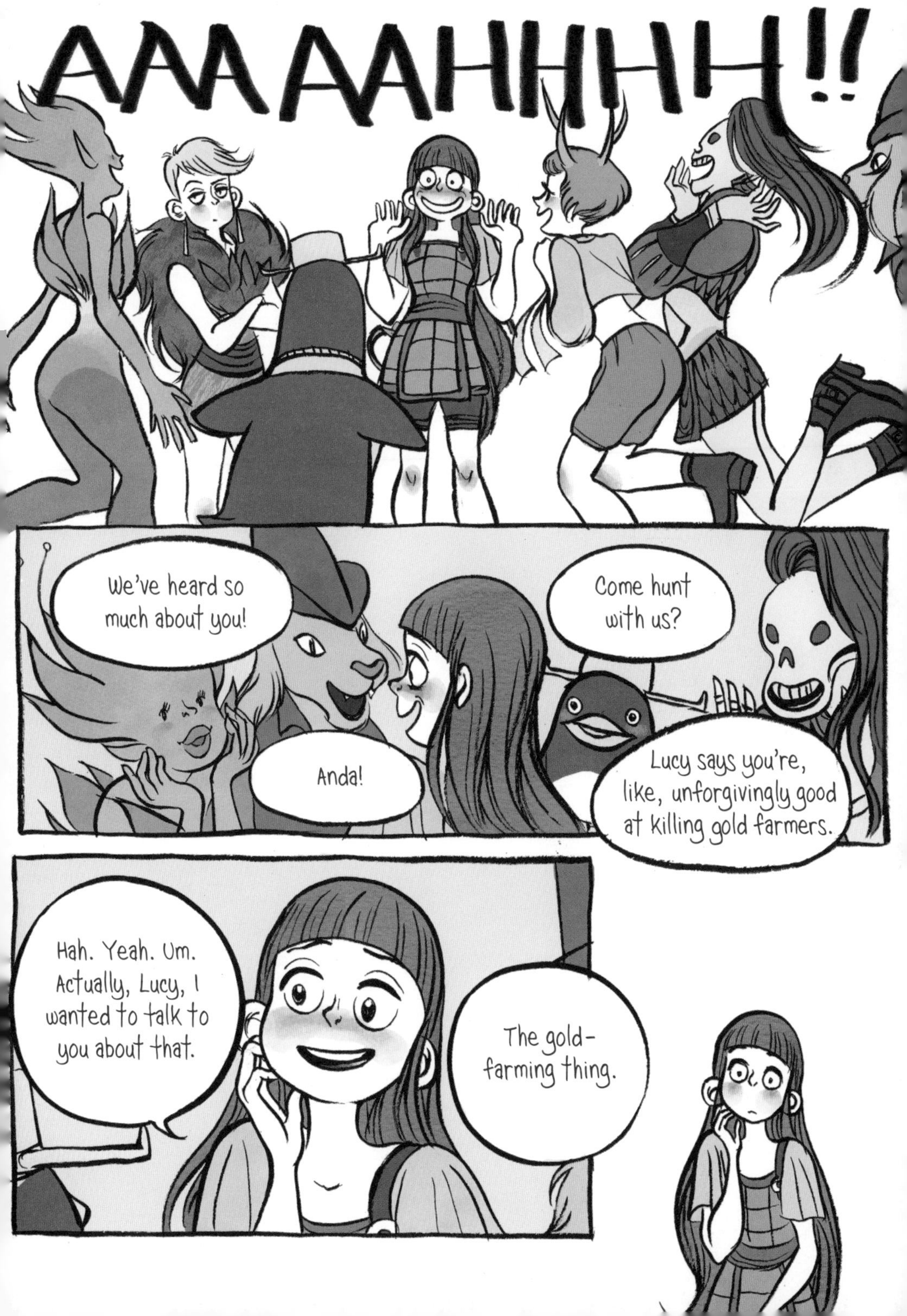
AAAAAHHHH!!
We've heard so much about you!
Come hunt with us?
Anda!
Lucy says you're, like, unforgivingly good at killing gold farmers.
Hah. Yeah. Um. Actually, Lucy, I wanted to talk to you about that.
The gold-farming thing.

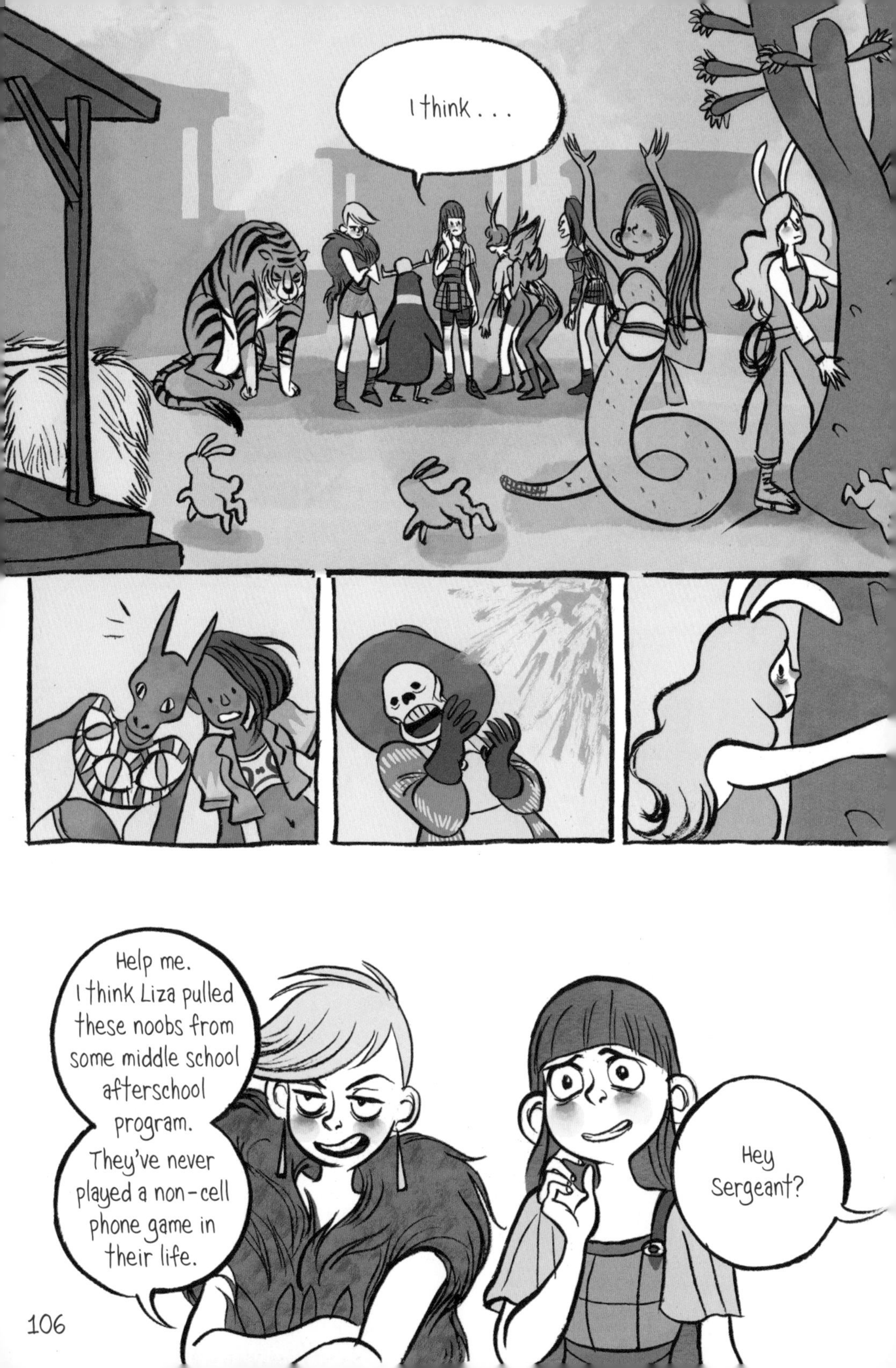
I think . . .
Help me.
I think Liza pulled these noobs from some middle school afterschool program.
They've never played a non-cell phone game in their life.
Hey Sergeant?

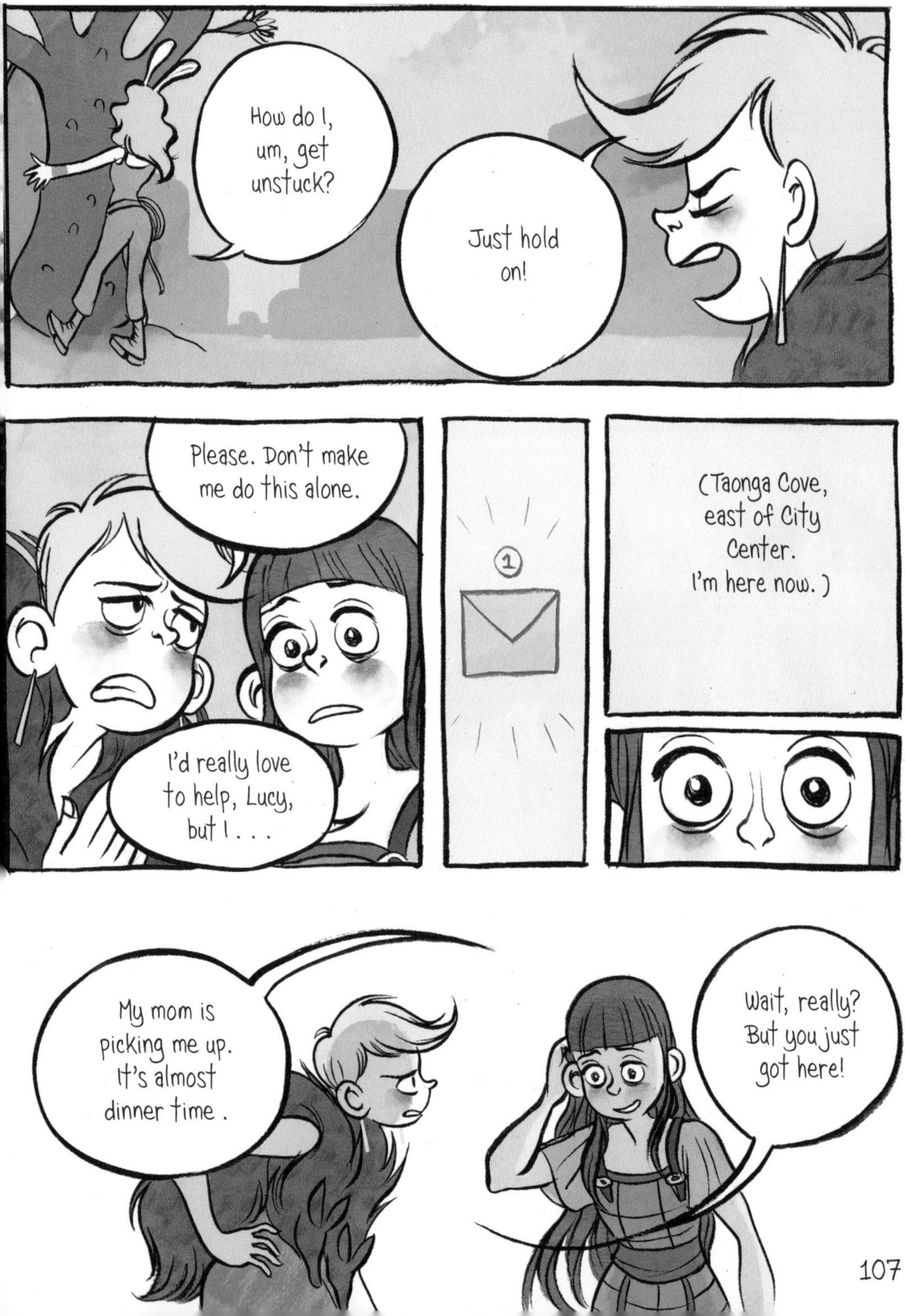
How do I, um, get unstuck?
Just hold on!
Please. Don't make me do this alone.
I'd really love to help, Lucy, but I . . .
1
(Taonga Cove, east of City Center. I'm here now.)
My mom is picking me up. It's almost dinner time .
Wait, really? But you just got here!

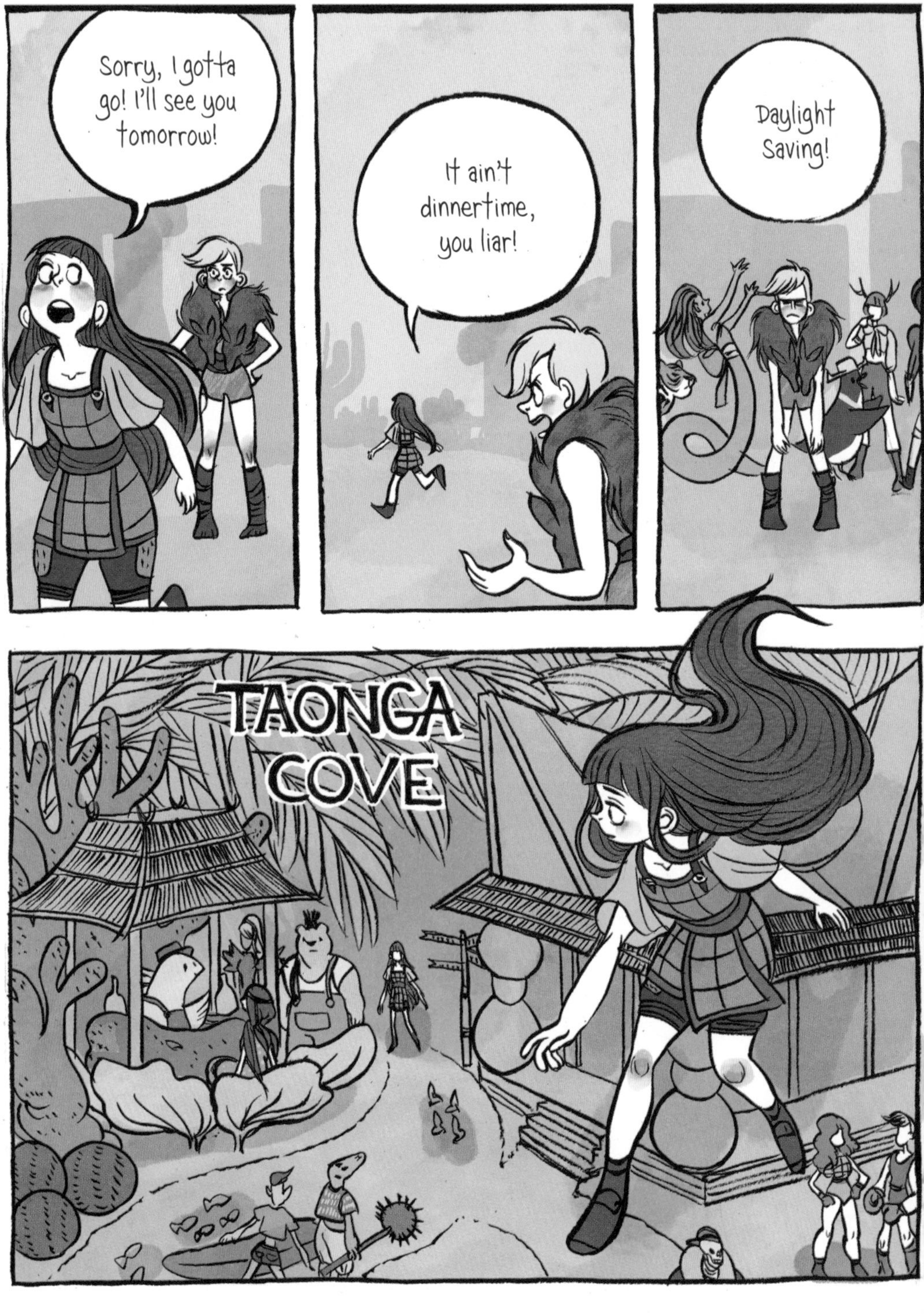
Sorry, I gotta go! I'll see you tomorrow!
It ain't dinnertime, you liar!
Daylight Saving!
TAONGA COVE

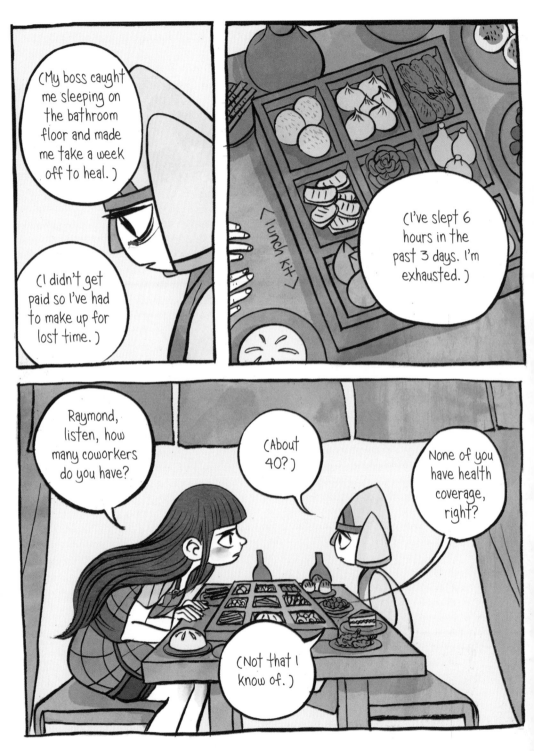

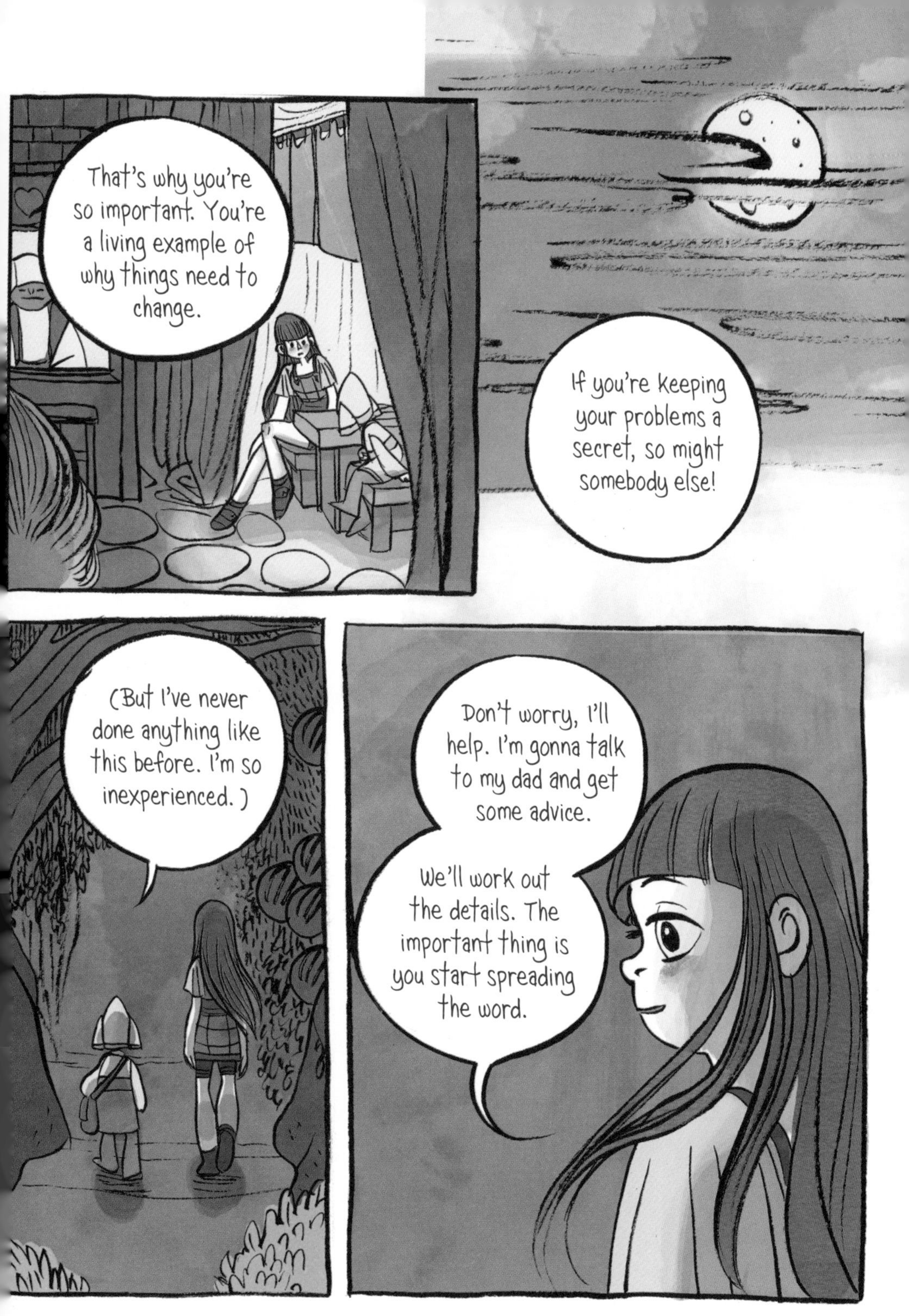

That's why you're so important. You're a living example of why things need to change.
If you're keeping your problems a secret, so might somebody else!
(But I've never done anything like this before. I'm so inexperienced.)
Don't worry, I'll help. I'm gonna talk to my dad and get some advice.
We'll work out the details. The important thing is you start spreading the word.

SLEEP

EXIT

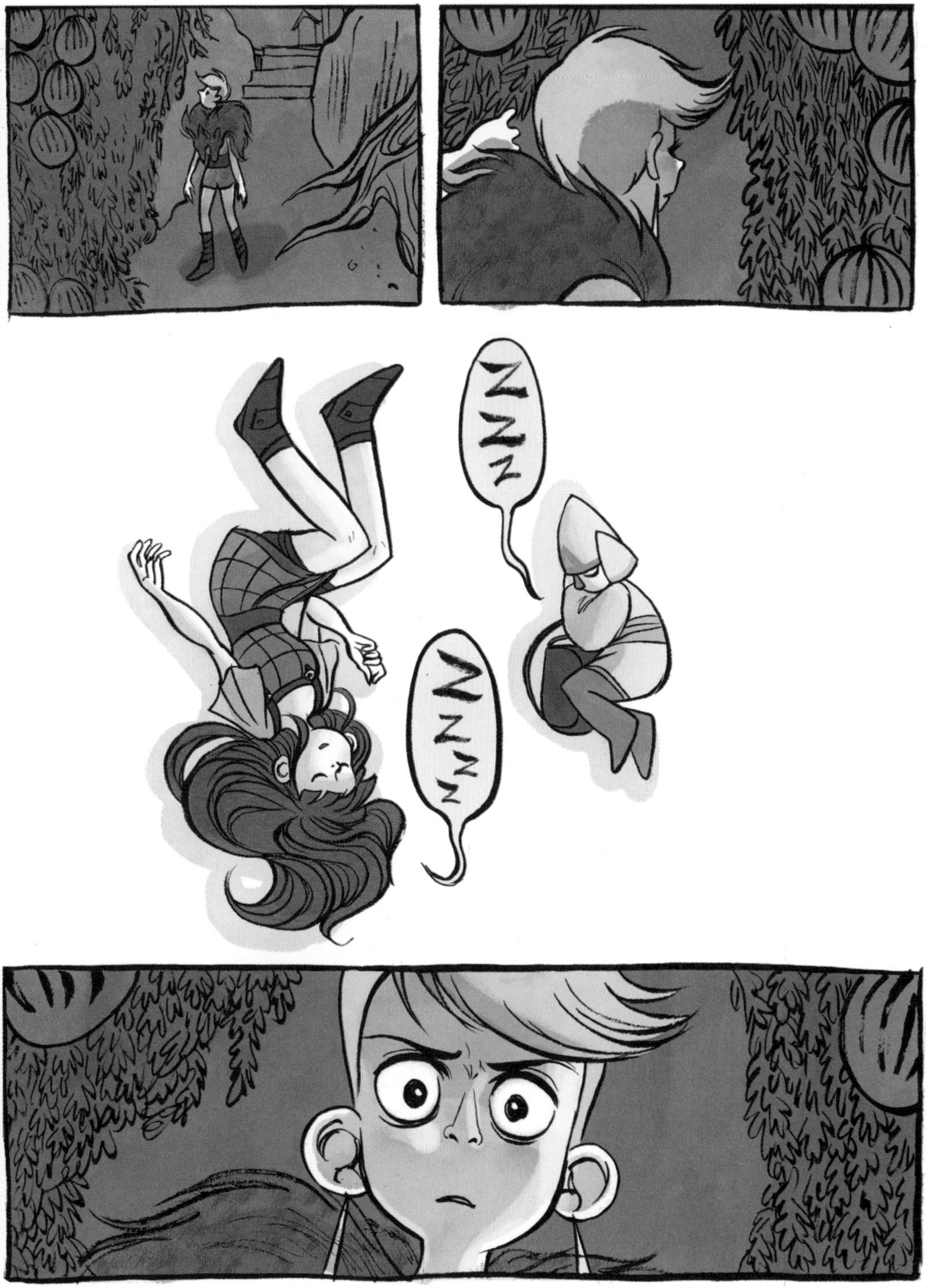

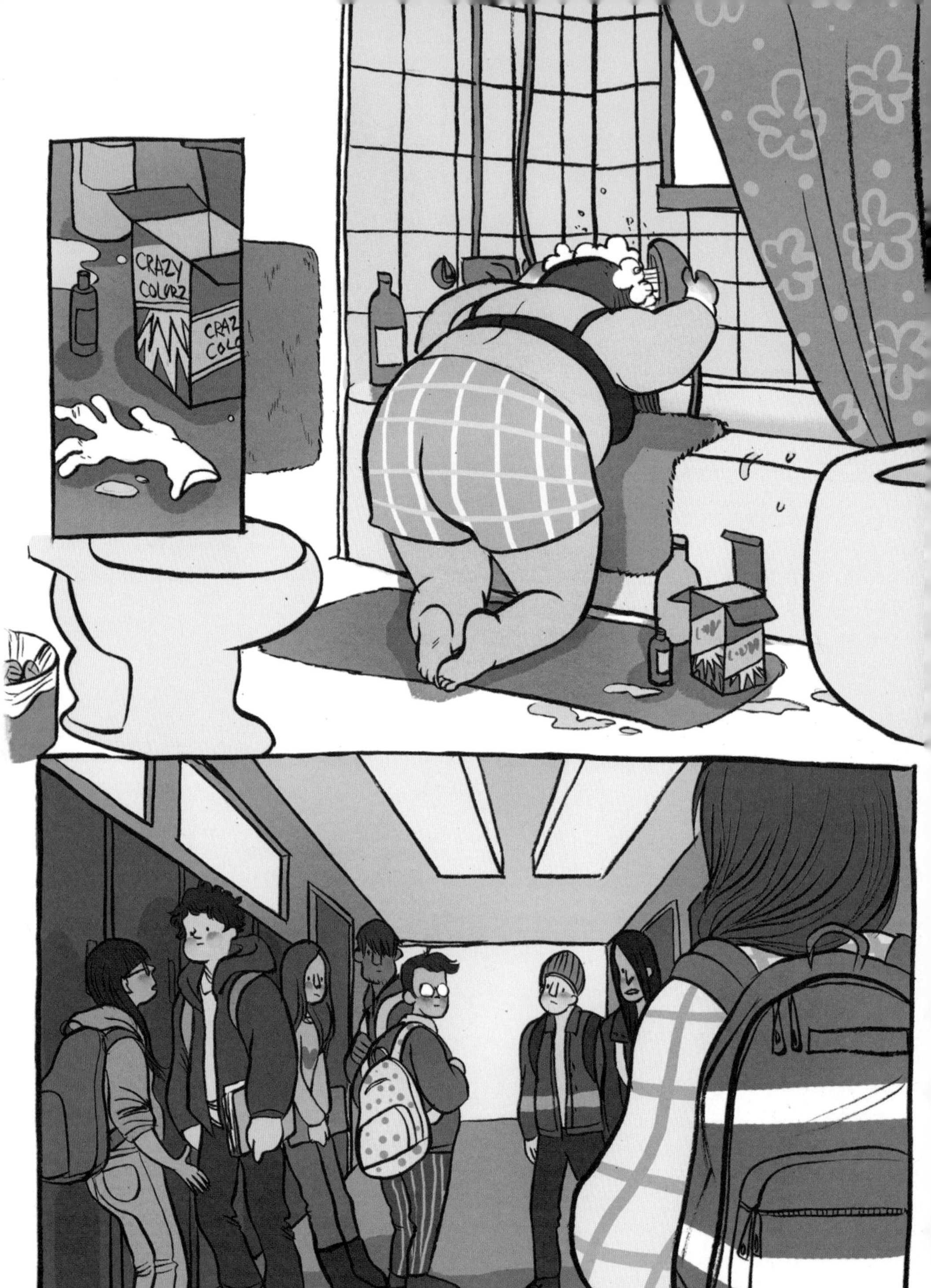
CRAZY
COLORZ

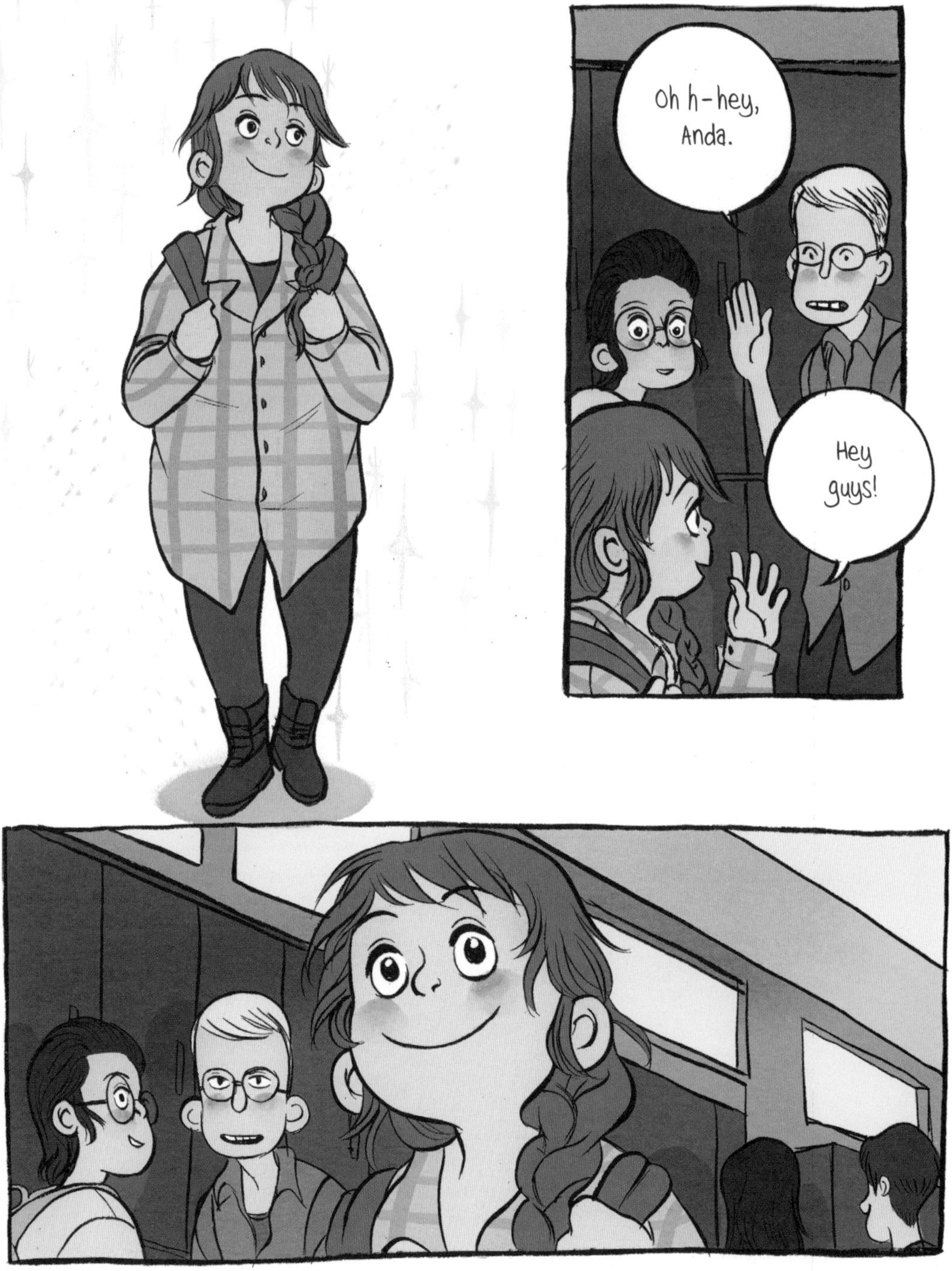
Oh h-hey,
Anda.
Hey
guys!

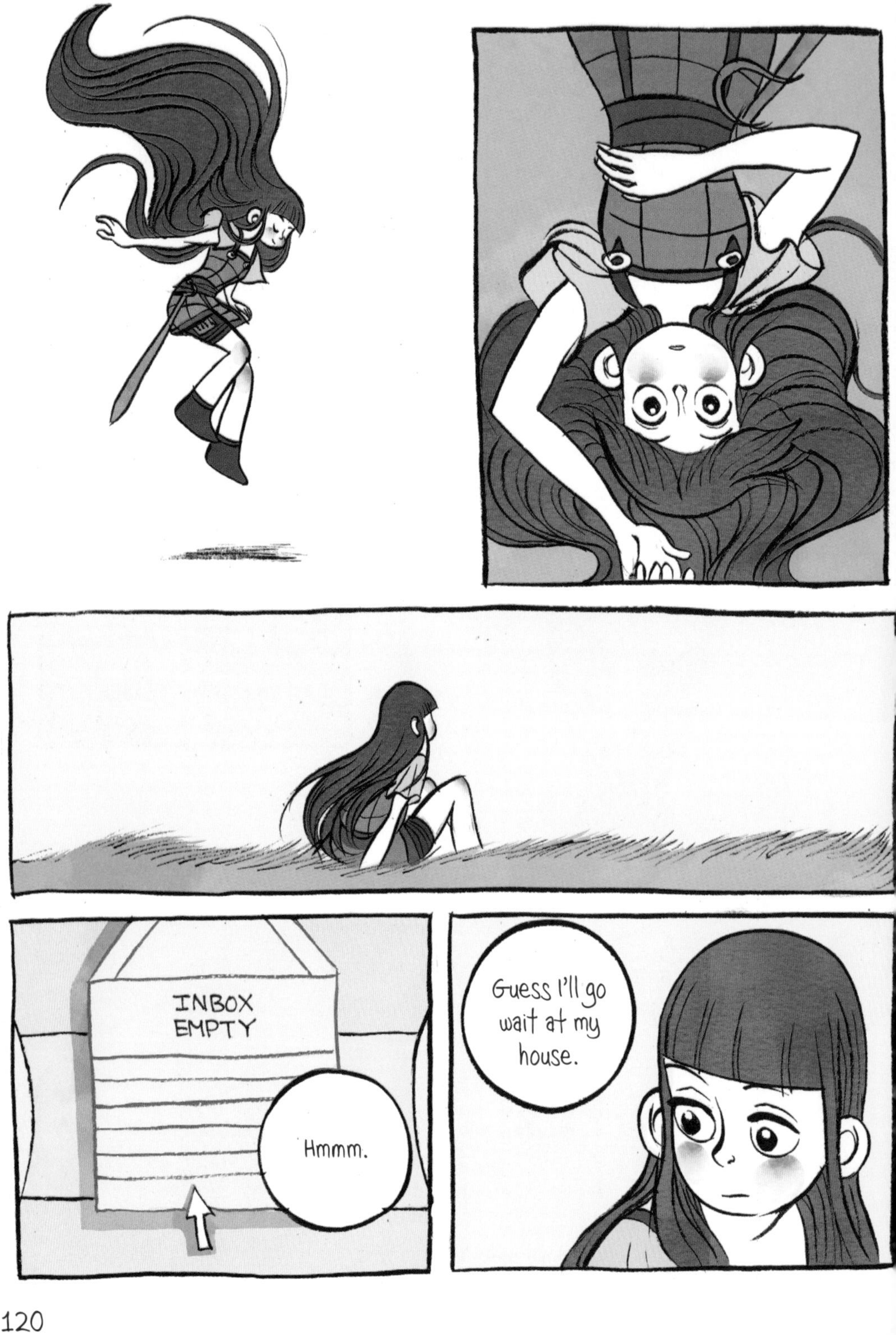
INBOX
EMPTY
Hmmm.
Guess I'll go wait at my house.

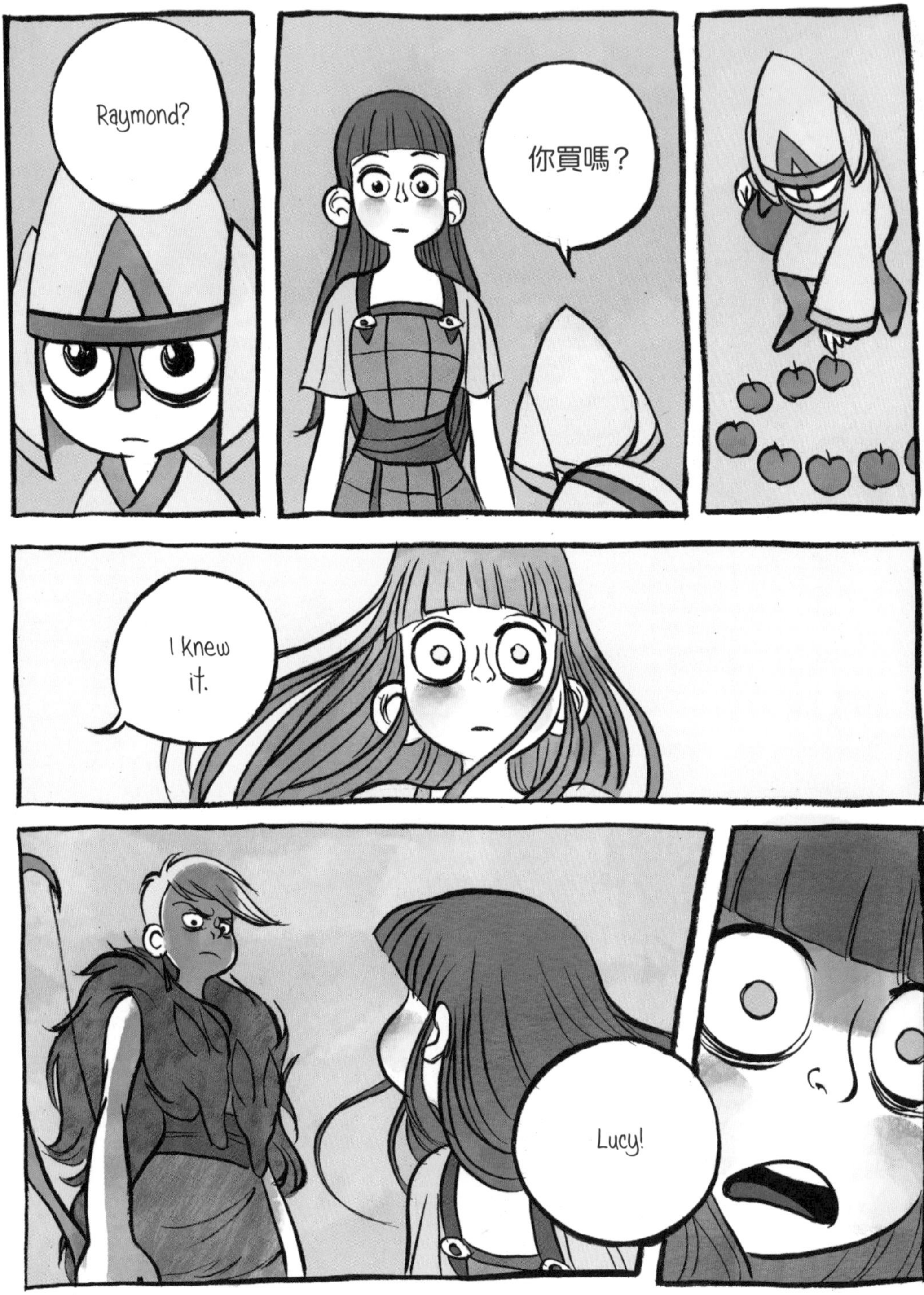
Raymond?
你買嗎？
I knew it.
Lucy!

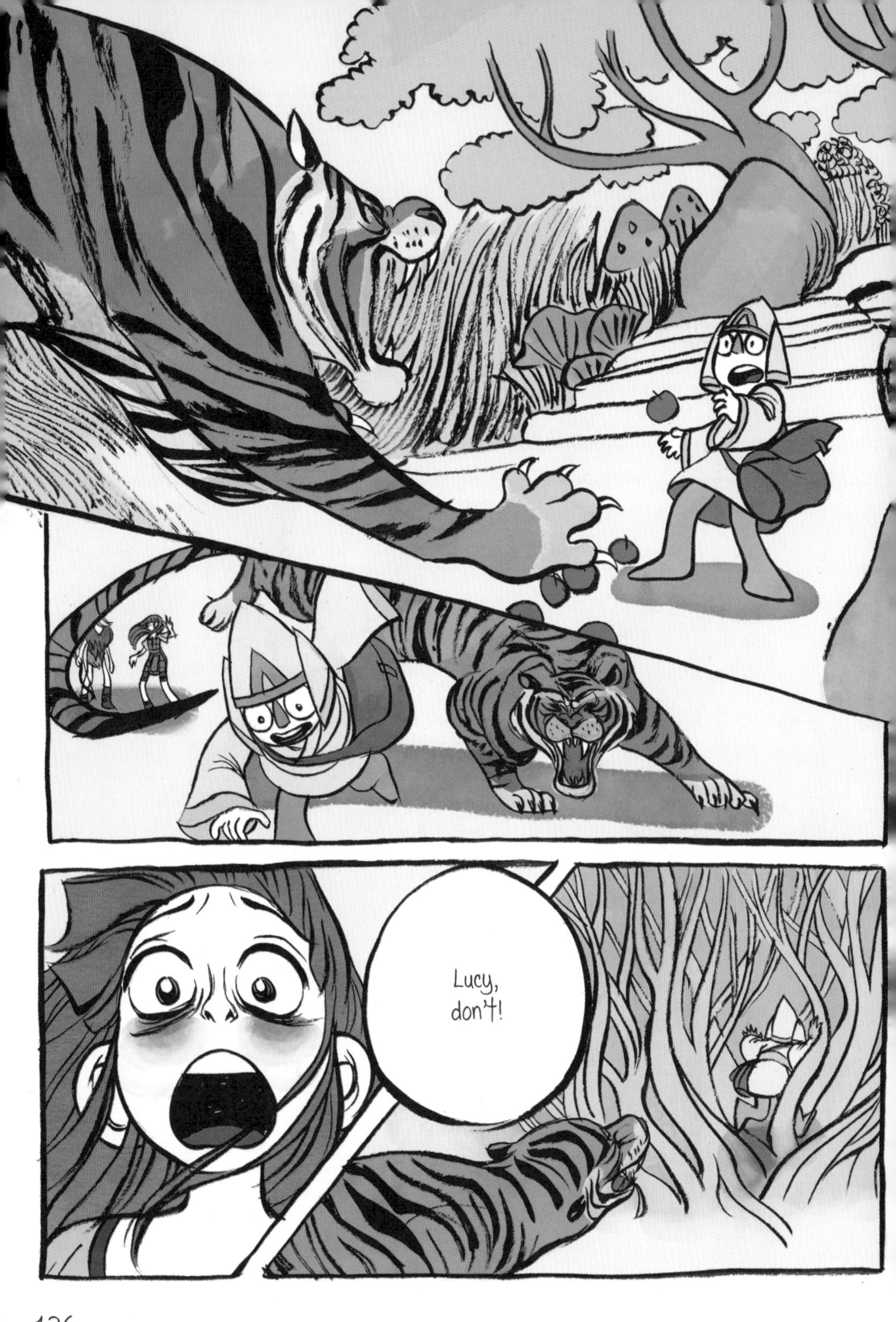
Lucy, don't!

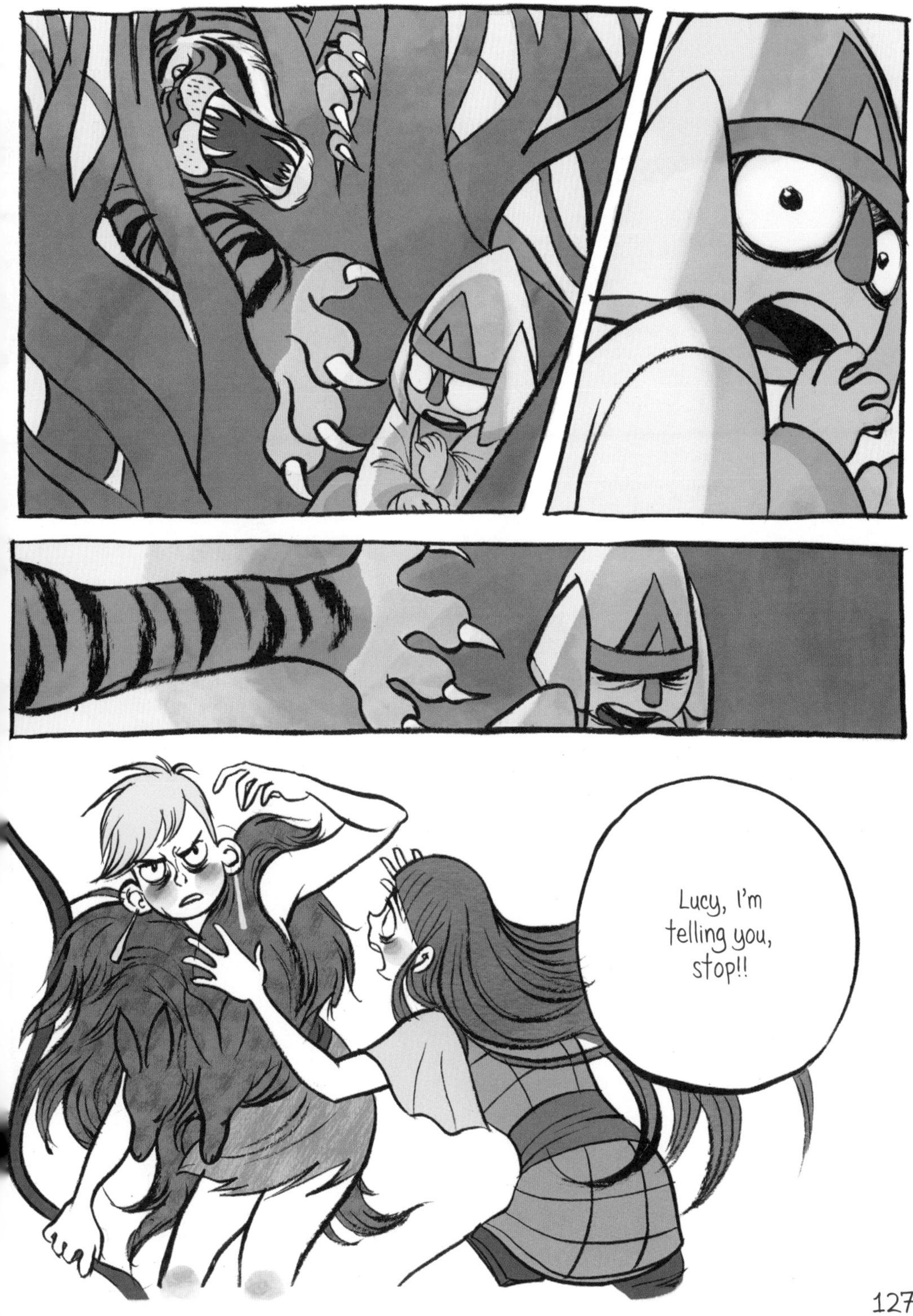
Lucy, I'm
telling you,
stop!!

129

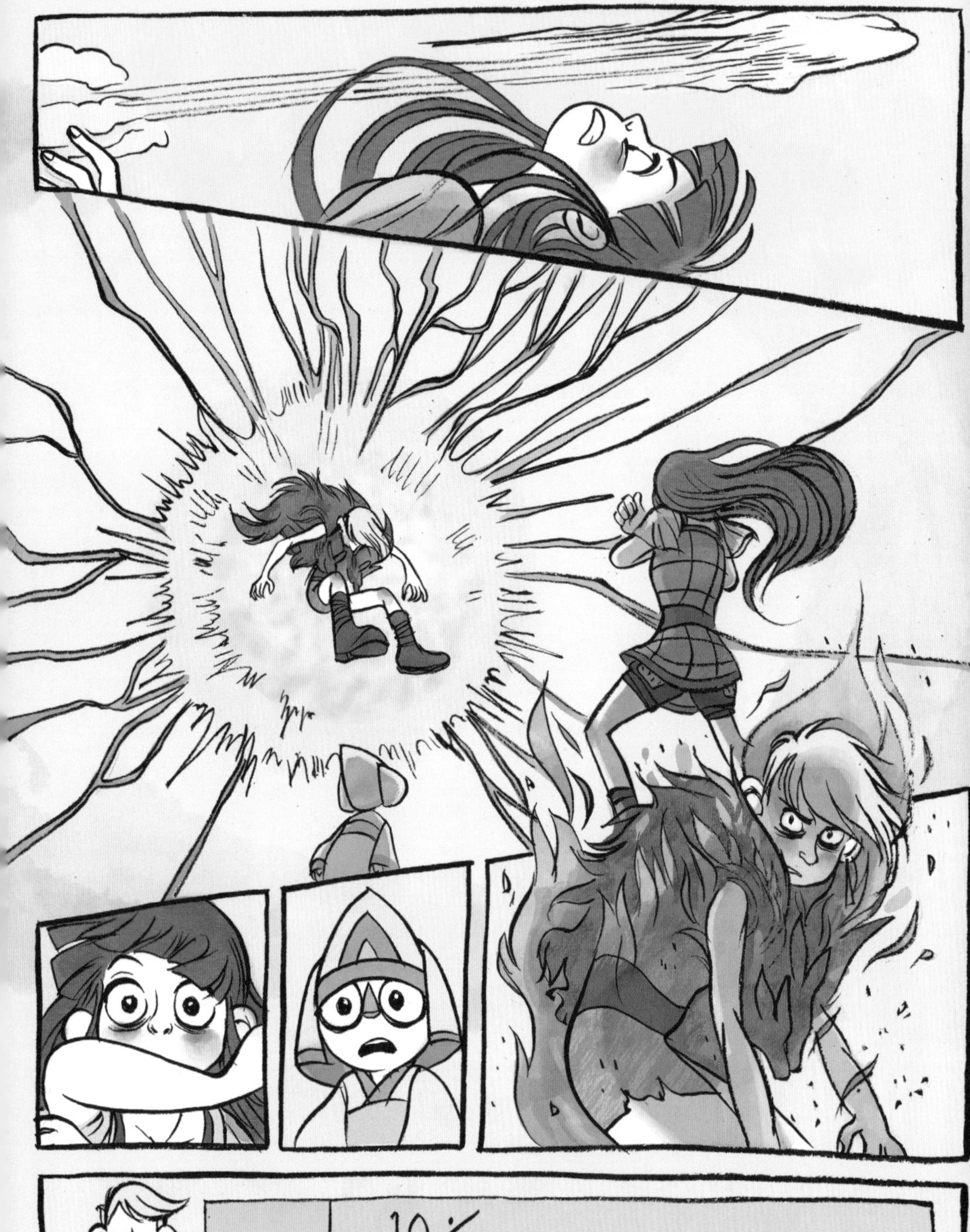
10%

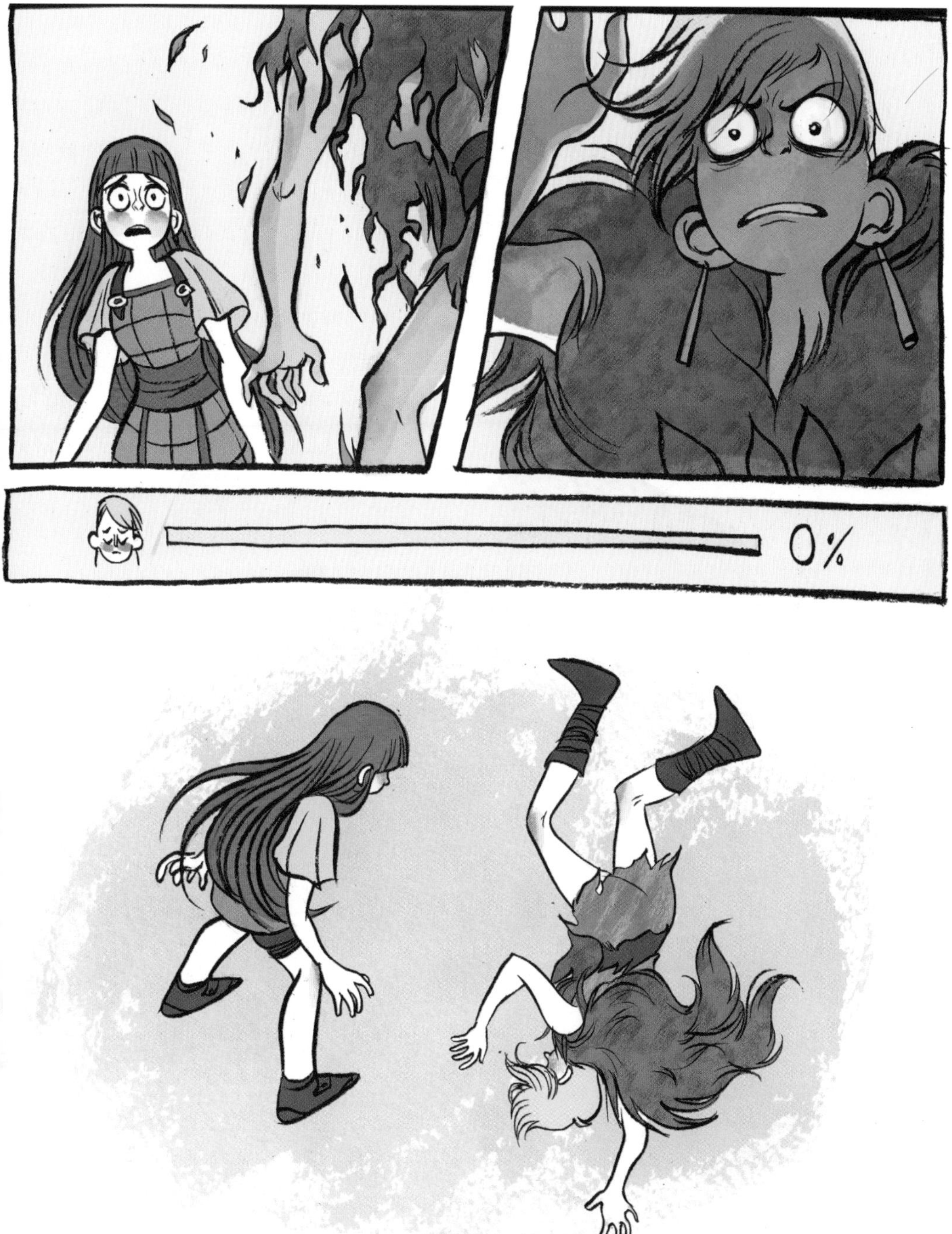
0%

132

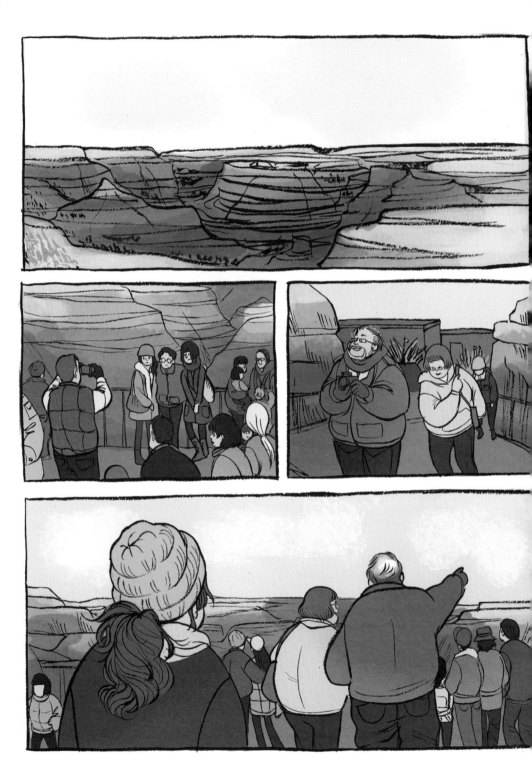

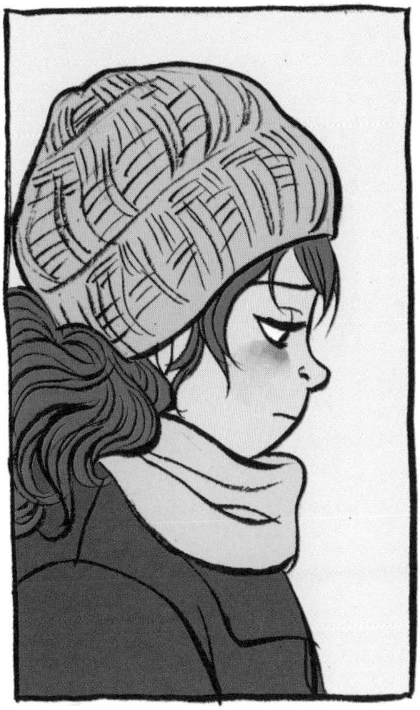

From: LIZA <liza@lizanator.com>
To: Anda

Anda,

I heard about your incident with Lucy yesterday. I've also been informed of the two of you dabbling in paid anti gold-farming missions. I wouldn't normally care what you do on your own time except you are representing the Fahrenheits, and harassing others is against our mission. You are both temporarily suspended until I've decided on a suitable punishment.

Yours,
Liza

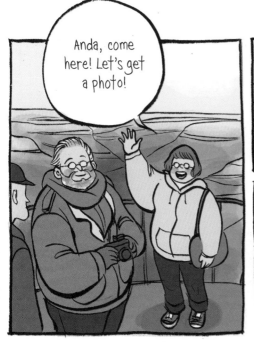

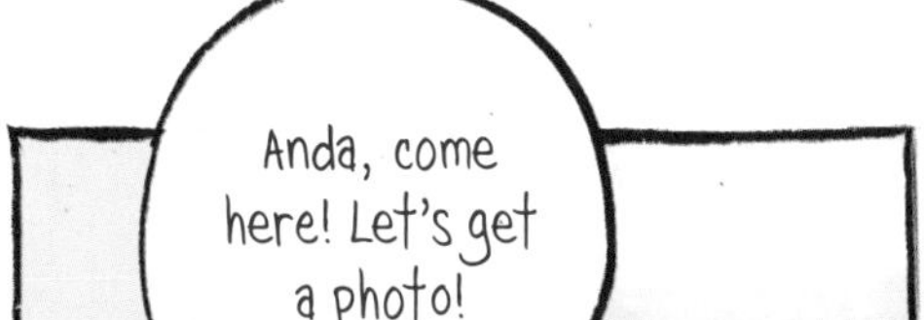
Anda, come here! Let's get a photo!

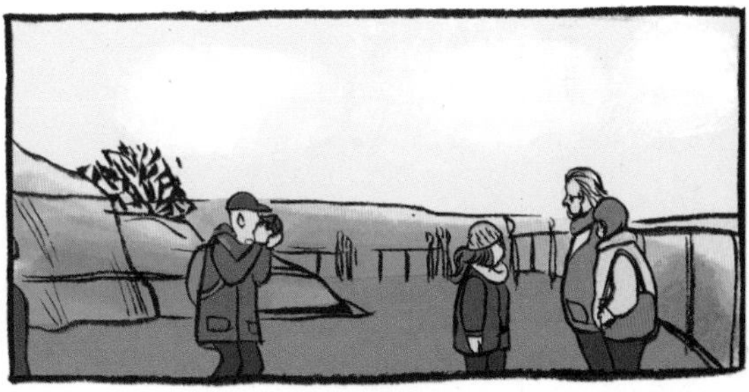

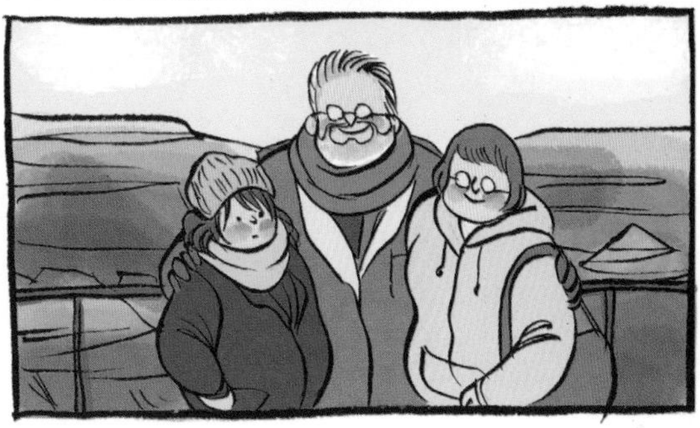

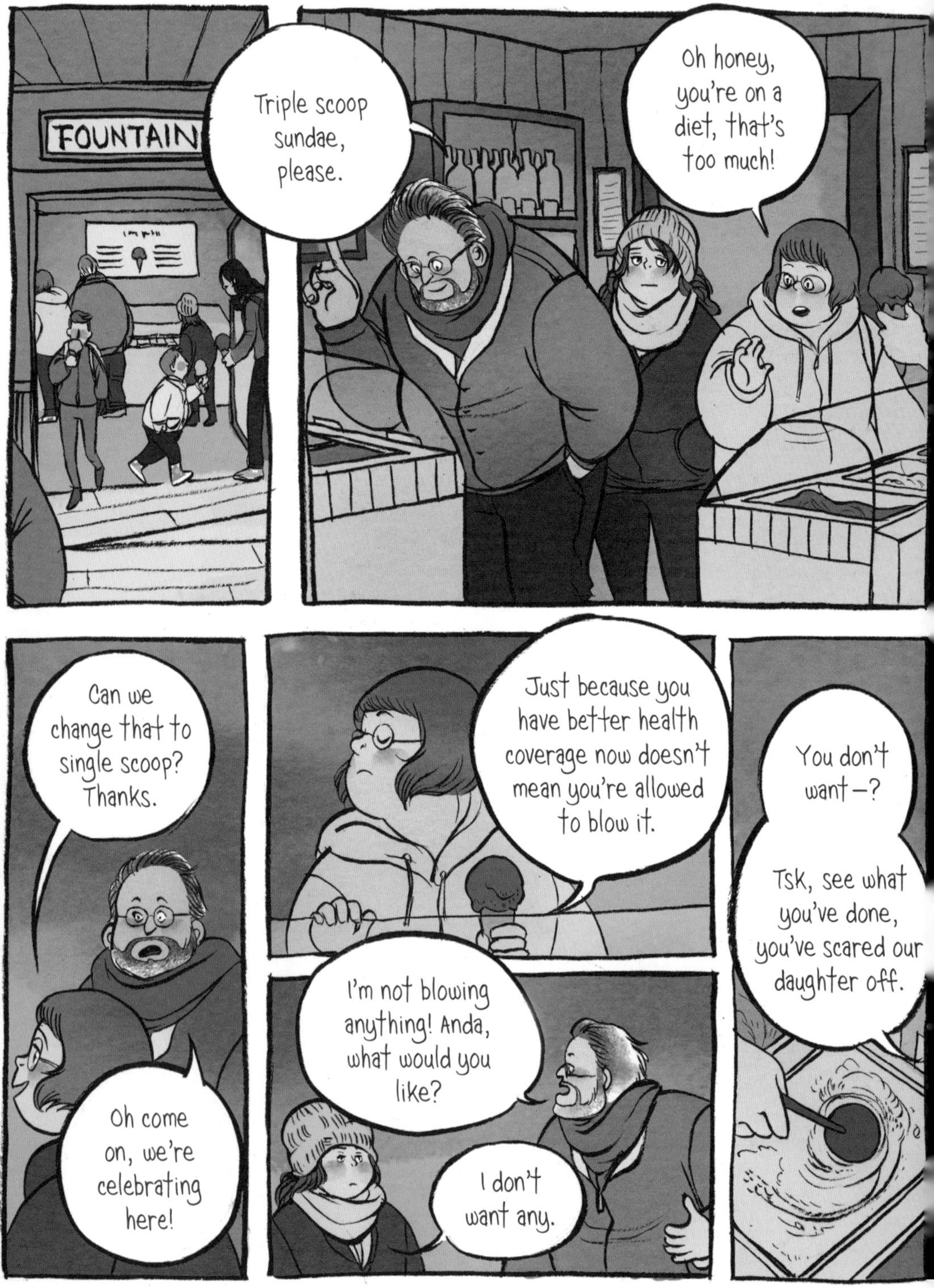
FOUNTAIN
Triple scoop sundae, please.
Oh honey, you're on a diet, that's too much!
Can we change that to single scoop? Thanks.
Oh come on, we're celebrating here!
Just because you have better health coverage now doesn't mean you're allowed to blow it.
I'm not blowing anything! Anda, what would you like?
I don't want any.
You don't want—?
Tsk, see what you've done, you've scared our daughter off.

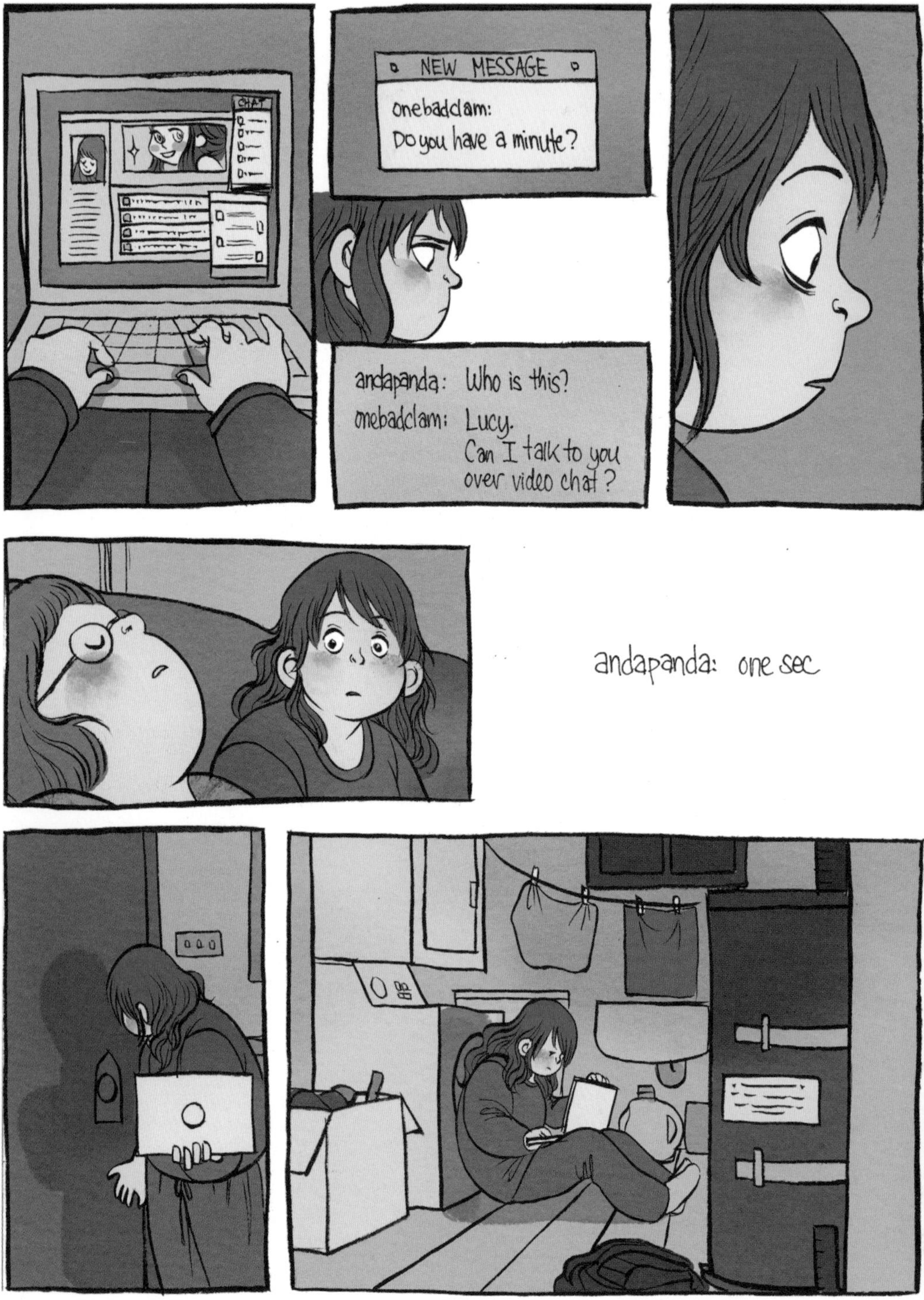
CHAT
NEW MESSAGE
onebadclam:
Do you have a minute?
andapanda: Who is this?
onebadclam: Lucy.
Can I talk to you
over video chat?
andapanda: one sec

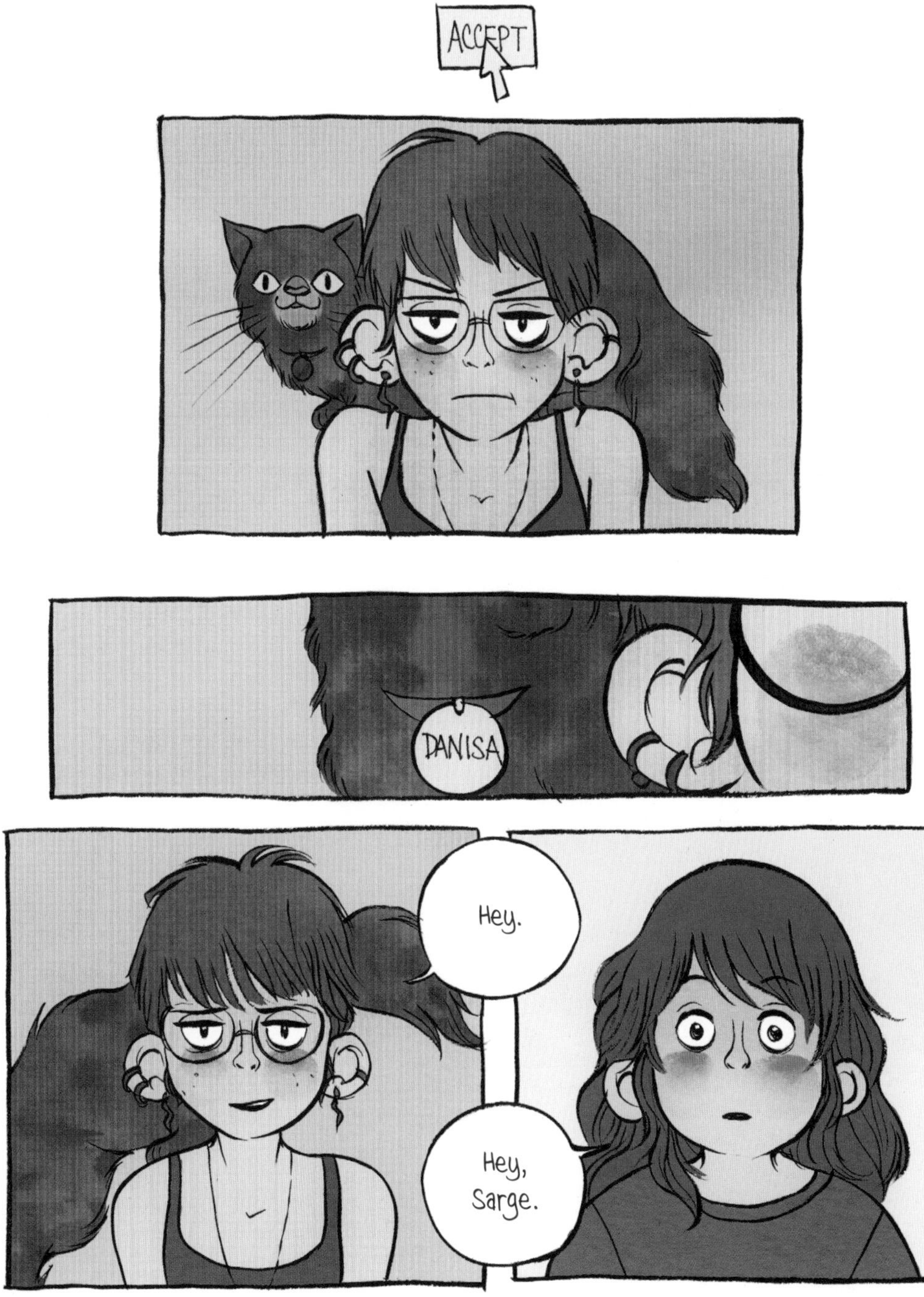
ACCEPT
DANISA
Hey.
Hey,
Sarge.

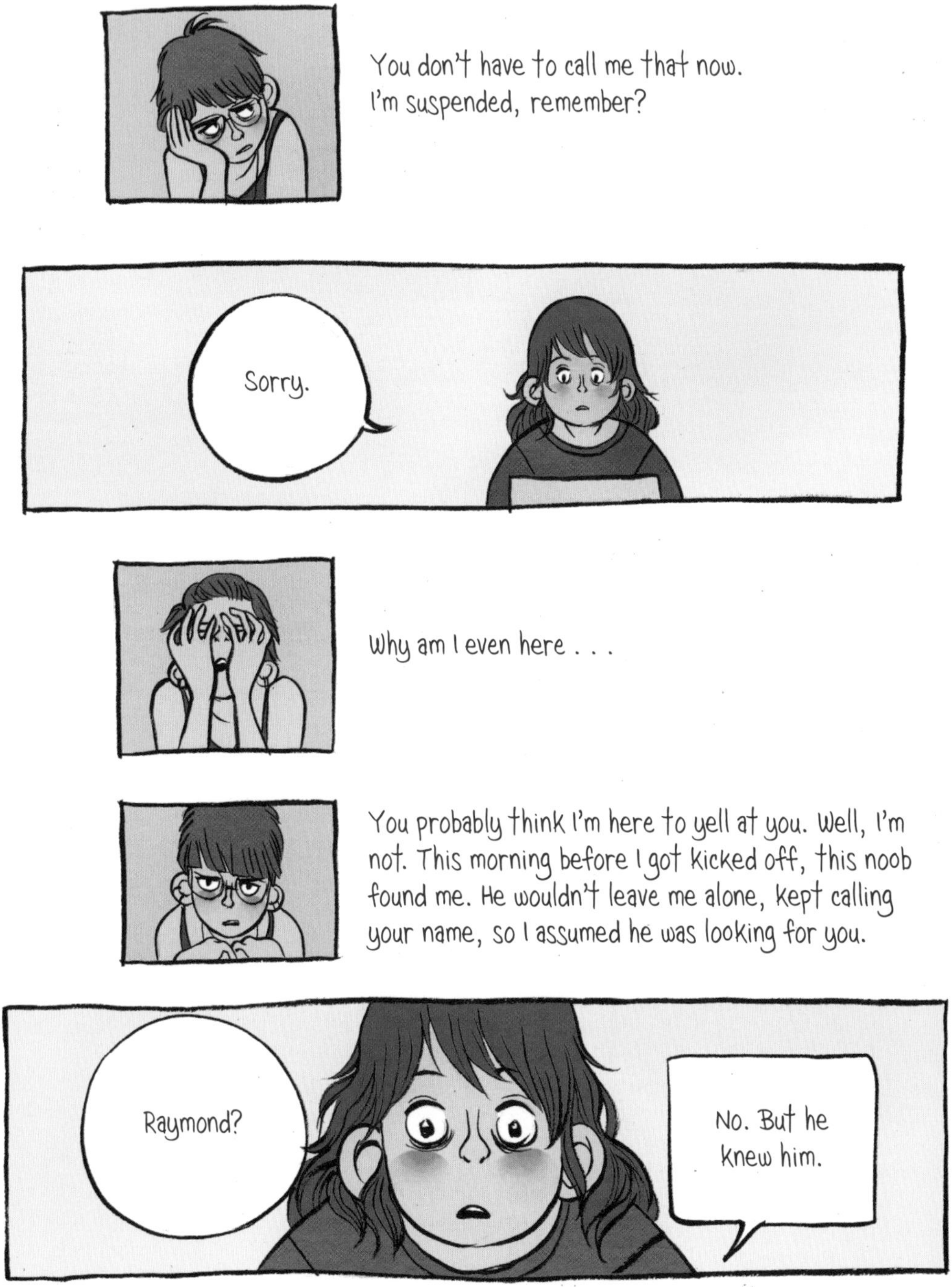
You don't have to call me that now.
I'm suspended, remember?
Sorry.
Why am I even here . . .
You probably think I'm here to yell at you. Well, I'm not. This morning before I got kicked off, this noob found me. He wouldn't leave me alone, kept calling your name, so I assumed he was looking for you.
Raymond?
No. But he knew him.

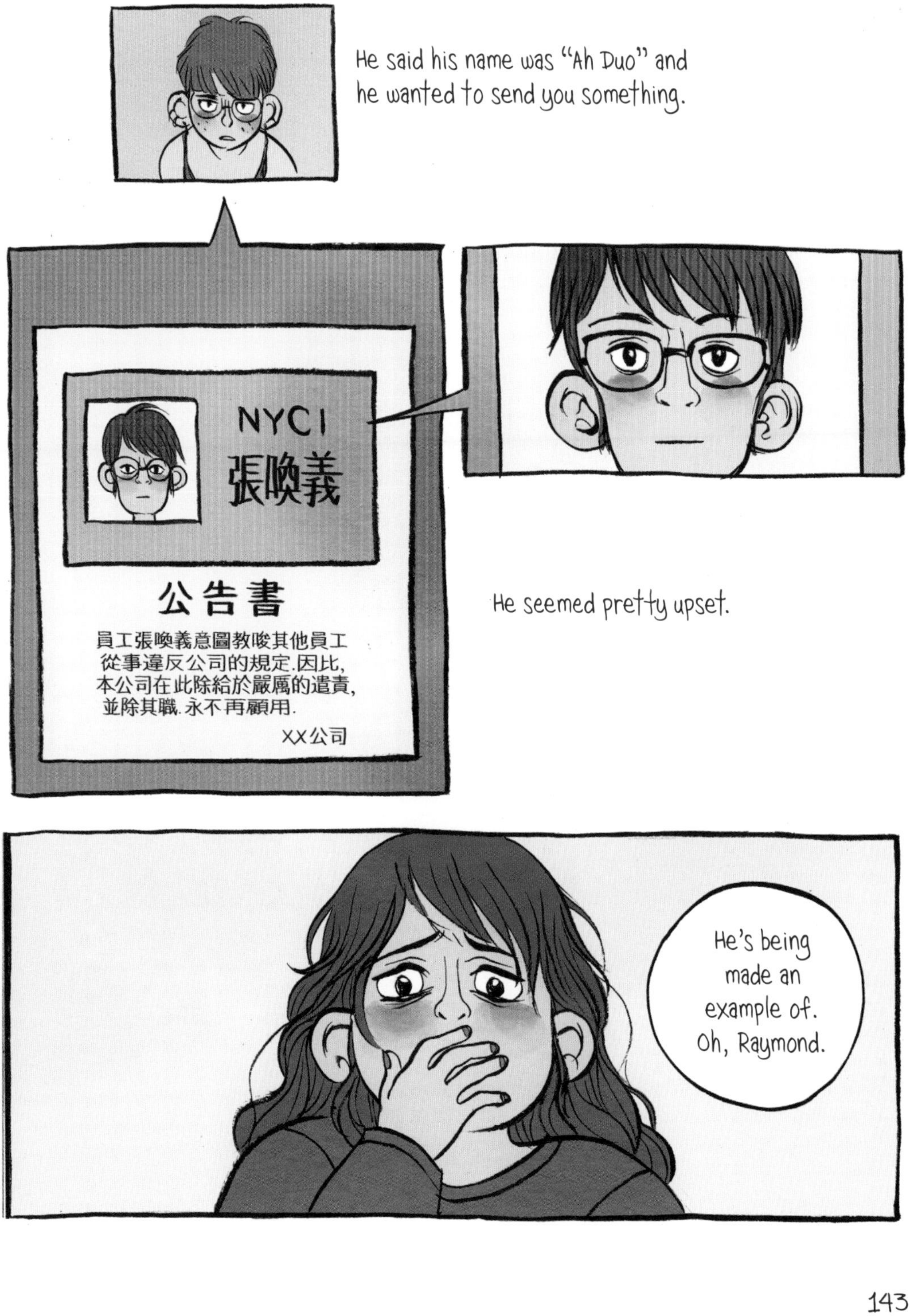

He said his name was "Ah Duo" and he wanted to send you something.
NYCI
張喚義
公告書
員工張喚義意圖教唆其他員工
從事違反公司的規定.因比,
本公司在此除給於嚴厲的遣責,
並除其職.永不再顧用.
XX公司
He seemed pretty upset.
He's being made an example of. Oh, Raymond.

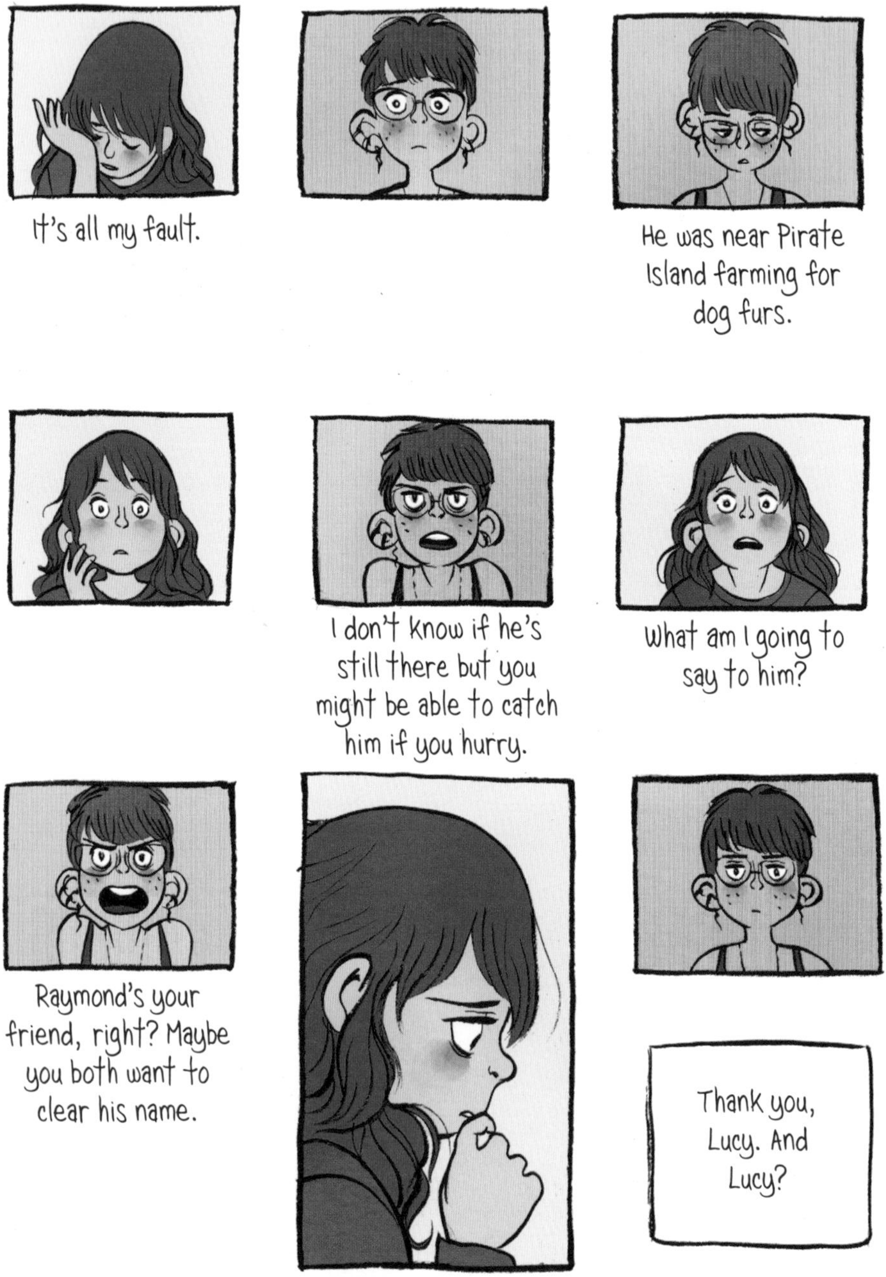
It's all my fault.
He was near Pirate Island farming for dog furs.
I don't know if he's still there but you might be able to catch him if you hurry.
What am I going to say to him?
Raymond's your friend, right? Maybe you both want to clear his name.
Thank you, Lucy. And Lucy?

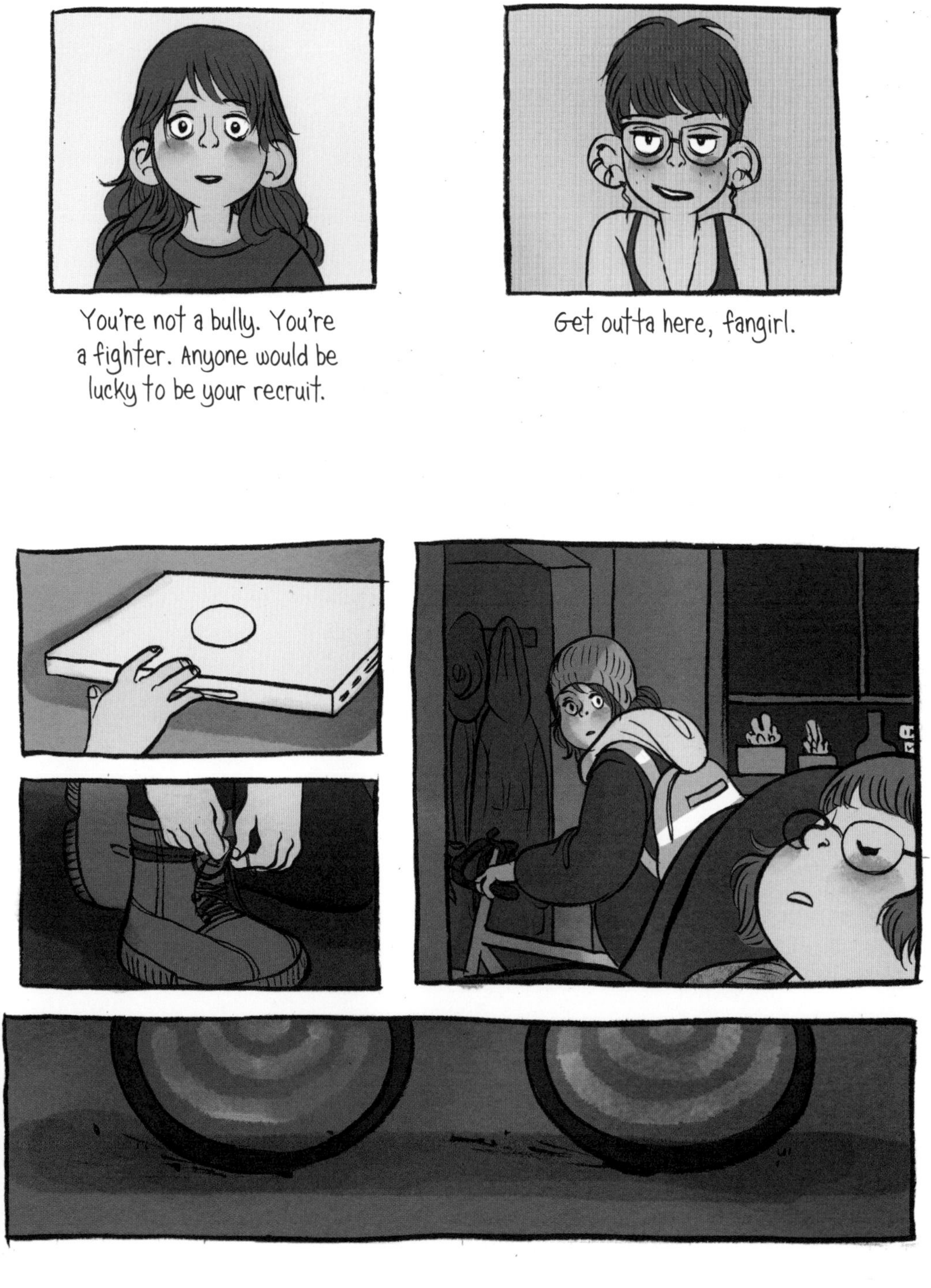
You're not a bully. You're a fighter. Anyone would be lucky to be your recruit.
Get outta here, fangirl.

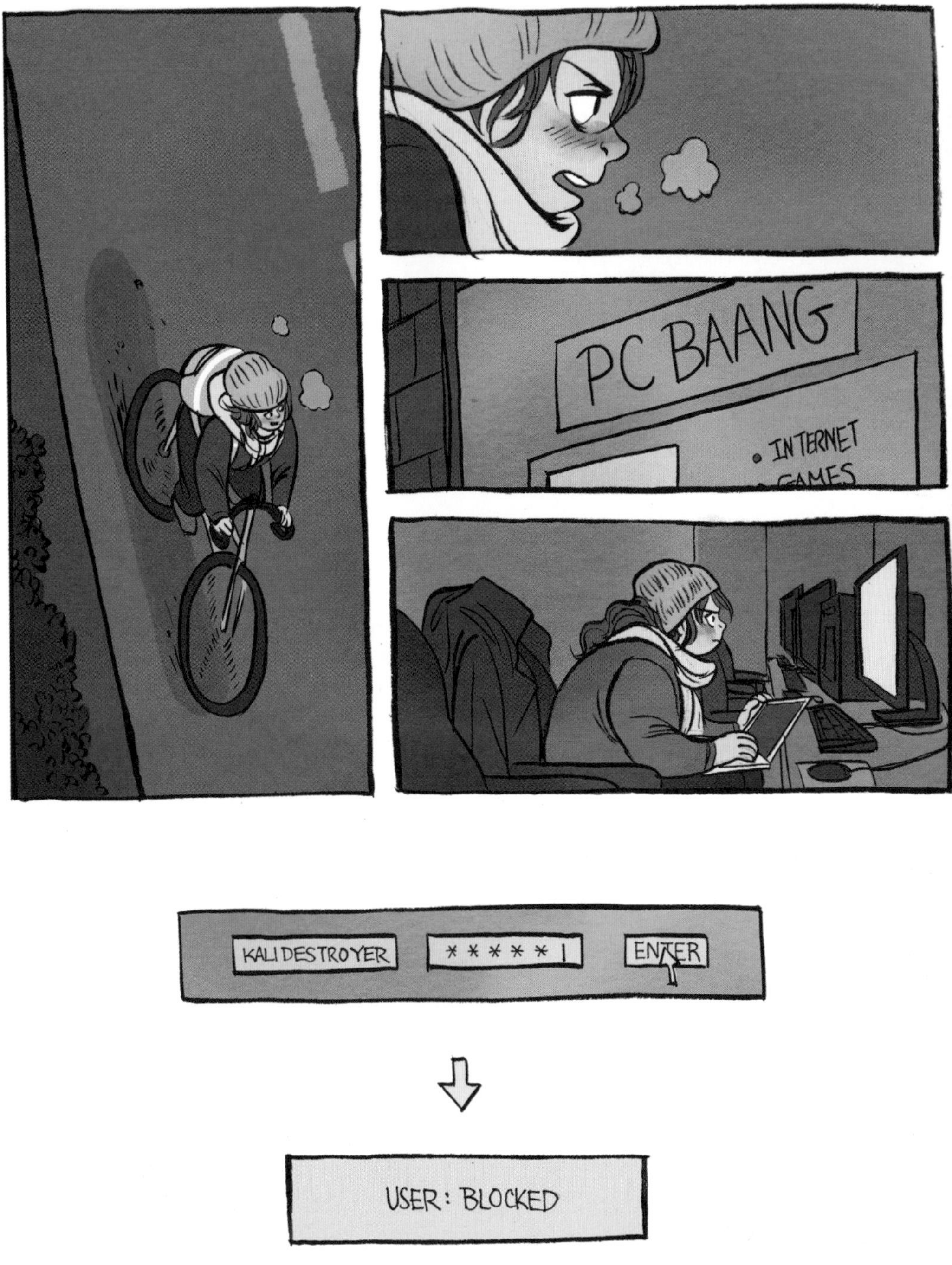
PC BAANG
• INTERNET
KALIDESTROYER
* * * * * 1
ENTER
USER : BLOCKED

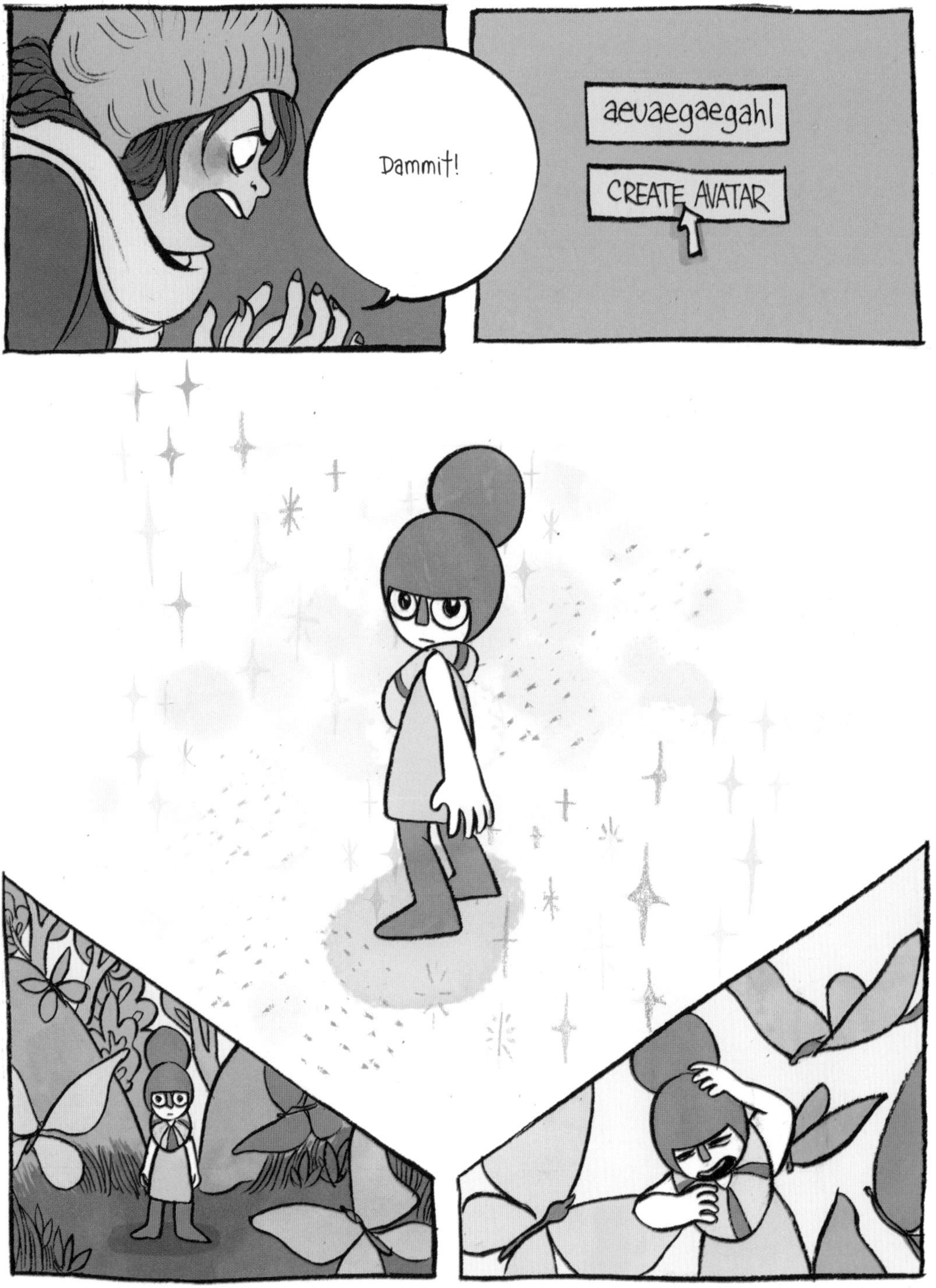
Dammit!
aevaegaegahl
CREATE AVATAR

149

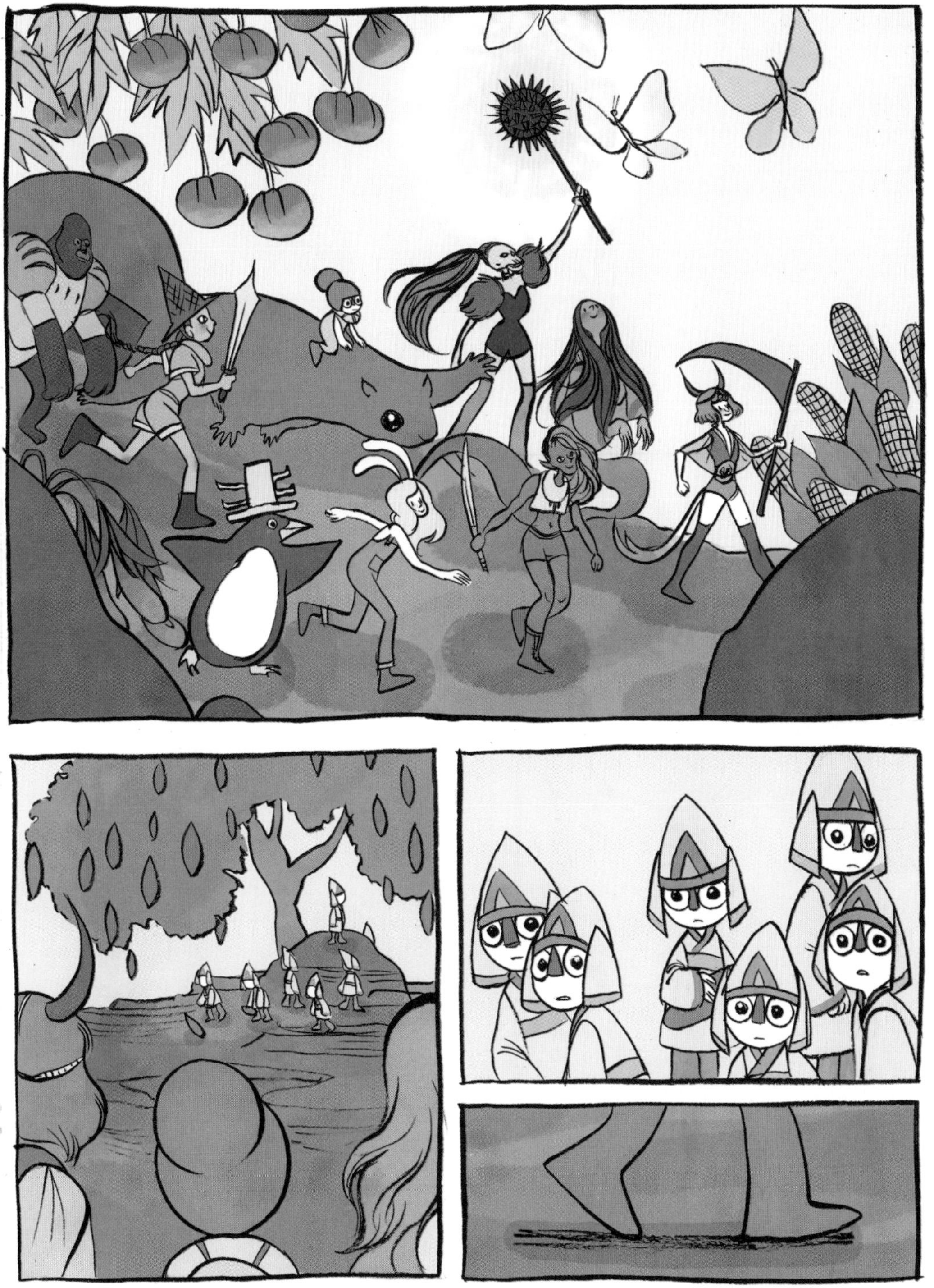

153

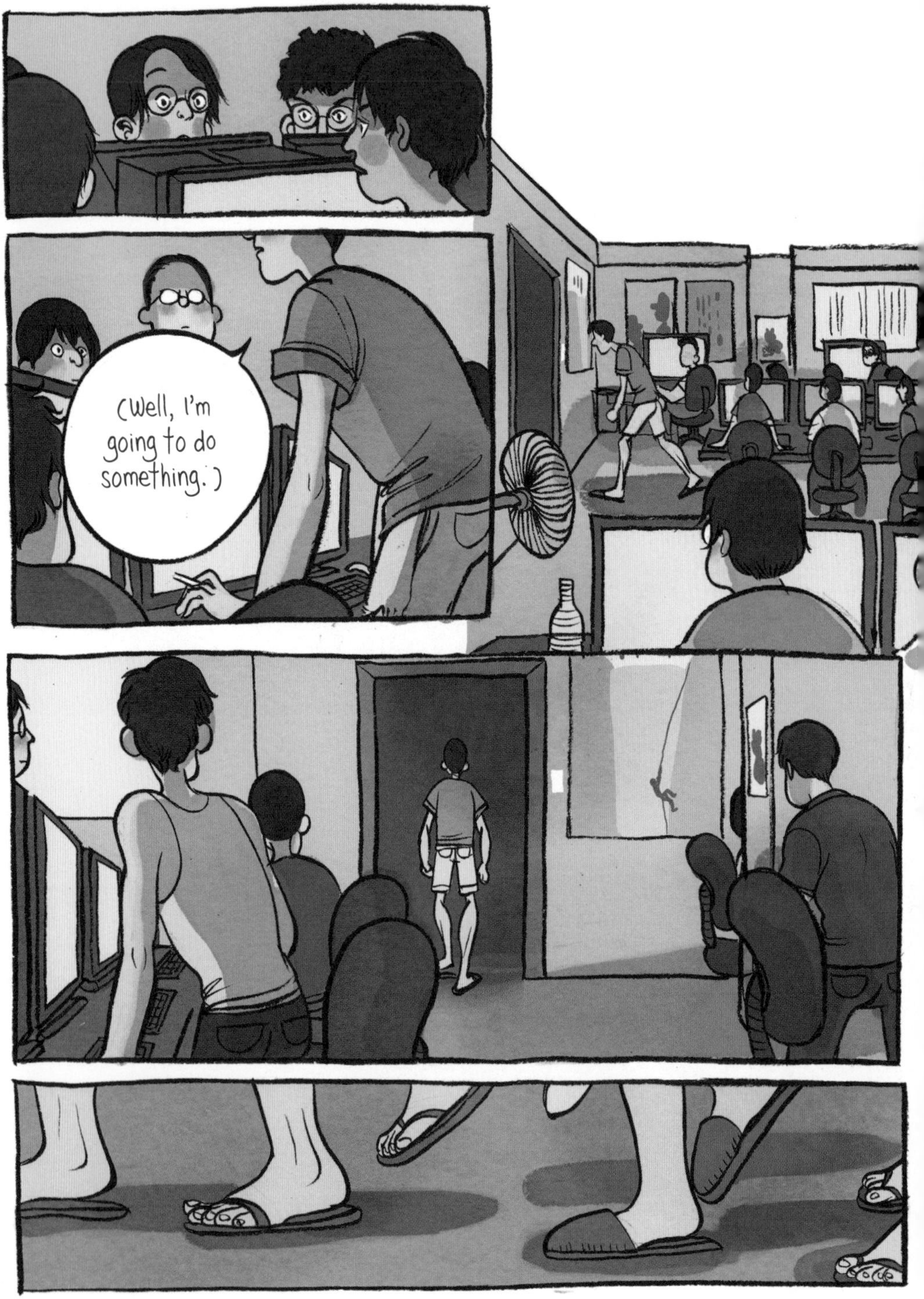
(Well, I'm going to do something.)

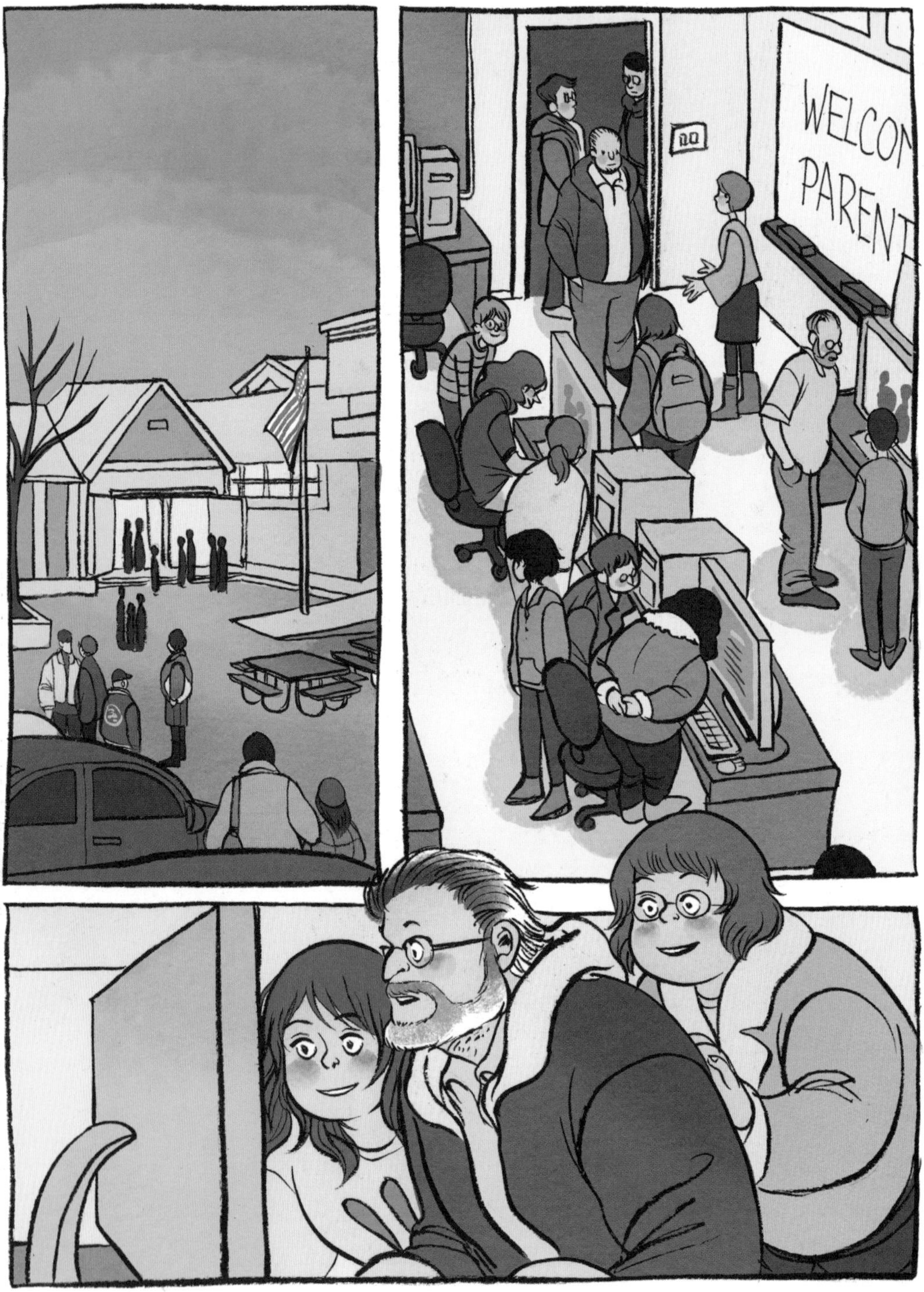
WELCOM
PARENT

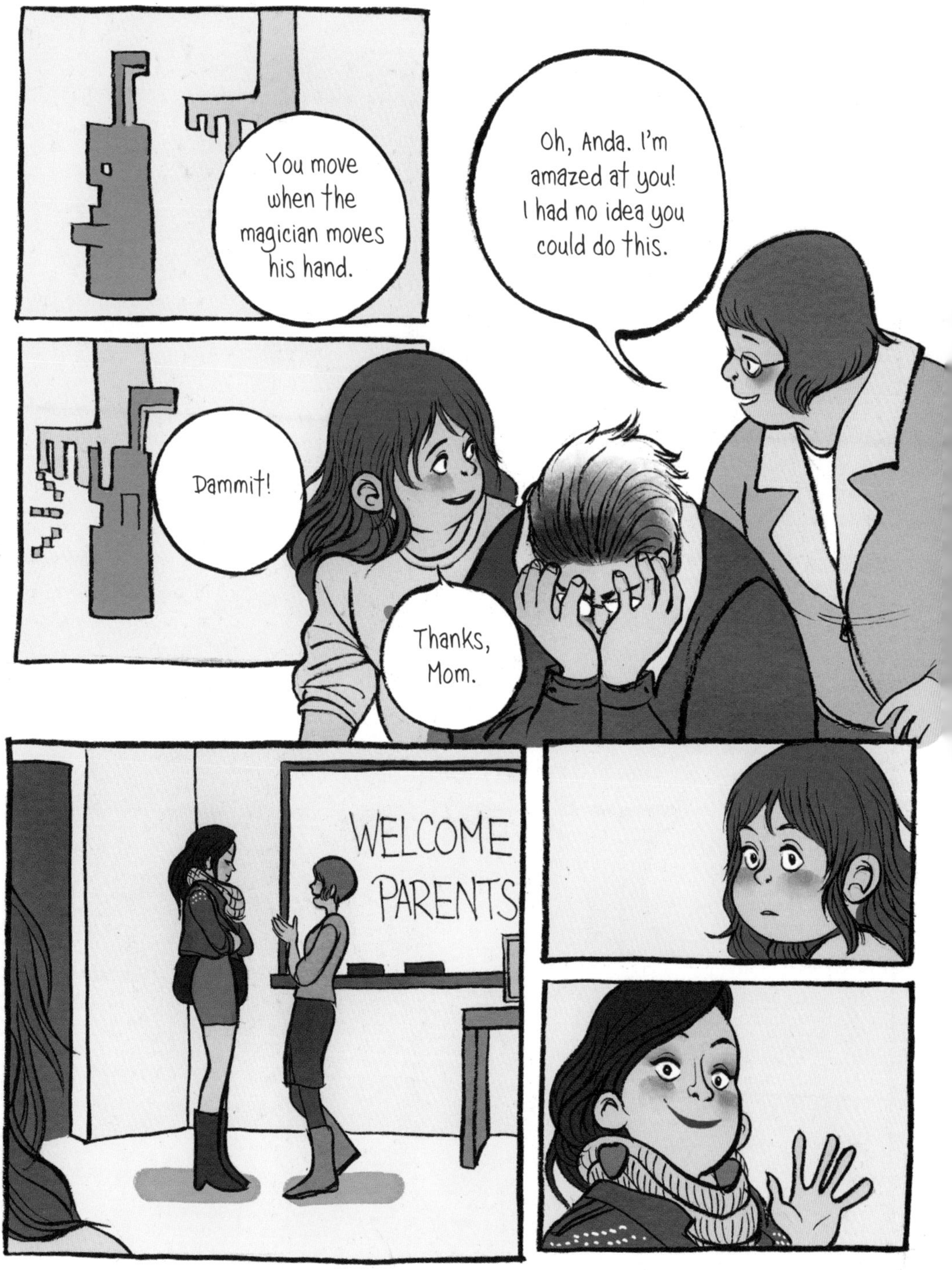
You move when the magician moves his hand.
Oh, Anda. I'm amazed at you! I had no idea you could do this.
Dammit!
Thanks, Mom.
WELCOME PARENTS

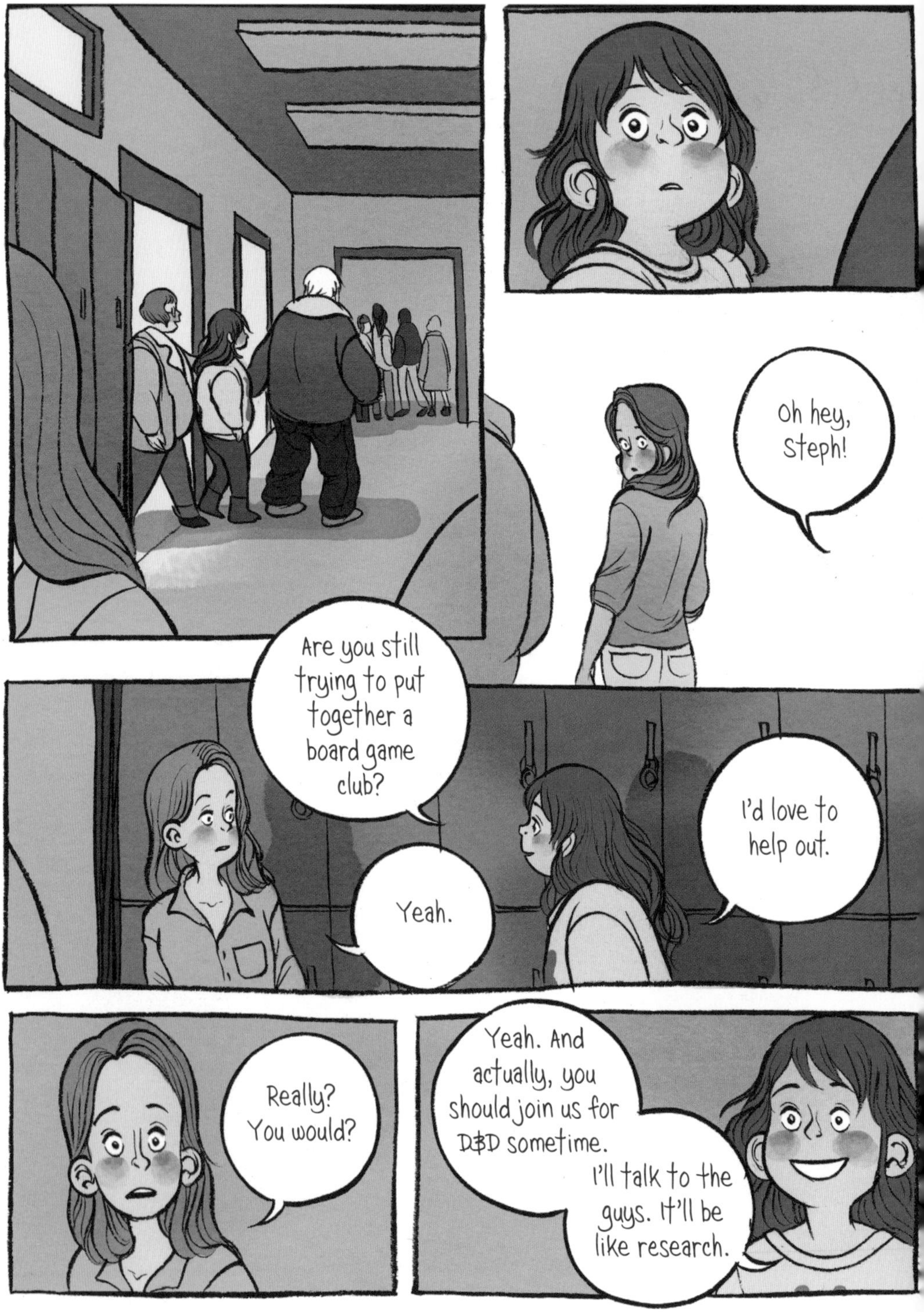
Oh hey, Steph!
Are you still trying to put together a board game club?
Yeah.
I'd love to help out.
Really? You would?
Yeah. And actually, you should join us for D&D sometime.
I'll talk to the guys. It'll be like research.

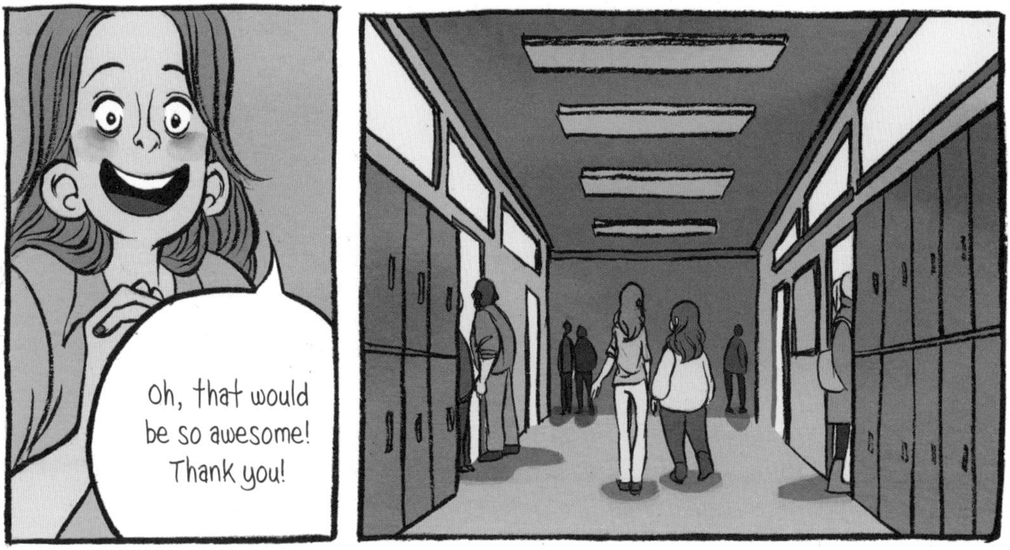
Oh, that would be so awesome! Thank you!

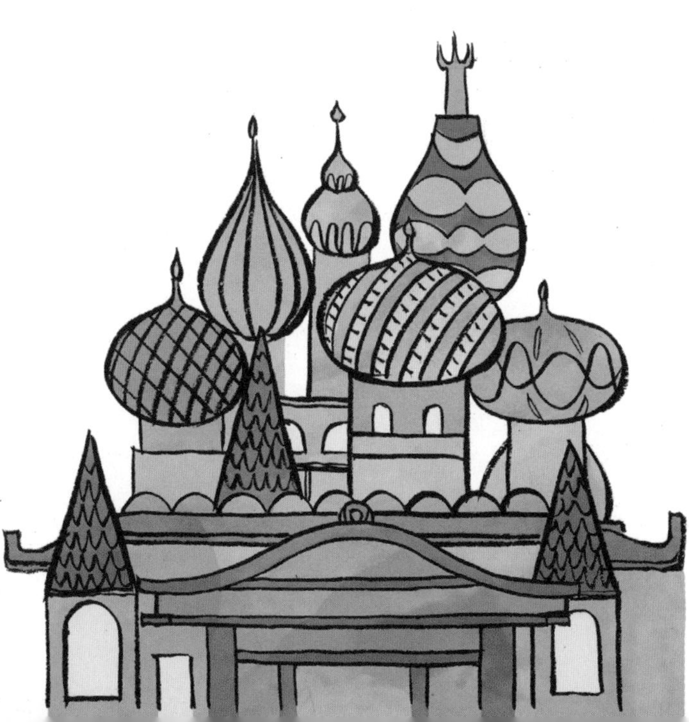

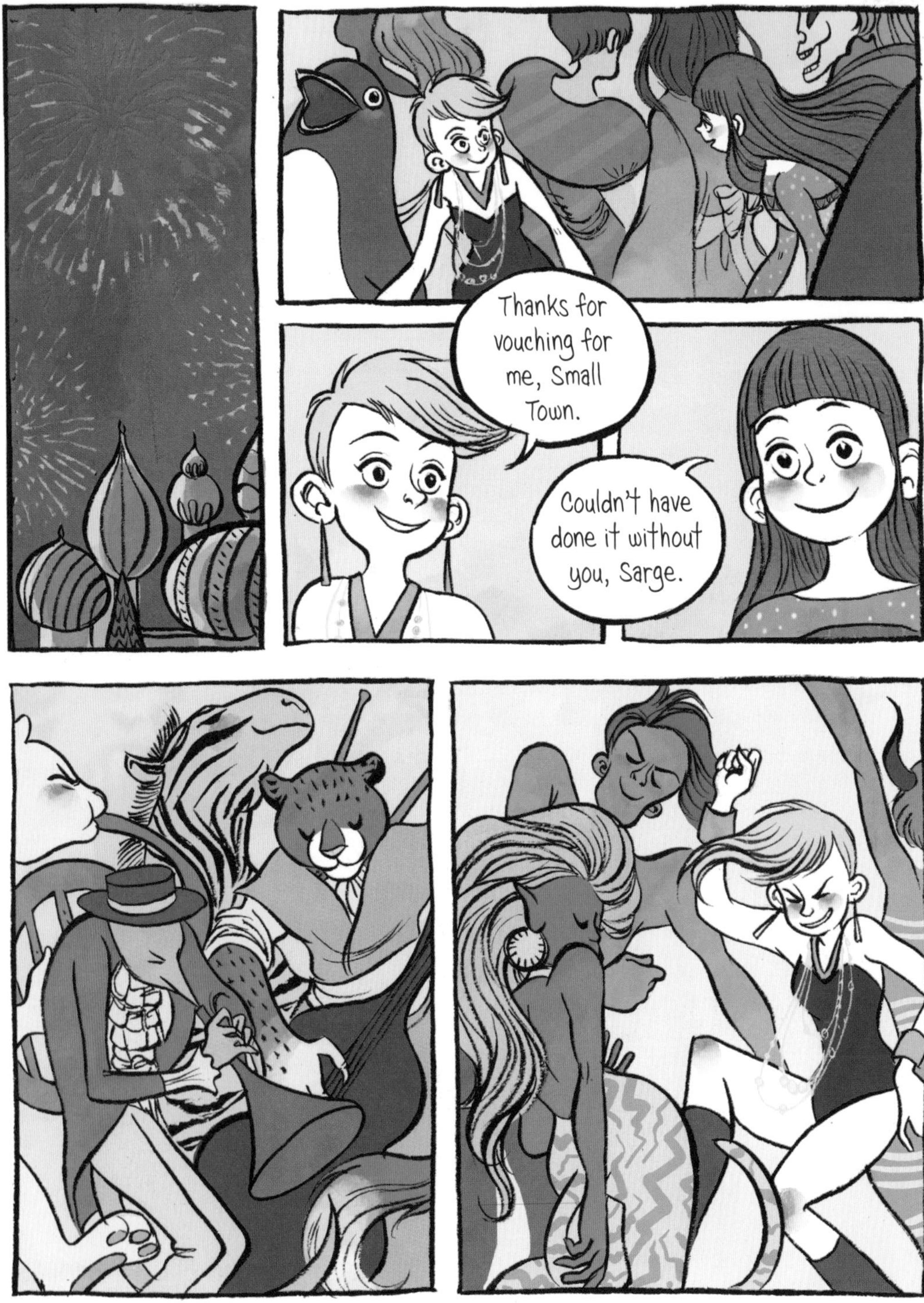
Thanks for vouching for me, Small Town.
Couldn't have done it without you, Sarge.

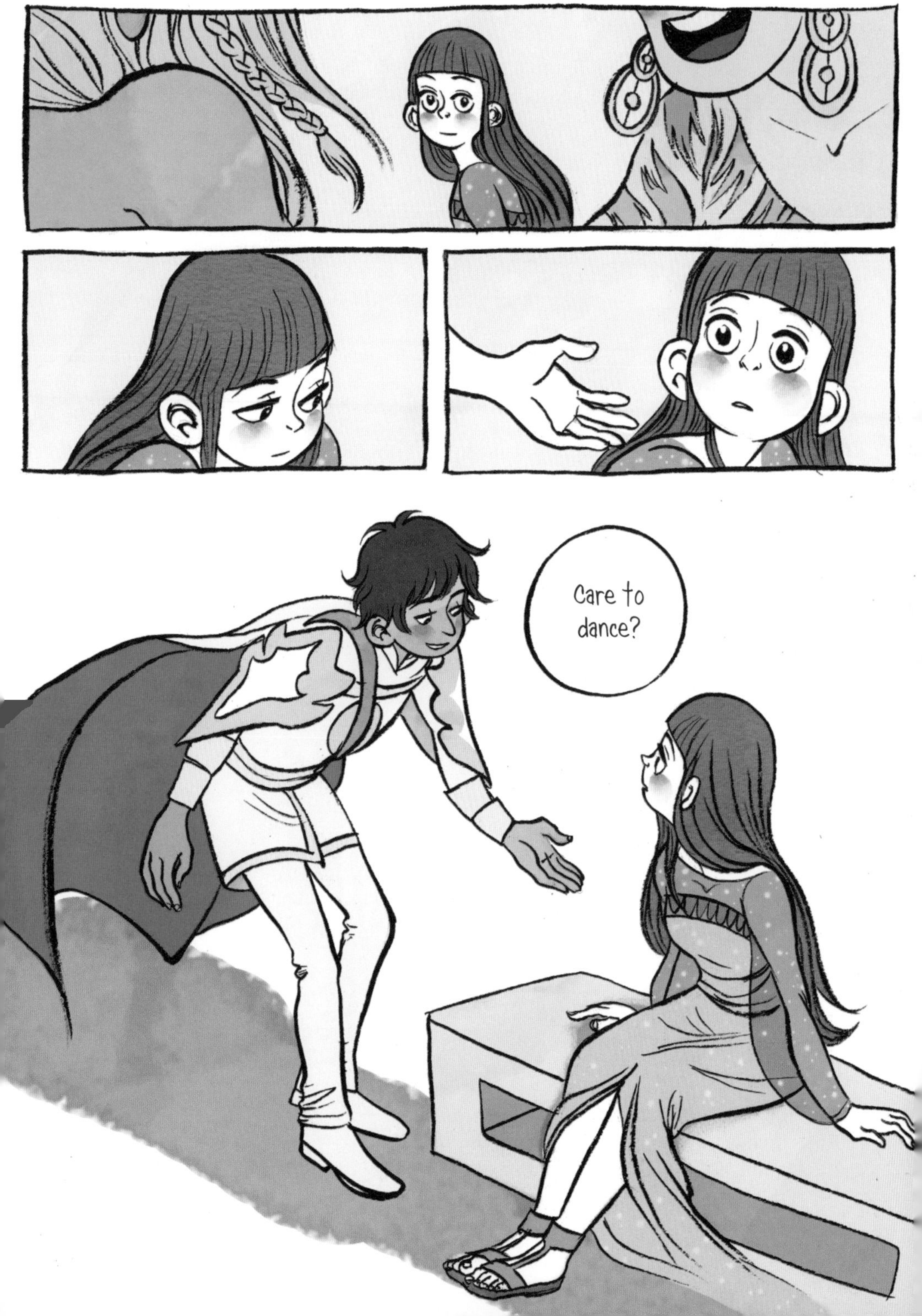
Care to dance?

173

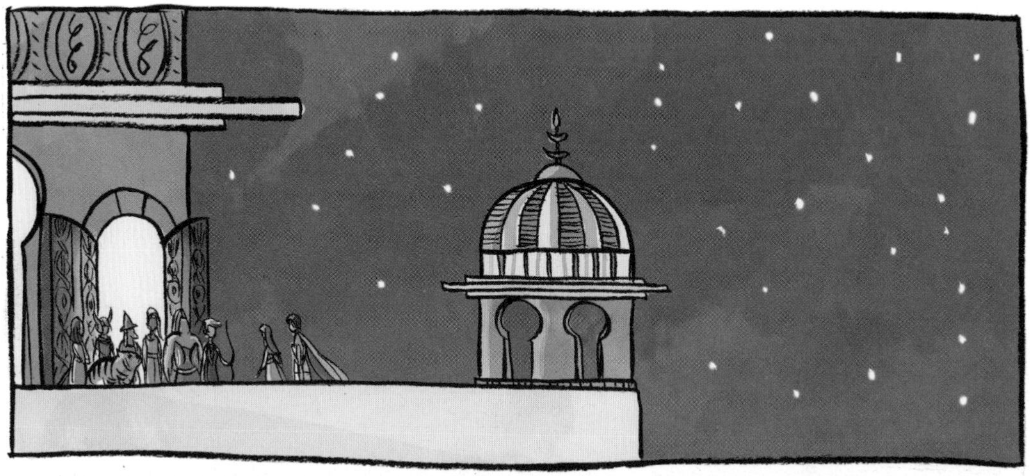
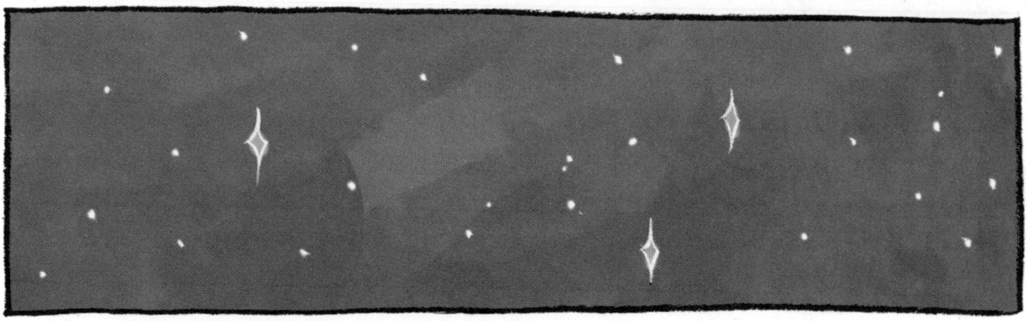
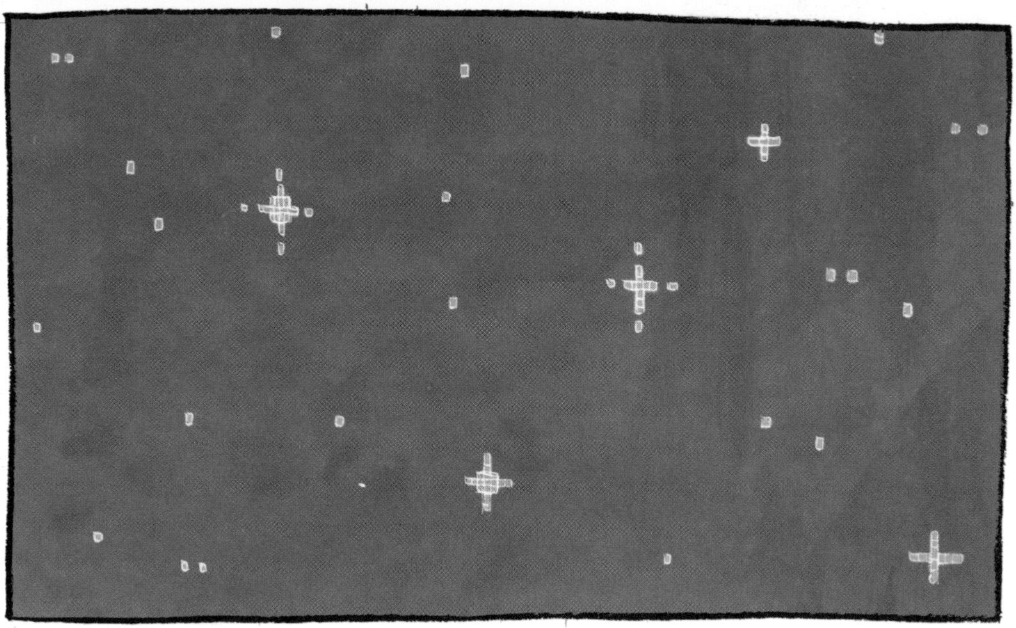

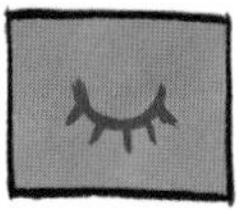

SLEEP

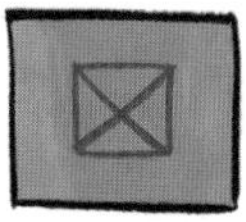

EXIT

First Second

Story copyright © 2014 by Cory Doctorow
Art and adaptation copyright © 2014 by Jen Wang

In Real Life was adapted from a story by Cory Doctorow called "Anda's Game"
first published on Salon.com in 2004.

Published by First Second
First Second is an imprint of Roaring Brook Press, a division of
Holtzbrinck Publishing Holdings Limited Partnership
175 Fifth Avenue, New York, New York 10010
All rights reserved

Cataloging-in-Publication Data is on file at the Library of Congress.

ISBN 978-1-59643-658-9

First Second books may be purchased for business or promotional use.
For information on bulk purchases please contact Macmillan Corporate
and Premium Sales Department at (800) 221-7945 x5442 or by email at
specialmarkets@macmillan.com.

FIRST

EDITION

First edition 2014
Book design by Colleen AF Venable

Printed in China

10 9 8 7